Kristi Gold has a fondness for beaches, baseball and bridal reality shows. She firmly believes that love has remarkable healing powers, and she feels very fortunate to be able to weave stories of love and commitment. As a bestselling author, a National Readers' Choice Award winner and a Romance Writers of America three-time RITA® Award finalist, Kristi has learned that although accolades are wonderful, the most cherished rewards come from networking with readers. She can be reached through her website at www.kristigold.com, or through Facebook.

Kathie DeNosky lives in her native Southern Illinois on the land her family settled in 1839. Her books have appeared on the *USA TODAY* bestseller list and received numerous awards, including two National Readers' Choice Awards. Readers may contact Kathie by emailing Kathie@kathiedenosky.com. They can also visit her website, www.kathiedenosky.com, or find her on Facebook at Facebook.com/Kathie-DeNosky-Author/278166445536145.

Lauren Canan, born and raised amid the cattle ranches of Texas, climbed a fence and jumped onto the back of her first horse at age three. She still maintains the punishment was worth the experience. She grew up listening to her dad tell stories of make-believe and was always encouraged to let her imagination soar. The multi-award-winning author and recipient of the 2014 Golden Heart® Award happily spends her days penning her favorite kind of stories: those of two people who, against all odds, meet, fall in love and live happily ever after—which is the way it should be. In her spare time she enjoys playing guitar, piano and dulcimer in acoustic club jams and getting lots of kisses and wags from her four-legged fuzzy babies. Visit Lauren's website at www.laurencanan.com. She would love to hear from you!

His Marriage Pact

KRISTI GOLD
KATHIE DENOSKY
LAUREN CANAN

MILLS & BOON

First Published in Great Britain 2018
by Mills & Boon, an imprint of HarperCollins*Publishers*
1 London Bridge Street, London, SE1 9GF

ISBN: 978-0-263-27458-5

0918

MIX
Paper from responsible sources
FSC C007454

This book is produced from independently certified FSC™ paper to ensure responsible forest management.

For more information visit: www.harpercollins.co.uk/green

Printed and bound in Spain
by CPI, Barcelona

THE RANCHER'S MARRIAGE PACT

KRISTI GOLD

To my childhood companion,
very best friend and surrogate sister,
Charlotte L.

One

The Last Chance Ranch...

Her first thought, as she left her compact sedan and strode toward the single-story white stone structure set somewhere between San Antonio and the middle of nowhere. Her second thought—the South Texas weather was ridiculously hot for March. She should never have worn the tailored black blazer and skirt. Fortunately she'd twisted her hair up and off her neck that was now damp with perspiration. Of course in part, her current predicament could be attributed to nerves, not the afternoon sun. And a good dose of desperation.

Once she reached the threshold, Paris flipped her sunglasses up onto her head and noted the wooden plaque to the right of the entry.

"Welcome to the D Bar C, where cowboys and hospitality rule. Take off your boots, hang your hat and come in to sit a spell. And if we don't happen to be here, just reach out and ring the bell."

Cute. Very cute. Unfortunately she wasn't wearing a hat or boots, but what she wouldn't give to kick off her three-inch heels and barrel in barefoot. Not a banner idea when applying for a job, and boy did she need this job. Of course, the position hadn't exactly been announced, yet that hadn't stopped her from showing up, uninvited, which could result in rejection. Nothing new there.

After smoothing a palm down her jacket, Paris drew in a calming breath as she clutched the strap of the teal briefcase hanging from her shoulder. She exhaled slowly before opening the heavy mahogany door to find the place blessedly cool, otherwise she might have shed her blazer to reveal the sheer sleeveless white shell. The area happened to be completely deserted, not one soul in sight behind the lengthy mahogany counter, yet she did spot the aforementioned bell.

She could ring it to summon someone, or she could wait. She could leave, or she could convene some courage and see this through. But she had come too far to give up now.

In a fit of sheer procrastination, Paris took a few moments to study the area with a designer's eye. Aside from the usual office equipment behind the counter, she discovered typical Western decor—burnt-orange-and-white cowhide chairs set about the waiting area, massive stone fireplace with a heavy wood mantel, a set of horns hanging above said mantel. She moved closer to read the bronze plaque below the sad symbol of human cruelty to find it etched with "Prize twelve-point buck bagged by J. D. Calloway."

Lovely. Just lovely. She supposed she should be thankful dear J.D. had only saved the horns as a souvenir and not the poor deer's entire head.

More than ready to see this spontaneous plan through, Paris turned back to the counter and reached for the bell with a trembling hand. But before she could pick it up, a tall, dark-haired man emerged from an entry at the far end of the office, looking as if he had walked right out of an Old West time warp and into the future. He kept his attention trained on a document clasped in his rather large and masculine hands as he strode toward her, the jingle of spurs echoing against the beige walls, providing her the prime opportunity to do a comprehensive inspection. He was every bit a cowboy, from the top of his tan hat to the tip of his brown leather boots. He wore a faded blue shirt and equally faded blue jeans, yet the large silver belt buckle drew her immediate focus. She noticed the word *Champion* before her gaze traveled lower to a place no self-respecting, professional woman should go.

"Can I help you, ma'am?"

At the sound of the incredibly deep voice, Paris's attention returned to the cowboy's face, her cheeks flaming from mortification. "Uh, actually, I'm..." Heavens, the impact of his silver-blue eyes caused her to forget her name. She'd seen several photographs of him, yet none had done Dallas Calloway justice.

He reacted to her momentary mental lapse with a

half smile, revealing a deep dimple creasing the left of his whisker-shaded jaw. "Are you lost?"

"Not really," she managed to say although in a sense she did feel a bit lost. "I'm Paris Reynolds."

He leaned over the counter and offered a hand. "Dallas Calloway. What can I do for you?"

That question was as loaded as a shotgun. But since this man could hold the key to her future financial security, she had to regain her composure. "I'm here about your new venture."

Before he could respond, a petite woman dressed in a plain tailored floral blouse covering faded jeans, her silver-and-brown hair twisted into a braid, strode into the room and pulled up short when she caught sight of the pair. She eyed Paris with suspicion as she made her way to Dallas's side. "Whatever you're selling, we're not buying."

Paris had the feeling no one crossed this woman and lived to tell about it. "I'm not selling anything but my services."

She huffed. "For your information, my stepson doesn't have to pay for it."

When awareness dawned, another bout of embarrassment plagued Paris. "You've definitely misunderstood my motives. I'm here to discuss a *business* proposition." Not that the explanation sounded much better, evidenced by the woman's raised eyebrows.

"Stop jumping to conclusions, Mom," Dallas interjected. "I'm fairly sure that's not what she's selling."

The woman propped a hand on her hip and sneered.

"Dallas deals on a daily basis with females who come here under the guise of business."

"Oh, so true, Maria," came from behind Paris. "Our stepson is a regular chick magnet."

Paris turned to find a pretty middle-aged blonde dressed in a chic coral sundress, standing at the front door. Apparently the place was rife with the now-deceased J. D. Calloway's wives. Determined to get off on the right foot with this one, she held out her hand and smiled. "I'm Paris Reynolds."

The blonde returned her smile and shook her hand with much more gusto than Paris expected. "I'm Jenny Parks Calloway, J.D.'s third wife."

"Not officially," Maria added in a sour tone.

Paris assumed there must be a story behind that comment, but chose to remain silent and await the fallout between the feuding former spouses.

It came out in Jenny's intense frown. "Please forgive the second missus. Sometimes Maria forgets her manners. What shade on the color chart is your blond, if you don't mind me asking?"

Paris's hand immediately went to her hair. "I wouldn't know. I'm actually a natural blonde."

Jenny chuckled. "Oh, so am I."

"And I'm the queen of Texas," Maria said with a smirk.

Ignoring the other mother, Jenny turned her smile back on Paris. "By the way, I love, love, love your suit, sugar."

Paris grasped to find a return compliment. "Thank you, and I love your bracelet."

Jenny twisted the diamond and silver leaf bauble around her wrist. "And thank you. I picked this up at a silent auction at the art center in San Antonio last month."

Unbelievable. "Really? I was there, too." But she hadn't had the funds to bid. She'd been there to drum up business. An unsuccessful plan that had led her to this remote ranch.

Jenny laid a hand beneath the strand of pearls at her throat. "A small, small world it is."

"Way too small if you ask me," Maria grumbled.

Jenny sent her another scowl. "No one asked you, Maria, and no one appreciates your attitude or your sarcasm. You really should learn some Southern decorum."

"I think we all can work on that," Dallas chimed in as he opened the half door built into the counter. "Ms. Reynolds, if you'll follow me to my office, we can get away from all this verbal sparring and you can tell me what you need."

"But make it quick," Maria added. "He has work to do."

"Oh, hush," Jenny replied as Paris stepped through the opening. "He's not too busy to entertain a pretty girl. Also, their names go so well together—Paris and Dallas. Sounds like a match made in heaven."

"Sounds like an airport flight schedule," Maria muttered.

"It's high time he meets a nice girl, Maria," Jenny added. "Don't forget what's coming up at the end of the week and we both know what that means."

If only Paris knew what that meant. Regardless, she

could tell Dallas wasn't comfortable with the conversation when he rushed toward an opening to his left without responding.

With her mind riddled with confusion, Paris followed Dallas down a lengthy corridor, all the while unsuccessfully trying to keep her eyes off his derriere. She found the way he dangled his arms at his sides, his perfect lean build and the roll of his hips quite fascinating.

Good grief. Evidently the lengthy amount of time she'd bccn without male companionship had her falling head over common sense over some cowboy. Okay, not just any cowboy. An extremely gorgeous, rich cowboy who had succeeded at everything he'd tried, from rodeo to ranching, according to what she'd read on the internet. A far cry from her seedy ex-husband who'd managed to screw up everything he'd endeavored, including their marriage.

Dallas soon paused to lead Paris into a well-appointed office that served as a tribute to his success. The lush brown leather sofa and love seat set near the window complemented his masculine aura, and the massive mahogany desk spoke to his rugged persona. The hand-scraped dark wood floors topped off the decor that couldn't have been done any better if she'd done it herself, even if it wasn't exactly her cup of tea.

"Would you like something to drink?" he asked as he crossed the room to the elaborate granite-covered wet bar in the corner.

"Water would be fine," she said, *although wine would be better*, she thought.

"Water it is. Have a seat."

After settling in a beige club chair across from the desk, Paris set her case on the floor, crossed her legs, adjusted her skirt and prepared to make her pitch. She decided to begin with casual conversation and in the same instant, assuage her natural curiosity. "If you don't mind my asking, what's coming up at the end of the week?"

"I turn thirty-eight on Saturday," he said as he retrieved a crystal highball glass from the upper cabinet.

Six years her senior. Not too bad. Not that it mattered. "Big party planned?"

Once he filled the tumbler with ice from a bucket on the counter, then poured water into it from a pitcher he pulled from the built-in stainless refrigerator, he returned to the desk and set the glass on a coaster before her. "I hope like hell that's not going to happen. I'm not one for having people making a big deal over my birthday."

She sensed he would be that kind of man. "I have a feeling your stepmothers might be planning a big deal."

He dropped down into the chair behind the desk, leaned back and affected a relaxed posture, but his expression said he didn't exactly appreciate her conjecture. "They know better than to pull that on me."

Paris gathered he might be suffering from a severe case of the birthday blues. "Are you sure? It sounded as if at least one of them wants you to have a date for some soiree, hence the *nice girl* comment."

He sent her that sexy, crooked smile again. "If that's the case, are you volunteering to fill the role?"

If she were only that brave. Then again, if it helped

her secure the job… "I generally avoid mixing business with pleasure, although your family seemed to jump to the conclusion that my business is pleasure."

He narrowed his eyes and studied her straight on. "Speaking of that, what exactly do you do for a living?"

The suspicion in his tone ruffled her feminine feathers. "It doesn't involve a nine hundred number or a pimp, I promise you that."

Now he looked amused. "Glad you cleared the air."

So was she, and she planned to be perfectly clear. "In reality, I'm—"

"Wait. Let me guess." He inclined his head and pointed at her. "You're a stockbroker and you want to get your hands on my investments."

She might like to get her hands on something of his that happened to be a far cry from his portfolio. Since when had she become a purveyor of naughty thoughts? "Not even close."

He rubbed a palm over his chin. "I would bet the back forty you have an accounting degree."

If he only knew about her lack of accounting skills, he would never have assumed such a thing. That downfall had landed her in deep trouble and served as another reason for being there, about to beg for employment. "Believe me, math is not my forte."

"Marketing?"

In an effort to clear her parched throat, Paris took a quick sip of water. "Try again."

His gaze landed on her fingers still wrapped around the glass. "Considering your perfectly manicured nails, I'm guessing you're not a ranch hand."

"I haven't even seen a cow up close."

"Not even on your dinner plate in the form of filet mignon?"

"I'm primarily a vegetarian."

"I'm strictly a meat-and-potatoes kind of guy."

What a shocker. "I won't judge your food preferences if you won't judge mine."

"Agreed." He took off his hat to place it brim up on the desk, then forked a hand through his dark brown hair that worked well with those deadly blue eyes. "If you're a beautician, I don't need one. Just a quick round with the clippers and I'm good to go."

Yes, he was. Good enough to go anywhere he might want to take her. "No, I'm not a hairstylist. Do you give up now?"

"Yep. I'm all out of guesses."

The time had come to lay all her cards on the table, less a few secrets he didn't need to know. "I'm a commercial interior designer." Disgraced designer.

"No kidding?" he said, sounding somewhat awed over the admission.

"No kidding. And that's why I'm here. I wanted to speak to you about—"

"Hey, Dallas, I'm about to head out."

Paris shifted in her seat to see a young, buff blond guy filling the doorway. Aside from the tattered jeans and worn cowboy boots, he looked more surfer than rancher. Or body builder in light of the fit of the lime-green T-shirt hugging his muscled arms and torso.

"Where are you going now?" Dallas asked, looking and sounding none too pleased.

"To the beach for the weekend," the stranger replied as he strode to the wet bar.

Aha! Paris had pegged him right on his surfer status, though she still didn't know his relationship to the Calloways. He certainly didn't resemble Dallas.

"Did you talk to Fort yet, Worth?" Dallas asked.

"I called him," the man with the unusual name said as he pulled a soda from the fridge and popped it open. "But he's still pissed I left him high and dry and came here. He refuses to call me back."

"Figures," Dallas muttered. "By the way, does Houston know you're leaving?"

"Yeah, and Austin's agreed to hang around in case any of the heifers calve."

"That's good because Tyler's going to be gone until Monday."

Paris felt as though she'd just gone on a Cities of Texas tour. Without further hesitation, she stood to face Surfer Worth and smiled, bent on introducing herself since her potential boss evidently wasn't going to do the honors. "Hi, my name is Paris Reynolds."

Worth grinned and shook her extended hand, revealing the same dimple Dallas sported. "Pleasure to meet you, ma'am. Are you a friend of my big brother's?"

That confirmed her supposition that he was a Calloway sibling, although she couldn't recall any mention of him in any of the press releases she'd recently read. "Actually, we just met today."

Worth winked. "Well, if he doesn't treat you right, you're welcome to come to Padre Island with me. I'm a helluva lot more fun."

And way too young for her, Paris decided. Plus, she had always been attracted to brown-haired men, like the one seated not far away.

Dallas pointed at the door. "Get out, Worthless. Ms. Reynolds doesn't need you coming on to her."

Worth backed toward the exit with hands held up, palms forward. "All right. And when you find out where the hell you left your sense of humor, let me know."

With that, the younger Calloway son winked at Paris again before striding out of the room.

"I apologize for his behavior," Dallas said as he resumed holding cowboy court from his place behind the desk.

Paris dropped back down into her designated chair. "No need. He seems relatively harmless."

"He's a skirt chaser, according to his mother, and I've seen more than enough evidence of that fact."

The identity of Worth's mother didn't require a lot of guessing. "Is that Jenny?"

"Yeah, my father's third wife. Maria is the second."

"And your mother is?"

Dallas's gaze drifted away for a moment. "Gone. She died when I was pretty young."

"I'm sorry, Dallas." And she sincerely was. "I'm sure that's been really difficult for you."

"Not so much," he said. "I barely remember her. Now let's get back to the reason why you're here."

Being summarily dismissed wasn't all that surprising to Paris. Most men clammed up when it came to emotional issues, including her own father. "Well, as I was saying, I'm a commercial interior designer, and since it's apparent you'll need my services soon, I'm here to apply for the position."

He frowned. "Why do you believe I need an interior decorator?"

She wasn't certain if he was kidding, or he really didn't have a clue. "Look, I saw an article in the San Antonio paper about this Texas Extreme project and how you're going to cater to people who want to enjoy the whole high-risk rodeo experience." Though she couldn't imagine why anyone would want to do that. "I also read about your plans to build a lodge to house your guests, and that's where I come in. I would like the opportunity to oversee the design of that lodge."

"We haven't even broken ground yet," he said. "In fact, we haven't seen the final plans from the architect."

That could definitely work to her advantage. "All the better. If I'm involved in the beginning, then I can make suggestions that will only enhance the guests' experience. I have extensive knowledge in hotel design. I have a strong attention to detail and—"

"Ms. Reynolds—"

"Paris."

"Okay, Paris, first of all, these guests are wannabe cowboys. They don't need a fancy room. They only need a bunk and a bathroom. Hell, they might be satisfied with an outhouse and a creek."

The thought made her shudder. Yet he had made a good point, darn it. Still… "What if some of them want to bring their wives? Women have much higher standards. What if some of the wives or girlfriends want to participate, too?"

He mulled that over a moment before addressing her again. "I hadn't thought about that."

Now she was getting somewhere. "Have you given any consideration to the kitchen? You are having one installed, aren't you? Or will you be roasting marshmallows and wieners?"

He favored her with a sexy grin. "That's a thought."

"Seriously? A wiener roast for every meal?"

"Maybe that's not a great idea. But the kitchen doesn't have to be all that elaborate. Just the basics."

He truly didn't grasp the concept of hospitality. "How many people do you plan to house at one time?"

"Fifty if we're at capacity, but we want to be able to accommodate more in the future."

"Feeding fifty hungry men and/or women will require more than a four-burner stove, a side-by-side refrigerator and a single oven. You'll need commercial-grade appliances, plenty of prep space—"

"I understand what you're saying," he said, effectively cutting her off. "But we don't plan to open for business for a year, maybe longer if we can't get all the facilities set up by then. Not only do we have to build the lodge, we have to build a new arena and catch pens, plus a first-aid station and acquire rodeo stock. I wouldn't even need you for a good six months."

She would be destitute in two months. The unwelcome sense of extreme anxiety came home to roost, prompting Paris to make a final plea. "Again, you would be better off hiring me now than fixing something later. That will only cost you more money. I could meet with the architect before the plans are finalized. I could take care of all the details from the ground up. Besides, I live in San Antonio and since that's only an hour and a half away, that's convenient for us both. And I'm going to work cheaper than many firms you might decide to hire, but I don't do cheap work or cut corners. To be perfectly honest, you can't do better than me. And most important, I really, really need this job."

He tilted his head again and eyed her suspiciously. "If you're so good at it, why is that?"

She'd gone too far with the tirade, and probably blown any chance at the opportunity to oversee his project. Yct she was somewhat bolstered by the fact he hadn't kicked her out…yet. "Due to personal circumstances beyond my control, I've been forced to start over, but I won't bother you with the details. I would like to show you my work."

As she drew a breath, Paris fumbled for the briefcase resting on the floor and lifted it up. "I have my portfolio right here if you care to take a quick look."

Dallas sat in silence for a few moments while Paris's pulse raced out of control. "I'm sure you're more than qualified for the job," he finally said, "but like I told you, I don't see the need to hire a decorator—"

"Designer," Paris corrected without regard to helping her cause.

"Hiring a *designer* right now doesn't make much sense to me."

Plagued with the bitter taste of defeat, Paris stood. "Fine, but you should be aware, in six months, I might not be available." She might even be in jail. Or worse—

living with her folks on a potato farm in Idaho. "It's been a pleasure to meet you."

Dallas came to his feet and rounded the desk. "One question before you leave. What exactly did you mean by having to start over?"

She certainly wasn't prepared to get into that, but if it meant he might possibly reconsider, she would tell him everything. Almost everything. "Okay, as long as you understand I'm not looking for pity."

"Understood."

Oh, how she hated having to explain the sordid details. "Almost two years ago, my ex-husband left in the middle of the night, took every penny I owned and then took off to the Dominican Republic to get a quickie divorce."

The anger that flashed in his eyes took her aback. "Where is the bastard now?"

"Still there, with my hard-earned money and a new girlfriend. Shortly thereafter, the firm where I'd been working for eight years laid me off. I have very few funds to maintain my apartment for much longer, so I might be forced to move in with my family until I get back on my feet." That last part had wounded her pride beyond belief. The part she'd left out—the reasons why she'd lost her job—had caused her great shame.

He attempted a slight smile. "I can relate to living with family."

"Your stepmothers live with you?"

"No, they live in the main house. I built my own place a few years ago. But I see them every day, whether I want to or not."

They just stood there in uncomfortable silence until Paris decided to end the meeting and escape from her humiliating revelations. She retrieved a card from her bag's side pocket and offered it to him. "If you happen to change your mind, here's my contact information. If not, I wish you the best of luck with your new venture."

"Good luck to you, too," he said as he escorted her to the door. "And if I happen to need a date to a surprise birthday party, I just might give you a call."

Oh, sure he would. In some ways she wished he would. Who wouldn't want to spend an evening with a gorgeous macho guy? And since he obviously wasn't going to hire her…"You know, I just might take you up on the invitation."

Without gauging his response, Paris worked her way back to the front office and out the door, pausing only long enough to tell both mothers to have a good day. Once she slid into her car, she experienced overwhelming dejection over the epic failure. But she refused to cry. She'd already done enough of that to last a lifetime.

"Why in the hell did you let her leave, Dallas?"

At the moment, a lecture from Maria—his long time maternal influence—was the very last thing Dallas needed. He still hadn't gotten over the impact of the pretty green-eyed, golden-haired, determined woman named after a European city who had landed on his doorstep. He didn't quite understand his reaction to her, either. A strong reaction that had had him wanting to suggest things to her that any man with an ounce of honor wouldn't dare mention to a woman he'd just met. And if Maria Leone Calloway could read his mind, she would nix the speech and wash his mouth out with homemade soap even if he hadn't uttered a dirty word.

He cleared the uncomfortable hitch from his throat and shifted in his chair. "I don't know why her departure is bothering you, Mom. I figured you didn't like her all that much."

Without invitation, the current burr in his backside took the seat Paris Reynolds had vacated a few minutes before. "She's a little too uppity in my opinion, *mijo*. But as bad as I hate to admit it, Jenny was right about one thing. You need to find a woman, and maybe this Paris is that woman."

Dallas rocked back in his chair and sighed. "First of all, you both need to forget about that. It's too late. Secondly, I've come to terms with staying single and you just need to accept it."

Maria narrowed her dark eyes. "You're telling me you're going to let your no-account little brother gain control over this ranch?"

The thought left a bad taste in his mouth. "Blame your husband for putting that stupid marriage codicil in the will, although it still doesn't make any sense why Dad would leave this place to Fort. From what Jenny says, the kid was a rebel most of his life, plus he already owns the horse farm in Louisiana."

Maria tightened the band securing her braid, a nervous habit for as long as Dallas could remember. "You're right. It doesn't make a damn bit of sense what J.D. did, particularly since Fort wants nothing to do with you or any of his brothers. Then again, what your father did to me and Jenny didn't make any sense, either."

Dallas would never forget that day six years ago when during the reading of his father's will, he'd not only discovered he had twin half-brothers, he'd learned his father had been living as a bigamist. "I'm hoping Fort's disdain for the family will be enough for him to ignore the stipulation." Even if he wasn't banking on it.

"That's a big chance you'd be taking, Dallas," Maria said. "If you're wrong, he'll put a stop to your dream of turning this place into Texas Extreme. Hell, he could even toss you and your brothers off the property, take over the houses you all built and legally he could do it."

He knew that all too well. He also knew Fort would probably turn the place into a subdivision just to spite them. "I don't have a choice, Mom. I can't find a proper wife in four days, nor do I even want to attempt it."

The other mother—every bit the Southern belle—suddenly breezed into the room and stood behind Maria. "I think Paris is quite proper and sophisticated, and a man of your financial means and social status needs that in a life partner. If you make an effort to get to know her, who knows what could happen in a few days? You might find yourself falling hopelessly in love for the first time in your life, sugar. Why, I met your father on a Saturday night and we were married two weeks later."

"And look how that turned out, Jenny," Maria said. "Don't give him reason not to give this a shot."

Over the past few years, Dallas had learned one important thing about Jenny Parks Calloway—she was a flighty romantic who spent most of her days with stars in her eyes. "That's good in theory, Jen, but the chances of it happening are slim to none. And even if I wanted to pursue a relationship with Paris Reynolds, who's to say she would agree? And even if she did agree to go out with me, do you really think she'd jump at the chance to marry me two days later? Get real."

"She sounded pretty desperate to us," Jenny chimed in, then clamped her mouth closed after Maria shot her a nasty look over her shoulder.

Dallas wasn't all that shocked, but he was pretty pissed off over the intrusion. "You two were listening to our conversation?"

"Just a little bit," Jenny said sheepishly. "Your phone's intercom was on."

He looked at the key pad, noted the button was depressed and then muttered a few mild oaths. "Why didn't you tell me?"

"We didn't want to disturb you, *mijo*," Maria said.

Dallas didn't buy that for a minute. "You wanted to eavesdrop. Regardless of how desperate Paris might be, I don't see her as the kind of woman who'd agree to marry a stranger in exchange for a job. And I'm not the kind of man who would ask that of any woman."

Jenny put on her sweeter-than-honey expression. "Sugar, I love my son, but I also know Fort doesn't deserve this place given how much grief he's showered on me and Worth. Why don't you just invite Paris to dinner tonight and see what happens?"

He'd like to see what happened, but not in the way she was thinking. "I'm sure she's already halfway to

San Antonio by now and I've got a lot do before I fly to Houston in two days."

"You can take one night off," Maria stated, a totally out-of-character comment.

"Yes, you can, for the cause," Jenny added. "Now go after her, sugar, and escort her back here. I can make you both my famous chateaubriand."

He saw one big problem with that, and a prime excuse to halt all the nonsense. "She's a vegetarian."

Maria shook her head. "Yeah, we heard her say that, but it's not normal. Not normal at all."

"We'll work around it," Jenny said. "I'll make a wonderful assortment of spring vegetables. That will allow Dallas and Paris to get to know each other better in an intimate setting, not a crowded restaurant."

Dallas barked out a laugh. "Sure, while the two of you hang out in the next room, listening to every word we say."

Jenny raised her hand like she was about to take an oath. "I swear I will leave as soon as the food is served. Maria will, too. Right?"

Maria stared up at Jenny. "Why do you need me there anyway?"

"For moral support," Jenny answered. "And you can make Dallas his usual T-bone, since that's not my forte."

Maria sighed. "It's easy. Remove the horns, slap it on the stove, make sure it's not mooing and put it on the plate."

Jenny ignored Maria and took his hand. "Sugar, we'll work out the dinner details. In the meantime, you just have to convince Paris to join you by telling her you want to discuss the particulars of the job, sort of like an interview. Then you can see what comes up after that."

He had a sneaking suspicion he knew exactly what would come up if he didn't get a rein on his libido. Logical or not, he did like the plan, if for no other reason than to spend a little more time with Paris. As far as the mothers' harebrained matrimony scheme was concerned, no way would that happen.

After pushing away from the desk, he stood and propped his hat on his head. "All right, you two. Get to cooking and I'll go get the girl."

Two

Seated in her compact sedan, Paris stared at the private number displayed on her phone. Normally she would ignore the call, but some mysterious force propelled her to answer. “Hello?”

“Where are you right now?”

Overcome with sudden paranoia, she looked around the almost empty lot for some seedy no-account who’d magically come upon her cell number. “Who is this?”

“Sorry. It’s Dallas Calloway. Are you back in San Antonio?”

“No,” she said after she’d regained enough composure to speak. “I’m at a convenience store somewhere between Cotulla and Dilley. Or maybe I’ve already passed Dilley and missed it when I blinked.”

“Right off the interstate?”

"Yes. It's a red-and-white building with some weird creature on the sign, but I can't see the name from here."

"I know the place. Stay put. I'll be there in a few."

Paris didn't have the opportunity to say another word before the line went dead, leaving her with a laundry list of questions bombarding her brain. Why would he want to come after her? Had she left something important at the office? She glanced at the passenger seat to verify the presence of her briefcase, although only a few moments ago she'd just carried it into the store to pay for gas and buy a snack. Speaking of snacks…she yanked down the visor and pulled up the vanity mirror to check for the presence of chocolate, which she found smeared in the corner of her mouth.

Paris scrambled around in the center console for a napkin, then swiped furiously over the offensive spot while cursing herself for being such a cliché. Have stress, grab candy. Preferably chocolate candy. Dark, light, didn't matter. As long as it contained cocoa and no nuts.

After reapplying her lipstick, and tightening the hair band securing the low twist at her nape, she waited for the enigmatic cowboy to arrive in a pickup, or possibly ride up on his trusty horse.

The first assumption had been correct, she realized, when a large dual-wheeled black monstrosity of a truck pulled in the space to her right and its dashing driver left the cab.

As Dallas approached the door, Paris powered down her window to find out what his surprise appearance was all about. "Did I forget something?" she asked as soon as he arrived.

"Nope," he said. "But I forgot to ask you something."

"What would that be, pray tell?"

"If you'd care to stay for dinner."

Only moments ago, she'd consumed a large bar of candy and washed it down with cola so dinner wasn't all that appealing. But maybe this was his way of saying he might be considering her for the position after all. "Dinner would be nice, but wouldn't it have been much easier for you to call me and ask me to come back rather than you drive all the way here?"

"Yep, that fifteen-minute drive was a real hardship, but here the West is still wild, and the men go after their women."

She'd give him a speech on the death of chauvinism if he didn't look so gorgeous displaying that grin and a delightful dimple. "Far be it from me to question archaic tradition."

He leaned over and folded his arms on the window's ledge. "Are you going to follow me home, or do you want to ride with me and I'll bring you back later to get your car?"

Although he seemed harmless enough, Paris wasn't stupid. If she didn't have her vehicle, she couldn't determine when it was time to go. "I know the way now. I'll drive."

He pushed away from the car and straightened. "Fine by me. See you in a bit."

In less time than it took Paris to fasten her seat belt, Dallas shot out of the lot on spinning tires, kicking up a flurry of dust in his wake as he turned onto the access road. She took a little more time following suit, still questioning the reason behind his surprise invitation.

Yet life wasn't without risk, and she'd taken plenty in her formative years. Some had turned out well, others, not so much. She hoped this risk proved to be a good one.

After traveling ten or so miles, she found Dallas had pulled over on the shoulder to wait for her. He seemed to slow down to accommodate her caution, and remained that way until they turned off the interstate and onto the rural road leading to the ranch.

Once they traveled through the elaborate stone entry containing the iron sign announcing their arrival at the D Bar C, Dallas drove past the office where the barren terrain took a dramatic turn. Paris glanced from the road long enough to ogle the massive white rock ranch house to her left as Dallas continued on. They passed by several other large houses set back off the road, each one appearing to include transplanted trees, lovely landscaping, first-rate barns and expensive vehicles, including one black Porsche that she would wager belonged to Worth. After Dallas took a left, pavement soon turned to gravel as they navigated through pastureland lined with barbwire fence and dotted with mesquite.

They soon passed a large pond lined with weeping willows where a two-story, expansive home came into view, dealing Paris another stunning mental blow. The structure was also stone trimmed with cedar accents, like the rest of the residences, only this one had a gleaming silver metal roof and seemed to be twice the size, as well as a tad more elaborate. If she didn't know better, she would have thought she'd happened upon a resort hotel.

Dallas pulled beneath the portico and Paris followed his lead, half expecting to be greeted by a parking attendant. When that didn't happen, she slid out of the car and joined her host for the evening at the entry. "Nice place you have here," she said as he opened one of the heavy pine double doors.

"It'll do," he replied with surprising nonchalance.

It would more than do, she realized after she stepped over the threshold. A grand staircase with a wrought iron banister centered in the soaring foyer, and dark slate floors could be deemed somewhat elegant. Yet that was where the elegance ended, right before the West began.

As Paris trailed behind Dallas into the great room, the cowboy culture came shining through in the floor-to-ceiling rock fireplace anchoring the room along with the macho leather furniture in shades of gray and black. And hanging from the towering ceiling, a chandelier, for lack of a better term, appeared to be made out of metallic animal horns, although she would swear they weren't authentic. At least she hoped not.

"Welcome to Dallas's little piece of heaven, Paris," Jenny said as she floated into the room wearing a frilly pink apron and a vibrant smile.

Odd that Dallas didn't have household staff and had to rely on his stepmother to play hostess. "Thanks for having me, and I have to agree. This place is paradise."

Jenny's grin deepened. "You should see the veranda overlooking the pool, which is where you two will dine so you can watch the sunset. The view is breathtaking."

Dallas frowned. "I'm thinking the dining room might be better since it's still fairly hot outside and the mosquitoes are big as airplanes."

Jenny waved her hand in a dismissive gesture. "Oh, posh, Dallas. You don't have a romantic bone in your body. Besides, the temperature will go down with the sun and it's too early in the year for a lot of bugs, including mosquitoes."

A sunset dinner was conducive to romance, but Paris was not in the market for wining and dining or mosquitoes. "The dining room will be fine." When Jenny looked absolutely disappointed, she added, "Or the veranda. I'm sure the sunset is very impressive."

"The veranda it is," Jenny said as she started to back away. "Dinner will be ready very soon and I assure you, Paris, I'm preparing a delectable vegetarian meal. In the meantime, Dallas can give you the VIP tour. His master suite is to die for."

She questioned the wisdom in viewing Dallas's bedroom. "I'm looking forward to it. The tour, I mean."

Jenny smiled before she hurried away, leaving Dallas and Paris standing in the middle of the great room cloaked in uncomfortable silence.

"Are you ready for the tour?" he asked.

As long as he didn't get too close to her in the boudoir; otherwise she might forget herself in the shadow of that smile. "I'm more than a little curious, so lead the way."

"Okay. Follow me."

And she did, up the stairs, trying desperately to avoid studying his butt before they took an immediate right at the top landing. They walked by several closed doors before reaching the end of the corridor where Dallas paused at a pair of double doors.

"Prepare yourself," he said. "You're about to see where all the action happens."

Holding her breath, Paris expected to discover a large bed, but she only saw what appeared to be a cowboy man cave with an at least seventy-inch television screen, a large old-fashioned bar straight out of a saloon and a series of round wooden tables and straight-backed chairs. She strolled toward a large glass display case to her right that housed trophies and belt buckles and trinkets from days past. "Is this the Dallas Calloway Hall of Fame?"

"Not exactly," he said from behind her. "If I had my way, those things would've stayed in the trunk in the tack room."

She glanced at him over one shoulder. "You should be proud of these. Not many men can lay claim to being a three-time world champion all-around cowboy."

"Funny, that's what Maria said." He came to her side, showing his handsome profile to full advantage. "She set this up after I built the house."

Time to get to know him a bit better. "You two are close, huh?"

He streaked a palm over his neck. "Yeah. She's the only mother I've ever really known. Then Jen came into the mix and now I have two mothers. Double trouble. They mean well but sometimes they're both a little too motherly."

"Right down to choosing your mate?"

He shot her a smile, throwing her for a mental loop.

"They try but I don't listen to them when it comes to my choice in female companionship."

That led Paris to a question she'd been dying to ask, perhaps at her own detriment if she dared. "You really don't have a girlfriend waiting somewhere in the wings?"

He turned those silver-blue eyes on her. "Nope. I've had a couple of steady girlfriends in the past, but rodeo and relationships didn't mix well."

"Apparently you no longer rodeo, so do you see yourself eventually settling down?"

He sent her an odd look before he brought his attention back to the mementos from his past. "Only if and when the time is right."

"I'm sure you're considered quite the catch in these parts. Probably throughout the state."

He turned and leaned a shoulder against the case. "I've had my share of propositions, but it's kind of hard to tell if they're more interested in my personality, or my personal finances."

Or his stellar physical attributes. "I'm sure more than a few are drawn to the cowboy fantasy and the notion you'll scoop them up and ride off into the sunset."

"Is that your fantasy?"

Not until that moment. Not until he favored her with that winning, dimpled grin again. "My exposure to cowboys has been nonexistent, so I'd have to say no."

He inched a little closer. "Now that you've been exposed, do you think you might change your mind?"

Heaven help her, he was flirting like a teenage jock. And she responded like an adolescent schoolgirl with a self-conscious smile. "The jury is still out. I'll let you know after dinner."

"And I'll do my best to show you there's something to be said for the cowboy way."

They stood there in silence, tension as thick as a morning haze hanging over them as Dallas's focus landed on her mouth. Paris sensed if she moved just a little closer, gave him just a little encouragement, he might actually kiss her. And she might actually hurl caution to the warm wind and let him.

The sound of staccato footsteps interrupted the moment and drew Paris back into reality and her attention to the doorway where Jenny now stood sporting a knowing look. "Dinner is served, y'all. Just come on out to the veranda when you're finished doing whatever it is you're doing."

As soon as Jenny disappeared, Paris turned back to Dallas. "Shall we go? I'm suddenly starving."

"So am I," he replied, keeping his gaze centered on hers. "Food sounds pretty good, too."

Paris released a nervous laugh. "I can tell you have a little bad boy in you."

"Yeah, darlin', I do. But don't ever doubt I'm every bit a man."

That wasn't up for debate. Paris had a sneaking suspicion if she hung around too long after dinner and let down her guard, she could very well see exactly how manly he could be.

She was getting under his skin, a dangerous prospect. He didn't need to lose all control around her, but he almost had. He didn't need a woman complicating his life, even if he couldn't deny he needed a woman. But not just any woman. *This* woman.

Dallas pushed his empty plate aside and watched as Paris sipped at the second mint julep Jenny had served her. He'd settled for a beer, but only one, in order to keep his wits about him. He didn't know enough about Paris to bring out the usual moves, even if those fantastic green eyes had reeled him in like a trout on a fly from the minute she'd walked into the office. He brought his attention to her hands, imagined those slender fingers raking across his chest, then traveling lower to the nagging place down south that craved some female attention.

Shaking off the images, Dallas thought it best to talk, not fantasize about her being naked beneath him. "How long have you been a vegetarian?"

She dabbed at her lips then set the napkin aside. "When I started college, I was determined not to gain the typical freshman fifteen. And honestly, when I was in my teens, I was somewhat...chunky."

He couldn't even imagine that. "Are you kidding?"

"It's true. I wasn't obese, but I was anything but thin. My family moved around a lot and I tended to use food to compensate for the fact I didn't have time to make friends. Before I knew it, I was a regular porker who lived on cheeseburgers and fries."

"The only way I'd believe that is to see some pictures."

She shook her head. "No way. Besides, I think I probably destroyed all evidence."

He downed the last of the beer and pushed the mug away. "You said you moved a lot. Why is that?"

"I was a navy brat. We were rarely in one place for any length of time."

"Do you have any siblings?"

"An older sister. She's living around the corner from my parents in Idaho with her husband and three kids. My folks are so proud."

"They're not proud of you?"

She rimmed a fingertip around the edge of the glass. "Let's just say they don't understand my creative nature. Or at least my father never did. He preferred I become a nurse or teacher."

"A traditionalist, huh?"

"More like a taskmaster. It was always his way or the highway."

He could relate to that. His father was still controlling his life from the grave. "My dad never liked me devoting all my time to the rodeo. That made him a damn hypocrite since he met my mother on the circuit."

"Really?"

"Yeah. She was a barrel racer and he was a bulldogger."

"Bulldogger?"

"Steer wrestler."

She frowned. "Why would you want to wrestle a steer? That sounds rather dangerous."

He chuckled over her lack of comprehension. "Sorry. I'm just surrounded by women who lived with rodeo cowboys. Most of the time they think they know more about it than I do."

After downing the last of her drink, she took off her jacket and laid it in her lap, revealing a sleeveless silk top that sparked his imagination. And suddenly he started to sweat.

"Well, you'll never have to worry about that with me," she began, "because obviously I know nothing about the rodeo. Not that I'm averse to learning. I'm a quick study."

Just seeing her bare arms, and a hint of cleavage, brought to mind a few lessons involving his second favorite sport. "I'm a good teacher."

Smiling, she bent her elbow on the table and supported her cheek with her palm. "When is my first lesson?"

He wanted to suggest tonight, but the fact her voice sounded a little thick led him to believe she might be feeling the effects of the alcohol. "You name the place and the time, and I'll be there."

After a moment's hesitation, she straightened and stared out at the horizon. "This place really surprised me. I was expecting a lot more desertlike terrain, not all this green pastureland. The scenery is really beautiful."

So was she, and the fact she didn't seem to realize that only elevated Dallas's opinion of her. "Yeah, when the sky turns orange at sunset, it makes all the mesquite trees look good."

She sent him a smile. "Where are you going to put the lodge?"

"On the east side of the property. We've surveyed about five acres that will be dedicated to Texas Extreme."

"How many acres do you have?"

"Ten thousand."

Her eyes went wide. "Wow. That's a lot of land."

He resisted reaching across the table and pushing the strand of hair away from her cheek. "We have a large herd of cattle. In fact, Texas Extreme is going to offer the experience of a good old-fashioned cattle drive, including a camp-out under the stars, complete with a chuck wagon."

"That actually sounds fun. I'd like to join you."

"You'd have to learn to ride a horse first."

"I'm game, as long as it's a gentle horse."

"That can be arranged. I have a good gelding. He's so broke I'd put a five-year-old on him."

"That would be about my speed."

"Something tells me you'd be a natural."

Her cheeks turned a light shade of pink. "Thanks, but don't count on it. I'm not sure I've ever been a natural at anything except designing."

That put all sorts of questionable images in his mind. "I doubt that. In fact, I'm fairly sure you're a natural at several things."

She barked out a soft laugh. "I can't think of one."

"I can, but I'm guessing your ex never tapped into your innate abilities."

"My ex rarely tapped into anything after our first year of marriage."

Without giving it a thought, Dallas reached over and pushed that sliver of golden hair away from her face. "The man had to be an idiot. Is that why you divorced him?"

She suddenly looked more than a little uncomfortable. "He divorced me, remember? Not that I thought the marriage had any chance of surviving at that juncture. Anyway, I should probably be going before it gets any later."

He really didn't want her to leave but he had no one to blame but himself for bringing up past history. "It's barely eight."

"And I still have to drive back to San Antonio."

When Paris pushed back from the table, came to her feet and swayed, Dallas stood and caught her arm. "Are you okay?"

She pinched the bridge of her nose with her fingers. "I was fine until I got up. Guess I'm a little tired. That drink went straight to my head."

As he'd predicted, Jenny's mint juleps had claimed another unsuspecting victim. He should've warned Paris that she could be heavy-handed with the bourbon. "Come to think of it, you had two."

She sent him a shaky smile. "I did, didn't I?"

"Yeah, you did, which means you're in no shape to drive."

Her stern expression didn't take away from her fantastic face. "I can't very well stay here."

"You can, and you will. I have several guest rooms. Five, in fact. Take your pick." If he had his way, she'd pick his room. But he'd been taught never to take advantage of a woman under the influence.

"I didn't pack a bag," she protested. "I'm sure if I lie down for a little while, I'll be fine."

He didn't have much faith in that. "We'll see how

you feel later, but I'm not going to let you get behind the wheel tonight if I think you're not fit to drive. End of discussion."

Clasping her elbow, Dallas led Paris through the double sliding doors, into the sunroom and guided her to the great room. He took one look at the towering staircase and decided showing her to his downstairs quarters would be the better part of valor.

He continued down the corridor and past the kitchen where he noticed Jenny cleaning up the dishes. He didn't dare stop although he knew he'd have to do some serious explaining if she caught sight of them heading to the bedroom. He'd wager his inheritance she had. Not a problem. He had a bone to pick with her over the booze.

Once they arrived at the back of the house, he let go of Paris long enough to open the double doors before grasping her arm to steady her.

She took him by surprise when she wrenched out of his hold and headed to the bed. "This looks heavenly," she said as she fell back on the mattress and laughed. "What a lovely guest room."

"It's my room," he muttered. "I wasn't sure you could make it up the stairs."

She giggled again when she kicked off her shoes and one landed on top of the dresser several feet away, barely missing the mirror. "Are you trying to ruin my reputation, sir?"

"I'm trying to keep you from breaking your neck." He crossed the room and held out his hands. "Hop up so I can turn down the covers."

She accepted the gesture but instead of stepping

aside, she stepped right into his arms. And then she did the one thing he'd been avoiding all night, yet wanted more than anything. She planted her mouth on his.

She looked like a saint and kissed like a sinner. Oh, yeah, she was a natural. She had mighty fine lips and met his tongue stroke for stroke. He roved his palms down her slender back and paused right before he reached her butt, which took a lot of effort.

He intended to stop it before they went too far. Stop short before it went too deep. But when she pressed that sweet body against his, he tossed all those well-intentioned plans to the plains. And the longer this went on, the more he wanted to take her back onto the bed… or ignore all formality and take her down to the floor.

Without warning, Paris pulled away and touched her fingertips to her mouth like she'd been burned. "I'm not normally that bold."

He liked her *that* bold. "You're not thinking straight."

"I'm a little bit tipsy," she said, her speech slurred. "I came here to convince you to hire me, not to drink and make out with you."

That made him feel like an oversexed teenager. "It was just a kiss, Paris." One knock-em-dead kiss. "And I'm the one who should've stopped it."

Paris dropped down on the edge of the mattress. "I'm really not…normally…like this." She followed the comment with a hiccup and a giggle.

"You've got a good excuse," he said as he pulled her up again and set her aside to turn down the comforter. "Now lie down and sleep it off."

"Okay," she said through a yawn. "But don't let me

sleep too long. I have to…" Her eyes drifted closed then opened again. "Hmmm. I have to do something tomorrow but I can't remember what."

Dallas suspected she'd be there all night, and he'd be spending the evening in another bed, wishing he was beside her. He hooked a thumb behind him. "The bathroom's there if you need it. Make yourself at home."

She pulled the band that secured her low ponytail and set it on the nightstand before she perched on the edge of the mattress. "Thank you, Dallas Calloway. You're a nice man, and I'm sorry I'm not acting like a nice girl."

He liked his girls a little naughty, he started to say, but began backing to the door when he noticed how sexy she looked with that blond hair curling around her shoulders. "No need to apologize. Just get some rest."

She stretched her arms over her head and sent him a sleepy smile. "Since I probably blew my chances at the job, I wouldn't mind another kiss good-night." She tapped her cheek and smiled. "Just a peck."

He might laugh at that if he hadn't been so damn uncomfortable, or tempted to do more than give her *just* a peck. "We'll talk later when you're sober. I'll check on you in a bit."

Before he traded in his honor and gave in to animal urges, Dallas rushed out of the room, closed the door behind him and then headed down the hall to confront the culprit who'd created the chaos. Once he reached the kitchen, he found Jenny loading the last of the dishes into the washer. "What in the hell did you put in those drinks?"

Jenny turned toward him and had the gall to look

surprised. "Why, honey, just the usual. A little mint, some sugar and water, bourbon. And maybe a touch of tequila."

That explained a lot. "You added tequila on top of the bourbon?"

She didn't bother to look contrite. "Yes. It gives the julep that special kick everyone raves about."

"It kicked my date right into drunk mode."

Jenny grinned. "Your date?"

"Guest," he corrected, although he didn't see much point in getting the details right.

"Maybe I put a little too much alcohol into the drink," she said, "but I thought it would help Paris relax."

"Hell, she's relaxed all right. She's passed out in my bed."

"Then why are you in here?"

He was asking himself that same question. "Because there is no way I'm going to seduce a woman who's intoxicated."

Jenny leaned back against the counter. "Of course you wouldn't, sugar. You're too good for that. However, she won't be drunk in the morning."

Of all the confounded suggestions. "I'm going to check on Paris and then I'm going upstairs."

"I'll have a nice breakfast waiting for the two of you in the morning."

"Great."

Without further comment, Dallas turned around and nearly ran into his other stepmother. "'Night," he muttered, looking for a quick escape.

Maria had other ideas, he realized, when she grabbed his arm. "Why is the woman still here?"

He didn't have the energy to explain. "Ask Jenny," he said as he brushed past her and headed toward his bedroom.

Once there, he opened the door to find Paris curled up on her side, the covers shoved to the end of the bed. She'd stripped down to a white strapless bra and damn if she hadn't taken off her skirt, giving him a prime view of a pair of lacy, black panties.

Damn, damn, damn...

He should probably turn tail and run, but he worried about leaving her all night in her current state. He could crawl in next to her, or he could be the man Maria had raised him to be. A gentleman.

With that in mind, he strode into the bathroom, dressed in his boxers and a T-shirt, then prepared to sleep in the lounger. But before he settled in for the duration, he paused a few moments to study the gorgeous woman in his bed.

With her arm crooked beneath her head, her hair a sexy, tangled mess, she looked somewhat innocent in sleep, and someone he wouldn't mind waking up to in the morning. He liked her wit, her brain and her body. Definitely her body. Too bad he hadn't met her a year ago, when he still had time to court a woman in an effort to meet his match, and circumvent the terms of the will.

But unfortunately that time had passed, and unless he wanted to propose to someone he'd met only a few hours ago, he could just let go of that pipe dream. Then something suddenly occurred to him. Something the mothers had suggested.

Nah. That would be too weird, not to mention she would never agree to it.

Following a quick shower, Dallas took one last look at the pretty lady, turned off the lights and kicked back in the lounge chair. He still had trouble shutting down his thoughts for several reasons, including the damned deadline on the will. He'd be better served if he accepted his fate—his youngest brother would have controlling interest over the ranch. Short of a miracle, that would come to pass. Unless…

Maybe the harebrained idea could work if he handled it right. If he made it worth Paris's while. Or she could laugh in his face and leave. Still, it couldn't hurt to ask, if he found the courage to do it. Hell, he'd ridden some of the rankest bulls in the world. He could propose a marriage pact to a woman.

Probably best to sleep on it for now and decide in the morning—if he actually got any sleep at all.

Three

Shaking off the fog of sleep, Paris came into consciousness slowly in reaction to a ribbon of light landing on her face. She opened her eyes and squinted at first, until she spotted the man with an open chambray shirt sitting in the chair in the corner, putting on his boots. Her eyes went wide when she remembered her current location—a stranger's bed.

Then it all came back to her, one frame at a time, like a mortifying slide show. Dinner with Dallas Calloway. Two drinks. Getting drunk. Getting into his bed. And that kiss she'd instigated.

Paris resisted the urge to pull the covers over her head and hide away until he left. Or she could choose the mature path and apologize again for her stupid behavior.

After scooting up against the tufted leather headboard, Paris pushed her hair away from her face and cleared her throat to garner his attention. "What time is it?"

He glanced at her, rose to his feet and began buttoning his shirt, but not before she caught a good glimpse of his toned chest, ridged abdomen and the thin happy trail leading to his open fly. "It's after nine," he said. "I thought for a minute there you might sleep until lunchtime."

She thought for a minute there she might swallow her tongue due to his sheer male perfection. "You should have woken me sooner."

"I tried."

"Apparently not very hard."

"I nearly shook your shoulder off, but you didn't budge." He cracked a crooked smile. "How's your head?"

"Fuzzy." But not so fuzzy that she couldn't recall what a fool she'd made of herself.

"Need an aspirin?" he asked as he tucked his shirt into the jeans' waistband.

She needed an escape route when she noticed her skirt and top hanging on the end of the bedpost. "No, I'm fine," she said as she clutched the covers tighter. "I do need to get dressed and go home."

He barked out a laugh. "That's usually my morning line."

It suddenly occurred to her she might not remember everything about their evening, although she couldn't imagine forgetting *that*. "Uh, we didn't do anything… you know."

He buckled his belt and approached the side of the bed. "Unfortunately 'you know' wasn't involved. You did strip down to your underwear, but I didn't look."

"I've definitely heard that before." She determined an amendment would be best before he assumed she slept around. "From my ex-husband, and he was telling the truth. He rarely looked at me the last few years of our wedded non-bliss."

"Your husband sounds like an idiot. No offense."

"No offense taken. You've pegged him right, although my actions last evening would probably qualify as idiotic. I'm so sorry I subjected you to that."

He grabbed an off-white straw cowboy hat hanging from a hook near the door. "Look, you had a little too much to drink. It happens."

"Not to me," she muttered. "I can't recall ever drinking so much that I took off my clothes and climbed into a stranger's bed."

"Darlin', since all you did was climb into my bed, I think you can stop worrying about your actions."

"But I kissed you. Or at least I think I did."

His grin expanded. "Oh, yeah, you did. And you won't hear me complainin' about that at all."

At least that was reassuring. "I want to be clear I have never done anything like this before."

"Kissed someone?"

"Kissed someone I just met."

"I kind of like knowing I was your first."

"I like knowing you're not completely disgusted with me."

"Nothing about you disgusts me, sweetheart." He

settled the hat on his head and smiled. "Stay in bed as long as you'd like, and I'll see you in a bit."

"In bed?" Now why had she said something so leading and ludicrous?

He didn't seem at all affected by the faux pas. "Is that an invitation?"

She shook her aching head. "No. Just proof that I sometimes speak before I think."

He winked. "That's too bad."

Paris fought the temptation to tell him she'd reconsidered. "Where are you going now?"

"I have to check on some of the livestock."

"Well, I guess I'll just say goodbye then. I'll probably be on my way home before you get back."

"You can't leave yet. Jenny went to town this morning and bought you a dress and some underclothes and laundered them. She left them in the bathroom along with some toiletries. She's also keeping breakfast warm for you."

Jenny could be nominated for Southern sainthood, in her opinion. But how embarrassing to have one of the Calloway stepmothers learn she'd spent the night in the stepson's bed. "Although I appreciate the gesture, that's not really necessary. I'll just put on the clothes I wore last night and get out of your hair."

"I want you to stay a while longer so we can talk."

"About what?"

"Business," he said as he clasped the knob and opened the door. "So don't go anywhere."

Paris fought the urge to salute over his demanding tone, but Dallas had already disappeared before she could deliver the gesture. Assured he had left the premises, she slipped out of bed and wandered into the bathroom. Spa bathroom.

The beige marble tub seemed as large as her whole apartment, and so was the stone shower. She had a good mind to take a soak, but she didn't want to prolong her stay in Dallas's domain or delay the breakfast Jenny had prepared.

She retrieved shampoo and shower gel from the basket on the double vanity, gathered a towel from the heated rack on the wall, then took a quick spray until she finally felt somewhat refreshed and energized.

She dressed in the aforementioned underwear, and donned the yellow sundress hanging on a hook on the back of the door. Evidently Jenny had thought of everything, right down to the matching sandals and hair dryer.

After completing the morning ritual, Paris strode back into the bedroom where she thankfully found her case that held her makeup bag. She didn't have her complete beauty arsenal, but she did have mascara and lip gloss, which would have to do.

After pulling her hair back into a low ponytail, Paris carefully folded her suit, shoved it into the bag and then headed toward the luscious scents wafting through the hallway. Once there, she found Jenny standing at the massive six-burner stainless stove, flipping pancakes, surrounded by a chef's dream kitchen. She had finally uncovered the one place that shouted ultramodern, not macho rustic.

"Good morning, Jenny," she said as she sent her a somewhat self-conscious smile.

The friendly stepmom favored her with a bright grin. "Good morning to you, sugar. Did you sleep well?"

"Like a rock." Like a drunken sailor. "The mint juleps saw to that."

Jenny pushed the spatula under one cake and slid it onto a plate. "I am so sorry, sugar. I didn't know you were such a lightweight."

Paris leaned against the cabinet adjacent to the huge fridge and rested an elbow on the gray quartz countertop. "I really don't drink too often. Just the occasional glass of wine."

Jenny sent her a sideways glance. "Would you like a mimosa? Or perhaps a screwdriver. Nothing relieves a hangover better than that old hair of the hound dog."

The thought twisted her stomach into a knot. "Heavens no. I mean, no thank you. I wouldn't mind some orange juice, without the champagne or vodka."

Jenny retrieved a pitcher of juice from the refrigerator, poured Paris a glass and handed it to her. "You're not from the South, are you, sugar?"

"No. Why?"

"Because good Southern girls like their toddies now and again."

Now and again could possibly be an understatement when it came to Jenny. "I'm not really from anywhere. My family traveled all over the country during my youth."

That earned Paris a sympathetic look. "Everyone

should have a place to call home, honey. Mine was the New Orleans area, until I moved here."

Paris had fond memories of New Orleans, the place where she'd headed her first hotel design project. Little had she known that a few years later, she would suffer a major fall from grace. "Do you miss Louisiana?"

Jenny shrugged. "At times, but I can always go back whenever I choose."

She gestured toward a small bistro table set near a bank of windows at the end of the expansive kitchen. "Have a seat, sugar. How many slices of bacon with your pancakes?"

Apparently Jenny had forgotten the meal she'd prepared the night before. "None, please. And only one pancake."

The woman looked as if Paris had uttered the ultimate blasphemy. "Oh, that's right. You're a vegetarian."

After setting her glass on the round table, Paris pulled back a cute red chair and sat. The color definitely indicated a woman's touch, and most likely an unwelcome concession on Dallas's part. "I do eat eggs and some seafood. I just avoid pork, poultry and beef."

Jenny slid a plate piled high with the cakes onto the table in front of Paris. "You'd have a hard time living here, honey. Beef is a mainstay with almost every meal."

She wrinkled her nose. "Sounds like a cholesterol catastrophe to me."

After claiming the chair across from her, Jenny smiled. "You'd be surprised how good old hard work keeps that in check. I tell you, Dallas is in prime shape and in perfect health."

From what she'd seen, Paris wouldn't debate the *prime shape* part. She grabbed the pitcher of warm syrup and poured only a small amount, ignoring the pats of butter to her right. "Is Dallas not joining us for breakfast?"

Jenny laid a hand on her throat. "Oh, sugar, he gets up with the chickens. He ate at five a.m."

Paris couldn't imagine dragging out of bed at that hour, much less eating a full breakfast. "What exactly does he do at that time of the morning?"

"He tends to the ranch," came from behind Paris. "He's a rancher and that's what they do."

She didn't have to turn around to recognize the voice, but she did glance over her shoulder to see Maria Calloway pouring a cup of coffee from the carafe on the counter. "I guess that makes sense," Paris said. "I'm surprised it requires working sunup to sundown."

Maria took the chair next to Jenny and leveled her stare on Paris. "Have you ever lived on a large parcel of land?"

Paris swallowed the bite she'd just taken and rested her fork on the plate. "No, I've never lived on a farm or a ranch."

"She's never really had a home, Maria," Jenny said sympathetically. "Isn't that just so sad?"

Maria appeared unaffected by the revelation. "Then you're not accustomed to working with your hands?"

She didn't understand the reasons behind the obvious interrogation. After all, she'd be leaving in hopefully less than an hour. Then again, Dallas had mentioned a business talk, so she could be coming back to the ranch, if luck prevailed. "Any work I do with my hands involves sketching designs and using a computer keyboard."

Maria took a long drink of coffee before speaking again. "It's a hard life on a ranch. Not for the weak of spirit or faint of heart."

"It's not that bad, Maria," Jenny said. "I've adjusted just fine, but then I did spend several years on a horse farm."

Maria turned her frown on the other mother. "You spent those years throwing garden parties, so your opinion doesn't count. And since you've been here, I don't recall you even picking up a garden rake, much less muck a stall."

"Don't listen to her, Paris," Jenny said. "I planted the roses in the hedges."

"Bully for you," Maria muttered.

Feeling the need to play peacemaker, Paris decided to change the subject. "Where exactly is Dallas now?"

"In the barn, of course," Maria said. "He told me to send you there as soon as you're done eating."

Wearing a pair of sandals in a barn didn't seem wise, but anything beat dueling stepmoms. After consuming only half her food, Paris dabbed at her mouth, put the napkin aside, pushed away from the table and stood. "Ladies, it's been a pleasure meeting both of you, and thanks so much for your hospitality. Now if you'll direct me to the barn, I'll be on my way."

Maria pointed behind her. "It's that way. Big building with a big door. Can't miss it."

Jenny rose and took Paris's hand. "Sugar, I am so glad you showed up here. I know Dallas is, too."

Paris only wished she could be sure of that. "Thanks, Jenny, and if we don't see each other again, I'll always remember our meeting fondly."

"Oh, you'll be seeing her again," Maria said from her perch at the table. "Me, too. A lot."

She wanted to jump for joy. "Then he's decided to hire me?"

Jenny and Maria exchanged a strange look before Jenny regarded her again. "You could say that in a manner of speaking. Now run along, sugar. Dallas doesn't like to be kept waiting."

If a chance existed that Dallas Calloway would soon be her boss, she would run all the way to the barn.

When he noticed Paris picking her way carefully down the rock path, Dallas propped the shovel against the rough-hewn wall and smiled. His amusement was short-lived when he realized what he was about to do, and what was at stake—his future as the head of the D Bar C Ranch and his project, Texas Extreme.

If he went through with his plan, some might consider him pretty mercenary. Or insane. Or both. But at the moment, he only cared about the opinion of the good-looking woman entering the barn.

"Maria said you wanted to see me," Paris said as she balanced on one foot and shook the sawdust out of her sandal.

"Yeah," he told her, although he was seeing a little more than he should, namely a nice glimpse of the curve of her breast when she leaned over and removed the other shoe.

After she straightened and tugged at the hem on the sundress, her attention turned to some focal point behind him. “What a beautiful horse.”

Dallas glanced over his shoulder to find the black gelding poking his head through the opening in the stall. “That’s Raven. Even though he lost his stud status years ago, he still knows a beautiful woman when he sees one.”

A slight blush colored her cheeks. “He must not get out much.”

Dallas still couldn’t get why she didn’t realize her worth. He’d be happy to take a turn at trying to convince her. But not now. Not yet. He had something more pressing that required her consideration. “How was breakfast?”

She leaned back against the opposite wall. “Wonderful. Maria said you wanted to speak with me.”

“Yeah. I thought I could show you around.”

“Around where?”

“The barn.” *Although the bedroom would be better*, a thought that luckily hadn’t jumped out of his mouth.

She folded her arms beneath her breasts. “You’re not going to ask me to be one of your ranch hands, are you?”

He couldn’t stop a laugh. “Not hardly. Just trying to be hospitable.”

“Oh. You said earlier you wanted to talk to me about business, so I assumed maybe that’s why I’m here.”

Obviously she wanted to get right down to it. Normally that would suit him fine, but this proposition would take some time easing into it. "We'll cover that in a minute. First, I want you to officially meet Raven."

She looked almost alarmed. "Is that necessary? I mean, he is rather big."

He crossed the aisle and took her hand. "He's big all right. A big baby. He won't hurt you."

"Are you sure?" she asked, a good dose of wariness in her voice.

"Positive."

He guided her to the gelding's stall, stood behind her and told her, "Just pet him on his muzzle."

"Huh?"

"His nose. Or rub him right between his eyes on that white part, which is known as a blaze. He'll follow you anywhere if you do that."

She glanced back at him and frowned. "I'm not sure I want him following me."

"Give it a try, darlin'. You'll see he's a gentle giant. Besides, if you're serious about going on that cattle drive, you better get used to being around a horse before you climb on his back."

After a moment's hesitation, Paris reached out and touched Raven carefully, then slowly began to stroke him. The gelding didn't move an inch, as predicted, and soon began to close his eyes like he'd been hypnotized. Dallas, on the other hand, began to twitch as he followed her movements and imagined her hands on him…

He had a dirty mind full of devilish thoughts that

could land him in trouble, or on his ass if he acted on them. To make matters worse, Paris suddenly turned and ended up way too close for his comfort.

He figured it would be best if he continued the tour, but when she wet her lips, he could only move toward her, not away. And this time, he took the reins. He lowered his head and kissed her like he hadn't kissed a woman in years.

The next thing he knew, he had her spun around and backed up against the wall. She had her hands wrapped around his neck and that sweet little body pressed against his. All thoughts of wedding pacts and proposing to a virtual stranger flew out of his brain in lieu of what was going on below his belt.

Without warning, Paris broke the kiss and ducked under his arm. "This should not be happening."

Dallas braced both palms on the wall and tipped his forehead against the wood. "Maybe not, but it did. Too late to take it back."

"I wish I could take it back," she said from behind him. "I don't understand what is wrong with me. I see no reason whatsoever why I keep acting this way."

That ticked him off a bit and turned him around to face her. "Are you going to try to ignore the chemistry between us? Because I'm sure as hell not going to even try. From the minute you marched into the office, I knew something was brewing."

She looked away for a few seconds. "It's immaterial whether we share chemistry or not. I've made it a point not to do anything rash, and I'm not inclined to sleep with someone outside a committed relationship."

Hell, not only was she sexy, she could read minds. "I don't remember asking you to sleep with me."

She sent a pointed look south of his buckle. "You might not have verbally asked, but the message was loud and clear."

That wasn't up for discussion. "Hey, I'm a man. We don't always have control over physical reactions."

She gave him a good eye-rolling. "That could be true, but I do have control over mine."

"Lady, you could've fooled me a few minutes ago. And don't forget that kiss last night."

"Evidently I forgot myself."

"Maybe you've just forgotten what it feels like to be with a man who really wants you."

Her indignant look told him he'd struck a nerve. "Look, I have a few rules. I don't believe in casual sex, and I don't become intimate with anyone I've known such a short time. Never have. Never will."

A good lead-in to his crazy scheme, *crazy* being the operative word. But for the first time in a long time, he saw a possible end to his dilemma. Not to mention being married to Paris Reynolds carried a couple of perks, the least of which would be some nice, hot lovemaking. First, he had to convince her to give his plan credence.

He paced down the aisle and back again before he paused in front of her. "No sex outside a committed relationship, huh?"

"That is correct."

He rubbed a palm over his neck and prepared to propose. “Then if that’s the case, I can only see one answer to the problem.”

“What would that be?”

“Marry me.”

Four

"Have you lost your mind?"

"Nope."

Paris found it difficult to believe a man like Dallas Calloway—a reputed confirmed bachelor—would blurt out a proposal to a woman he'd known less than twenty-four hours. "Let me get this straight. You'd be willing to marry me in order to sleep with me?"

"Yep."

This simply had to be a joke with an impending punch line. "Shouldn't we go steady first?"

"I'm serious, Paris, and I'm not asking just so I can get you into my bed."

From the somber look on his face, she could tell he was dead serious. "If it's not only the sex, then why would you want to rush into a marriage?"

"Because I need a wife and I need one fairly fast."

Her head started spinning from confusion. "Could you be any more vague?"

"It's kind of complicated. But I believe getting married would benefit both of us."

In what universe? "This doesn't make any sense to me, Dallas. As I said before, you could probably have any woman you wanted and—"

"I don't want any other woman. And in all honesty, I'm running out of time to find a bride."

Paris entertained visions of gloom and doom. "Is there something physically wrong with you?"

"Do you mean a terminal illness?"

"Yes."

"No, but I am suffering from an incurable codicil."

"Now I'm really perplexed."

"Join the club." He gestured toward the end of the lengthy barn. "Let's go into the office. You're going to need to sit down while I explain."

That sounded like a good plan. Her knees were still weak from their mini make-out session and the bombshell proposal. "Lead the way."

Paris followed Dallas into the office that was surprisingly simple and blessedly cool. She took a black-and-chrome chair situated in the corner while he leaned back on the industrial metal desk opposite her.

Dallas released a rough sigh as he centered his gaze on her. "Before I launch into this mess, I need to know I can trust you with the information I'm about to disclose."

She braced for deep secrets, an all too familiar concept. "I promise I won't say anything. Besides, I really don't have anyone to tell, at least not around here. And I promise you I have no intention of mentioning any of this conversation to my mother and father."

"No best friend?"

"Not really. I basically lost touch with my friends from college." A sad commentary on the state of her life.

"Good, because some of my current predicament involves a scandal."

Her curiosity was considerably piqued. "Go ahead."

After looking away a few moments, Dallas finally regarded her again. "A few years ago, during the reading of my dad's will, we discovered he had another family we didn't know a damn thing about."

"You mean Jenny?"

"Yeah, and the twins."

Both shocking and scandalous. "I didn't realize your dad and Maria divorced."

"They didn't."

The cogs started spinning in her head as she added outrageous to the adjectives describing the situation. "You mean he was—"

"A bigamist."

"How did he get away with that?"

"By leaving the state to screw around on Maria. He bought a horse farm in Louisiana when Maria was pregnant with my half brother Houston. He met Jenny in New Orleans, married her and proceeded to get her pregnant not long after my other half brother Tyler was born. For over twenty years he lived the lie and no one was the wiser."

Paris felt as if she'd been thrust into a spaghetti Western soap opera. "I can't imagine keeping a secret of that magnitude for weeks, much less decades."

"J. D. Calloway was a conniving, cheating, lying son of a bitch," he said, venom in his voice. "Pardon my French."

She couldn't believe he would be concerned about cursing in light of what he'd just told her. "No worries. My father speaks the language fluently."

Her attempt at humor obviously fell flat when Dallas didn't even crack a smile. "But that part of the sorry story isn't even the worst of it."

Paris had a difficult time believing it could get much worse. Then again… "Please don't tell me he had another wife."

"Not that we're aware of, although I wouldn't put it past him. But he did have it out for me."

"Why is that?"

"Because he never could control me in life, so he decided to do it in death."

She definitely didn't think she'd care for the late Calloway patriarch. "How exactly did he manage that?"

"By using ownership of the ranch. He knew my grandfather insisted the controlling interest of the D Bar C be passed down to his first-born grandson, and my dad was forced to adhere to that request. But then he added a condition that would allow me to continue to run this place only if I did his bidding."

She was almost afraid to ask. "Such as?"

"I have to get married before my thirty-eighth birthday. If not, controlling interest reverts to my half brother Fort who doesn't give a tinker's damn about this place. He's so ate up with anger he'd like to see all of us fail."

So now she knew why that milestone held so much importance with the mothers. And she suspected she knew the reason behind the spontaneous proposal. "Am I correct in assuming you want me to prevent that from happening by entering into a bogus marriage?"

He scowled. "When you put it that way, it makes me sound like a jerk. But after I met you yesterday and learned about your current situation, I figured it would benefit us both."

"How am I going to benefit from a lie?"

"Financially."

She'd begun to feel a bit like the prostitute Maria had believed her to be. "Marriage for money. Interesting. And out of the question."

"Will you at least hear me out?"

"I wouldn't miss it for the world. But first, I have to know one thing."

"Go ahead."

"How could you put that much faith in this plan when you know so little about me?"

He paused for a brief moment. "Your parents are Howard and Sheila Reynolds. You were born in San Diego thirty-two years ago on November second. You graduated from a prestigious college, worked for an equally prestigious firm in Nevada and you married Peter L. Smith in Vegas eight years ago. I didn't find any record of your divorce though."

She was floored he'd gained so much information in such a short time. "I have the documents although they're in Spanish, and a photo of the book where the registrar recorded the divorce. And exactly when did you do this background check on me?"

"I couldn't sleep last night so I did an internet search. This morning I called a friend who's in security. He took it from there."

Security meant criminal history. Momentary panic set in. "Did he find anything interesting?"

"Nope. Not one felony or misdemeanor or even a speeding ticket."

She relaxed for a moment knowing he hadn't discovered her primary secret, but then no one knew about that. No one ever would, thanks to a nondisclosure order arranged by her attorney. "I'd expect you to thoroughly investigate someone you intend to hire, but not someone you intend to marry."

"I'm a businessman, Paris, and this is a business proposition. Maybe that sounds kind of crass, but before we go any further, I wouldn't want you to have expectations of it being anything else."

For some odd reason that stung like a hornet, as if she was stupid enough to think it might be more. "Really? Again I ask, what's in it for me? Aside from being wed to the object of many a woman's lust, of course."

He didn't seem affected at all by her sarcasm. "First of all, you have a fairly substantial debt you're dealing with."

Had he somehow discovered the money she owed

her former firm? Impossible. Or so she hoped. "Did you run a report on my finances?"

"No. I figured that out when you came begging for a job, and confirmed it when you mentioned your ex taking your money and cutting out of the country. I also recall some issue with staying in your apartment and possibly having to move to Idaho. Am I wrong?"

If he only knew the true magnitude of her problems. "No, you're not wrong."

"Exactly how much debt are you carrying?"

"That's really none of your—"

"Business? If you want me to help you, you'll have to be honest about the money aspects."

He had a lot of nerve making the request when she hadn't agreed to anything. "I believe I asked you for a job, not for your help."

"Yeah, but I'm asking for yours. We could help each other. How much debt?"

She momentarily swallowed her pride. "Over seventy thousand dollars." Most of which she owed to her former firm.

"Are you a chronic shopper?" he asked.

"No, but my ex is. He left me with all the bills." Including money he'd stolen that she was having to reimburse.

"Okay. If you agree to this, I'll make sure you're debt-free. I'll give you twenty thousand up front and you can live here rent-free. You can also design the lodge and I'll pay you monthly for that. If you see that through, I'll provide a reference and the seed money to start your own company."

Wow. She would finally be solvent, liberated from her former employer and on her way to a bright future. But at what cost? A nagging voice told her to go for it. Her mother's voice told her to proceed with caution. "If I did agree to this, and I'm not saying I am, how long would I be expected to remain in this marriage?"

"The will states a year," he said. "It's going to take at least that long to get Texas Extreme up and running and the lodge ready for guests. If you'll stay until then, I'll throw in another bonus. I'll buy you a new car so you can put that rusty sedan out to pasture."

She took offense to him insulting her car. "Bubba is not rusty."

He chuckled. "You gave that clunker a name?"

"Yes. He's been very reliable, unlike most men I've known."

"Bubba sounds like he's barely running."

"He does need a little work." Now for a very pertinent question. "There is the very important matter of dissolving the marriage. I'm personally not keen on being labeled a two-time loser with another divorce."

"We could look into an annulment."

"Under what grounds after we've hung in there for a year?"

He streaked a palm over his shaded jaw. "I'm not sure."

Neither was she, but she intended to find out. "Mind if I borrow your laptop to do a little research?"

He reached behind him and offered her the computer. "Knock yourself out."

After setting it on her lap, Paris began the search

for annulment criteria. She selected the most official-looking article and began to read. "Let's see here. The first condition states the parties are family members, but I highly doubt we're related to each other."

"Did you not pay attention to me telling you about my father's philandering ways? I wouldn't be surprised to discover you're the sister I've always wanted but never had."

"Very funny and kind of creepy."

"I'm kidding, Paris. I don't harbor any brotherly feelings for you whatsoever."

She looked up to see Dallas's smile before scanning the text again. "On to the next point. I guess one of us could get drunk during the ceremony and claim we weren't coherent enough to consent. We could then say we didn't sober up until after our first anniversary."

His low laugh gave her pleasant chills. "Sounds like you could handle that with a couple of Jen's mint juleps, pre-ceremony. I'm sure she'll keep you supplied for the next twelve months."

This time she didn't bother to look up. "Clever, but not anything either of us should consider. Coercion is out because I wouldn't agree to this unless we're both sure. Bigamy is also out. And fraud unless one of us is lying about our age."

"Nope," he said. "But back to that bigamy thing. Are you sure you're divorced?"

Realizing she'd inadvertently hit a nerve bringing up bigamy, Paris closed the computer and frowned. "Yes, I'm sure I'm divorced. Peter couldn't get out of the marriage quick enough. He's a CPA so he's fastidious and detail oriented." As well as a con artist, a fact she chose to withhold. "That leaves us with the final possibility. Do you have issues with impotence that would lead to the old standby, failure to consummate?"

He looked more amused than insulted. "You and I both know the answer to that after what happened a few minutes ago."

She'd realized very quickly he hadn't been poking fun. "That's too bad since it would make the whole failure to consummate much easier, which appears to be our only option. Get married, no whoopee."

He looked like he'd just bitten into a dill pickle. "You expect me to go without sex for a year?"

Paris thought that would be the greatest challenge of all, and a possible reason for him to rescind the offer. "Cowboy up, cowboy. You can handle it if you want to keep the ranch. Which leads me to another question."

"Shoot."

"Does maintaining control of this place mean so much to you that you would enter into a fake marriage that requires celibacy for a year?"

"I don't like the celibacy clause one damn bit, but I can only promise I'll try. And it would have to be a real marriage in order to meet the will's requirements."

She saw a possible alternative. "Who would know if we only pretended we married?"

"Fort will make a point to check it out."

The decision would be so much easier for Paris if that weren't the case. "You're obviously a rich guy, Dallas. I imagine you could buy a ranch just like this one anywhere in the world. Maybe even a bigger and better ranch. Then you wouldn't have to resort to this ruse."

"It wouldn't be the same," he said. "To risk sounding like Jenny, the D Bar C is equivalent to losing the plantation that's been in the family for generations."

"Wouldn't it still be in the family if Fort takes over? Have you even bothered to work out some agreement that wouldn't force you to go to such extremes?"

Anger flashed in his eyes. "Fort doesn't talk to anyone but Worth. He'd have the power to do anything he pleases, including selling it off piece by piece. I wouldn't put it past him to do that just for spite. He hates anything associated with the Calloways, including me. Especially me."

A family feud of grand proportions. "Because I grew up traveling the world, I've never experienced having a real home place. But I do understand why it would be difficult to give up a legacy."

"And even harder to give up the memories."

"Of your dad?"

"Of my mother. I have very few as it is."

That revelation yanked hard on her heartstrings. At times her own mother could drive her insane with her penchant for being overprotective, yet Paris couldn't imagine not having her mom in her life. "How old were you when she passed?"

"Not quite five years old, but I still recall the little things. If I'm forced to leave here, I'm afraid the memories might fade completely."

Hearing the pain in his voice almost pushed Paris over the marriage edge. But she couldn't let emotions rule common sense. She'd done that too often as it was. "You've given me a lot to consider," she said as she handed him the laptop.

"Then you're not completely ruling it out?"

"No, but I have to think about it long and hard. And you'd have to promise we'd find some way to go the annulment route."

"Believe me, my lawyer will find a loophole if that's how we want to end the marriage. And I'd be willing to put all the terms in writing if that would make you feel better."

She'd feel better if she had more time to weigh the verdict. "When do you want my answer?"

"I'm flying to Houston on Friday and I thought we could just do it there. It'll be easier to blend in at that courthouse rather than do it around here. Word travels fast in small towns."

"I don't know if I can make such a serious decision that soon."

"That's all the time I have since my birthday's Saturday," he said as he pushed off the desk. "When it comes right down to it, it makes sense to get it done the day before."

If only she could be so sure. "I'm going to go home and think it over," she told him as she stood. "But if I were you, I wouldn't get my hopes up. I'll call you as soon as I've made up my mind."

After leaving him behind in the barn, Paris managed to return to Dallas's house, gather her things and sneak out without being detected. She drove the ninety miles home in a haze, ticking off a mental list of pros and cons. She entered her barren apartment and thought about how she'd hoped to settle in a loft downtown, with a view of the River Walk. Yet her budget had only allowed her to rent a one-bedroom in a cookie-cutter complex outside the magic of the city.

Her life had turned into an absolute mess, devoid of security and absent of even a shred of a sincere social life. She had a closet full of expensive shoes and nowhere to wear them, a large stack of unpaid bills, including one that if ignored could take away her freedom, and a solid sense of defeat. But she still had an option—accept Dallas's proposal. What was the worst that could happen? Paris could think of one thing—she might lose her heart to a man who didn't return the sentiment. Again.

Not this time. Not if she approached the proposal as strictly business. She married for love the first time, why not marry for financial gain the second? A lot of people did it. Unfortunately she'd never imagined herself fitting into that mercenary mold. But she'd never dreamed she would be caught in this dire position.

Damn her bad luck. Damn Peter Smith for his criminal acts and betrayal and leaving her to take the fall. Damn Dallas Calloway for putting her on the verge of accepting his offer.

Knowing she needed advice had her reaching for the cell phone, although she would have to be very, very careful.

On that thought, Paris dropped down onto the sofa and pounded out her parents' number. After two rings,

"Reynolds residence" filtered through the line in Sheila's usual sing-song voice.

"Hey, Mom. It's Paris."

"Well I'll be, it's the prodigal daughter checking in and it's not even a holiday."

Her mom did have a tendency to make her kids feel guilty at times. "I know, Mother. It's been a while since I called, but I've been rather busy."

"Do you have a job?"

That depended on whether she took a husband. "Actually, I have a good prospect." Now for adding that other little tidbit of information. "I also have a new man in my life."

"Oh, Paris, are you sure that's a good idea? The ink has barely dried on your divorce decree."

"It's been twenty-two months, Mom." And four days.

"Oh. Time does fly, doesn't it?"

"Yes, it does. Anyway, I think you and Dad would like him."

"Does *he* have a job?"

"Yes, he does. He's a rancher. An honest to goodness cowboy."

"Interesting. Does he have a nice butt?"

Heavens, leave it to her matriarch to bring that up. "What difference does it make?"

"Believe me, it does. I married your father for his butt and we're approaching forty years of marital bliss."

Definitely too much information. "Yes, he has a nice butt and a nice house and a lucrative ranching operation. Are you happy now?"

"I'm happy if you're happy, dear."

Now for the moment of truth. A prelude to what possibly could be in the offing. "Good, because the *M* word has been mentioned."

"Meatloaf? Manners? *Mistake*?"

"Very funny, Mom. Marriage."

"Darn, I'd hoped that wasn't it."

"Nothing is set in stone yet, but I didn't want you to be blindsided if it does happen."

"I certainly hope we get to meet this one before you take that step."

Not likely that would occur in two days. "I'm sure you'll have the opportunity in the near future."

"Paris, if this man treats you well, then you'll have our blessing. Just make certain this time you're doing the right thing."

An obvious slam on her lack of judgment when it came to her former relationship. "Believe me, I'm going to be very certain before I end up at the altar. A part of me says I should go for it. Another part tells me maybe I'm not cut out for matrimony."

"I don't want to ever hear you say that again," her mother said in a no nonsense tone. "You have the capacity to make a marriage work, as long as you can trust and love your mate for life."

Therein lay the problem—love didn't figure into the deal. "How do you ever really know that, Mother? Marriage doesn't come with guarantees."

"True, but it does come with certain risks if it's not right. If you happen to be lucky enough to find your soul mate, then don't be afraid to take the chance. One bad apple named Peter shouldn't spoil the whole bunch. By the way, what is this man's name?"

"Dallas." And sadly he would never be her soul mate, though he could be her financial savior.

"How nice that he carries the moniker of your father's favorite football team. That should earn him a few points."

They shared in a laugh before Paris decided to end the conversation. "Thanks for listening, Mom. I'll take all your advice to heart."

"You're welcome, dear. And don't forget to follow that heart. If it feels right, do it. It's high time to leave the past behind and look forward to a brighter future."

"You know, Mom, you're right. Love you bunches and tell Dad I love him, too."

"We love you, dear. And don't wait so long to call, okay?"

"I won't." And that next call could be a bombshell that might blow up in her face.

After Paris hung up, she mulled over her mother's words and clung to one thing in particular—leaving the past behind and looking forward to a brighter future.

Maybe she should choose a different direction, journey down a new path, even an unorthodox one. Maybe marriage to Dallas Calloway could provide all of that, and more. Maybe his offer would be the best way to start over.

Too much to consider, and far too little time.

Right then, Dallas only wanted enough time to enjoy his lunch alone. But the two women hovering at the dinette where he now sat had no intention of giving him some peace. Maybe if he ignored them, they'd go away. And pigs would probably sprout wings first.

Jenny propped one hand on her hip and stared at him. "Well?"

He swallowed the last bite of the barbecue sandwich before he responded. "Well what?"

"Where is Paris?"

"She went home."

Maria flipped her braid over one shoulder and folded her arms. "Are you gonna ask her out again, *mijo*?"

"Nope."

Jenny sighed. "Sugar, you really should have given her another chance. A lot of women get drunk on a first date."

He saw an opportunity to rattle their chains and jumped on it. "I decided I didn't need to ask her for a second date."

Jen looked crestfallen. "Why not?"

"Because I asked her to marry me. I figured we'd pretty much moved past the dating game at that point."

That effectively shut them up for the time being, but he suspected not for long.

"You really did it?" Jenny asked, confirming his suspicions.

"Yeah, I did."

"Don't just sit there, *mijo*," Maria said. "Give us all the down and dirty details."

Jenny took on that same old wistful, romantic look. "Did you get down on one knee? Did you give her a ring?"

That beat all he'd ever heard. "No, I didn't get down on one knee. I approached it as a business proposition, which it is. And when would I have found time to buy a ring?"

"You have your mother's ring, Dallas. It's in the safe."

Maria didn't have to remind him of that. He'd thought about it often, even though he'd never really looked inside the blue velvet box. Giving it to Paris under the circumstances would be as false as the marriage. Ironically, that trinket had been reserved for true love, according to his dad. "A ring is the least of my concerns."

Jenny's face fell like it had weights attached to it. "She said no?"

He pushed back from the table and came to his feet. "She said she'd think about it."

"Then it's not a lost cause?" Maria asked.

"Okay, you two, don't get your hopes up." Exactly what Paris had said to him before she'd left. "My guess is she's going to think it over and then refuse the offer."

"You should have knelt before her," Jenny said. "Women like that."

"And given her the damn ring," Maria added. "I'm not sappy like Blondie here, but I do know most gals like to be treated with dignity when a man pops the question. Even your father knew that."

"That's true," Jenny began. "J.D. could be quite the romantic even if he was a jackass."

He didn't want to hear anything else about the aforementioned jackass since he was the reason Dallas found himself in this predicament. "It wasn't going to matter to Paris if I rode in on a white horse, considering what I'm asking of her."

"A white horse would have been nice," Jenny added. "That would be hard to resist."

He wanted to shake some sense into the woman and dislodge her visions of hearts and flowers. "Again, the ball is now in Paris's court. If she wants to agree to the marriage terms, then she'll let me know."

"Maybe you should go after her," Maria added. "Give her a little nudge in the right direction."

He had actually thought about doing that very thing before deciding he didn't want to pressure her more than he already had. "If she wants to go forward, she'll come to me. I'm not going to coerce her into a decision." Although that would be a reason for ending the marriage, provided it actually happened. Nah. His sense of honor wouldn't allow him to use that tactic.

"I hope she does say yes," Jenny said. "We could plan a grand wedding on the grounds of the main house. I could make canapés and my famous mint juleps."

That's all he needed—a drunk bride. Then again, that would be grounds for the annulment. He really had to get a grip. "If she decides to go through with it, and that's a big *if*, there won't be any wedding. Just a simple courthouse ceremony and no publicity."

Jenny pretended to pout. "That's no fun, Dallas. You should have your family present for the nuptials."

Before she called a caterer, Dallas had to get out of there. "You ladies have a good afternoon talking about me behind my back."

With that, he left the kitchen and headed to the barn,

all the while recalling how he'd watched Paris drive away. Probably for the last time.

In reality, the marriage pact was the craziest thing he'd ever conjured up. He sure as hell couldn't imagine keeping his hands to himself for a day in her presence, much less a year. If everything fell through, he'd be better off. He'd just turn the place over to Fort and find somewhere else to start up Texas Extreme, even if it wouldn't be the same.

Accepting the fact that Paris would turn him down flat would be best. He'd bet his last buck that's exactly what she'd do.

Five

"With the power vested in me by the state of Texas, I now pronounce you husband and wife."

The man should probably be pronouncing them certifiably insane. Four days ago she hadn't even known Dallas Calloway. Two days ago she'd packed up her limited belongings and moved in with him. Today she wore a diamond-encrusted wedding band and vowed to be his wife. Unbelievable.

Paris waited for Dallas to follow the justice of the peace's declaration, expecting a peck on the cheek. Perhaps a brush across her mouth. She got a full-on, well-deep kiss that curled her toes in the white satin pumps she'd purchased with the sleeveless matching dress before she'd left San Antonio.

After Dallas pulled away and winked, she automatically touched her tingling lips. "That certainly sealed the deal."

He leaned over and whispered, "There's more of that to come if you want more of it."

Yes, she wanted more. Much more than she should. "Now that we've made this official, what's the next step?"

"I have a driver waiting outside the north entrance. He'll take us back to the plane."

The private plane that had whisked her to Houston a few hours ago to meet up with the groom following his appearance at the grand opening of his newest saddle shop. An elaborate aircraft that could pass for a flying motel with a high-class bar and sleeping quarters, of all things.

Dallas clasped her hand to guide her through the courthouse vestibule and when they stepped outside, Paris was shocked to find hoards of reporters milling around the steps outside. "What is going on?"

"They're here for us," Dallas muttered, followed by a few strong oaths. "Just keep walking and stay close to me."

"Not a problem." She had no intention of crawling into the lion's den without a proper escort.

As soon as they started their descent, cameras immediately began to flash, film began to roll and some woman with red hair as big as Jenny's started hurling questions at Paris. "How does it feel to be married to one of the most eligible bachelors in the state?" she asked as she thrust a microphone in Paris's face.

Before she could respond, Dallas practically dragged

her toward the black limo waiting at the curb as he shoved his way through the crowd. She could swear someone tugged at the hem of her dress right before the chauffeur helped her into the car and away from the chaos.

Dallas slid in bedside her and immediately began to loosen his tie. "Dammit, I wanted to avoid all this nonsense. I'd like to know who the hell tipped them off."

"That's anyone's guess. Maybe someone in the courthouse when you obtained our marriage license. By the way, how did you manage to circumvent the normal waiting period?"

He shrugged out of his beige jacket and laid it on the seat beside him. "I know people. Obviously people that can't be trusted."

She imagined he did know a lot of people in high places. She also imagined him taking off the white tailored shirt, his best pair of jeans and cowboy boots, and laying her down on the leather seat. Maybe she'd request he leave the boots on. Maybe she should exit the car now before she found herself in a lot of trouble. As if she wasn't already. "You know, marriages are a matter of public record, Dallas. I'm sure that's how the media learned about us."

"We haven't even been married fifteen minutes. Someone at the courthouse must've leaked the info. Probably an employee who wanted to make a buck selling a story."

Curious over how far the news had traveled, Paris pulled her cell from her silk bag and did a quick internet search of their names. In less than five seconds, she had her answer from a renowned celebrity gossip site. "Oh, my gosh. I can't believe this headline. Sexy Former Rodeo Superstar Dallas Calloway Marries Longtime Girlfriend Paris Reynolds."

"Don't know why you're so shocked," he said with a grin. "Some women think I'm sexy. My truck, too."

He was just too darned cute not to tolerate his wry wit. "I'm referring to the *longtime* part. Talk about a misprint. It should read His Girlfriend of Three Days. Or more accurately, His Business Partner."

He scooted a little closer to her, providing another heady whiff of his clean-scent cologne. "I wouldn't be surprised if they didn't get hold of Jenny for an interview. She'd say something like that to make the situation more socially acceptable."

"I suppose she would do that since she's definitely all about decorum."

"She's also still mad she wasn't invited to witness the wedding. So is Maria." After his cell began to ring, he pulled it from his jeans' pocket and said, "Speak of the devil."

"Which one?"

"Jen."

When he simply stared at the phone, Paris wondered why he was hesitating. "What are you waiting for?"

"I'm tryin' to decide if I want to speak to her."

"Of course you do. It might be an emergency."

"Yeah, her pantyhose could be shot or her hairdresser canceled her appointment."

"Answer it, Dallas."

"Fine." He swiped the screen and grumbled, "What's

up, Jen?" followed by a few *yeahs* and couple of *yeps* and one *big deal*. Then he added, "I'll take that into consideration, and I don't give a horse's rear what he thinks. And yeah, I forgive you but only because he's your kid. Talk to you later."

"What was that all about?" Paris asked after he disconnected.

Dallas forked a hand through his hair and sighed. "It seems Jen decided to call Fort and tell him we were getting married and where. When she saw the story at five a couple of minutes ago—"

"Why does our marriage warrant coverage on the news channels?"

He looked at her as if she'd lost her mind. "She was watching some tabloid channel, not the national news. But be prepared for that to happen. Weddings, babies and divorces of the rich and infamous equal good ratings."

Apparently their surprising little wedding was worthy of major coverage, thanks to the notoriety of the man sitting beside her. The man who happened to legally be her husband. "I knew you were popular with the ladies, but I had no idea losing your bachelor status would have such an impact on the general public."

He shrugged. "No one thought it would ever happen. Anyway, Fort evidently called the press just to piss me off. Jen says a lot of reporters are camped out near the ranch. Maria's doing her best to run them off, hopefully not with a shotgun. Like I suspected, Jen also said it was her idea to claim we've been a couple for a long time."

"How long?"

"Three years, and she's real proud of the plan."

The *plan* could be a major problem. "Unfortunately that would make me an adulteress since I've been divorced less than two years. I hope that doesn't come back to haunt us."

He reached into the built-in cooler centered between the opposing rows of seats and withdrew a bottle of high-dollar champagne. "If it does create problems, we'll deal with it. In the meantime, let's celebrate our nuptials."

Celebrating wasn't foremost on her mind. Not when she continued to worry that somehow someone might dig up the dirt from the debacle at her former firm. But she couldn't concern herself with something that happened to be beyond her control. Besides, if Dallas found out, she'd simply explain she'd only been guilty of being too gullible. "Nice touch," she said after he poured them each a glass of the bubbly and offered one to her. "But I wouldn't peg you as a wine drinker."

"Normally, I'm not, but I think we deserve a toast." He held the glass aloft. "To an arrangement that will allow us to both win in the end."

As long as *the end* didn't include an emotional hijacking, she'd drink to that. "To winning," she said as she touched the flute to his.

After taking a few sips, Paris leaned back in the seat, looked out the window and noticed the slow-moving traffic. "It's going to take forever to get to the airport."

Dallas downed the rest of the champagne and grimaced before setting the glass aside. "That's what happens in Houston during rush hour. Guess we should have planned better."

The situation could work to their advantage. "Since we have the extra time, we should probably use it to get to know each other."

He scooted closer, draped his arm over the back of the seat and grinned. "I'm game."

"I don't mean that." Even though *that* would be tempting.

He slid a fingertip down her cheek. "Are you sure? I mean, we are newlyweds and we're in this big old limo with all this room. The driver can't see a thing with the window up."

More very vivid images filtered into her thoughts. Risqué images that caused her face to fire up. She didn't know whether to fan herself or faint. "I'm referring to discussing details about each other, in case anyone asks. After all, we've presumably been together for three years."

He released a rough sigh. "Talking wasn't what I had in mind."

"Of course not. You're a man. You're averse to conversation."

He traced a random pattern on her knee. "Not always. Just at the moment."

She slapped her palm on his hand and placed it on the seat between them, even though she considered sliding it up her thigh. "Now, now. Be a good groom. We both know the terms."

"I don't like the terms one damn bit."

In reality, neither did she. But she liked the thought

of another divorce even less. "First get-to-know-you question. What's your favorite color?"

"Brown. Yours?"

"Coral. Favorite pastime?"

"I thought I made that clear right before you threw the no-sex terms up in my face."

Definitely a bad boy. "Your second favorite then."

"Taking a long, hard ride on a—"

"Dallas," she said in a scolding tone.

"Bull." He tried on an innocent look that didn't quite erase the devilish gleam in his blue eyes. "What did you think I was going to say?"

The man knew exactly what she'd been thinking, and with good reason. "Moving on. Favorite food?"

"Steak."

She knew the answer to that before she'd asked the question. "I love hummus with red peppers."

He frowned. "I'd rather eat hay. Your favorite vacation spot?"

"I haven't been on a vacation in so long I couldn't really say. I do know it's not Vegas. I've seen enough of that place to last a lifetime."

"Never been a big fan," he said. "Except when I was at the National Finals Rodeo. Now that I've retired, give me a fishing trip any day."

"I've never been fishing," she said.

"Never?"

"No. My father spent his career on boats so he avoided taking us anywhere that involved water."

Dallas remained quiet for a while before he asked, "How would you feel about going fishing?"

"Today?"

"Sure. We've got to spend our honeymoon somewhere, not to mention the press is hanging out at the ranch, waiting for our return. We could just kick back a couple of days. I can teach you how to cast a line and we can just relax."

Had this been a traditional marriage, she might have preferred a tropical paradise in lieu of a fishing excursion. However, that fit Dallas's cowboy persona, not consuming fruity drinks with umbrellas during an island escape. Avoiding any more media coverage for the time being sounded like a good idea no matter where they went. She did see one problem. "I didn't pack a bag, Dallas."

"Just leave it all up to me. I promise you'll have everything you need."

She trusted he would make good on that promise. "Okay. Exactly where will we go?"

"Lady, this is your lucky day. I just happen to know this little cabin on a lake."

It had to be the biggest log cabin she'd ever seen.

When they'd arrived at the airport an hour ago, they'd been greeted by a fiftysomething-year-old man who'd delivered Dallas a tricked-out black truck, complete with leather seats, satellite radio and a high-tech computer. They'd immediately set off for Texas Hill Country, northwest of San Antonio, luggage on board as promised, for their impromptu honeymoon. And now they traveled up a steep drive lined by a myriad of trees toward another magnificent property.

"This place is really yours?" Paris asked as Dallas pulled into the circular drive and stopped before the front door.

He turned off the ignition and gave her a prideful smile. "Yep. I helped build it with my own two hands a couple of years ago. It's a nice place to escape, although I don't get to enjoy it often enough. Now wait right here."

After undoing her seat belt, Paris remained in her seat while Dallas rounded the hood and helped her out. He only let go of her hand to open the pine door, and then caught her completely off guard when he picked her up into his arms.

She had a little trouble catching her breath as he stepped inside. "What on earth are you doing, Dallas?"

"Carrying my bride over the threshold."

Even her *official* first husband hadn't done that. "Isn't this a bit of overkill considering our situation?"

"The caretaker doesn't know our situation," he said as he set her on her feet atop the wood plank floors. "And I don't know if he's left yet. I'm going to check the place over then I'll bring in the bags."

After Dallas left her alone to her devices, Paris readjusted her dress and tightened the band at her nape. The man had literally swept her off her feet. Imagine that. If not careful, she might actually start viewing him as a real husband. Not wise at all.

Pushing the concerns aside, she surveyed the great room with floor-to-towering-ceiling windows that afforded a view of the wooded terrain. Or what she could see of it now that the sun had disappeared. The place was rustic, like its owner, but charming all the same. Most of the accent pieces appeared to be antiques, with a lot of Western art and bronze statues. The heavy wood furniture with tufted cushions could have been handmade, and the decor most likely had been strictly selected by Dallas. She could also tell it wasn't nearly as large as his ranch house, but just as masculine if not more so. In fact, she saw no evidence whatsoever of a woman's touch.

A few minutes later, Dallas came back through the front door, toting the suitcases, and startling her senseless. "All clear."

"How did you manage to sneak by me?"

He set the suitcases down by the oversize sectional. "I went out the back door then walked around to the front."

Logical, though she couldn't lay claim to much logic of late. "Oh. Makes sense."

He pointed to his left. "Kitchen and dining room are in there, along with the back door." He then pointed to his right. "Bedrooms are that way. All have their own private bath. You can pick whichever one you want."

"Which one is yours?"

He cracked a crooked grin. "I was hoping you'd pick that one."

Apparently he didn't intend to give up on the sex thing very easily. "You and I both know that's not a good idea, sleeping in the same bed."

"I know no such thing. I think it's a great idea. That way if someone comes calling, we'll at least appear to be the happy couple."

Stubborn man. "Do you routinely have people randomly show up in your bedroom?"

He rubbed his chin and looked as if he had to think about that. "Maybe a time or two back when I was a teen and managed to sneak a girl into my bedroom. But I'm fairly sure Maria isn't going to make a trip down here for that. In fact, she would expect us to be sharing a bed. Jenny, too."

"Do they not know the terms of this marriage?"

"Not exactly, but they do know me."

She had begun to know him, too. She'd also begun to realize resisting him would prove to be a major challenge. "Humor me and show me to my own room, okay?"

He gave her that little boy shrug. "Okay. But this isn't like any honeymoon I've ever read about."

This wasn't like any marriage she'd ever heard of, either. "You'll survive."

"Maybe, but I will be walking funny."

"Ha, ha."

She shadowed Dallas's steps as he led her into a hallway, bags in hand, and stopped at the first open door. "This is probably the smaller of the three, but I think it suits you."

Paris stepped into the room to find the four-poster queen bed draped in an orange-and-white cowhide. "I refuse to sleep with a dead animal."

Dallas chuckled behind her. "It's not real, just made to look that way."

She turned around and scowled. "It's not very tasteful."

"It's my taste. Get used to it. Are you hungry?"

Not anymore. "The little vegetable sandwiches they served us on the plane will tide me over. Right now I'd like to get these shoes off and get into something more comfortable."

"Need any help with that?"

"No, but I do need my suitcase."

He laid her bag on a bench at the foot of the bed. "Lady, you seem to be lacking in the fun department."

"And you seem to have an overabundance of testosterone."

"That I do, and I won't apologize for it."

"I wouldn't dream of asking for an apology." She brushed past him and unzipped the case, only to find some skimpy barely-there bright red nightie. "Who packed this?"

He leaned over her shoulder, his warm breath filtering over her neck. "I'd guess Jenny. She wants to make sure the groom is happy."

"I'm never going to wear this, you know."

He slid his arms around her and whispered, "Stranger things have happened."

She couldn't argue with that. This whole marriage pact was incredibly strange. The butterflies in her tummy were stranger, still. She couldn't recall the last time she'd been so sexually charged she wanted to jump out of her own skin. Or jump into bed with a man she barely knew. Easy. Never.

For her own protection, Paris wrested away from Dallas and strode to the door. "Now run along like a good boy, and take your suitcase with you."

He headed toward her, a determined look on his face.

"They're both yours. I have everything I need in my bedroom. Almost everything."

She didn't have to ask what he meant by that. "Before you go, is it safe to take a walk before bed?"

"Sure. Go out the back door and you'll find a path to the lake."

"Is it well lit?"

"The moon is full tonight. That's enough light for you to see where you're going. Just don't fall into the water. And watch out for snakes."

She cringed. "Snakes?"

He had the gall to grin. "Just kidding. The cats keep them away."

"Cats?"

"Yeah. Big ones. Attack cats. But they've been trained not to bother pretty girls."

With that, he exited, closing the door behind him, leaving Paris alone to unpack, and ponder how she would find the strength of will to ignore his overtures, and her own needs.

She returned to the suitcases, thankful to find something other than naughty negligees in the mix. In the smaller one, Jenny had packed every toiletry known to womankind, and enough underwear to last two months, not two days. The woman had also packed jeans and a few T-shirts, and from those Paris picked her favorite coral knit top and pair of seen-better-days denim with a slash above the right knee, a small hole on the inside of her left thigh, and a pocket that was barely hanging on. That suited her current state of mind.

After exchanging her formal dress for comfort, she

kicked out of her heels and donned the slide-on sneakers that had been stashed in a side pocket. Now she felt more human, if not more calm. Too bad they'd left the champagne in the limo.

She didn't need alcohol, she needed some peace and quiet. Time alone to reflect. With that in mind, she headed into the hall and located the well-equipped kitchen—which was almost as nice as the one back at the ranch—then made her way out the back door.

Dallas had been right about the moon. It cast the manicured lawn in an amber glow and helped guide Paris down the dirt path toward a copse of trees. Fortunately someone had had the foresight to cut a wide clearing in the woods, otherwise she might have been hesitant to continue. A few yards away she could see the shimmering lake and headed in that direction, all the while aware of the sounds of nature, including what sounded like an owl. She managed to make it to the dock without stepping on a critter or coming upon the attack cats.

Once there, she strolled to the end of the pier and lowered herself onto the wooden slats, then hugged her knees to her chest. A slight breeze blew across her face, bringing with it the pleasant scent of cedar. She heard the sound of chirping and an occasional rustle of leaves, which might have unnerved her if she would have still been walking.

On afterthought, she rolled up her jeans, took off her shoes and dangled her feet in the water that was much colder than she'd predicted. But after a while she acclimated to the temperature change and rocked back on her elbows to study the host of stars in the night sky.

For the first time that day, she experienced true tranquility. A sense of well-being as she soaked her sore feet in silence.

"Mind if I join you?"

Paris gasped and nearly vaulted right into the water. She shifted around, palm against her pounding heart, to find Dallas standing above her. "Jeez, you scared me to death!"

He sat beside her without waiting for an invitation and draped his arms on bent knees. "Did you think I was a snake? Or maybe one of the tomcats. Just so you know, they don't talk."

"You startled me because I wasn't expecting you."

"Next time I'll whistle."

Like that would help her anxiety over being accosted by random wildlife. "I'm surprised I didn't hear you."

"No kidding. This dock creaks like box springs on an old iron bed."

No real shock he would bring up a bed analogy. "I was very deep in thought."

"About?"

"Today. This whole thing seems so surreal."

He shifted slightly, leading Paris to believe maybe he was suffering from bride remorse. "Yeah, I know. Never thought it would happen to me."

Her conjecture could very well be right. She wouldn't know what might be on his mind unless she asked. "So what brings you here, other than this bizarre situation?"

"I owe you an apology."

That she hadn't expected. "For what?"

"I'm sorry for coming on too strong. But I won't apologize for wanting you so badly I ache."

She'd never felt so flattered in her life. "Apology accepted, and I'd be telling one colossal lie if I said I wasn't extremely attracted to you. But—"

"But what?" He gave her a meaningful look. "If you're worried about the whole annulment thing, I won't tell if you won't."

"I won't lie under oath. And I have a feeling your integrity won't allow that either."

His sigh cut through the silence. "You're right about that. One thing I learned from my father, deception takes no prisoners. I do think we can find other ways to answer our needs."

Was he suggesting an open marriage? "If you're going to ask if you can see other women, that's your call, but rest assured I wouldn't feel right seeing other men."

"I'm not saying that at all," he said. "We can explore each other without going beyond the limits."

"You mean only foreplay?"

"You got it, darlin'. It's my favorite kind of play."

The thought of his hands on her made her shiver in a very nice way. "That would certainly be new and different for me."

He frowned. "Your husband wasn't into foreplay?"

The understatement of the millennium. "Let me sum up our sex life in a few words. Hi, Paris, just passing through, only have a minute, got to go, see you later. That happened about once a week unless he wasn't in the mood. He always said I was too uptight about my body, but what did he expect when all he did was criticize me?"

"Why in the hell were you with that ass?"

The sheer anger in his voice took her aback. "I was young and stupid. He was my first lover and the first man who really paid attention to me. At least in the beginning. When I got him hired on at the firm, everything changed. I'm fairly certain he cheated on me, although I didn't have any proof. Eventually I didn't even care."

Dallas let go a litany of curses. "You're damn special, Paris. You deserve to be treated that way. And if you want me to show you how good it can be between a man and a woman, all you have to do is ask."

When he rose to his feet, Paris realized she didn't want him to leave. "Where are you going?"

"To grab a snack, take a cold shower and then head to bed."

"Could you stay a little longer?"

"I could, but being so close to you and not being able to touch you is killing me."

She recognized the risk she'd be taking, but she truly craved his attention because she knew with all her heart he would treat her with respect. "I want you to touch me, Dallas. I *need* you to touch me."

He stood statue still and after a few moments asked, "Are you sure?"

She held her hand toward him. "If you'll help me up, I'll go back to the house with you."

"No need for that."

Paris had no idea what he planned to do next when he, too, rolled up his jeans, sat back down, pulled off his socks and boots, then positioned himself behind her, his legs on either side of her thighs. Right at that moment, Paris felt something at her feet beneath the water and gasped again.

"Just relax sweetheart," he told her as he pulled the band away, pushed her hair aside and kissed the back of her neck.

"It's not you. Something was nibbling on my toes."

His slow laugh sent pleasurable chills down her spine. "Darlin', I can do that, but you'll have to wait until it's warmer or until you have your feet out of the lake."

She smiled back at him. "You mean you wouldn't jump in the water if I asked you?"

"Not unless you're waiting for me, naked."

Interesting concept, albeit not logical. "We probably should put that on hold for a couple of months."

"It's a deal."

He kissed her then, thoroughly, stroking her tongue softly with his in a heady rhythm that made her want to climb all over him. If she reacted so strongly to this simple show of affection, she couldn't imagine what she would do if he did anything else.

She would soon find out, she realized, when he broke the kiss and rested his cheek against her cheek, reached beneath her shirt and unclasped her bra. For a moment she felt like a schoolgirl making out with her first real boyfriend in a backseat, an experience she'd never really had. But when Dallas tugged the tee up over her head, taking the bra with it, she knew she was in the hands of a real man. Naked from the waist up. In wide-open spaces.

She should be mortified over being so exposed, but she honestly didn't care. She should have been self-conscious when Dallas whispered, "Watch," but instead she waited with excited anticipation. And the minute he began to circle her nipples simultaneously with his fingertips, she grew hotter than blazes in places still unseen.

As much as she wanted to continue to see what Dallas was doing, Paris closed her eyes and leaned back against him to savor the sensations.

"Feel good?" he asked, his voice low and grainy.

"Yes."

When Dallas slid his palm down her belly, Paris held her breath. And when he began to toy with the button on her jeans, she automatically tensed.

"Just tell me to stop and I will."

She frankly hoped he kept right on going, but then he suddenly halted everything, much to her disappointment. She opened her eyes and stared at him blankly. "I didn't say anything."

He moved from behind her, rolled down his jeans, put on his boots then stood. "I think that's enough for tonight."

She snatched the discarded shirt and clutched it to her bare breasts. "I don't understand."

"Put your shirt on and I'll walk you to the house."

Somewhat miffed, Paris slid the tee over her head,

stood and shoved the bra in her back pocket. "I can find my way."

"Are you mad at me?"

"No. I'm mad at myself for falling into your trap. Nothing good could ever come of mixing business with pleasure and in reality, this is a business arrangement as you have reminded me several times."

"Between two consenting adults who have the hots for each other." He had the nerve to wink. "Darlin', a lot of good could come from it, as soon as you realize sometimes you can't control chemistry. Just let me know when you're ready to explore all our options."

"Don't count on that happening," she said to Dallas as he strode away, leaving her alone to wonder why she couldn't resist him. Why she had let him go so far. Why he could so completely splinter her coveted control, and she welcomed it.

He might have caught her in a moment of weakness, but from that point forward, she vowed to reclaim her power. Call all the shots in this sexual game he seemed determined to play. Turn the tables on him. The time had come to shed her insecurities and prove to him—and to herself—that she could be a strong woman capable of going after what she wanted, wisdom be damned. Business be damned. Fact was, she wanted him.

Perhaps she hadn't been born a natural seductress, or acquired any real skills in thirty-two years, but it was never too late to learn. When it came right down to it, celibacy wasn't the least bit fun.

Six

Celibacy sucked swamp water.

Dallas had discovered that recently but learned long ago the lack of merit in a cold shower. He'd taken one anyway at dawn, following one helluva restless night. Afterward, he'd headed to the kitchen, made a strong pot of coffee, a couple of scrambled eggs and ate them at the kitchen island like he did every morning at the cabin. But his normal news catch-up routine had been disrupted by visions of the woman sleeping down the hall. Just the thought of touching Paris again, going further, going all the way, kept him from focusing on the state of the global markets. But he had to remember the annulment terms—no sex in the real sense.

If he had any hope of maintaining his sanity for the next twelve months, he had two options—take care of the problem himself, or convince Paris they should take care of each other, even if it meant not fully consummating the marriage. He liked the second plan best. Taking it slow seemed to be the only way to accomplish that goal, even though it would damn sure prove to be real hard. Literally. Now if he'd been a dishonorable jerk, he would've crawled into bed with her last night to solve the problem, knowing he'd had her exactly where he'd wanted her before he left her on the dock.

The *problem* only grew more obvious when Paris padded into the room on bare feet, wearing some short flimsy peach-colored robe, her hair piled on top of her head in a messy ponytail. On one hand, she was about as cute as a newborn foal. On the other, she looked sexy as hell, even with her face free of makeup.

She sauntered over to the counter, poured herself a cup of coffee, then turned a sleepy smile on him. "Happy birthday and good morning, handsome husband."

She looked like a birthday gift he wanted to thoroughly investigate. "Mornin', pretty wife." He'd never dreamed those words would ever leave his mouth. But then he'd never imagined meeting anyone like her, either. He liked the way she moved. The way she talked. Her intelligence. Her body. And he knew he would seriously like the way she loved if she gave him the chance to partake of all the benefits that most married couples enjoyed.

Wait a minute. For all intents and purposes, they'd entered into a fabricated union. They weren't playing house, they were doing business. If it was up to her, that's all they'd ever be doing.

Maybe not, he decided, when she sauntered over to the island, sat on the barstool across from him and didn't bother to close the opening of the robe, allowing him a nice view of the curve of her breasts. "Sleep well?"

Not hardly. "Fairly well. And you?"

"You mean after you left me alone topless on the dock? I've had better nights."

"Sorry," he muttered, although he really wasn't all that sorry, except maybe about the leaving part.

She then leaned completely across the granite surface to study the newspaper in front him, causing the robe to gape more and giving him full view of her bare breasts, nipples and all. "*Wall Street Journal*, huh? I expected you to be reading some ranching magazine."

He expected to elevate the island at any moment. "I've been interested in financial news since I acquired my MBA."

Her green eyes went wide as she sat back down, taking his fun away but giving him some moderate relief. "I had no idea you have a graduate degree. Where did you go to school?"

He couldn't resist rattling her chain a little. "Got it online from the University of Dumb Cowpokes."

She laughed softly as she rimmed a fingertip around the coffee cup, drawing Dallas's undivided attention. "Be serious for a change."

He had a serious need to see what else she might be wearing underneath that robe. Or what she wasn't wearing. "I got the undergraduate degree at a small college in Stephenville, Texas, while on a rodeo scholarship. A few years later, when I decided to open the saddle shops, I decided to go for the masters at a bigger university in Fort Worth."

"Impressive. Why saddle shops?"

Recounting his history could calm his rowdy libido. "When I was growing up, a ranch hand named Gordy taught me how to tool roping saddles. I used his design, started my own line of saddles and began to market it."

"Gordy doesn't have a problem with that?"

"Nope. He's happily retired living off the royalties."

"You are a man of many talents, I must say. Do you have any sugar?"

Ignoring the urge to tell her he could give her something really sweet, Dallas nodded toward the cabinet behind her. "Right next to the coffee maker."

She glanced over one shoulder before sending him another smile. "Oh. I didn't see it," she said as she slid out of her chair.

She sure had great legs, he realized, when she walked to the counter to sweeten her coffee. The robe was so short that if she lifted her arms, he felt sure he could see her bottom. He should've told her the canister was in an upper cabinet. He'd give a month's worth of pay to find some excuse for her to bend over. He didn't have to let go of a dime when she dropped the spoon on the floor and reached down to pick it up.

Damn if she didn't have on a thing. Damn if she didn't have one fantastic butt. And damn if he didn't have the mother of all erections.

She turned around and leaned back against the counter. "What are your plans for the day?"

He could offer up a few that involved staying horizontal for the next twenty-four hours, but remembered his aim to take it easy. "I thought we'd go fishing."

She sipped her coffee then set the cup aside. "Sounds like fun. When do you want to do it?"

Right now on the kitchen island. "We need to get going before it gets much later, while the fish are still biting."

"Then I should hurry. What should I wear?"

Not a damn thing. "T-shirt and jeans, I guess. Or shorts. It's going to be close to eighty degrees today."

While Dallas sat there suffering from lack of sex, Paris rinsed her cup out in the sink and put it in the dishwasher, unaware of his predicament. "I'll take a quick shower and be back in a few. Where should I meet you once I'm finished?"

In my bed. Your bed. Any bed. "The dock."

"The dock it is. Maybe I'll just show up without my top to save time."

Taking Dallas totally by surprise, Paris untied the sash at her waist, turned around and let the robe fall from her shoulders onto the floor as she walked away.

The image of her slender back and shapely butt remained burned in his brain long after she disappeared. Was she just trying to torture him, or give him a taste of his own medicine? He didn't know the answer, but he sure as hell intended to find out.

Paris wondered what effect, if any, her little attempt at seduction had had on Dallas. If he only knew how difficult it had been to completely let go of her inhibitions, then maybe he might have said *something.* When she'd left him in the kitchen, she hadn't had the fortitude to wait around. He certainly hadn't sought her out in the shower, or showed up at the bedroom door. Only time would tell what he might have in store for her during their little excursion, and the closer she came to the dock, the more the excitement escalated.

She discovered him waiting for her, dressed in khaki cargo shorts and a sleeveless army-green tank, revealing a pair of very masculine legs and muscled biceps that sent her heart on a marathon. A few moments passed before she noticed the sleek silver-and-red boat with the covered hull tied to the side of the pier.

After sliding her sunglasses into place, Paris stepped onto the creaky planks and made her way to her tour guide for the day. "Is this yours?"

"Yep," he replied.

"How did it get here?"

"George."

Clearly he'd decided to be cryptic. "Who is George?"

"My neighbor. He looks after the place when I'm not here, and in exchange I let him use the boat. I called and had him deliver it a few minutes ago."

Evidently George wasn't going to join them, a very good thing. "I see. I've never been on this kind of boat before. It looks like it costs a pretty penny."

"About eighty grand."

Paris nearly swallowed the gum she'd been chewing. "Eighty thousand dollars? For that price, it should clean the house, or at least do more than float around the water looking pretty."

"It can fly," he said as he held out his hand. "If you're lucky, I might let you drive it."

As long as he had sufficient insurance since she'd never been behind the wheel of a boat before. "I might take you up on that, if you're lucky."

He cracked a crooked grin. "I have a feeling we could both be lucky today."

She returned his smile. "Could be." Or not, depending on how far she wanted the seduction scheme to go.

After Dallas helped Paris down into the space-age looking seat, he untied the boat then claimed the space next to her. One hand on the wheel, he backed away from the dock slowly, said, "Hang on," then turned the craft around and shot off into open water.

Yes, the thing could fly, and she couldn't hold a conversation with him due to all the wind noise. She basically clutched the sides of the seats, gritted her teeth and only breathed easier when he navigated the boat into a secluded cove fifteen minutes later.

She pulled away the band securing her high ponytail and finger-combed her hair. "You need to turn around and go back."

He frowned. "Why?"

"Because I think I left my stomach a few miles back."

He barked a laugh. "I take it you're not much of a thrill seeker."

Only partially true. She'd married him on a moment's notice, hadn't she? And she was definitely seeking some thrills today. "I've ridden a few roller coasters on several occasions, but I wasn't quite prepared for this."

Paris *had* prepared to turn on the charms and hopefully turn him on in the process. On that note, she crossed her arms, grabbed the T-shirt's hem and tugged it over her head, leaving her clad in a red bikini top.

Dallas cleared his throat and shut down the ignition. "Didn't know you had a swimsuit."

"Actually, I didn't either," she said as she stood. "Jenny thought of everything." Including massage oil and lubricants, a veritable sex shop in a bag.

"No surprise there," he replied, his voice sounding somewhat grainy.

Paris realized she didn't have a lot of room to maneuver, so she pointed to the enclosed hull. "What's under there?"

"A live well to keep fresh bait and fish and a place to store equipment." He climbed over the smoked glass minidash and stood on the decking to toss an anchor overboard into the murky green water. "You basically turn on the trolling motor and stand here to fish, but we're going to stay stationary until you learn how to cast."

"Or I could sunbathe," she said as she retraced his steps and stood before him. "I can do that while we fish, right?"

"Not a whole lot of sun with all the trees, but whatever floats your boat, pun intended."

She shimmied out of the shorts and tossed them back onto the seat, revealing the scant swimsuit bottoms. "I'm ready for a pole now."

That earned her a wily grin. "I can fix you right up."

"Fishing pole, Dallas."

"I've got one of those, too."

"You have an evil mind."

"You have an unbelievable body."

She felt a head-to-toe blush coming on, and the same old belief he'd simply been trying to be nice. "I bet you say that to all your first mates."

He tucked one side of her hair behind her ear. "You're technically my first mate."

If only she could say the same for herself. If only she could erase Peter from her past and if only this arrangement with Dallas was real. "Well, I suppose we should start fishing before they stop biting."

He stared at her a few moments before leaning over, opening a hatch and pulling out a rod. "I've got this rigged to catch a bass. I also have some blood bait for catfish if you'd prefer to try for one of those."

She wrinkled her nose. "Any bait that includes *blood* in the name is out."

"Good call, because it's also known as stink bait."

Ewww... "Definitely bass."

"Bass it is. Now move to the edge of the boat."

After she complied, Paris surveyed the wooded bank and noticed not a house, or soul, in sight. "How many people live on this lake?"

"Just me and George," he said. "It's a private lake."

Of course it was. "So there's no chance anyone will see me making a fool of myself?"

"Not likely." Dallas came up behind her and handed her the pole with the little yellow frog-looking thingy dangling from the end. "Hold this in your left hand, and grasp the reel in your right."

Simple enough. "Like this?"

"Yep. Now push that button with your thumb, pull the rod back to the side and let it go, but not over your head or you'll hook me."

She did exactly as he'd instructed, yet nothing happened. "I knew I wasn't cut out for this."

"I don't mind helping you out." He moved behind her, wrapped his hand around the rod below her hand and replaced her thumb on the release with his. "It's just one smooth action," he said as he cast the line in the water with ease.

He didn't make a move away from her. In fact, Paris would swear he moved closer. "Okay. What now?"

He rested a palm on her belly and pushed her hair to one side with the other. "It's a top-water jig, so the fish will hit it on top of the water."

"How long does that take?"

"Until the fish decides to bite."

When Dallas rimmed the shell of her ear with his tongue, Paris almost dropped the pole. "So it might take a while."

"Probably not."

After Dallas dropped his arms from around her, Paris glanced back to find he'd removed his shirt. And oh, what a sight to behold. He had a board-flat belly and a chest that wouldn't quit. "Hot already?"

"Lady, you have no idea how hot."

She had a sneaking suspicion she might soon find out when he came back to her and began kissing her neck again. "What are you up to, Dallas Calloway?"

He moved flush against her back. "Pay me no mind and watch your line, in case you get a bite."

"Aren't you going to fish?"

"Maybe later. I have something I'd rather do at the moment."

Paris held her breath when he tugged the string at her neck and unclasped the strap at her back. Now the bikini top lay in a pool at her feet and she found herself exactly where she'd been last night—naked from the waist up.

"Dallas, are you sure no one will see us?" Her voice sounded tinny, thanks to the cowboy's hands roving over her breasts.

"George left for Kerrville this morning to visit his mother." He feathered more kisses along her neck. "Besides, the possibility of getting caught makes this a little more exciting."

Her legs began to shake like a leaf in the breeze. "Any more excitement and I might actually not be able to stand."

"I'll make sure you don't fall. Just relax."

Relaxing proved to be impossible when his palm came to rest on her midriff and began to drift lower… and lower. "What are you doing now?"

"Scratching your itch."

When he slipped his hand beneath her bathing suit bottoms, Paris was powerless to stop him. When he began to stroke her softly, she could no longer hold onto the fishing pole. After she dropped it on the deck, she reached back and wrapped her hand around his nape to ground herself. She briefly envisioned how this would look to a passerby—him with his hand down her pants and her in the throes of a sexual frenzy—and that only amplified her need for release.

In a matter of seconds, her pulse accelerated and her respiration picked up speed as the impending climax began to build. The orgasm slammed into her hard with a series of strong spasms that seemed as if they went on forever. She literally shook from the force of it and Dallas, as if he sensed she might not remain upright, turned her into his arms and kissed her.

She came back to reality slowly and broke the kiss to tip her forehead against his shoulder. "Wow."

"Been a while, has it?"

"Try never. At least not with Peter."

He set her back and stared at her. "He never got you off?"

She shook her head. "Sadly no, because he really didn't try, or care. And go ahead and say it. I'm a fool for staying with him as long as I did."

His expression turned somber. "Then why did you?"

"Because I'd convinced myself I couldn't do any better." An admission she'd not made to herself, much less to another soul.

He hugged her for a few moments then pulled away to study her eyes. "Sweetheart, you deserve better. You deserve to have a lover who takes care of you first and puts himself second. That's the way a man should treat his woman, especially a woman as special as you."

His woman? Once upon a time she would have made a snide comment about beating his chest, but oddly she liked the sound of it. "Thank you. That means more than you know. But I'm nothing special."

He looked mock serious. "Yes, you are, and don't argue with me."

"I wouldn't dare, Mr. Macho. Not after what you just did for me." That brought about an important question. "Speaking of that, what about you? You've clearly got an itch that needs scratching, too."

"True, but I'm fine for now." He grinned. "Later this evening is another story altogether. We still have a whole lot of exploring to do, if you're game."

Paris imagined giving him the pleasure he'd just given her and that made her tingle. "I'm definitely game." The sound of the reel suddenly drew her attention and prompted her to snatch the rod off the ground. "I think I have something. What do I do now?"

"Bring it in, darlin'."

"How?"

Without responding, Dallas stepped to her side, took the pole and turned the reel's handle until he brought up the line, a smallish silver fish dangling from the hook. "Not quite big enough for dinner."

"It's so cute, but hurry and take it off."

"It's a baby," he said as he unhooked the bass, crouched down and released it into the water. "Grow up, bud, and maybe I'll catch ya later."

That made Paris smile. "I'm glad you let him go."

"I don't like fishermen who hang on to undersized fish just because they can. It's a waste, and I don't like waste."

She liked him more and more with each passing moment. She predicted that beneath the tough-guy exterior resided a heart of gold. "It's nice to know you have respect for wildlife. And women."

He offered her the pole. "Want to try for something bigger?"

"Are you referring to a fish?" she teased.

"Well, sweetheart, what else do you have in mind?"

"Maybe I'll show you later this evening." She took the rod and this time managed to cast it all by herself. "How was that?"

"Looks like you're a fast learner."

She handed him back the pole. "But I'm not very patient. You fish, I'll just kick back on the deck, get some sun and watch you bring in dinner."

He nodded toward the hatch. "There's a towel in there, so have fun. But don't get too comfortable because we might not be here much longer. It's almost time for lunch."

Paris realized she hadn't eaten a thing since the whole grain bar she'd consumed in the bedroom following her novice strip tease. "I admit I'm getting a little hungry, too."

After casting toward the bank, Dallas shot her a grin. "From this point forward, you can always depend on me to take care of all your appetites. How am I doing so far?"

She returned his smile. "Best fishing trip ever."

And she couldn't wait to find out what else he had planned.

Seven

His plans for Paris had unfortunately been put on hold.

The woman had been so relaxed that immediately after she'd eaten lunch—if you wanted to call a tomato and lettuce sandwich *lunch*—she'd taken a nap. A long nap.

His mind whirled back to earlier in the day, when she'd been as hot as a branding iron and quick to fire. The bastard she'd married had done a number on her, and he really wanted to right the wrongs. Show her all the ways a man could please a woman. Convince her that she was as close to perfect as they come. No doubt he'd be up for the challenge, in every way possible.

Dallas had thought about joining her in bed, but he'd taken a trip to the nearest grocery store—fifteen miles away—then returned a few calls, including one from his attorney. As a result of that conversation, he had to break some serious news that wouldn't make Paris happy in the least. She might not want anything more to do with him.

And now, with the sun working its way down the horizon, Dallas grabbed a beer, fired up the grill and contemplated how he would tell her the sorry news. He didn't have a lot of time left, he realized, when Paris made an appearance on the back deck a few minutes later, looking like she'd walked right off the cover of a fashion magazine.

Her straight blond hair fell past her shoulders like homespun silk. She wore just enough makeup to show off her features to full advantage, and a short blue dress with thin straps that showed enough cleavage to make him want to growl. He couldn't believe his luck in finding such a good-looking fake wife.

She kicked off her flip-flops, curled up on the wicker sofa and pulled her legs beneath her on the blue cushions. "Whatcha doing, cowboy?"

Imagining what it would be like to make fast, hard love to you on that sofa. For the sake of distraction, Dallas turned the burgers before lowering the lid on the grill to regard her again. "I'm making us some dinner. You must've been really tired considering how long you slept."

"I only slept about an hour. I spent the rest of the time rehearsing what I would tell my parents about our marriage and then I called them."

He would have liked to have been a fly on the wall during that conversation. "How did it go?"

She shrugged. "As expected. My mom bemoaned the fact that once again she didn't have the opportunity to throw a lavish wedding for her youngest daughter due to a whirlwind courtship. The conversation with my dad wasn't much better."

"What did he say?"

"He said, and I quote, 'This guy better not treat you as poorly as that other SOB.' And then he went on to say to let him know where he can find Peter so he can beat the…well…some sense into him."

Although Dallas could understand her father's attitude toward the ex-husband, he didn't like the thought of winding up on the wrong side of a retired military man when that man learned his daughter's latest marriage wasn't permanent. "How big is your dad?"

"How tall are you?"

"Six-two."

"He's five inches shorter and stocky. My mom is five-seven, and so is my sister. I fell on the shorter side at five-five."

"I would've guessed you to be a little bit taller. Must be those long legs."

"Must be your imagination."

Yeah, his imagination was running amok when he thought about having those legs wrapped around his waist. Again he looked to his cooking duty to keep him from acting on his fantasies. At least until he could confess…after dinner.

"Speaking of family dynamics," Paris began, "I assume all your brothers know about the will, but do they know that our marriage isn't exactly the real thing?"

"They're all pretty busy right now so I'm not sure what Jen or Maria have told them. I plan to say as little as possible when we get back to the ranch."

"Do you think they would actually believe you would rush into a marriage on a whim because of a will?"

Probably not. "It doesn't matter what they believe. It's an unspoken rule that we don't get into each other's business."

After a span of silence, Paris leaned slightly and studied the grill. "Color me crazy, Dallas, but those look a lot like beef patties."

"Only two of them," he said as he flipped them again before turning back to Paris. "I found some kind of veggie burgers at the store. I figured they couldn't be too bad. Heck, you could serve up a boot as long as you've grilled it with mesquite wood chips."

"Heavens, I hope it doesn't taste like a boot."

Honestly, so did Dallas. He didn't want to let her down, although he suspected he eventually would before night's end. "The cashier who checked me out told me she loved them."

"I'll bet she checked you out thoroughly."

The jealously in her voice surprised him, and in some ways pleased him. "She had to be at least sixty-five."

She lifted her chin. "Just because a woman matures doesn't mean she can't recognize a sexy cowboy when she sees one."

"And just because I'm a man doesn't mean I'm gonna flirt with a grandmother."

"Men flirt with any woman who'll flirt back."

At least she'd said it with a smile. She wouldn't be

smiling when he lowered the legal boom. "Do you want something to drink?"

"I wouldn't turn down a glass of white wine, if you happen to have some. If not, water will work."

"I have wine." Thankfully he'd had the foresight to stock up a few months ago, the last time he'd had a female guest at the cabin. The last time he'd had a woman, period. Tina, or maybe it was Terry. What the hell did it matter? He'd only spent one weekend with her. Plus, she couldn't hold a candle to Paris in any way, shape or form.

When Paris came to her feet, Dallas caught a good glimpse of a thigh and one stubborn part of him stood, too. He needed to get the hell out of Dodge before she noticed. He'd begun to wonder if any man had ever expired due to a perpetual erection. "Sit. I'll bring it to you. In the meantime, you enjoy the sunset."

"If you leave, you'll miss it since it's almost gone."

So was his sanity. "I've seen it before." He'd also seen a feminine leg before, but for some reason, viewing even an inch of her bare skin kicked his libido into overdrive.

After one last look at the burgers, Dallas rushed into the house, braced both palms on the kitchen island and took a few deep breaths. If he didn't calm down and get with the program, all his plans for the evening would go up in smoke. He couldn't act on his need for her until she knew all the truth.

When he finally gained his composure, he took the plate full of lettuce, tomatoes and pickles from the fridge, along with the bottle of chardonnay. He thought about popping the top on another beer but figured that wouldn't help his predicament at all. He needed to keep his guard up and his sex drive down for the time being.

He brought the hamburger fixings and put them on the wooden picnic table, then handed Paris the wine. "Sorry about the plastic cup. I don't have any fancy barware here. Hell, I don't have any fancy dinnerware, either. That's why we're eating on disposable plates."

She took a drink of the chardonnay and rested the cup in her lap. "Not exactly environmentally friendly, but I suppose they'll do if we don't have a choice."

He didn't want her to believe he was a total Neanderthal. "They're plastic, too. I throw them in the recycle bin before I leave so George can properly dispose of them."

"That's good to know. How is dinner coming along?"

He checked the burgers, all the while considering giving her a kiss. Only one kiss. But like the potato chips resting on the red checkerboard tablecloth, he wouldn't be able to stop with just one. "Looks like they're about ready. Do you want cheese on yours?"

"Sure. I'm in the mood to splurge a little."

Dallas hadn't realized she was standing behind him until that moment. After laying the cheese slices on the burgers, he put the spatula down and turned around, only to run headlong into some fairly fantastic green eyes and a mouth that looked like it wanted to be kissed. Maybe that was just wishful thinking. "What else are you in the mood for?"

She slid her arms around his neck and pressed her great body against his, indicating she might be willing to make his wish come true. "Oh, I don't know. Maybe a little slap and tickle after we eat. Maybe a little of that before we eat."

Man, she was killing him. "Aren't you hungry?"

"Yes, but not only for food." She rubbed against him and it hadn't been an accident. "Just humor me, okay?"

With the last scrap of his control in shambles, Dallas gave her a full-throttle, no-holds-barred kiss. A tongue-dueling, fire-starting kiss that gave the barbecue grill behind him a run for its money.

But damn, he wanted more. He wanted to use his mouth somewhere else, and that meant disregarding his original plan of ignoring her. To hell with it.

He pushed the straps off her shoulders and then lowered the dress's bodice to do what he'd wanted to do earlier that day. He bent his head and took one breast into his mouth while Paris threaded her hands through his hair to hang on. When he circled her nipple with his tongue, she released a purely sexual sound that made him so hard he wanted to strip out of his jeans then and there. Instead, he slid his palms down her back, clasped her butt and pulled her against the erection that wouldn't die unless he did something about it. But if he acted in haste, he could make a mistake of monumental proportions. As bad as he wanted to be inside her, he thought of all the reasons why he couldn't.

Dallas let her go and took a step back. He had to look her straight in the eye when he made the revelation. "We need to have a serious talk before this goes any further."

Paris's lips looked swollen and her eyes hazy, but she

didn't seem to be too mad over the interruption. Yet. "Talk about what?"

"A change in the marriage terms."

"I'm sorry, Dallas, but I'm confused."

She wouldn't be confused much longer, but she sure as hell might be ready to slug him. He saw no choice but to blurt out the sorry truth.

"Darlin', we're going to have to get divorced."

Surely she hadn't heard him correctly. "Are you serious?"

"Yeah, I am."

Paris pulled the dress back into place as her mind reeled from Dallas's proclamation. "Now? We've barely been married a day."

"No, not now. When the year ends."

She could not believe he would go back on his word. So much for trusting another man. "We both agreed we would get an annulment. In fact, you promised your attorney would find some way to accomplish that goal."

Dallas took her by the hand and showed her to the table where they sat on opposing benches. "I spoke to him today," he began, "to ask him why it was taking so long to get the final agreement drawn up. He informed me that if we annul the marriage, that would be like it never existed in the first place, and that would go against the terms of the will."

Darn the family feud. She struggled to remain calm and sensible when she wanted to shout from frustration. "Then Worth could take control of the ranch and this charade would have been for naught."

"That about sums it up."

And she didn't like it one iota. "Great. We'll be forced to get a divorce and I'll be marked as a woman who just can't make any marriage work."

"Not if the divorce is my fault and I take the fall."

She supposed at this point they didn't have any choice. "How would you do that?"

"You could tell everyone I cheated on you."

Impossible. "That would be two cheating husbands. People could interpret that as I'm a total fool, or a cold fish in bed. What else do you have?"

"Maybe I drink too much."

She'd never seen him have more than one beer. "Anyone who knows you could disprove that. Any other brilliant ideas?"

"Yeah, I could tell the truth. I don't want any kids and that's a deal breaker for you."

Shock rendered her momentarily silent. Under the circumstances, that shouldn't matter to her, but it did. His disclosure did put the kibosh on any future with him, as if she'd really believed that would happen. "You don't want a child to continue your legacy?"

"Nope. I have five brothers who can take care of the procreating."

For a man who appeared to be all about family, he certainly seemed opposed to having one of his own. "Why exactly do you feel this way?"

He stared at some unknown focal point behind her. "When you have the misfortune of being born to a man like my dad, it makes you doubt yourself and your ability to be a good husband and father."

She reached over and touched his hand to garner his attention. "As far as I know, infidelity isn't genetic, and I sense you'd be a great father."

"You don't know me that well."

True, but she believed she was getting there. And she still had twelve months to learn even more, although she realized that was all she would ever have with him. "I know you love animals and you're willing to set a baby bass free. That speaks to your patience and compassion and some paternal instinct."

"I'm basically married to someone for the sake of a parcel of land. Some might say that speaks to my selfishness."

Obviously both of them put a lot of stock in other people's opinions. "I don't see you as selfish, just desperate. Besides, I'm basically in the same situation since I married for financial stability. Mr. and Mrs. Desperation. It has a nice ring to it."

He rubbed his chin then grinned. "Yeah, it does. So you're not too mad at me over the annulment issue?"

She wanted to be angry, but in essence she could only blame faulty research and jumping in feet first before they knew all the facts. "Let's just say I'm disappointed we rushed into this before I fully investigated our options"

"Would you have changed your mind if you'd known?"

She had to think about that a few seconds. "Possibly, but it doesn't matter since we can't do anything about it now. Besides, we still have twelve months to figure out how we're going to end it."

"Yeah, you're right, unless you can't tolerate me that long."

She gave him a mock stern look. "That's a strong possibility if you don't finish those burgers. I'm suddenly so hungry I could eat the tablecloth."

"No more slap and tickle?" he asked, clear disappointment in his tone.

She wanted to say definitely, but she hadn't quite digested the divorce issue. "Let's worry about dinner right now, okay?"

He stood and leaned over to kiss her forehead. "Sure thing, sweetheart."

Something suddenly occurred to her. "Since it is your birthday, I should have cooked for you."

He studied her a long moment before speaking again. "You know what I'd really like from you to make this day special?"

"Does it start with an 's' and rhyme with vex?"

He shook his head. "No. I want you to tell me you believe that I didn't know the annulment wasn't going to work."

"I'm going to give you the benefit of the doubt." And she hoped her faith wasn't misplaced again. "I only wish we'd had more time to think things through before we rushed into this arrangement."

"Unfortunately time wasn't on our side. But I'll try to make it up to you after dinner."

That could create more problems from an emotional standpoint if she succumbed to her strong desire for him. "How are you going to do that?"

"You'll have to wait and see."

* * *

The sound of a sultry country ballad drew Paris from the kitchen back onto the deck. As the music filtered through the outdoor speakers, the sun had disappeared from the horizon, washing the sky in an orange glow, providing the perfect backdrop to the man leaning back against the railing. A cowboy knight wearing a crisp light blue shirt rolled up at the sleeves, slightly faded jeans and the usual boots, one substantial hand wrapped around a beer.

"Did you shower?" she asked as she approached Dallas, immediately catching a whiff of his clean-scented cologne.

"I wanted to get rid of the barbecue smells."

"I really don't mind that at all." And she didn't, though she still worried she'd made a mistake with their fake marriage. She worried she might make another if she didn't keep her wits about her.

"Thanks for cleaning up the mess," he said.

"After those great veggie burgers, it was the least I could do."

A few moments of silence ticked off as they stood there steeped in palpable tension. Dallas shifted his weight from one leg to the other before setting the bottle atop the nearby table. "Let's dance," he said as he offered his hand to her.

Paris was plagued with a serious case of nerves. "I'm not very good. Not when it comes to country dancing."

He pulled her gently into his arms. "You just have to hold on to me."

And she did as they swayed in time to the tune, moving easily through the last of the song and onto the next, his palms roving softly over her back, her cheek resting against his shoulder.

She briefly wondered how many women had fallen under his spell. How many would have given anything to be in her shoes right now. That shouldn't matter. After all, they were married, at least for a year until it all came to an end.

Maybe they could take the time to learn more about each other. Perhaps she should spend the months finding herself, without getting lost in him. But she felt lost right then as they moved closer, held each other tighter.

When Dallas paused, Paris lifted her head and met his mesmerizing blue eyes. "Mind if I kiss you?" he asked.

She found that odd. "You've never needed my permission before."

"Yeah, but I do now since I didn't keep my promise to you about the annulment."

"It's done, Dallas. We can't go back and undo it. We can only move forward."

"True. You didn't answer my question."

She did, but not with words, despite the lack of wisdom. Instead, she wrapped her hands around his neck and kissed him. A soft, almost quiet kiss that seemed strangely emotional. The way newlyweds who had entered a real union would kiss. A kiss that took a drastic turn toward mutual need in a matter of moments.

Dallas broke the contact first and sighed. "I wish I didn't want you so damn bad."

In some ways she wished the same for herself. But

life was short, and their time limited. She could reject his advances, or take another risk that would most definitely come with rewards. Foolish as it might be, she wanted to experience all that he had to offer, and suffer the possible consequences later. "Maybe we shouldn't overthink this too much."

He frowned. "I'm not following you."

"Do you know what this divorce requirement means?"

"Yeah. I'm going to be padding my lawyer's pockets even more."

Evidently he was having a lapse in comprehension. "No. What it means for us."

He grinned. "We don't have to stop with only slappin' and ticklin'?"

She did a little smiling, too. "Correct."

His smile faded into a serious expression. "That's a big step, Paris."

A step she hadn't planned to take, but… "As you've said, we're both consenting adults and we'll be spending a lot of time together. Since the consummation issue no longer exists, we have no reason not to let nature take its course." And during the journey, she vowed to keep a good grip on her heart.

Taking her by the hand, he led her back to the table, claimed the bench across from her, folded his hands and gave her a somber look. "Are you sure you want to do this? I don't want you to feel like you're being pressured into something that makes you uncomfortable."

Evidently he didn't get it. "Let me put it to you this way. For the first thirty years of my life, I walked a straight line. I ignorantly thought if I followed all the rules, did what was expected, didn't make waves, everything would be rosy. I learned a painful lesson when I realized that wasn't always the case two years ago."

"After your divorce?"

She wanted so badly to tell him the whole truth, but only one person could verify that, and Peter wasn't talking. "The divorce turned out to be only the beginning. Once I lost my job, I recognized that no matter how well you walk the line, situations arise that steer you off your path. I determined then and there I would make my own decisions and guide my own future. As ridiculous as it seems, this agreement we made happened to be a step in the right direction. Otherwise, I would not have entered into it."

He frowned. "You still haven't answered my concerns."

"Actually, yes I have. If I want to be carefree and enjoy intimacy with my pseudohusband, then I'm going to do it. More importantly, I trust you, Dallas. I know you're going to treat me well and make me feel respected. So there."

He finally sent her that wonderful smile again. "Okay then. You've convinced me you're ready."

She wondered if maybe he was experiencing a little hesitation. "Are you ready?"

"Darlin' that is not a question you should have to ask."

Paris felt a disclaimer coming on. "We can do this as long as we go inside and turn off the lights since I assume I'm going to be completely naked."

He stood, rounded the table and held out his hand to help her up. "Inside is okay and we're both going to be naked. Besides, I've already seen a lot of your body, and I want to see it all, so I won't promise I'll turn off lights."

"Dallas—"

He cut off her protest with a quick kiss. "If you really trust me, then let me show you the benefits of seeing all the details."

Exactly what she wanted to avoid. But maybe the time had come to shed her self-consciousness in earnest. Maybe she could actually take charge of the situation and finally relax.

Mulling that over, Paris followed Dallas inside, expecting to be led into the bedroom. Instead, he went to the opposite end of the house and past the kitchen to an all-glass sun porch with rustic, wide, cushioned chaises and plush, rug-covered slate floors. Through the wall of windows, she glimpsed a small creek and two deer foraging in the grassy area in the last remnants of daylight. "Why have I never seen this place?"

"Because you haven't been here long enough to explore," he said. "During the day, you get sun. At night, you can see all the stars. If you notice, there aren't any light fixtures."

She looked around to confirm that fact. She also noted the room was illuminated enough to view all those details she preferred he not see. "Is this where you bring all your dates?"

He didn't appear too pleased over the question. "This is where I come to wind down."

"It's a good place to do it. Unwind, I mean."

He cupped her cheek with his palm. "It's a good place for us to get to know each other in every way."

They stood there face-to-face, as if neither knew what to do next. Dallas broke the standoff by taking her back into his arms and holding her for a long moment. He pulled away and searched her eyes. "If you change your mind at any point, let me know. I want you to be totally comfortable."

She very much appreciated his consideration. She also felt confident he would show her great care, and probably a very good time. "I'm not going to change my mind."

He sent her a soft smile. "Good. I've been waiting all night to see you undress for me."

Oh, mercy. "Are you going to watch?"

He flashed a grin and a dimple. "Do politicians lie?"

"All right. I suppose I can do that. As you pointed out, you've seen almost all of me anyway." And now he would see it all—from head to toe and too-wide hips in between.

You're too uptight, Paris.

The ghost of that chunky, awkward girl came back to haunt her, along with the voice of her ex criticizing her butt and in his opinion, inadequate breasts. She lowered her eyes to avoid Dallas's scrutiny. "I'm not sure I can do this while you're staring at me."

He came to her then, tipped up her chin with his fingertips and kissed her softly. "Yeah, you can. Don't forget the boat."

"That was different. I had on a bikini until you took the top off me. And that was only the top."

She could tell by his expression that his patience was waning. "You're a beautiful woman, Paris. All of you. Now we can talk about this all night, or we can act on this all-fire need between us."

"Okay, I admit there is a tad bit of chemistry."

"You know we've both been hot for each other since we met. You can keep denying it, but you know I'm right. I figured that out in the kitchen this morning when you dropped the robe. If that wasn't a hint, then I don't know what is."

She couldn't be shocked when she'd intentionally been transparent. She'd also allowed him a peek of her backside, and he hadn't run away yet. "Okay, I'll make a deal with you. Since you've already seen more of me than I care to admit, it's only fair you go first."

Without hesitating, he stepped back and lowered his fly. "Just so you know, something's come up. It's been up for days."

She managed a smile. "Nothing I haven't seen before."

After stripping out of his clothes and underwear, he looked no less proud. Every inch of him. And frankly, her very limited sexual experience had not included such an absolutely impressive…man.

"It's your turn, sweetheart."

Okay, she could do this. She'd been pretty gutsy this morning. Why not carry that over to this moment?

Following a deep breath, Paris shimmied out of the dress and let it fall to her feet, then shoved her panties down and kicked them aside. And there she stood, totally nude in the middle of a dimly-lit, glass-walled room with a fantasy man raking his gaze over her, clear approval in his eyes.

He inclined his head and pointed at her. "Lady, if I had my choice, you'd never wear a thing again when you're with me."

She released an anxious laugh. "Something tells me that could be awkward with both the mothers darting in and out all the time."

"True. Now come here and let me give you the time of your life."

Paris felt much less ill at ease and very ready to be in his arms. "Gladly."

Dallas grabbed a pillow from one chaise, set it down on the largest rug, then signaled her to join him on the floor. He laid her back and hovered above her a few moments as he stroked her cheek. They kissed for a long while as if they didn't have a worry in the world. She did find it strange that he hadn't exactly ravished her, and very curious when he said, "I need to get something."

When Dallas left her embrace, Paris felt bereft. "Hope you hurry back."

"Darlin', you won't even know I'm gone."

Perhaps he wasn't quite that quick, but he did return in less than two minutes, carrying that "something" in his hand. She sat up and braced on bent arms. "Just so you know, I am on the pill."

"Doesn't matter," he said as he stretched out next to her on his side. "No birth control is fail proof so having both is better. Nothing wrong with a double bucket, as we say in the horse world."

The seriousness in his tone told Paris he truly didn't want a child, and she found that sad. However, getting pregnant in this situation would be completely inadvisable and cause for great concern. "I totally agree with using both. Besides, in this day and time, safety should also come into play."

"I'm safe, just don't want to be sorry."

After Dallas tossed the condom aside, he kissed his way down her throat, pausing to pay special attention to her breasts, barring all thoughts or concerns from her brain. But he didn't linger very long before sending his talented mouth down her torso, lower and lower, causing Paris to shift with anticipation.

He lifted his head and rested his chin on her belly. "Are you okay?"

Apparently he'd misinterpreted her movement. "Never better."

"Just wanted to be sure this is something you want."

"It's something I've never had before." Only one more admission that pointed to the sad state of her sex life and the severe lack of intimacy with her former husband.

Her current husband, on the other hand, looked as if she'd awarded him the grand prize for being such a gracious lover. "I will almost guarantee you're going to like it. But if not, let me know."

When Dallas's mouth hit home between her trembling legs, Paris couldn't speak if her life depended it. She could barely even breathe. She couldn't manage to keep her eyes open, though. Every featherlight stroke of his tongue brought her closer to the brink of madness. Every pull of his lips drove her further into oblivion, but not enough to tune out the steady build of the climax as he lifted her hips with his palms, bringing her closer to his expert mouth. And then came the strongest, mind-blowing climax she'd ever experienced.

She almost screamed but somehow quelled it. She couldn't stop the slight moan that drifted from her mouth or the inadvertent movement of her hips. She did miss the moment Dallas rose up, she realized, when her eyes fluttered open to discover him tearing at the silver package with his teeth.

He seemed to be quite in a hurry and that might have made her smile except she wanted him to hurry, too. He also seemed to be a pro when he had the condom in place in a matter of seconds.

Paris refused to think about his past conquests. She wanted only to concentrate on all the sensations as Dallas shifted over and eased inside. She rubbed her palms over his muscled back as he moved in a slow, delicious rhythm. She circled her legs around his waist, allowing him to go deeper with each thrust. He demonstrated his stamina, his control, as they continued this dance she'd been determined to avoid. And when that control slipped, his body tensed and he collapsed against her with a low groan.

Paris truly cherished the feel of his weight, the feel of this man who'd entered her life and turned her world upside down. She honestly mourned the loss of him when he rolled onto his back and draped one arm over his eyes.

"That happened way too fast," he said.

She shifted to her side and studied him a few minutes. "Out of ten, I'd give that a twelve."

"A twenty," he muttered. "You're definitely a natural."

"And you're definitely an expert."

He turned to face her. "Don't ever doubt that you're special, sweetheart."

Funny, he made her feel that way. "I must admit I did surprise myself."

He could move mountains with that grin. "I'm ready for another round. How about you?"

"Maybe we could do it under the table outside since we have yet to explore that scenario. Heck, maybe we could do it *on* the table."

He narrowed his eyes and tried to look disapproving. "Have I turned my good girl bad?"

My good girl... If only that were true. "You know, I think you have."

"I'm glad. I wouldn't want you any other way."

She wished he wanted her for all time.

The sudden thought took Paris by storm. She had to emotionally stand firm and avoid any fuzzy feelings if she wanted to protect herself. Yet when Dallas held her again, she worried she might travel straight into the land of heartache.

Eight

During the past week, his good girl turned bad had pretty much worn him out. Not at all a complaint, just an accurate observation. But as soon as they returned to the ranch today, Dallas had to resume his usual routine.

He'd let a lot of things slide, including joining Tyler to search for prime rodeo stock for Texas Extreme. But as he felt his wife's hand beneath the sheet, he didn't give a damn about duty. He had to have her. Now.

They came together in a rush of kisses, a hot, quick roll. A morning drive-by, as Paris had put it. He knew exactly how to touch her to give her what she needed. She knew exactly how to move to send him over the edge. By the time they were done, they were both pretty much exhausted.

Dallas rolled onto his back and studied the ceiling,

waiting for his breathing to calm and his heart to slow down. "You're incredible, darlin'."

"You're not so bad yourself, cowboy." She draped her arm across his belly. "I wish we could stay here a little longer."

He stacked his hands behind his head and sighed. "I didn't intend to be here this long, but a pretty little lady decided to hold me hostage."

She playfully slapped at his arm. "I didn't hold you hostage, Dallas. You were free to go at any point in time."

"Let me rephrase that. You made me a prisoner with your good loving."

She remained quiet for a moment before asking, "What's going to happen after we're back at the ranch?"

"Business as usual."

"I meant with us. Do I sleep in the guest room or in your room?"

He hadn't given that much thought, but he didn't like not having her in his bed. "We should probably give the appearance of the happily married newlyweds."

She laid her head on his shoulder and sighed. "Honestly, I can't remember the last time I've been this happy. It's been a wonderful week."

Uh-oh. If she got stars in her eyes, that could spell trouble. "It's been great, but it's not reality. You and I both know this arrangement comes to an end in a year."

She rose up and stared at him. "You don't have to remind me of that. But if I'm going to be stuck in this pretense, I don't see any reason why we can't enjoy each other's company, unless you decide that once we leave here, the party's over."

He saw a major reason why they shouldn't enjoy it too much. "I still want to be with you, just as long as you know I'm not looking for anything permanent."

The comment sent her out of the bed to grab her robe and slide it on before she faced him. "Of course it's not permanent, Dallas. If I learned anything about you at all since we met, it's that for some reason you run from emotional commitment."

That made him sound like a coward. "Look, I'm not running from anything. I just know who I am, darlin', and if you expect too much, I'll break your heart."

She tightened the sash and pushed her hair away from her face. "Don't flatter yourself. I'm much tougher than you think."

Spinning around, Paris headed into the bathroom and shut the door a little harder than necessary. Dallas remained in the same spot, pondering her words. Maybe in some ways she'd been right. Maybe he had been running away. But one thing he'd learned in life—aside from most of his immediate family, people never stayed around for very long, if not physically, then emotionally. He recalled the loneliness following his mother's death. He'd witnessed both Maria's and Jen's devastation when they'd learned of his dad's betrayal. He wasn't going to put himself out there to be hung up to dry.

He'd been a loner much of his life, and he liked it that way. Even a special woman like Paris couldn't change his mind.

* * *

Little by little, everything had begun to change over the past few days. Even though Paris had opted to stay in his suite, he hadn't touched her. She'd gone to bed before him, and he'd started getting up before her. No more predawn lovemaking. No more joking around. In fact, he'd barely spoken to her aside from general conversation over meals. When she'd asked Dallas if something was wrong, he'd only said he'd been busy playing catch-up. It seemed as if everything they'd shared at the cabin had all been a dream. Today she planned to get to the bottom of his sudden turnaround.

After a futile search for him in the barn, Paris hopped into her new black luxury sedan—a wedding gift from her new husband—then drove to the main office and marched in, bent on seeking him out. "Is Dallas here?"

Jenny patted her big hair and smiled. "No, sugar, he's not here. He left for the house about a half hour ago. I believe he's in the media room."

Oh, for heavens sake. She should have checked there first. "Are you sure?"

"That's what he told me when I put your dinner in the oven. I made a nice vegetarian lasagna. It should be ready in ten minutes or so and you'll find a salad in the fridge."

Eating alone didn't exactly appeal to her. "Thanks, but I need to talk to Dallas before I even think about dinner."

Jenny took on a concerned look. "Is something wrong, sugar?"

"No." She reconsidered when she realized the stepmom could be a solid sounding board. "Actually, yes. Since we returned from the cabin, he's been rather aloof."

"Oh, that. I'm not surprised."

Clearly everyone else in the Calloway family held the key to Dallas's mood. "Could you let me in on the secret?"

"I will gladly fill you in, since my stepson isn't one to talk about his feelings."

Paris knew that all too well. "Go ahead. I'm all ears."

"First of all, his mother died on April second, which happens to be tomorrow. Coincidentally, J.D. died April third. According to Maria, and I've seen it myself since I've been here, Dallas goes into this funk. Give him a week or so and he'll come back around."

Most of that made sense, but she believed there could be more. She also found it hard to believe he would do a one-eighty when it came to their floundering personal relationship. "Maybe it's time someone encourages him to get in touch with his feelings."

"Be careful, Paris," Jenny cautioned. "If you push too hard, he'll only withdraw more."

Not if she could help it. "I'll approach the issue slowly. Thanks for telling me."

"You're welcome, sugar, and good luck. By the way, you never said if you enjoyed your honeymoon."

She had been intentionally guarded in what she'd revealed for fear Jenny would read too much into it. Regardless, the honeymoon phase was basically over before it had really begun. "We had a very nice time. I'll see you later."

Paris rushed out of the office before Jenny began requesting details. After she made it back to the house, she hurried up the stairs and headed to the cowboy cave, only to find the door closed. She considered knocking but since he might not answer, she decided to walk right in.

Dallas looked surprised to see her, but she happened to be more surprised to see him seated at a round table, a slew of photographs spread out before him.

"I thought I might find you here," she said as she pulled out a chair. "What are those, if you don't mind me asking?"

He slid a picture of a brown-haired, blue-eyed young woman holding a toddler, a black horse grazing beside them. "That's my mom, Carol."

The first time she'd heard him mention his mother's name. "And you?"

"Yeah and her mare, Kenya."

"She's beautiful. Your mom, not the horse, although the horse is pretty, too. You definitely have her eyes. Your mom's eyes, not the horse."

Finally she'd unearthed his smile but it faded fast. "That's the horse that killed her."

Paris swallowed around her shock. "How did that happen?"

He leaned back in the chair and streaked a hand over his jaw. "She was training her for speed events. Kenya spooked one day and threw her into a barrel. She sustained a serious head injury and died two days later."

The pain in his voice was palpable. "Do you remember any of that?"

"No. I just recall she was there one day and not the next. I didn't find out what happened until I asked my dad when I turned thirteen. Of course, he didn't want to talk about it so Maria told me."

Thank heavens he'd been spared the details when he'd been too young to understand. She leaned over and picked up a photo of a twentysomething, tall, handsome man with a single prominent dimple. The resemblance to Dallas was almost uncanny. "I assume this is your father."

"The one and only. That was taken right after he married Maria."

She'd always wanted to know how that had come about, and now she had her chance. "When and how did they meet?"

"He hired her as our nanny after my mom died. Next thing I knew, they married a few months later. Then came Houston and Tyler."

"No doubt about it, your dad didn't waste any time."

"No. He just wasted the truth."

Paris wished he could find a way to heal, and she could find a way to help. "Don't waste your life being bitter, Dallas. I had to tell myself if I let my anger toward Peter continue to rule my life, I would lose and he would win."

He nailed her with a stern look. "Maybe I'm not the eternal optimist, like you."

"Then it seems to me you're very much like Fort."

He mulled that over for a moment, as if he'd never considered that notion, before the ire returned. "I'm nothing like him. I didn't abandon the entire family due to the sins of the father."

She might as well beat her forehead against the table. "No, but you might be abandoning your happiness by keeping yourself closed off to it. And shutting me out isn't going to make me go away, if that's what you're thinking."

He failed to look at her. "I'm not shutting you out."

"Oh, really? I don't remember the last time you kissed me, much less touched me. I wake up in the middle of the night and you're on the edge of the bed as if you can't stand to be near me. If you find it so appalling to sleep with me, just let me know. I'll be glad to move to a guest room."

"I don't find you appalling, dammit. It's just that—"

"What?"

"I never wanted to hurt you, Paris, but it sure looks like I'm doing that now. I'm worried maybe you have expectations I can't meet."

Feeling a bit more benevolent, she laid a palm on his arm. "You can't hurt me unless I allow it, and I'm not going to do that. And I don't expect anything from you that you can't give. I'm a big girl and I know what I agreed to when I married you. But I would like better communication between us."

"I'm not real good at that and I'm not sure I can change."

With a retort on the tip of her tongue, Paris suddenly remembered she hadn't removed the food from the oven. "Dinner should be ready by now. We can continue this conversation while we eat."

"I'm not hungry," he said. "You go ahead. I'll grab something later."

Paris's frustration began to mount. "I don't deserve this, Dallas."

He shuffled through the pictures to avoid her gaze. "Deserve what?"

"Your disregard. I'm trying to be your friend but you're making it pretty darned difficult."

"Don't need a friend," he said. "I need to be left alone."

She shoved back from the table and stood. "Sure you do. That's the way you operate, isn't it? Always the tough guy. But let me tell you something, Dallas Calloway. A future with the prospect of happiness is a terrible thing to squander, and you're the one who's afraid of getting hurt, not me."

Without awaiting his response, she rushed out the door and slammed it behind her. She despised the overwhelming disappointment. Hated that she couldn't reach him and probably never would. Most important, she detested the emotions welling inside her. She couldn't save him from himself and for some reason that made her so sad.

Somehow, someway, she had come perilously close to falling in love with the wounded cowboy, or at least the one she'd known while they were away. If she let the cycle complete, she would most surely collide head-on with devastation.

To prevent that from happening, and for self-protection, she would let Dallas continue to brood, and in the meantime, she would get out of his bed. But as far as their arrangement went, she vowed to see it through. No matter how hard he might try to drive her away, she wasn't going to budge until she saw the arrangement through.

When he retired at midnight, Dallas found nothing but a deserted room and an empty bed. He also discovered all her clothes were gone, and the toiletries, too. Not one sign that Paris had ever been in his life.

Unexpected panic set in and sent him to the garage first, where he found the Mercedes parked next to the truck. That didn't mean she hadn't abandoned the car and found another way to leave him.

He wouldn't blame her if she'd left. He'd been a moody bastard and he'd pushed her away. He couldn't stand the thought of her taking off without telling him goodbye. Taking off at all.

He took the stairs two at a time, flipped on the hallway lights and started opening doors to the additional rooms. By the time he reached the final one at the end of the corridor, he'd all but given up…until he found her in the black sleigh bed wearing a pink nightshirt, a pillow propped behind her back, her legs crossed before her and a computer in her lap.

"Mind if I come in?"

"Depends on why you're here," she said without taking her attention from the laptop.

"I'm here to talk."

Finally she looked up. "Wow. That's new and different. Are you ill?"

Sick over hurting her feelings. He perched on the edge of the mattress near the footboard and sighed.

"First, I want to say I'm sorry. You're right, I haven't been treating you well and it's not fair. My problems aren't your fault."

"Apology accepted. Go on."

"Secondly, I suck at being a boyfriend."

That made her laugh. "In case you've forgotten, we kind of skipped the boyfriend-girlfriend stage and went right to the marriage. Besides, I wasn't looking for a boyfriend when I entered into this mess."

The "mess" thing didn't bode well for him. "Okay, I suck at relationships. And I didn't come looking for you, either. But here you are, and honestly, it does scare me."

She closed the computer and set it aside. "Why?"

Now for the admission he didn't count on making. "Because I do care about you, Paris. I don't think I realized how much until I thought you'd left."

"I promised you I'd stay until the bitter end."

"And I promised you an annulment."

"As I've previously stated, that was due to faulty research and an unreasonable timeline."

"Do you regret marrying me?"

She paused for a few seconds. "I regret that more couldn't exist between us aside from you keeping the ranch and me alleviating my debt. But hey, I'm a realist. This is a unique situation. I don't regret our time at the cabin, even if it was only temporary and apparently over."

"It doesn't have to be."

She frowned. "All signs point to the contrary, Dallas. I refuse to make love to a man who won't give me the time of day."

"What if I try to do better?" He drew in a breath and released it slowly. "What if I told you I want to see where this thing goes between us in the next year?"

He green eyes widened. "Do you mean exploring the possibility of making it permanent?"

"Yeah. There's no guarantee it will work, but I'd like to try. It would require starting over, since we put the cart before the horse."

"You mean like dating?"

"I guess you could call it that. I want to take you out to dinner and maybe go see a movie or two. I definitely want to teach you how to ride if you're going to be a rancher's wife."

She held up her hands, palms forward. "Wait a minute. I'm still trying to digest the whole dating thing."

So was he. "Okay. I'll slow down. But just so you know, I've never had a relationship that lasted longer than six months. Maybe that's because I don't know what it takes."

Paris unfolded her legs, draped them over the bed and scooted next to him. "My mother always said that when you evaluate who you're going to have as a life partner, you have to ask yourself, *Will they make me a better person?*"

Solid advice. "I believe that could be true when it comes to you making me a better man. You'd probably be getting the short end of the stick with me."

She hooked her arm through his and kissed his cheek. "I think we could make each other better."

For the first time in two weeks, he felt optimistic

and not quite as afraid of making her life miserable. "As long as we both can trust each other."

"We can do that."

"Can we still have sex while we're dating?"

That earned him a mild punch in the biceps and her smile. "Is that all you men think about?"

"Pretty much."

She released an exaggerated sigh. "Oh, all right. I suppose we can tango between the sheets now and then."

He came to his feet, ready for the dance to begin. "Let's get back to our bedroom, wife."

She stood, grabbed the nightshirt's hem and pulled it over her head. "We have a perfectly good bed here, husband, so let's mix it up."

Up would be the operative word when she slid her panties down and tossed them onto the nearby chair. "You won't catch me arguing with a naked woman."

Dallas undressed in a rush, took her down on the bed, kissed her thoroughly and then sent his lips and hands on a mission over her body. She responded strongly to his touch and climaxed quickly beneath his mouth. He realized he didn't have a condom, but this time he didn't care. He trusted Paris completely, not to mention he'd seen her birth control pills.

When he started to move over her, Paris said, "Not this time," before nudging him onto his back. "I want to play cowgirl."

Damned if she wasn't full of surprises. "Lady, ride away. I just hope this lasts longer than eight seconds."

It took all his strength to hold back the orgasm when

she climbed on top and guided him inside her. Having no barriers between them only increased the sensations, and he realized he'd never had sex without protection, a lesson that had been drilled into his brain by his dad. The wait had been worth it. But it also happened to be playing hell with his control, and no matter how hard he tried to hold back the tide, the dam broke all too soon.

After Paris collapsed against him, Dallas rubbed her back and felt a strong sense of peace, like this is where they belonged. Like the way love might feel.

Whoa. He sure as hell wasn't going to go there yet.

"Did you enjoy that?" Paris whispered in his ear.

"Hell yeah. I always like new adventures."

She lifted her head and smiled. "So do I."

He brushed her hair away from her cheek. "Darlin', get ready for all the adventure you can handle."

For the past three weeks, the adventures had kept coming like hits on a radio. She'd learned to ride a horse—kind of—spent three days holed up in a cabin in Wyoming with Dallas and attended a country music award ceremony on his arm in Nashville.

Paris couldn't remember when she'd had so much fun, or so much fantastic sex. No place had been off-limits, from hot tubs to home-theater chairs to pickup trucks. And yesterday, when she'd walked in the office to show Dallas the latest plans for the lodge, she ended up with her dress hiked up to her waist and her panties down at her ankles while her husband ravished her on his desk without taking off his boots.

Memories of those moments brought about a blush

when she returned to the office today and came face-to-face with both the mothers. "It sure is getting hotter outside," she said as she entered the opening at the counter.

"Hotter inside, too," Maria muttered while Jenny giggled. "Real hot yesterday."

Mortified, Paris rushed toward Dallas's study, hurried inside, closed the door behind her and leaned back against it. "They know."

Dallas glanced up from a document and frowned. "Know what?"

She walked to his desk and collapsed into the chair. "They know what we did in here yesterday."

"Why do you say that?"

"Because Maria just made a comment about it being hot inside when I said it was hot outside." She snapped a finger and pointed. "You pressed the intercom and told Jenny to hold all your calls and I bet the button got stuck. You need to get that fixed before we do it in here again."

He grinned. "Darlin', are you ready for another round?"

Yes. "No. I came here to tell you to schedule the groundbreaking for the lodge next week. I've been working with the architect and we've almost finalized the design. If you have a few minutes, I want to fill you in on the details."

He stood and rounded the desk. "We might not be ready to build yet, but that's still cause for celebration."

When he bent down and nibbled her ear, Paris shivered. "Stop it, you bad, bad cowboy, and let your fake wife tell you about the lodge."

He pulled her out of her chair and brought her into his arms. "You like me when I'm bad, Mrs. Calloway."

"And you like me bad, too, Mr. Calloway."

"That I do."

Just as Dallas planted his mouth on hers for a hair-curling kiss, the pesky intercom sounded. When the buzz repeated twice, Paris pulled back. "Aren't you going to answer that?"

"Do I have to?"

"It could be important."

He looked thoroughly put out. "You're right. I have an appointment in about fifteen minutes with a supplier. He's probably early, dammit."

She stood on tiptoe and kissed his chin. "I suppose I'll see you at the house for dinner."

"Yep, and when I get there, be naked."

"I can do that."

He let her go to depress the pesky button. "Yeah, Jen."

"There's someone here to see your wife."

Dallas sent her a confused look, prompting Paris to say, "I'm not expecting anyone."

"Who is it, Jen?" he asked.

"Maybe she should just come out here, sugar."

"A name, Jen," Dallas said. "Stop beatin' around the bush."

"He says he's her husband."

Nine

From the panic on Paris's face, Dallas figured she hadn't expected this blast from her past. "What the hell does he want?"

"I have no idea," she said as she started toward the door. "But I'm going to find out."

"Don't go out there," he said as he pushed the button. "Send him in, Jen."

When she spun, fear flashed in her eyes. "I need to handle this myself."

"Fine, but I want to be there when you do." In case he needed to take matters into his own hands with the bastard.

The loud rap obviously startled Paris, sending her around to open the door to a lanky, blond-haired guy wearing a prissy pink polo shirt, chinos and a smirk. "Hello, Paris."

"Hello, jerk."

Dallas wanted to applaud when the idiot reached for her and she sidestepped him. He also wanted to punch the guy and wasn't ruling that out.

Paris held on to the doorframe but didn't invite him into the room. "Why are you here?"

He leaned over and eyed Dallas. "I have information that would interest you and your new *husband*." He had the nerve to push past Paris, stride to the desk and stick out a bony hand. "It's a pleasure to meet the other husband."

Dallas ignored the gesture. "Pleasure's all mine, Dick."

"It's Peter."

"Whatever. Now state your business and get the hell out of here."

The bastard dropped his arm and sneered. "You might not be so quick to dismiss me once I say what I have to say."

He fought the urge to wrap a hand around that skinny neck and toss him out. "Hurry up."

"Dallas, could I have a few moments alone with him?" Paris asked.

No way. No how. "Not on your life, sweetheart. But I am going to step out and tell Jen to reschedule my appointment." He intended to tell her more than that. "In the meantime, don't say anything to him until I get back."

He hated to leave Paris alone, but he didn't trust the

son of a bitch or his motives. For that reason, he strode to the reception area and gestured Jen aside. "Do you still have that digital recorder?"

She looked a little clueless. "Yes. Why?"

"Because as soon as I get back in there, I want you to turn it on and press the intercom. Can you handle that?"

"Of course."

"Good. I also want you to go outside, call the sheriff on your cell phone and have him send a deputy over to be on standby."

Now she looked alarmed. "Are you afraid he's going to harm you, sugar?"

"No. I'm afraid I might hurt him. And I'm also thinking he might be up to no good."

He turned around to head back to the office and hoped like hell Jen followed his instructions to a tee. If the bastard tried to pull anything at all, at least they'd have proof and the law on their side.

When he entered the room, he found Paris seated in the chair under the window while the ex roosted in the one across from the desk. They both sat silent like they'd been engaged in a standoff.

Dallas decided to stand next to his wife. "Okay, the floor's yours, Pete," he said. "Have at it."

The guy crossed one leg over the other, looking every bit the wimp he was. "How much do you know about Paris, Mr. Calloway?"

"All that I need to know," he answered before Paris could open her mouth.

"Then she told you about her criminal history."

"I don't have a criminal history," Paris shot back. "I covered for yours."

Dallas didn't care for where this was heading. "What is he talking about, Paris?"

"He embezzled funds from our former employer," she said. "He led them to believe it was all my idea, which it was not. I'm only guilty of being gullible and stupid."

The SOB let go a grating laugh. "Don't play innocent, Paris. You had no problem spending the funds that I borrowed from the company."

"You mean stole, don't you?" Paris scooted up to the edge of the chair. "I didn't have time to spend a dime other than what we needed for bills. I was too busy working. You, on the other hand, were hitting on every woman in Vegas. They reaped the benefits of your ill-begotten gains and now I'm charged with paying off your debt or risk going to jail."

Dallas wasn't at all pleased that Paris had withheld this level of information. "Looks like I'm a walking example of 'the husband is the last to know.'"

"About that husband thing," Peter chimed in. "There's a bit of a problem with that."

Dallas leveled his gaze on the bastard. "What kind of problem?"

"Paris and I are still married."

A strong wave of nausea hit Paris, driving her to take a few calming breaths before she could respond. "I don't understand."

"It's simple," Peter said. "I didn't complete the divorce process in the Dominican Republic for leverage."

Dallas released a few unflattering oaths aimed at the once-believed-to-be-ex-husband. He then turned his obvious anger on her. "You told me you had the documents, Paris."

She'd never felt so hopeless, or foolish, in her life. "I did. I do."

Peter's laugh sounded maniacal. "Since I knew you know very little Spanish, I sent you a record of a civil lawsuit that I obtained from the internet and I altered a photo of the official record from the Dominican Republic to include our names. You should have hired an attorney to protect your interests, dear. You did have that option."

She had the strongest urge to dump him out of the chair. How could she have been so blind to believe he was a decent guy when she'd married him? Easy. He'd been a chameleon and a con, and she'd been a naive girl. "I spent all the money I had left on attorney fees to stay out of jail, all because of you."

"Someday perhaps you will learn not to be so trusting, Paris."

She had another urge to slap that condescending grin off his face but settled for a verbal slug. "You should get help for your short man's syndrome, although it does apply in every sense of the word, you miscreant con artist."

Dallas took a step toward Peter. "You could've told her this in a phone call, which leads me to believe you're up to something."

"I considered calling," he replied. "But I couldn't be certain she would tell you everything."

Paris shot out of the chair. "You're the liar, not me."

"What do you want?" Dallas asked, his fists balled at his sides.

"Well, for starters," Peter began, "I'm sure you wouldn't want this scandalous secret to taint your good name. If you give me fifty thousand dollars, I won't go to the media and tell them you married another man's wife. A hundred thousand buys Paris a proper and legal divorce so you two can resume your life together."

Before Paris could react, Dallas had Peter by the collar and backed up to the wall. "Listen, you son of a bitch, I strongly suggest you take your blackmail attempts and get the hell out of here before I forget there's a lady present and I throw you out the window."

For the first time she saw fear in Peter's eyes. "It's your choice. If I don't have the money by tomorrow, in cash, I will notify the press. As far as the divorce is concerned, it's immaterial to me what you do. It's no skin off my nose to stay married to the most gullible woman I've ever known."

Dallas balled his fist but before he could throw a punch, someone said, "Don't do it, Calloway, or I'll have to arrest you, too."

Paris looked straight ahead to see a deputy filling the doorframe, Jenny cowering behind him.

Dallas shoved Peter toward the officer. "Did you get it all recorded?" he asked Jenny.

"Every bit, sugar."

He addressed the deputy then. "Did you hear it, Rowdy?"

The man patted his rounded belly. "Every word, Dallas."

The deputy stepped toward Peter and withdrew a pair of handcuffs. "Turn around and put your hands behind your back."

Peter stood in stunned silence for a few seconds. "Why are you arresting me? He should be cuffed for assault."

"I don't see any signs of assault," Rowdy said as he turned him around and snapped the cuffs into place. "You, my man, are in a heap of hot water."

Peter shot a menacing look in Paris's direction. "What are the charges?"

"Extortion. Embezzlement," Rowdy answered. "Take your pick. You want me to lock him up, Dallas?"

"Not yet." He stared at Peter for a long moment. "I'll make you a deal, Pete. If you never show your face here again, I'll let you slide for now. But if I ever lay eyes on your sorry self, and if I learn you uttered one word about this to even the clerk at the convenience store, I'll have you thrown in jail so fast your head will spin. I'll also play your confession to your former boss."

Peter practically cowered. "All right."

"And as far as that divorce goes," Dallas continued, "I want you back on a plane to finish the procedure and I plan to hire that lawyer to make sure you follow through this time. Understand?"

"Yes, I understand."

"Good. Rowdy, get him out of my sight before I forget why I didn't coldcock him the minute he opened his mouth."

As the deputy led Peter away, Paris waited for the shock to subside before facing Dallas again. "I am so, so sorry."

His somber expression spoke volumes. "Sorry about which part? That we're not legally married or that you lied to me about your past?"

She should have seen this coming. "I didn't exactly lie about the theft at the firm since I legally couldn't tell you. When Peter left the country before he could answer to the allegations, both parties signed a nondisclosure in exchange for my agreement to pay off the debt. My former employer was convinced I played some role, but I swear I didn't."

"You mean to tell me that you lived and worked with the man and you didn't know a damn thing about it?"

His distrust burned like a hot poker to the heart, though she couldn't exactly blame him under the circumstances. "I didn't have a clue because we had separate checking accounts. He was double billing vendors and depositing the excess in various places. Of course, he did give me funds to pay his half of the bills, so in essence I did benefit from his illegal activities, but I didn't know that's what I was doing."

Skeptical would be the best way to describe the look Dallas gave her. "Well, darlin', at least you won't have to worry about getting our divorce now. You're free to go do what you please."

She expected him to be angry. Livid even. But not to be totally written off. "You're being unreasonable."

"I'm being practical."

His attitude absolutely floored her. "Look, I understand why you're upset. I even understand why you might question my role in the embezzlement. But I can't quite comprehend after all we've been through why you can't give me the benefit of the doubt when I afforded you that courtesy over the annulment issue. I've never given you any reason not to trust me."

"You just did, by deceiving me. Lying by omission is as bad as a bald-face lie."

She truly wanted to scream. "So that's it? All the time we've spent together means nothing?"

"If you're worried about losing the money I fronted you, keep it. Keep the car, too, since I sold the old one for scrap. I'll even give you a good reference for what you've already accomplished on the lodge design."

"I don't want your money or the car or the job. I also don't want any more of your excuses."

"Excuses?"

"You've been looking for an out and I handed it to you on a silver platter. In fact, you lied to me when you said you wanted to see where our relationship might go. You never had any intention of making this marriage work. You only told me that to keep me in your bed."

"That's not true, Paris."

"Oh, really? Well, listen up, cowboy. You were right when you said you don't know how to commit because committed couples weather the storms and forgive all the flaws. But then you don't know the first thing about forgiveness because you certainly haven't forgiven your father. Since he's a blood relative, and I'm little more than your playmate, I don't stand a chance."

Before she started to cry, she had to leave. But she still had one more thing to tell him. "Even after knowing what I know about you now, I still believe in you, because Dallas, I've fallen in love with you although that's the last thing I wanted to do. I only wish you believed in me, too. I'll be out of here tonight." She removed the wedding band from her finger and laid it on the desk. "Have a nice life."

As she walked away, tears began to flow, yet she managed to get outside before the dam completely burst. She left the Mercedes parked in front of the office and started to the house on foot, hoping that maybe Dallas would come to his senses and come after her. But by the time she reached the front door, she realized that wasn't going to happen.

Now all she had left were the memories, a few mementos, some money and a severely shattered heart.

"What in the hell are you doing, *mijo*?"

An hour after the sorry scene, Dallas turned from the office window to see the mothers filing into the room, led by Maria, along with a band of merry brothers. All his brothers—Austin, Tyler, Houston, Worth—except one. Judges and jury members all wrapped into one family unit, thanks to his matriarchs' role as family criers.

"Why are you all here?"

"We're here to talk to you about Paris," Maria answered.

Figured. "Nothing to talk about, so you can leave and take the boys with you."

"We've filled them all in on the details, sugar," Jen said. "We're worried about you."

He had a good mind to walk out before the show started, but they'd probably follow him. "If you're going to take turns taking potshots and me, that's the last thing I need at the moment."

Austin stepped forward first. "I'd personally like to knock some sense into you. Do you have any idea what you've done to that little gal?"

"He's stomped on her heart," Tyler replied for Dallas. "I saw her walking up the road, crying like a baby."

"And now he's lost the ranch in the process," Worth added.

Houston took a step forward. "Hell, Dallas, Fort is going to have a field day with this once he knows you're no longer married."

Dallas had about had enough. "We weren't married in the first place, dammit, and that's not my fault."

"It's not Paris's fault either, sugar," Jenny chimed in. "She was victimized by a man and the fact that you dismissed her so easily means you've done the same thing to her."

He hadn't done that. Or had he? "You all know how much I hate deception. She could've told me what happened with her former employer because I wouldn't have told a soul. I didn't have to hear it from that SOB ex-husband. Oh, yeah. Her current husband."

"And you're so damned perfect, Dallas," Austin added. "You tossed her out before you gave her a chance."

His temper was close to reaching the boiling point. "And you're a damned hypocrite, Austin. You were married to Lilly, what, less than a year?"

Austin looked like he wanted to throw a left hook. "At least I made it to a year. Plus we both decided the marriage wasn't working."

"That's what happens when you get drunk and get hitched."

"Kiss my—"

Maria clapped her hands and pointed toward the door. "Everyone out. This kangaroo court is dismissed."

"Yes, boys, you should all go because we need to talk to Dallas alone," Jenny said.

Maria scowled. "When I said everyone, that means you, too, Jenny. I'm going to handle this."

Jenny looked dejected. "But—"

"No buts. Go."

After the crowd disappeared, Maria gestured toward the desk chair. "Sit down, *mijo*, and I'm going to tell you how the cow ate the cabbage."

Great. Just great. "I'd rather go work off some steam in the barn."

"I don't care what you want, Dallas Calloway. You're going to hear me out. *Comprendes?*"

He understood all too well. He was about to get a butt chewing. "Fine. But make it fast."

Maria took a seat in front of the desk. "I will make it very fast because you're running out of time. If you don't get your head on straight, Paris is going to leave and she won't be coming back."

The thought left a bitter taste in his mouth even though it's what he wanted. Or what he thought he wanted. "The damage is done and it can't be repaired, Mom."

"Love fixes anything."

That nearly shocked him out of his boots. "I've never said I love her."

"I'm sure you haven't, but that doesn't mean you don't. I've seen the way you look at her, *mijo*."

"You're seeing lust."

"Like hell I am. I've lived long enough to know the difference. She walks in the room and you hang on her every word. You open doors for her and you put your hand on her back when you're walking out together. You always let her speak without interrupting and you're always asking if she needs anything, and I don't mean sex. I've even heard you say hurry back if you're watching TV and she goes into the kitchen."

"And your point?"

Maria muttered a few choice words in her native tongue. Words he'd learned from some of the hands. "Let me ask you something. Do you wake up every morning thinking about her and go to bed every night glad she's going to be by your side?"

As bad as he hated to admit it, all that was true. "Yeah."

"Do you imagine growing old with her?"

Damn. "Maybe."

"Do you wonder what it would be like if she had your babies?"

"I've always made it clear I don't want kids."

"Answer me."

He released a rough sigh. "Not at first, but lately, yeah."

"Have you ever felt this way about any other woman?"

The answer was easy, and pretty damn telling. "Nope."

Maria slapped her palms on the desk and stood. "You're in love, although you're too damn hardheaded to admit it to yourself. If you don't get to the house, get on your knees and beg Paris for forgiveness for being a *cobarde*, you're going to live the rest of your life with a belly full of regrets. She'll forever be known to you as the one who got away when she should be the one who saved you from one helluva lonely life."

Deep down he recognized everything Maria had said made sense. He also realized he had one major problem. "What if she doesn't accept my apology?"

"She will if you offer her the ring."

He didn't have to ask which ring. The one meant for his true love. And damned if he hadn't found her. But... "You think it's a good idea I propose?"

"Do you still want to marry her?"

Did horses like hay? "Yeah."

"Then I'll go get the ring, and you go get the girl."

Ten

"Sugar, are you sure you can't wait until the morning before you go?"

Paris kept right on packing. And sniffling. And occasionally sobbing. "He doesn't want me here, Jenny, so the faster I leave, the better it will be for all concerned, myself included."

"Not as far as we're all concerned," Jenny said. "You should have seen the boys take him on for his cruelty. I thought Austin and Dallas were going to actually fight."

Wherever she went, clearly trouble followed. "I'm sorry this has caused a divide in the family. I never meant for that to happen."

Jenny handed her a tissue. "Honey, none of this is your fault. If Dallas wasn't so darned pigheaded, he'd realize you had no choice but to lie. He would also realize what the two of you have together is worth fighting for."

"You can't fight for something you don't care to win. Dallas has already decided what he wants, and it's not me. I need to be with someone who's willing to accept me for who I am, an imperfect woman."

"Sugar, he believes in you. He just doesn't believe in himself."

After dabbing at her eyes, Paris zipped the last suitcase and set it next to the other two at the foot of the bed. "Dallas hates deception, justified or not. And he doesn't feel he's capable of a long-term commitment. He has his father to thank for that. No offense."

"Oh, sugar, we all know J.D. was a lying philanderer, but we loved him all the same."

"That's because you know how to forgive. Dallas hasn't learned that lesson yet."

"Dallas hasn't figured out everyone lies now and then. Why, my mother passed herself off for years as the consummate Southern lady when in fact she grew up in the Bronx. She got away with it because she mastered the accent perfectly. And she learned how to make those luscious mint juleps. Would you like me to make you one before you go?"

It would only delay her departure if she passed out. "No, thank you, but if you could call a cab I would definitely appreciate it."

"Dallas bought you a perfectly good car."

"I don't want it." She didn't want anything more from him aside from some good memories to override the bad.

"Honey, there aren't any cabs that come out here. But

I would be glad to drive you anywhere you want to go, although I don't see why you won't take the Mercedes since it was a gift from Dallas."

A gift that came with conditions—marry me, make love with me but don't get too close. "He can give it to the next faux bride. I'm sure he'll get to work on that first thing in the morning, before Fort finds out we aren't married."

Jenny drew her into a hug. "I promise you, he won't go looking for someone else. Besides, the birthday deadline has passed, not to mention he doesn't want anyone but you."

If only that were true. "He doesn't want me, Jenny. I'm no longer of any use to him."

"I guess we'll see, won't we?" She sounded as if she knew a secret.

Paris pulled the handles from the rolling bags and slid the duffel's strap over her shoulder. "I won't see anything since I'm ready to go. If you could just drop me off in the nearest town, I'll find a room and rent a car tomorrow." At least she had enough money to get her to Idaho to stay with her parents and explain once again how she'd been duped by another man. Oh, joy.

Jenny gave her a pretend pout. "Are you sure you won't change your mind about that drink? Or how about some dinner? I could make you a nice vegetable frittata."

Her stomach roiled over the thought of choking down any food. "You've done enough already. And by the way, Dallas has enough money to hire a private chef, so why doesn't he?"

"Because he knows I like to make sure all the boys are fed. It makes me feel useful."

Unbelievable. "You make dinner for the other four?"

"Almost every night unless they're out of town or engaged in activities with women that no mother should be exposed to. Which is sometimes quite often with Worth. That little apple didn't fall far from the family tree."

They shared a laugh and another hug before heading out of the bedroom…and running right into none other than her erstwhile pretend husband. Her heart sank a little over the sight of him, and the regrets tugged at her soul.

When Paris muttered an apology and tried to push past him, he clasped her arm, halting her progress. "We need to talk."

"I think we've said all we have to say. No need to belabor the point and my shortcomings."

Jenny took the duffel from Paris. "Hear him out, sugar."

Maria appeared in the hall to give her two cents worth. "It's important, *mija*. Let's go to the kitchen, Jenny."

"No, stay," Dallas said. "I don't care if the whole damn county hears this, as long as the two of you don't interrupt. Besides, you're going to eavesdrop anyway."

Paris wasn't at all certain how to take any of this. "Then make it quick so I can get out of here."

"I don't want you to go. It's going to kill me if you go."

A stunning development. "I can't stay with a man who can't trust me, Dallas."

"I trust you, darlin'. I don't always trust me. But I'm going to learn if it's the last thing I do. And you were right, I got cold feet and blamed you for it."

Oh, how she wanted to believe him. "If that's the case, why the sudden change of heart?"

He looked somewhat sheepish. "I had a little help with that."

"From me," Maria stated without regard for the non-interruption directive. "I verbally beat him over the head."

"She just said things that made sense," hc countered. "She made me take inventory of my feelings for you, and it led to a fairly obvious conclusion."

"Which is?"

"I love you, sweetheart."

She lost her grip on the bags' handles, sending the upright suitcases onto the floor. "Could you repeat that, please?"

He circled his arms around her. "I love you more than this ranch. More than I ever thought I could love anyone. We'll find our own place and build a house, along with a future together."

"And we'll all go with you if we have to," Jenny said.

"Don't give her any reason not to stay with him," Maria scolded.

She let that proposition soak in for a moment. "I love you, too, but is that enough?"

"It's a start. And we won't know unless you stay."

"You do realize we're not married anymore and it's bound to get out."

"We can fix that real quick." He pulled a blue velvet

box from his shirt pocket, opened it to reveal a gorgeous marquise diamond that had to be at least two carats and lowered to one knee. "Paris, this belonged to my mom and it was given to me to give to the woman I want to spend my life with. That woman is you. So will you marry me again and have our babies and make this miserable cowboy a better man?"

Paris stood there, mouth agape, basking in the emotion in his eyes, the sincerity in his words, until reality jumped into the euphoria. "I'm not divorced yet."

"We don't have to be in a hurry. We're going to need time to plan a proper wedding anyway."

"I can't wait," Jenny practically shouted.

A proper wedding would be wonderful. However, another issue still remained. "But you'll lose the D Bar C if Fort finds out we're not married anymore. Maybe we should hurry up and do it."

"I don't care about Fort or the will. I only want to be with you. This isn't about keeping the ranch—it's about keeping you close, always."

As much as she wanted to accept his heartfelt proposal, she still had one more question. "You're serious about wanting babies?"

"Yep. I actually like them. I help with the rodeo club at the local high school and I plan to have a summer riding camp for the younger ones. If I can ride a bull, I can take on a baby. Or babies."

Paris managed a smile around the mist forming in her eyes. "As long as you don't expect us to keep them in the barn."

"I promise. And by the way, I have a bum knee,

thanks to a rank horse that bucked me off two years ago, so if you could give me an answer, my joints would appreciate it."

She laughed through the tears. "Yes, I will marry you, bad knees and all, so you can get up now."

After sliding the ring on her finger, Dallas rose and drew her into a soft kiss. "We're going to have a lot of adventures. And when we find our own place, you can design the house to your liking."

"Actually, you probably won't have to move after all, sugar."

Dallas let her go long enough to stare at Jenny. "Fort will probably say otherwise."

She shook her head. "No, he won't. I told him if he wouldn't pursue the terms of the will, I'd give him my half of the horse farm in Louisiana."

"I thought you'd already done that," Dallas said.

Jenny grinned. "I conveniently forgot to do it, just in case I need some leverage, even though he didn't know that. Sometimes you just have to tell a little white lie."

"When did this happen?" Paris asked.

Jenny stared at her pink peep-toe pumps. "The day you arrived here after the wedding. I had a feeling you two would be a good fit if given the chance. Also, around these parts, available women are few and far between."

"And you just let the marriage plans go on without telling me?" Both his tone and expression revealed Dallas's displeasure.

Jenny propped her hands on her hips. "Yes, sugar, and you should thank your lucky stars I didn't tell you.

Otherwise, you wouldn't be engaged to the woman of your dreams."

Dallas turned his attention to Maria. "Did you know, too?"

"Yep. I figured it was the only way to get you hitched so you can have me some grandbabies."

He pointed to the hall behind him. "Both of you can leave now."

Ignoring the order, Maria gave Paris a hug. "Welcome to the family, *mija*. Get ready for one wild ride."

After Jenny and Maria departed, Dallas pulled Paris back into his arms. "Looks like everything is going to work out after all. I keep the ranch and the girl. Who would've guessed that would happen?"

Not Paris. Not in a million years. "Did you know I almost decided to settle in New York? If I had, we would never have met."

"What changed your mind?"

"Actually, I'd picked out an apartment to rent and the landlord decided to sell it right before I left Vegas. Then I turned on my computer to search for another one, and I saw an ad for San Antonio. Something told me I needed to be in Texas, and here I am with my very own cowboy whom I love with all my heart."

He kissed her again, a little longer and deeper this time. "Care to take that cowboy and show him how much you love him?"

"I'll race you to the bedroom."

"Who said anything about the bedroom?"

"We're not going to do it here in the hall, Dallas. Not

with the probability that Jenny and Maria are somewhere nearby."

"True, and we're going to set some ground rules about that. But I'm actually thinking I want to make love to you in a place we haven't tried yet."

Paris tapped her chin with a fingertip and pretended to think. "I can't recall a place where we haven't done it."

"It's the place where we won't be keeping the kids."

They exchanged a smile and simultaneously said, "The barn."

Most women wouldn't agree to get hitched in front of a barn. But Paris Reynolds Calloway wasn't most women, Dallas decided. She'd turned out to be one in a million, and now she belonged to him. And he definitely belonged to her.

He stood next to Maria, choking down one of Jenny's gut-burning brews so he wouldn't hurt her feelings, even if he preferred beer. As he watched Paris visiting with her parents beneath the tent's canopy, he noticed she'd only been drinking punch.

"She looks beautiful, *mijo*. And very happy."

"Yeah, she does." When he'd seen Paris coming down the makeshift aisle an hour ago, wearing that form-fitting, long, sleeveless silk gown, sparkling tiny flowers sprinkled through her hair, he couldn't believe he'd gotten so lucky. "Her folks seem fairly nice, too."

"Her dad's a piece of work," she said. "He told me he brought a shotgun in case you bowed out. I told him I had one handy, too."

Dallas couldn't help but laugh over the image of his stepmom wielding a weapon while wearing a dress. "In-laws and outlaws. Works for me."

At that moment, Paris caught his eye, smiled and started toward him. Once she arrived, he leaned over and kissed her. "Do you think we can have a few minutes alone before dinner is served?"

"I'm going now," Maria said. "I've got to make sure Jen isn't putting too much tequila in those drinks."

After his mom disappeared into the tent, Dallas wrapped his arms around his wife. "How are you holding up?"

"Pretty well for a woman who planned a wedding in less than two months."

"Any regrets so far?"

"No, other than we have to wait another four hours or so before we can start the honeymoon. Actually, second honeymoon. And speaking of that, are you going to tell me where you're taking me?"

"I'll give you a hint. It involves a boat."

"The cabin?"

"No. It involves a big boat. Worth offered his yacht with a full crew and captain. I figure we can mosey on down to the Mexican Caribbean for two weeks where I've rented a private villa."

She hugged him hard and kissed him soundly. "That sounds wonderful, honey."

"And since I'm not getting any younger, I also figure we can get on with the baby-making."

She glanced at the ground before raising her gaze

to his. “Now that you mention it, I probably should tell you it’s too late for that.”

For a second he couldn’t speak. “How? When?”

“Well, *how* is pretty obvious, although exactly where is up for grabs. I estimate it happened around six weeks ago. And in case you’re wondering why, it’s been crazy with the wedding plans and I might have missed a pill or two. But I swear on my mother’s favorite blue flats, which she’s wearing now, I did not plan this.”

He waited for the urge to head for the hills, but it didn’t come. He might be a bit nervous, but he wasn’t spooked. “I believe you, darlin’. And I’m looking forward to being a dad.”

She immediately relaxed. “I am so glad. I wasn’t sure how I was going to tell you after I confirmed it this morning.”

“This morning?”

“Yes. I looked at the calendar on my phone and thought something’s missing, and it ain’t only my mind.”

“Ain’t? Looks like you’re picking up the cowboy vernacular. I’m impressed.”

“Vernacular? Now I’m impressed.”

“Hey, I might be a hayseed, but I have a little class in me, too. I also have a hankering to kiss my bride and the mother of my baby.”

She draped her arms around his neck. “Kiss away, cowboy.”

Before he could, he felt a tap on his shoulder and turned to find his brother standing there. “What do you want, Austin?”

“We want you both in the tent for a toast.”

"Are you going to make it?"

"Nope. Worth drew the shortest straw."

Paris laughed. "This should be interesting."

"Or a train wreck," Dallas said.

When they walked beneath the canopy, Dallas spotted his youngest brother standing on the stage reserved for the band, Jenny standing at his side. A roving waiter offered them champagne, which Paris nixed for a glass of water, while Dallas picked up a flute.

Worth held his glass up and cleared his throat. "To my brother Dallas, who had the good sense to wed a woman like Paris. And to my new sister-in-law, I hope you own a pair of boots because he'll probably have you muck the stalls before you know it. Best of luck to you both and may your trail ride together be a long one."

After the applause died down, Dallas put down the wine and grabbed his wife's hand to lead her to the stage.

"Dallas, what are we doing?" she asked once they reached their destination.

"You'll see." He circled his arm around her waist and prepared to say a few words. "We'd like to thank all you folks for sharing in this day with us. I'd also like to thank Jen for pulling together one heck of a party in a short amount of time, and my mom, Maria, for being there for me through thick or thin after I lost my own mother. If my dad were here, he'd pat me on the back and tell me *You did good, son*, and I did." He looked into Paris's eyes and saw honest-to-goodness love there. "And Paris, I never expected to find someone as special as you, and I sure as hell never really thought I'd settle down, but I'm damn glad I did. Thank you for honoring me with your vows, and for carrying our baby."

That caused a spattering of gasps among the onlookers and another toast from Houston. "To the Calloway sperm, known for being good swimmers."

"And I hope it's not catching," Tyler said, spurring a lot of laughter in the crowd.

Dallas guided Paris through the maze of guests offering their congratulations and managed to get her alone again, this time in the barn. "I hope you don't mind me telling everyone," he told her after they arrived. "I just couldn't wait to let everyone know."

"It's okay," she said. "I would have liked to have waited a little while since it's so early."

He held her again. "Darlin', I will do everything in my power to protect you. I promise you won't have to muck any stalls and I'll make sure you stay off your feet and get plenty of rest—"

She pressed a fingertip to his lips. "I'm having a baby, honey, not suffering from an incurable illness. Women do it every day. And I just know everything will turn out well with our little girl."

"Or boy."

She sighed. "You're probably right if you inherited the Calloway sperm that not only swims fast, it produces male children."

"Stranger things have happened. After all, the woman of my dreams said yes."

"Twice," she said. "And I am so glad I did. I love you, Mr. Calloway."

"I love you, too, Mrs. Calloway."

Maybe he had too much pride and too many trust issues. Maybe he still had a lot of learning to do about love, women, and most of all, himself. But with Paris by his side, Dallas felt confident he would master those lessons in time. One thing he did know for sure, when this beautiful blonde breezed through his door three months ago, that turned out to be the best day of his life. He expected to have many, many more.

* * * * *

THE RANCHER'S ONE-WEEK WIFE

KATHIE DENOSKY

This book is dedicated to my editor, Stacy Boyd.
Thank you for being my cheerleader and for waving
those pom-poms when I need them the most.

One

Blake Hartwell shook his head in disgust when he heard the low-slung sports car bottom out in first one, then another of the many potholes pitting the dirt lane leading up to the foreman's cottage. As he brushed the sorrel gelding he'd tied to the side of the corral, he decided right then and there that whoever was behind the steering wheel of that little red toy couldn't be from the area. Folks in rural Wyoming had better sense than to drive a vehicle that sat that low on unpaved mountain roads. It was a surefire way to knock a hole in the oil pan or tear up the exhaust system on a car.

"Whoever he is, he'd better be prepared to hitch a ride on the back of an antelope if he breaks down because I'm not driving his fool hide back to town," Blake muttered as he glanced at the afternoon sun sinking toward the taller peaks to the west.

The car stopped at the side of the foreman's cottage next to Blake's truck. When the driver's door opened, a leggy blonde stepped out, causing his heart to stall and the breath to lodge in his lungs.

Blake clenched the grooming brush he'd been using on Boomer so tightly he wouldn't have been surprised if he left his fingerprints in the wood. He swallowed hard as he watched her walk toward the corral as fast as her spiked heels would allow on the uneven ground.

Slender and sleek in her formfitting black dress, her delicate body moved much like a jungle panther on the prowl. Blake's lower body tightened and he wasn't sure if it was in response to the sight of her now, or the memory of how those long legs felt wrapped around him when they made love.

"Aw, hell," he cursed under his breath. "What does *she* want?"

Boomer stamped one of his front hooves, then looked over his shoulder as if to ask if Blake knew her.

Reminding himself to exhale, Blake released the breath he'd been holding and went back to brushing the gelding's rust-colored hide. He knew her all right. Back in December, he'd met Karly Ewing in Las Vegas. She'd been on vacation from her job—whatever that was—and he'd been in town to com-pete in the national bull-riding finals. He'd accidently bumped into her in the lobby at Caesar's Palace and barely managed to catch her before she fell. As a way of apologizing for his carelessness, he'd convinced her to let him buy her a drink. They'd ended up talking for hours and the chemistry between them had been explosive. By the end of the day they'd been lovers. By the end of the week they'd been husband and wife. And one week after that, they'd been filing for a divorce.

When she stopped a few feet from the horse, she looked a little uncertain, as if she wasn't sure what kind of reception she'd get from him. "H-hello, Blake."

Her voice flowed over him like a fine piece of silk and reminded him of the way it had sounded when she'd said his name as he pleasured her. Blake gritted his teeth against the heat building in his lower belly and continued to brush Boomer.

He wasn't about to let her get to him. Not again. It had taken months after that fateful phone call on New Year's Eve, when she told him she wanted a divorce, for him to get a decent night's sleep. If possible, he'd just as soon avoid repeating that.

She'd made the choice to end things between them and although he hadn't agreed with her, he had accepted it. The way he saw it, there wasn't anything they hadn't already covered and there was no sense in rehashing it now.

"What brings you to the Wolf Creek Ranch,

Karly?" Without waiting for an answer, he added, "Eight months ago you weren't even willing to come here to see it. In fact, you said you weren't the least bit interested in learning anything about the backside of no-man's-land."

As long as he lived, he would never forget the sting of her rejection, or her scorn for the land he loved. The ranch had been in his family for the past hundred and fifty years and he'd spent the majority of his adult life trying to get it back from his gold-digging stepmother after his father's death. He'd finally accomplished that goal almost two years ago and once he'd made Karly his wife, he'd been looking forward to showing her the place that he was proud to call home. But she hadn't cared enough about him or it to even see the place before she refused to live there with him.

Meeting her startled gaze head-on, he did his best to ignore the effect she had on him whenever he looked into her incredible blue eyes. "Why the sudden interest in a place you had no desire to learn anything about?"

Color rose on her cheeks and it seemed as if she might be slightly embarrassed. "I, um, I'm sorry if I left you with the wrong impression, Blake. It's not that I didn't think the ranch would be beautiful..."

When her voice trailed off as she looked around, Blake stopped grooming the gelding and rested his forearms on the gentle animal's broad back to give her an expectant look. "Then what was it?"

As he stared at her, awaiting an answer, a slight breeze fluttered her long, honey-colored hair and reminded him how the silky strands had felt when he'd threaded his fingers through them as he kissed her. His body came to full arousal and he was damn glad the horse stood between them. At least she wouldn't be able to see the evidence of how he still burned for her.

Turning back to face him, her eyes couldn't quite meet his. "I've always lived in the city and I was…" She shook her head. "It doesn't matter."

"What are you doing here, Karly?" Seeing her again was heaven and hell rolled into one neat little bundle, and the sooner she laid her cards on the table and went back to Seattle, the sooner he could get back to the business of trying to forget her.

When she took a deep breath, he did his best to ignore the rise and fall of her perfect breasts. "We need to talk, Blake."

He shook his head. "I don't know what you think we need to discuss now. We pretty much covered everything that needed to be said eight months ago. I wanted you to give us a chance to make our marriage work. You didn't want that. End of story."

"Please, Blake." She took a step back when Boomer blew out a gentle breath through his nose and turned his head to gaze at her. Looking a little apprehensive, she continued. "I wouldn't be here if it wasn't important. Could we please go somewhere we can sit down and talk? I promise I won't take up too much of your time."

Blake sighed heavily. It was clear she wasn't going anywhere until she'd said her piece. And truth to tell, he did need to talk to her. He hadn't yet received a copy of their divorce papers and he needed them for his records.

"The door's open," he finally said, motioning toward the foreman's cottage. "Make yourself at home. I'll be in as soon as I put Boomer in his stall for the night."

She opened her mouth as if she intended to say something more, then with a short nod she turned on her black spiked heels and slowly walked toward the back porch. Watching the gentle sway of her slender hips as she navigated the hard-packed, uneven ground in those ridiculous shoes, Blake shifted his weight from one foot to the other in an effort to relieve the pressure in his now too-tight jeans. He'd spent the past eight months trying to forget how her soft curves had felt beneath his hands and how her kisses were the sweetest this side of heaven. Seeing her here—where he'd wanted her—was bringing back all the memories he thought he'd left behind.

Shaking his head, he untied the gelding's lead rope from the top fence rail. He had no idea what she thought they needed to discuss, but if it had brought her from Seattle all the way to his remote ranch in Wyoming, it had to be pretty damn important.

Leading Boomer into the barn, he decided to get

this meeting over with as soon as possible. Then, after he watched Karly drive off his land and away from him for good, he had every intention of getting his brother, Sean, to come over from his ranch on the other side of the mountain and go with him to the Silver Dollar Bar in the tiny community of Antelope Junction. Sean could be the designated driver, while Blake finally finished the job of forgetting he'd ever met the petite blonde who'd turned his world upside down from the moment he'd laid eyes on her.

Karly opened the back door to Blake's home and walked into the kitchen on shaky legs. It had taken every ounce of courage she possessed to face him again, and although she had thought she'd put their brief relationship in perspective and moved on, his effect on her had been no less devastating today than it had been eight months ago, when she'd agreed to become his wife.

Blake was every bit as handsome, every bit as masculine and even sexier than she'd remembered. With wide shoulders, narrow hips and long muscular legs, he had a physique women drooled over and men spent endless hours in a gym trying to attain. But the steely muscles covering his tall frame had been honed from years of ranch work and competing in rodeos, not from lifting weights or working out on fitness machines. He was the real deal—the epitome of every woman's cowboy fantasy, and then some.

That was something she hadn't even realized she

possessed until they ran into each other in Las Vegas. But when he caught her to him to keep her from falling, all it had taken was one look at the cowboy holding her to his wide chest and she'd come close to melting into a puddle at his big-booted feet.

A delicious little shiver slid up her spine when she remembered how it had felt to be held in his strong arms, to taste the passion of his masterful kiss and experience the power of his desire as he made love to her. Her breathing grew shallow and her heart sped up. She forced herself to ignore it.

The hardest thing she'd ever done had been making the call to tell Blake she thought it would be in both of their best interest to call off their brief marriage. But when she had returned home, she'd thought about how little they knew about each other and she couldn't think of a single thing they had in common besides not being able to keep their hands off of each other. Her breath caught and she had to swallow hard against the sudden wave of emotion threatening to overtake her.

"Get a grip," she admonished herself. "Nothing has changed. He lives here and you live in Seattle. It would have never worked."

To distract herself, she glanced around Blake's neatly kept home. Even though the appliances were ultramodern, the rest of the kitchen appeared to be as rugged and masculine as the man who lived there.

A wooden butcher-block island sat in the middle of the kitchen with a variety of copper bottom skillets, pots and pans hanging above it from a wrought-iron rack. The cabinets were a warm oak with hammered black hinges and door pulls; the countertop was polished blue marble. A wagon wheel suspended from the ceiling with old-fashioned-looking chimney lamps served as a chandelier over the round oak dining table, while the windows on the wall behind the dining area framed a panoramic view of the Laramie Mountains, which surrounded the ranch.

"Beautiful," she murmured as she gazed at the picture-perfect landscape. It was as rugged and fascinating as the man she was here to see.

Wandering into the living room, she wasn't at all surprised to see a stone fireplace with a rough-hewn mantel surrounded by a grouping of heavy leather furniture and rustic wooden end tables. The room was so cozy and inviting, she felt as if she belonged there, which was absolutely ridiculous. She belonged in Seattle, in her own apartment with its modern decor and view of the city. And try as she might, she couldn't imagine how it would have been living here with Blake. If that wasn't enough to convince her that she'd made the right decision, she didn't know what was.

But as she looked around at the colorful Native American throws on the back of the large leather sofa, and the pieces of vintage tack and Western accents hanging on the walls, she had to admit that Blake's home had a warm, friendly feel to it that her place had never possessed. An uncharacteristic loneliness suddenly invaded every part of her. She did her best to tamp it down.

She loved her life in Seattle. She had a great job as buyer for a large import/export dealer and although she didn't have much of a social life, she did occasionally go out with some of her coworkers for happy hour after work. But as she thought about how long it had been since that had happened, she took a deep breath. She really couldn't say she had a lot in common with any of them anymore. They were all either married or in committed relationships and were more interested in going home to their significant others than hanging out to talk shop.

It was odd she hadn't noticed that before she met Blake. And she had to admit that when she did realize it, she might have had second thoughts about her decision to end things with him. In the end, she hadn't let that sway her and resigned herself to being the only one in her office with no one to go home to.

But the more she thought about it, the more her loneliness increased. Shaking her head to dislodge the unsettling feeling, Karly turned to go back into the kitchen to wait for Blake and walked right into his broad chest. Stumbling backward, she would have fallen if not for his big hands encircling her upper arms to steady her.

"I'm sorry. I didn't mean to—"

Her voice failed her as she gazed up into his sexy brown eyes. For a split second, she thought she caught a glimpse of the warm, compassionate man she'd thought she was in love with. But just as quickly as it appeared the glimmer was gone, replaced by a closed-off stare.

"You'd better watch your step," he said, his deep baritone sending a shiver coursing through her. "One of these days those ridiculous shoes are going to cause you to fall and break an ankle." Before she could find her voice and tell him that she didn't need his input on what she should or shouldn't wear, he released her and motioned toward a door across the room. "Let's go into the office for this talk you seem to think is so important."

Blake stepped back for her to precede him into a study off the living room, and as she seated herself in the burgundy leather armchair in front of his desk, Karly forced herself to stay calm. The heat from his calloused palms through the fabric of her dress when he caught her had set her pulse racing and made breathing all but impossible.

She tried to calm herself as she stared at the outdoor scene intricately carved into the oak desk's front panel. She'd just as soon face off with the bear fishing in the stream as she would having to deliver the news she'd traveled over a thousand miles to give Blake.

"So what brings you all the way to Wyoming, Karly?" He removed his hat and hung it on a peg by the door. "I'm betting you didn't make this trip by choice."

He wasn't going to make their meeting easy and

she really hadn't expected him to. When they'd decided to dissolve their marriage eight months ago, they had both said things out of hurt and frustration that she was sure they both regretted.

"Please, Blake. Can't we at least—"

"What do you expect from me, Karly?" he interrupted, sinking into the chair behind his desk. "I haven't seen or heard from you since just before the first of the year. After we spent Christmas in Las Vegas, I came home expecting my wife to be joining me here for New Year's Eve. Instead, I get a call telling me you'd changed your mind. If I wanted to stay married, I'd have to give up my life on the Wolf Creek Ranch, quit riding bulls and move to Seattle because you decided you couldn't live out in the middle of nowhere."

"That isn't exactly what I told you," she said, defending herself.

"Close enough," he stated flatly.

"You were just as adamant that you couldn't live in the city," she reminded him, feeling a little guilty. He hadn't been as insulting in his assessment of Seattle as she'd been about where the ranch was located. But dredging up what he said and what she said wasn't getting to the point of her visit. When they continued to glare at each other for what seemed an eternity, she sighed and shook her head. "I didn't come here to argue with you, Blake."

"Why *are* you here? I thought we settled things when I signed the papers without contesting the divorce." He frowned. "By the way, I'd like to get a copy of the final decree. You said your lawyer was supposed to mail that to me, but like everything else you promised, it didn't happen."

Karly stared down at her tightly clasped hands. She supposed he was right. She had made several promises that she hadn't been able to keep. She'd meant to keep them at the time. But once she went back home to pack her things and close her apartment, her sanity returned and the fear of failure had her second-guessing everything that had happened in Las Vegas.

"When I took the documents back to Mr. Campanella after you signed them, he suggested that I file for the divorce myself in Lincoln County on the eastern side of the state," she finally said. "Which I did."

Blake frowned. "Why?"

"The dockets in Seattle are filled with other domestic matters and it can take up to a year or more just to get a court date," she explained. "All I had to do was mail the signed documents to the courthouse in Lincoln County and after the ninety-day cooling-off period the divorce would be final."

"Mail them?" His frown darkened. "I thought a lawyer and at least one of the petitioners had to go before a judge for a divorce. At least that's how I think it is here. Is it different in Washington State?"

Rubbing her temples, Karly tried to concentrate. This was what she'd come here to tell him. It was also where everything got extremely complicated.

"If the petition had been filed in Seattle, Mr. Campanella would have been present. But Lincoln is one of only two counties where residents of Washington State file uncontested divorces by mailing the paperwork to the county clerk. Neither petitioner has to be present, nor do they have to have legal representation." When she noticed his skeptical expression, the tension headache she'd been fighting began to pound unmercifully. "It's really quite simple. The judge looks over the papers, signs a final judgment and sends it back."

"That sounds out of character, for a lawyer to pass up a case like this," Blake said, frowning. "Most of the ones I know would jump at the chance to make some easy money."

"Mr. Campanella is the grandfather of one of my coworkers," she explained. Karly really appreciated the woman's offer of help. When she'd come back from Vegas and realized the enormity of what she'd done, she'd been in a panic to fix her mistake. "Jo Ellen asked him to guide me through it all and he agreed. He suggested that I use the courts in Lincoln County since ours was a simple, uncontested divorce. He said it would save time and cost a lot less than going through the court system in Seattle. I agreed, and followed his instructions."

Blake nodded. "I guess that makes sense if you're in a hurry to rid yourself of an unwanted husband."

His words were bitter and cut like a knife. She had to swallow around the lump forming in her throat. He had no idea how hard it had been to make the decision not to follow her heart and move to the middle of nowhere with him. She had witnessed the unhappiness and resentment created when her mother followed her heart and it had ultimately ended her parents' marriage. Karly had reasoned that it was better to end things before it came to such hard feelings between herself and Blake. But there was no sense in dwelling on the mistakes and heartaches of the past now.

"I never said I was in a hurry to get rid of you."

He stared at her for a moment before he shrugged. "That's debatable, but it's not the issue. I need a notarized copy of the final decree."

Karly nibbled on her lower lip as she nervously met Blake's fathomless brown eyes. The time had come to lay out the reason for her visit and apologize for making such a mess of everything. "Actually, I don't even have a copy of it myself."

"Didn't they send you one?" he asked, his frown turning to a scowl.

"No, but I'm sure they will," she said evasively. She needed to explain what happened before she told him the reason she'd traveled all the way to Wyoming. "The import company I work for sent me to their offices in Hong Kong for several months shortly before the ninety-day cooling-off period was up and I wasn't able to check on it from overseas." Her head pounded as she thought about how badly she'd handled something as important to both herself and

Blake as their divorce. But she'd been sad and unsure as to why she'd felt so badly about a logical, sensible decision that should have brought only relief. "When I got back last week, I called to inquire about our copies of the final decree."

He must have been able to sense that there was more to the story because Blake's scowl darkened. "What did they say?"

Shaking her head, Karly took a deep fortifying breath in order to tell him the rest of what had happened. "I called the Lincoln County courthouse to see if I could get a copy of the final decree..."

When she let her voice trail off as she searched for the right words, he prompted, "Yeah, I got that. You called about the papers. And?"

Karly briefly closed her eyes as she tried to gather her courage for what needed to be said. Opening them to meet his suspicious gaze, she did her best to keep her voice steady. "Apparently the papers were lost in the mail because the court clerk has no record of us ever filing for a divorce." She had to take a deep breath before she could finish. "It appears that we're still husband and wife, Blake."

"We're still married," he repeated as if he had a hard time grasping what she'd said.

"Yes." She hurried on as she reached into her purse to take out a new set of divorce papers. Her hand trembled slightly as she placed the envelope on the desk in front of him. "I'm really sorry for the inconvenience. Once you sign these, I'm going to fly to

Spokane and drive over to the Lincoln County courthouse to file them with the clerk myself."

"So all this time, I've been thinking I'm a free man and I wasn't," he said, sitting back in the desk chair.

"Have you met someone?" she asked before she could stop herself.

He raised one dark eyebrow as he stared at her. "Would it matter if I had, Karly?"

Yes! "No," she lied. Thinking quickly, she added, "I was, um, afraid this snag might have derailed plans you might have made with someone else."

He continued to stare at her for a few moments before he smiled, shook his head and opened the envelope to remove the document. Reaching for an ink pen, he signed where she had flagged the papers with colored sticky notes.

"Well, you're stuck with me for at least another ninety days," he said, sliding the pages back into the envelope and pushing it across the desk's shiny surface toward her.

Karly winced at his acidic tone. She knew he was disillusioned and extremely unhappy with the situation. "I'm really...sorry, Blake. I never meant for any of this to happen." At least, not the mishandling of their divorce.

"Yeah, well, it did," he said, sounding resigned. "When you file these at the courthouse, make sure they send me copies of everything."

"Of course," she said, nodding as she slid the envelope back into her shoulder bag. She hesitated a moment as she tried to think of some way to say goodbye. Deciding there wasn't anything she could say that wouldn't make matters worse, she rose to her feet. "I'll be in touch if there's anything else we need to do."

"Did you drive all the way from Seattle or is that little toy in the driveway a rental?" he asked, standing up.

"I rented it when I flew into the Cheyenne Regional Airport," she answered, wondering why he wanted to know.

"I'll check under the car before you leave to make sure you didn't do some kind of damage to the undercarriage," he said, taking his wide-brimmed hat from the hook as they left the room. "You hit quite a few potholes on your way up the lane. Drive slower on the way back. You'll be less likely to damage the car."

"Who's responsible for taking care of the roads around here?" she asked. "They're in terrible condition."

"The county is responsible for the roads leading up to the ranch property lines, but ranchers have to keep the roads on their land plowed in the winter and graded in the summer," he explained. "We took care of grading the road after the snow melted off in the spring. But once the rainy season hit it washed out a lot of places. We were waiting until it dried up to work on the road again, when we have time."

"I think it's safe to say it's dry enough," she said

as they walked out of the house. She didn't know much about caring for a ranch or tending to roads, but she did notice the red sports car was coated with a thick layer of Wyoming dust.

His deep laughter sent heat racing through her veins and reminded her of the carefree man she'd met eight months ago. The man he'd been before she'd told him she couldn't be his wife after all. "It won't be an issue much longer," he stated. "The new owner is having it asphalted all the way to the county road."

"Why didn't the previous owner do that?" she asked, walking across the yard with him to the rental car.

"After her husband died, she wasn't interested in anything but trying to sell the ranch to a land developer. When she tried for a couple of years and failed to find a buyer, she finally sold it to one of her husband's sons from a previous marriage," he answered, sounding a little angry as he kneeled down to peer under the car.

She briefly wondered why he would be upset by a property dispute between the owner's heirs, but she abandoned her speculation when her cell phone chirped. Taking it out of her shoulder bag, Karly looked to see who was texting her. Her heart sank as she read the message. It was an alert from the airline, informing her that due to a contract-workers strike at the Denver airport, all flights had been canceled until further notice. Since the only commercial airline going in or out of the Cheyenne airfield was from Denver, she wasn't going anywhere until the labor dispute was settled.

"Lovely," she muttered sarcastically. Now what was she supposed to do?

She'd packed light because she hadn't expected to be away from home for more than a couple of nights. And she certainly hadn't planned on having to find a local place to stay indefinitely while the strike was settled.

"Looks like everything is intact," Blake said, unaware of her dilemma. He straightened to his full height as he dusted off his hands. "When does your flight leave?"

"It's not leaving," she said disgustedly as she opened the browser on her phone to see what lodging was available in the nearest town. "All flights in and out of Denver have been canceled due to an airport workers' strike."

He remained silent for several long moments and when she looked up, he was staring at her. "Looks like you'll be spending some time on the Wolf Creek Ranch after all," he said, folding his arms across his wide chest.

"No, I'll get a room in town," she said determinedly. It had been hard enough to see him again, to sit across the desk from him. She couldn't imagine spending the night in the same house with him, knowing he was so close and not being able to touch him or have him hold her.

He pointed toward the mountains to the west.

"Not tonight you won't. I can't, in good conscience, let you drive on unfamiliar mountain roads in the dark. Hell, it would be a miracle if you didn't get lost or end up hung in the top of a tree after missing a curve and going over the side of the mountain."

"You *can't allow* me to drive back in the dark?" she demanded indignantly. "I have news for you, buster. If I choose to go, you aren't going to stop me."

He closed his eyes and shook his head as if trying to gather his patience. When he opened them, he looked directly at her. "I realize we won't be married for much longer, but right now, I'm still your husband," he finally said. "I take my vows seriously. It's my job to keep you safe until a judge says otherwise. I'd feel a lot better if you would at least wait to make the drive until tomorrow morning. It's safer."

Karly was surprised by his grudging admission that he thought he should protect her. There hadn't been anyone who'd cared about her safety since her mother passed away several years ago. But as nice as it was to have someone worry about her well-being again, she needed to remember that Blake was only doing it because he felt it was his obligation. He'd signed the divorce papers. He must be as ready to undo their mistake as she was.

Sighing heavily, she tried to decide what to do. Everything about this trip had gone awry. Her flight from Denver to Cheyenne had been delayed for over two hours due to a dangerous storm front moving through, the drive to the ranch had taken three times as long as she had anticipated due to the car the rental agency had provided and her meeting with Blake hadn't gone as quickly as she'd thought it would. The way her luck had been running, it was very likely that she'd end up in one of the disastrous scenarios he mentioned.

"Eagle Fork is only twenty miles away," she said, glancing at the sun rapidly sinking behind the mountains to the west.

"It takes a little over an hour in the daylight to drive down the mountain to get there. How long do you think it would take you to get back at night?" Blake pointed toward the road. "Do you really want to drive on unfamiliar, rough mountain roads in the dark? At least stay tonight."

"If I take it slow, I shouldn't have a problem," she hedged. Sleeping in the same house with Blake—even if it was in different rooms—wasn't a good idea. He was six feet two inches of male temptation that had proved almost impossible for her to resist in the past. It had taken going all the way back to Seattle for her to realize the effect he'd had on her good sense. What crazy decisions would she make if she stayed here with him?

"And what happens if you have a deer or elk run across the road in front of you?" he persisted, oblivious to her inner battle. "I've got news for you, sweetheart. If you hit one of those in that little toy car, you're going to lose."

Karly stared at him as she weighed her options. Driving up through the mountains during the day with all the switchbacks and ninety-degree curves had been a challenge. And of course, there had been the last several miles to the ranch, which had become a dirt-and-gravel road pitted with more holes than a piece of Swiss cheese. But at night?

She hated to admit it, but her choices were extremely limited. Since she didn't know another soul in Wyoming, she either had to risk going down the mountain in the dark to find a motel room in Eagle Fork, or stay with Blake.

As she watched the evening shadows begin to overtake the high mountain valley, she decided she had run out of time. There simply wasn't enough daylight left to make it back to town before it got completely dark.

"I suppose I could spend the night here and then drive back down to Eagle Fork tomorrow to get a room for however long it takes the strike to be resolved," she said, talking more to herself than to Blake.

"Then it's settled," he said, walking to the back of the car. "I'll carry your luggage inside."

"I wasn't expecting to spend more than two nights away from home and only have an overnight case," she said, using the keyless remote to open the trunk as she walked over to take the small bag from him. "I can bring it inside."

He shook his head as he lifted it from the trunk.

"Grandma Jean would have my hide if she got wind of me letting you carry your luggage yourself."

"Does she live close by?" Karly had never known what it was like to be close to a grandparent. Three of hers had passed away before she was born and her paternal grandmother had lived so far away, she'd only seen her a handful of times.

"She lives down in Eagle Fork," he said as he placed his hand at the small of her back to guide her into the house. "There were several of us who lived with her during the winter when we were still in school."

"Because of all the snow?" she mused as they climbed the stairs to the second floor. If the roads were so difficult to navigate in the summer, she couldn't imagine trying to get around in a heavy snowfall.

"It was easier to stay down there where we could get to school than have to miss and make up all of the schoolwork when we were finally able to get back to class," he said, nodding as he stepped back so she could enter a bedroom. When he set her small suitcase on the bed, he hooked his thumb over his shoulder toward the door. "While you get settled, I have to drive over to the main house to see about a few things the owner needs me to take care of."

"Was that the huge log home I passed just before I got here?" she asked, unzipping the overnight case to remove her flip-flops. She loved wearing heels, but she had been in them all day and her feet were beginning to hurt.

Blake nodded. "The owner had that built a couple of years ago. Right after he bought the ranch."

"It's beautiful," she said, removing the heels to put on the flip-flops. "And it's perfect for the rugged surroundings."

He stared at her a moment before he turned and walked out into the hall. "I guess I'd better go on over to the main house. Make yourself at home. I won't be long."

As she heard him descend the stairs, she began to realize just how little she knew about the man she had married. In Las Vegas, Blake had literally swept her off her feet and charmed her into a fairytale week of romance, lovemaking and a wedding. But as idyllic as their time together had been, they hadn't talked about their families or jobs, their hopes or their dreams.

"It would have never worked between us," she murmured as she sat down on the side of the bed.

The realization was not a new one. So Karly had no idea why the words made her feel so sad. This was what she'd chosen—the way it had to be. She wasn't about to make the same mistakes her mother had made. She wasn't going to give up everything—her home, her lifestyle, her job—for a man and then resent him for her choices.

No matter how beautiful it was here or how cherished and safe Blake made her feel when he took her in his arms, she couldn't live on this ranch with him any more than he could live with her in Seattle. And the sooner she accepted that truth, the better off she would be.

Two

Blake glanced over at his backpack, the thermal food carrier and the jug of iced tea on the truck seat beside him as he drove away from the main ranch house. *His* house.

He had never lied to Karly, not eight months ago and not today.

But he hadn't been completely honest with her, either.

When they met in Las Vegas, he'd told her that besides competing in rodeo, he was the boss at the Wolf Creek Ranch in Wyoming. She had assumed that meant he was the foreman and he hadn't bothered to set her straight. For one thing, they'd been so hot for each other, they hadn't talked at length about their jobs or much of anything else. And for another, he didn't go around flaunting the fact that he owned the Wolf Creek or that he was a multimillionaire.

He had firsthand knowledge of how the lure of money could influence people and he intended to avoid that kind of shallowness at all costs. He didn't want the money to affect his relationships, and he'd been especially careful about what he'd shared with the woman he'd married so quickly. In the past, both he and his father had seen the ugly side of women hell-bent on getting their hands on a hefty bankroll and once had been enough to leave Blake more than a little cautious.

But he was fairly certain Karly had no knowledge about the size of his bank account. She had fallen for him—without the influence of his money. He had figured that when she joined him at the ranch it would be a nice surprise to let her know that they would never have financial worries like a lot of other couples starting out. Unfortunately, he hadn't had the chance to tell her the truth because she'd decided that living in a big city without him was preferable to living on the ranch with him. She'd made that decision without the influence of his money, too.

In hindsight, he wished he'd told her right after they got married in Vegas. He didn't want her thinking that he had been trying to hide his assets because of their pending divorce. That wasn't the case at all. And he had every intention of telling her the truth, as well as providing her with a nice settlement for the very brief time they'd been married. He just needed to figure out the right time and way to go about doing that.

He could have told her about his wealth when she called from Seattle to tell him she thought they'd made a mistake and that ending the marriage would be for the best. But he'd decided against that because she might have assumed it was a desperate attempt on his part to get her to reconsider their divorce, to give them a chance. Him begging for a second chance was something that would never happen. Even if his pride had allowed it, it probably wouldn't have made a difference. She'd had her mind made up and nothing he could have said would have changed it.

So he'd kept his secret and signed the papers. But he could have told her the truth today, too, when she'd mistakenly assumed the foreman's cottage was his house and that the main house and ranch belonged to someone else. But he'd held back without really knowing why.

All he knew was that his ego had taken enough of a hit eight months ago, when he'd learned that while she might have been the woman of his dreams, he obviously hadn't been the man of hers. And if he was perfectly honest with himself, there had probably been a little fear holding him back, as well. He hadn't wanted to tell her he was rich and end up finding out that he'd been wrong about her—that Karly could be swayed by the temptation of his money.

As he steered his truck up the lane leading to the foreman's cottage, he reached up to rub the tension building at the back of his neck. He wasn't sure how something that had originally felt so right had gone so wrong. When he'd married Karly after only knowing her a week, the decision had seemed as natural as taking his next breath. Their whirlwind wedding carried on the Hartwell family tradition. Blake's Grandma and Grandpa Hartwell had been married three days after meeting and his father and mother tied the knot two weeks after their first date. Both couples had successful marriages until death separated them and Blake had been sure it would be that way with himself and Karly. It was obvious now that he had been wrong.

Parking his truck beside the little red sports car, Blake took a deep breath and reached for his backpack, the thermal carrier full of food and the gallon thermos of iced tea he'd had his cook pack for their supper. There was no sense in trying to figure out how he could have misjudged Karly's commitment to their relationship. He had and there wasn't anything he could do about it now. Besides, he'd never been one to dwell on his mistakes.

As he walked toward the cottage, she opened the door and stepped out onto the porch. His breath caught and his heart thumped against his ribs. He felt the same pull that had drawn him to her the first time he'd laid eyes on her in Vegas. He forced himself to ignore the feeling. She might be the most exciting woman he'd ever known, but the sting of her rejection and her disdain for his lifestyle told him in no uncertain terms just how unimportant he was to her. She'd walked away from him once. He wouldn't give her another chance to do it again.

Distracted by his turbulent thoughts, it took him a moment to notice the frown on her pretty face. "Is something wrong?" he asked as he climbed the steps.

"Where do you keep your food?" she answered his question with one of her own as they entered the house. "I was going to make something for dinner, but the refrigerator and pantry are both empty. If you live here why isn't there anything in the house to eat?"

"I usually eat down at the bunkhouse with the single men or over at the main house," he said truthfully as he set the cooler and jug of iced tea on the kitchen island, then turned to hang his hat on a peg by the door. He did eat with his men at the bunkhouse occasionally, just not as often as he ate what his cook made for him in the main house.

She looked doubtful. "Even in the winter when you're snowed in?"

He couldn't help but laugh at her erroneous assumption. "Sweetheart, there's no such thing as getting snowed in around here. A ranch is a twenty-four-hours, seven-days-a-week operation. It never shuts down because the livestock are depending on us to take care of them. If it rains we get wet. If it snows we wade through it no matter how deep it gets or how cold it is."

"I hadn't thought of that." Looking a little sheepish, she shook her head. "I'll be the first to admit I don't know anything about ranching."

"Don't worry about it." He motioned toward the thermal carrier. "And don't worry about cooking. I had the cook over at the main house pack up what he made for supper. Why don't you set the table while I go wash up?"

He didn't mention that he'd had to endure an interrogation and a stern lecture before old Silas finished loading the carrier with containers of food. A retired cowboy turned cook after his arthritis prevented him from doing ranch work, Silas Burrows had some definite ideas on how Blake should conduct his life and he didn't mind sharing them every chance he got. Having a wife show up unexpectedly, one that Blake hadn't told Silas about, definitely got the old boy started. As sure as the grass was green, Blake knew he hadn't heard the end of what Silas had to say on the matter, either.

"I'll have dinner on the table by the time you return," she said as she started removing the food from the carrier to set it on the butcher-block island.

Blake watched her for a moment before he gritted his teeth and left the room. Karly had changed into a pair of khaki camp shorts and an oversize T-shirt while he was gone. She shouldn't have looked the least bit appealing. But he'd be damned if just seeing her in the baggy shorts, shapeless shirt and bright pink flip-flops didn't have him feeling as restless as a range-raised colt.

Disgusted with himself, he marched up the stairs and down the hall to the master bedroom. How could he want a woman who had rejected him? Who had rejected his way of life and the land he loved?

Setting his backpack on the cedar chest at the end of the bed, he walked into the adjoining bathroom to wash up. As he splashed cold water on his face to clear his head, he couldn't help but think about the irony of the situation.

When Karly called him a few days after they parted in Vegas to tell him that she had changed her mind about being his wife, she hadn't even been willing to discuss coming to Wyoming in order to see if they could save their brief marriage. Yet almost nine months later, here she was—in the very place she said she never wanted to see—with papers to end the union.

But as he dried his face and hands with one of the fluffy towels from the linen cabinet, he couldn't help but think there had to have been something that happened when she got back to Seattle that had caused her change of heart. But what could it have been? Was there someone else she hadn't told him about? Maybe an old flame or someone she had been seeing before they met?

He'd asked himself the same questions a hundred times—and just as often told himself to forget about solving the mystery. He had no way of knowing what went through her head. And no reason to ask once she'd been determined to end things between them.

But now that Karly was here, he had a golden opportunity that was just too damn good to pass up. All he had to do was convince her to stay at the ranch a few days, until the strike in Denver was settled. That would give him time to ask her what had happened, to find out what had changed her mind and why.

It might not be the smartest thing he'd ever wanted to do. And he knew that whatever he found out wouldn't change the state of their marriage; he'd already signed the papers and let her go. Hell, he'd probably be better off not knowing. And he certainly wasn't expecting anything about him or his ranch to change her mind, even if he did learn the answer.

But some perverse part of him felt that it was his right to know why she'd refused to even try to make a go of things with him.

With his mind made up, Blake went back downstairs to the kitchen to help Karly set the table. "I've been thinking. It doesn't make any sense for you to spend money on a motel room when you can stay here for free," he pointed out as he got two glasses down from one of the cabinets.

"I can't do that," she said, looking at him like he had sprouted another head.

"Why not?" he asked, pouring them each a glass of iced tea from the thermal jug.

"I don't want to impose," she said, placing a container of country-fried steaks on the table.

"How would you staying here be an imposition?" He carried the glasses to the table, then held her chair for her to sit down. "We're still married and the last time I heard, a husband and wife staying in the same house isn't all that unusual," he added, laughing.

"We're not going to be married that much longer," she insisted. "We're practically divorced already."

"It doesn't matter." He shrugged as he seated himself at the head of the table and reached for the container of steaks. "You're still my wife and that gives you the right to stay here."

"We really don't know each other," she said, taking a bite of a seasoned potato wedge.

"That didn't seem to be a deal breaker when you said 'I do,'" he pointed out, before he could stop himself. He felt like a prize ass when he saw the wounded expression on her pretty face.

She stared at him for several long moments before she shook her head. "I think it would be best if I get that motel room tomorrow as planned."

"Look, I'm sorry about what I just said." He took a deep breath. "That was out of line."

She stared at him for a moment longer before she shook her head again. "Not entirely. We were both—" she paused, as if searching for the right words "—caught up in the moment in Las Vegas. And I don't think one of us was more at fault than the other."

Maybe she had been caught up in the moment, but he had known exactly what he was doing and the commitment he was making when he vowed to take care of her for the rest of their lives. But arguing that point wasn't going to accomplish what he had set out to do.

"That's all water under the bridge now," he said, shrugging. "But if you stay here, I'm sure you'll be more comfortable than in a motel room. And you won't have to drive the mountain roads more than once to get back to the airport."

She gave him a suspicious look. "Why are you being so persistent about this, Blake?"

"I figure it will save you a few hundred bucks or so," he said, thinking quickly. She obviously had to watch her finances. Otherwise, she wouldn't have mentioned that by filing the divorce herself instead of having a lawyer do it for her she was saving money. But he wasn't going to point out that he knew she was on a tight budget. She had her pride, the same as he did, and bringing up the state of her financial situation would probably send her back down the mountain as fast as that little red car could take her. "Besides, staying here beats sitting in a motel room for several days with nothing to do but stare at the four walls."

He almost groaned aloud when she nibbled on her lower lip as she mulled over what he'd said. She wasn't trying to be seductive, but it seemed like everything about her had his libido working overtime.

Maybe it was due to the memories of making love to her that haunted his dreams at night. Or, more likely, it was the fact that he hadn't been with a woman since they'd parted ways in Las Vegas. Whatever the reason behind his overactive hormones, he had every intention of ignoring them.

"I suppose not having anything to do would be pretty boring," she finally conceded. "But I wouldn't have anything to do here, either."

"Sure you would," he said, careful not to sound too eager. "There's never a lack of things to do around a ranch. You could help me feed the horses and a couple of orphaned calves. And tomorrow afternoon, you can ride up to the summer pasture with me to check on a herd of steers we'll be moving back down here in a couple of weeks."

"You mean ride a horse?" When he nodded, she vigorously shook her head. "That's not an option."

"Why?"

"Other than a pony ride at the grand opening of a grocery store when I was five, I've never been on a horse," she said, taking a sip of her iced tea.

That explained her skittish reaction to Boomer when she'd first arrived. "Don't worry about it. I've got the perfect horse for you and it won't take any time to teach you how to ride her."

"I don't think that would be a good idea," she commented, reaching for a roll. "Horses don't like me."

"Why do you say that?" he asked. "You just admitted that you've never really been around horses. How would you know if they like you or not?"

She frowned. "Your horse snorted and stomped his foot at me this afternoon. If that wasn't an indication he didn't like me, I don't know what is."

"Hoof," he countered, correcting her. "Horses have hooves and he was just shooing away a fly when he moved his leg." Blake took a bite of his steak. "And for the record, Boomer didn't snort. Gently blowing through his nose like that is a horse's way of sighing. It signals that he's relaxed, curious or in some cases just saying hello. Boomer was just being friendly."

"His name doesn't exactly instill a lot of confidence," she said, shaking her head. "Boomer sounds rather…explosive."

Blake laughed out loud at her inaccurate assumption that the gentle gelding's name reflected his temperament. "Boomer is short for Boomerang and the reason he got that name is because he likes people so much he can't stay away from them. I can turn him out into a pasture with other horses and before I know it, he turns around and comes right back to me."

"That's great, but it doesn't mean he likes *me*," she said, looking doubtful.

Blake grinned. "I'll introduce you tomorrow morning when we go out to the barn to take care of the calves. You'll see. He's as gentle as a lapdog."

She looked skeptical, but didn't comment until

they had finished their meal. “I can help you feed the babies, but I’m afraid riding a horse tomorrow is out of the question. I didn’t expect to be away from home more than a couple of nights and I really don’t have anything to wear that would be suitable for a horseback ride.”

He smiled at the relief he heard in her soft voice. He’d bet every dime he had that she’d spent the entire meal trying to think of a way to get out of riding.

“We’ll remedy that tomorrow morning after I get the feeding done,” he said, smiling as he helped her clear the table. “We’ll make a trip down to Eagle Fork’s Western store and get everything you need.”

“That sounds like a lot of time and trouble for a pair of jeans,” she said as she put containers of leftovers into the refrigerator. “And besides, I don’t want to interfere with the work you need to get done.”

“It won’t be any trouble at all,” Blake said, barely able to keep from laughing at her attempts to escape his plans. He was not only determined to find out what she wasn’t telling him, he was also going to give her a ranch experience she’d never forget. “I need to get a new shirt for a Labor Day barbecue on Monday anyway and you’ll need something to wear to that as well. In fact, it would probably be a good idea to get you enough clothes for a few days since there’s no telling how long the strike will last.”

“I can’t crash your friend’s party,” she said as she turned to wipe off the kitchen island.

“You won’t be crashing the party.” Blake wasn’t

about to take no for an answer. "You'll go as my date."

"That would be rather awkward," she insisted.

"Only if you make it that way," he said, even though he knew she was right.

"How on earth would you even introduce me?" She gave him a pointed look. "We may be married right now, but we're little more than strangers on the way to a divorce. We wouldn't even be married if the papers had arrived as they should have. I'd just as soon avoid a lot of questions about our hasty marriage and the upcoming divorce."

"Easy. I'll just tell them that we met in Vegas and you came for a visit," Blake explained.

She stared at him before she frowned. "Do you really think it will take that long for the strike to be settled?"

He shrugged. "It's a holiday weekend. There's really no telling. Even if they come to an agreement over the weekend it's going to take at least a day or two for the airlines to get all of the schedules lined up and the passengers from the canceled flights who haven't found other means of transportation on their way again. And with Labor Day on Monday that's going to delay things even more."

"I suppose I could drive from here to Lincoln County," Karly said, looking thoughtful.

"I know you want to get this divorce over with, but do you really want to drive fifteen or sixteen hours in holiday traffic?" he asked. "You couldn't possibly get there tomorrow before the courthouse closes and it won't reopen again until Tuesday. By that time the strike might be settled and you'd be able to fly."

She didn't look happy about what he was saying, but she finally nodded. "You're probably right."

"I know I am." When she yawned, he pointed toward the hall. "I can finish cleaning the kitchen. Why don't you go ahead and turn in for the night? Mornings around here start early."

"How early are we talking about?" she asked, hiding another yawn with her delicate hand.

"I'll start feeding the livestock in the barns around dawn," he said as he loaded the dishwasher. "That will take about an hour. Since you don't really have suitable clothes for that yet, I'll wake you up after I get finished."

She looked horrified. "Good Lord, are the animals even awake at that time of day?"

"They're not only awake, they're usually making a lot of noise because they know it's time for breakfast," he said, laughing.

When she yawned again, she started toward the hall. "In that case, I think I'll follow your advice and go to bed." She stopped at the door and turned back. "Thank you, Blake."

"What for?" he asked, walking over to her.

"For giving me a place to stay until the strike is settled and for being so nice about all of this," she said quietly. "You really didn't have to be, considering how badly I handled filing for the divorce."

He barely resisted the urge to reach for her. As he stuffed his hands into the front pockets of his jeans to keep himself from doing something stupid like taking her in his arms and kissing her until they both gasped for air, he shook his head. "Don't be so hard on yourself. You had no control over what happened after you put the papers in the mail. And like I told you earlier, I'm old-fashioned. As long as we're married it's my job to provide you with a roof over your head and something to eat."

She stared at him for several long moments before she finally nodded. "Well, thank you anyway. Good night."

"Yeah, see you in the morning," he mumbled as he watched her walk down the hall to the stairs.

Taking a deep breath, he waited until he heard her close the door to her bedroom before he started the dishwasher and turned out the kitchen light. As he slowly climbed the stairs to his own guest room, he couldn't help but wonder how everything had become so damn complicated. Eight months ago, things had been simple. He'd found the woman he was going to spend the rest of his life with and she'd told him that he was the man she wanted to share hers with, too.

He had no idea what had changed from the time they left Vegas until she called him a few days later from Seattle to tell him she wasn't joining him at the ranch as planned. But one thing was sure—before she left this ranch to file for divorce and return to her life in the city, he had every intention of getting an explanation and settling the matter once and for all.

The following morning, as Karly sat on the passenger side of Blake's truck, she looked out over the side of the mountain. On her drive up the winding road the day before, she'd been so focused on getting Blake to sign the new set of divorce papers and returning to Cheyenne to make her connecting flight back to Denver that she hadn't taken the time to notice the scenery. Although the mountains surrounding Seattle were more lush—with tall, straight conifers, beds of ferns and thick moss carpeting the forest floor—the ruggedness of the Wyoming landscape was no less beautiful. The pine and aspen trees didn't seem to grow as thick as the forests of the Northwest, but the jagged, snow-capped peaks and vast valleys of thick prairie grass, with colorful late-summer wildflowers, were utterly breathtaking.

"It's really beautiful here," she murmured aloud.

"Imagine that." Grinning as he steered the truck around a tight switchback, Blake added, "It's amazing how different things turn out to be from our preconceived notions, isn't it?"

When she'd called to tell him she'd changed her mind about the marriage, she'd said some things about the land he so obviously loved that she deeply regretted. In hindsight, she'd been trying to convince herself that living in a remote area of Wyoming was unsuitable for her. She'd been trying to create enough distance between them to make divorce the best option. But that didn't change the fact that he'd taken offense at her comments. She'd hurt him unintentionally.

"I guess I might have been a bit hasty in my assumption that the area had nothing to offer," she finally admitted. "But you have to understand. I've lived most of my life in a city, where everything I want or need is close by."

"I understand that," he said, nodding. "But it's not the backwoods, off-the-grid type of living you envisioned, is it?"

"No," she admitted. "But you helped to create that misconception."

"How do you figure that?" he asked, frowning.

"You said the ranch was in a remote location and I naturally assumed..." She paused when she realized that with the closest neighbors at least ten miles away at the bottom of the mountain and only one way to get to the ranch, it really could be considered isolated. "I guess I thought that you meant it was without some of the modern conveniences."

"Tell the truth," he said, laughing. "You thought that a trip to the bathroom in the middle of the night would involve a flashlight and a little shed with a half-moon carved into the door."

She laughed. "Well, not quite. But I didn't expect it to have a main ranch house that looks like a log mansion, or the house you live in to have such a cozy feel to it. I guess I was thinking it would be more rustic."

"You've been watching too many old Westerns on television," he said, steering the truck onto the main road as they reached the bottom of the mountain. "Living on a ranch is like living anywhere else. We have modern appliances, satellite TV and high-speed internet. About the only difference is having to drive a few miles to get to a store instead of it being just down the street."

"Maybe I have been thinking it would be like the Old West," she admitted thoughtfully.

They fell silent for the rest of the drive and by the time they reached downtown Eagle Fork, Karly had come to a conclusion that she wasn't overly proud of. She wasn't going to tell Blake, but it wouldn't have mattered if the ranch was rustic and isolated or sat right in the middle of a town. Her choice to divorce him would have been the same. It wasn't the challenges of living on a ranch that had held her back. It had been the fear she would turn out to be like her mother and discover that a husband and family weren't enough for her—that her career was more important.

A few minutes later, when Blake parked his truck in front of the Blue Sage Western Emporium, Karly noticed that the store looked as if it had been in business since hitching posts were used instead of parking meters. Abandoning her disturbing thoughts, she focused on their shopping trip. She hoped the clothing wasn't going to be too expensive. She wasn't poor, but she did live on a budget and hadn't planned on buying clothes that she probably wouldn't wear past the few days she was stranded at the Wolf Creek Ranch.

Blake grinned as he opened the passenger door to help her out of the truck. "Are you ready to get your cowgirl on?"

"Whether I'm ready or not, it looks like I'm going to," she said, feeling breathless.

She was in real trouble if his smile alone was enough to take her breath away. But it was the feel of his hand pressed to the small of her back as he guided her into the store that caused her knees to wobble.

Stepping away from him, she took a deep breath and the rich scent of leather assailed her senses. It reminded her of the man at her side and sent a shiver of longing straight through her. It would definitely be in her best interest to forego the shopping and make plans to drive to Lincoln County.

But even as she thought it, she knew that probably wasn't going to happen.

"Pick out as many pairs as you think you'll need," he said, ushering her over to a wall with large cubby-holes filled with folded pairs of women's jeans. He pointed to a couple of racks holding T-shirts and blouses. "And don't forget to get some shirts and something special to wear to the barbecue."

Before she could tell him that she wouldn't be needing clothes because she was going to leave the next morning to drive back to Washington State, a middle-age woman walked over to them. "It's good to see you, Blake," she said, smiling. She shot a curious glance toward Karly, as if wondering who she was. "How arc things going at the Wolf Creek?"

"I can't complain, Mary Ann," he answered. "The hay crop was good this year and we should have more than enough to make it through the winter."

"That's always a relief," she said, nodding. "Eli Laughlin was in the other day and said pretty much the same thing about the Rusty Spur."

While Blake and the woman discussed what was going on at some of the other ranches in the area, Karly gave up on the idea of driving back to file the divorce papers. For one thing, she wasn't all that fond of spending so many hours in the car. And for another, sitting in a hotel room for a couple of days with nothing to do while she waited for the courthouse to open wasn't her idea of a good time, either.

Just as Blake had said, she'd be better off waiting here and looking for a way home after the holiday weekend. Most likely the strike would be done, and the courthouse would definitely be open. She didn't want to consider why the decision to stay here, with Blake, made her feel so warm inside.

By the time she found jeans and a few shirts that weren't too pricey, Blake joined her. "Are you ready to try on boots?"

"I hadn't even thought about footwear," she said, wondering how long it would take for her budget to recover from all of her unplanned purchases. She glanced down at her feet. "I know I can't wear these heels and I don't suppose flip-flops are suitable for helping you feed the orphaned calves, are they?"

He shook his head as he led her toward the back of the store, where boxes of boots were stacked on shelves from the floor all the way to the ceiling. "Not unless you want to risk a nasty cut or broken toes when one of them steps on your foot."

"Not hardly," she said, deciding that a financial headache was preferable to physical pain. Since she'd decided to stay the long weekend at Blake's ranch, she supposed she had to go all in and as he so eloquently put it, "get her cowgirl on."

A half hour later as she and Blake walked out of the store, Karly frowned at all the bags and boxes he carried. She knew she couldn't really afford all the things she'd bought, but she hadn't expected Blake to pay for her shopping spree. This was probably another obligation for him, because he was her husband. And the only reason she'd said yes was because her bank account wouldn't let her reject his kind offer. But she seemed to be getting deeper into the role of a wife even though the whole point of this trip had been to finalize their divorce.

"You should have let me pay for all of this," Karly said. If he had, she would have definitely gone with fewer and more economical selections. "I doubt the owner of the ranch will be all that happy about you putting my clothes on his charge account."

"Don't worry about it. He doesn't mind me charging things on the ranch account. And, like I said, you're my wife. If you lived with me, you'd be charging things all the time." Grinning, he shrugged as he put the purchases onto the backseat of the club cab truck. "It's one of the perks of being the boss."

"There's a difference between charging one or two items and loading up the account." She pointed to the two boxes he added to the pile. "That hat was outrageously expensive and those boots alone cost more than I've ever paid for a pair of shoes in my entire life."

"A good hat and a comfortable pair of boots are worth whatever price you have to pay for them," he stated as he helped her up into the passenger seat.

"But I won't be here that long," she argued, trying to make him understand. "Something cheaper would have served the purpose just as well."

She'd tried to tell him when he insisted she put them on that they were far too expensive. But when he gently wrapped his hand around her calf as he took her high heel off to put one of the boots on, her brain had short-circuited. Somewhere between her vocal cords and opened mouth her objection had turn into a gasp of awareness. His smile and the twinkle in his sexy brown eyes indicated that he'd noticed, but he didn't comment as he worked the boot onto her foot and she couldn't get her voice to work long enough to protest further.

He closed the door, walked around the front of the

truck and got in behind the steering wheel. "Let's get something straight. As long as you're at the ranch and we're still married, I provide for you. That includes the clothes and hat you'll wear and the boots on your feet. There are some things that I won't skimp on, no matter how expensive they are, because in most cases, you get what you pay for. Hats and boots are two of those things." He surprised her when he reached over to cover her hand with his. "And don't worry about me charging all of this on the ranch account. When the bill comes in, I'll pay for it."

The feel of his calloused palm on her skin and the memory of how his hands had felt on her body when they made love sent a shiver of longing straight up her spine. She tried her best to dismiss the reaction as nothing more than nerves. But as they continued to stare at each other, she knew it was going to take everything in her to keep from falling under his charming spell again.

She quickly slid her hand from beneath his and concentrated on what he'd said. "Blake, I appreciate that you feel it's your responsibility to see that I have what I need," she said, choosing her words carefully. "But I don't feel right about you buying a whole wardrobe for me."

He gave her a cursory glance as he started the truck and steered it out of the parking lot onto the street. "Why not?"

"If I had handled the divorce differently, you wouldn't be in the awkward position of giving me a place to stay or feeling obligated to buy things for me," she said, feeling guilty. For that matter, if she hadn't been so impulsive and made promises she hadn't been able to keep when they were in Las Vegas, neither of them would have found themselves in their current situation.

"Don't beat yourself up over this," he said, surprising her. "You did what you thought was best and it didn't turn out the way you planned." He stared straight ahead as he added, "It happens to the best of us."

Her guilt increased when she realized he was talking about his own plans for them to live together as husband and wife. He had every right to be bitter about how she'd ended things, but instead he was treating her like the wife she'd never been to him. Suddenly, she was wishing things could have worked out differently—but she quickly squashed that traitorous thought. "I suppose you're right," she murmured.

They fell silent for several minutes as Blake drove out of town toward the ranch. "Why don't we start over?" he suggested, breaking the silence.

She frowned. "What do you mean?"

"There's no sense wasting time pointing fingers or feeling guilty about what went wrong between us," he said pragmatically. "We've both signed the papers already. So why don't we forget the real reason for your trip to the ranch and look at this holiday weekend as a friendly visit? I'll show you what ranch life is all about." He laughed. "And you can look on your time here as one of those vacations people take just to play cowboy."

Her chest tightened at his offer, at the consideration he was showing her. They both knew she was to blame for the entire fiasco and that he had been terribly disappointed with her decisions. But he was willing to put aside any hard feelings in order for her stay at the Wolf Creek Ranch to be more pleasant. If she hadn't been so afraid that quitting her job and moving so far away from the city would turn her into her mother, she would have loved having this man for her husband.

"Thank you, Blake," she said, blinking back tears. "I think I'd like that."

"Then it's settled." His grin caused her pulse to flutter. "Let's get back to the ranch so we can get started on giving you the ranching experience of your life."

Three

The lingering shadows of night were just giving way to the misty light of dawn when Karly followed Blake out of the house and across the ranch yard toward one of the barns. Wearing a new pair of jeans, a hot pink T-shirt, her hat and a flannel-lined denim jacket he had insisted on buying her the day before, she stepped around puddles left by the thunderstorm that had popped up yesterday afternoon to keep from getting her expensive new boots wet.

The rain had prevented her and Blake from riding up to check on the herd of cattle in the upper pasture when they returned from the store and that had been just fine with Karly. It had given her a day's reprieve from having to learn to ride a horse.

It was probably too much to hope for that it would rain again today.

"How long does it take to feed the animals?" she asked when they entered the barn.

"It takes longer right now than it usually does because of the bucket babies," Blake answered, opening the door to a room filled with large sacks of grain and assorted sizes of buckets. "But we're usually finished in about an hour."

She assumed the bucket babies he was talking about were the orphaned calves. When he set two pails with large nipples protruding from the bottom edge on a small table outside of the door, she understood why he called them bucket babies.

"Why don't you use big bottles?" she asked. "Wouldn't that be easier?"

He laughed. "Two reasons. One, we'd be stopping to refill the bottle every few minutes. And two, calves tend to be extremely enthusiastic when they eat. Holding a bucket can be hard enough when they get going. But holding a bottle would be damn near impossible."

"How old are they?" she asked, when he started scooping cream-colored powder into each bucket. "If they're still on baby formula, they must be quite young."

"They're almost four weeks old," he said, adding premeasured jugs of distilled water to the buckets. He handed her a smooth wooden paddle. "If you'll stir the formula, I'll measure up the grain starter."

"They're already eating solids?" she asked, frowning. "Aren't they a little young for that?"

He laughed. "You know what they say. Kids grow up real fast these days."

She rolled her eyes. "Will you be serious? It was a legitimate question."

"Sorry," he said, continuing to chuckle.

"No, you're not." She couldn't help but laugh with him.

"Not really. I just couldn't resist." As he shook his head, his charming grin sent goose bumps shimmering over her skin. "Calves usually start nibbling on grass out in the field when they're a day or two old. But that's when they have their mamas with them and are able to nurse whenever they want. Because these calves are orphaned and have to be fed on a schedule, we start them on a little bit of hay a few days after they're born and grain starter about a week after that. When they're up to eating about a pound or two of grain a day we start weaning them away from the milk replacer. That's when they are about six to eight weeks old."

"They really do grow up fast," she said, marveling at how quickly the animal babies progressed.

While she stirred the calf formula, he went back into the feed room and began scooping grain into shallow pails. Glancing through the doorway to watch him, Karly decided that Blake Hartwell was without a doubt the most handsome, charismatic man she'd ever met. She was going to have to be extremely careful not to fall for him all over again.

That thought should have sent her speeding down the mountain as fast as the red sports car she'd rented could take her. But she had told him she would stay until the strike was settled and she'd already broken enough of her promises to him. She wasn't going to add another, especially after he'd been so nice about everything that had happened between them.

When he rejoined her in the wide barn aisle, he handed her the lighter pails with small amounts of grain starter in them and picked up the heavier buckets with the formula she had finished mixing. "Are you ready for your first lesson in the fine art of feeding calves?"

She nodded. "I guess I'm as ready as I'll ever be."

Other than the pony she'd ridden at the grocery store grand opening when she was in kindergarten, she'd never been around an animal larger than a cat or a dog and she was definitely feeling a little intimidated. Did calves have a tendency to bite? She didn't remember hearing of anyone suffering a cow bite. But that didn't mean anything. She knew absolutely nothing about livestock. And other than Blake, she didn't know anyone else who did.

That was another reason that she'd gotten cold feet about their marriage. She'd not only feared quitting her job and finding herself feeling as displaced and resentful as her mother, she would have also been living on this ranch with animals large enough to squash her like a bug.

The first time she'd ever seen those animals in action had been in Las Vegas when she met Blake and he'd invited her to watch him ride in the rodeo events. After returning to Seattle and remembering what the huge animals were capable of doing and the injuries their actions caused, she'd known for certain that ranch life wasn't for her. Yet, here she was doing the very thing that she'd feared—interacting with the beasts.

But when they reached the stall where the calves were, Karly couldn't help but smile. The two bucket babies immediately started bawling and pushing at the gate as she and Blake approached, as if they knew their breakfast had arrived.

"They're so cute!" she said, looking over the top board at the black calves. They seemed too little to do much damage. "Do they bite?"

Blake laughed as he set the two buckets of milk on a bale of hay outside of the stall, then took the pails of grain starter from her. "Cattle would have to have upper front teeth before they could do that."

"They don't have teeth?" she asked, doubtfully. She thought most all animals needed teeth to eat.

He shook his head. "They only have bottom incisors and a tough, thickly padded top gum, so it's highly unlikely that one could bite you and cause an injury. And even if they tried it, which they aren't prone to do, it would be more of a pinch than a bite."

"That's good to know," she said when he opened the stall door.

"I'll take care of feeding them the grain starter and then we'll give them the milk together," he said, entering the enclosure.

He was immediately accosted by the calves and she was amazed at how quickly the pair finished off the grain in the pails Blake held. "You were right about them being enthusiastic eaters," she said, laughing. They reminded her of two rather large, clumsy puppies.

When he walked out of the stall to get the buckets of calf formula, he chuckled. "Just wait until they see these. They'll be like sharks in a feeding frenzy."

Karly opened the door to the stall for him and cautiously followed him inside. The calves nudged up against her as they looked for the buckets Blake held. One of them even took two of her fingers in its mouth and started sucking.

"Oh, my." The calf hadn't hurt her and she laughed as she pulled back her hand. "They really are in a feeding frenzy."

Grinning, he nodded. "Just wait."

He showed her how to hold the bucket and she immediately understood what he meant. The calf she was feeding started butting its mouth against the bucket as it sucked on the nipple.

"Why is it doing that?" she asked, frowning.

"It's instinctive," he explained. "Out in the pasture, calves butt their mother's udder to help bring down the milk."

The calves had the buckets drained in no time and Karly couldn't help but wonder if they had to be on a four-hour schedule like human babies. "When will they need to eat again?"

"One of the other guys will feed them again in about twelve hours." He put a couple of flakes of hay in the stall, then washed the buckets and put them into plastic bags. When he finished, he smiled. "So what do you think of your first ranch experience?"

"I can't believe I'm going to say this, but I actually liked taking care of the orphaned calves," she admitted as they walked out of the barn. "They were so cute and when they looked up at me with those big brown eyes, I couldn't help but fall in love with them."

"If I remember correctly, you said something similar to me when we were in Las Vegas," he said, his voice low and intimate.

Karly swallowed hard as she gazed up at him. When they'd met, she had told him how much she loved his eyes. Gazing into the fathomless depths now, she found it hard to look away. Just as in Las Vegas, she felt as if she saw her future in the sexy warmth of his dark brown eyes and it took monumental effort to look away.

Blinking to break the spell, she gave herself a mental shake. That way of thinking was the exact reason she found herself in her current predicament and why she was facing the dissolution of their brief marriage instead of just ending a whirlwind affair.

Forcing herself to remember all the reasons why she had to stand firm in her decisions, she took a deep fortifying breath and attempted to change the subject. "Will my next ranch experience be breakfast?"

He stared at her for several long moments before he pointed toward the foreman's cottage. "While you go inside and wash up, I'll walk over to the bunkhouse and get something for us from the cook." Without another word, he turned and walked toward a building on the other side of the barn.

As she watched him go, Karly knew she should leave the ranch as soon as she could load the car. But she also knew she wasn't going to do that. For reasons she didn't want to think about, she felt compelled to stay with Blake until the strike was settled. Maybe it was due to the fact that she really didn't relish the idea of driving such a long distance. But more likely, it was the fact that every time she looked into his warm brown eyes she lost every ounce of sense she possessed.

Turning, she slowly walked to the house. Staying with him wasn't smart and she anticipated more than a few awkward moments over the course of the next several days. But with few other options open to her and a budget that couldn't really withstand a long stay in a hotel, she really didn't have much choice.

Now all she had to do was be strong and resist

falling under his spell again. Unfortunately, that might prove to be a monumental challenge, considering that it only took a look from him for her to feel as if she would melt.

When Blake finished saddling the gentle buckskin mare, he glanced over at Karly, who was sitting on a bale of hay by the tack-room door. She looked about as nervous as a long-tailed cat in a room full of rocking chairs. All through breakfast, she had questioned him about riding a horse. She'd wanted to know what would happen in a number of situations—all of which were highly unlikely.

She'd looked so darned cute as she interrogated him about riding that it had been all he could do to keep his hands to himself. But as much as he'd like to take her in his arms and reacquaint himself with his wife's sweet taste, he resisted the temptation. Papers had been signed and it was just a matter of time before she went her way and he went his.

Besides, giving into his need for Karly wasn't going to get him any closer to finding out what had changed her mind about them. That's why he was going to do his best to ignore the fact that she still turned him on like no other woman ever had and concentrate on showing her the beauty of his ranch and the wonderful life they could have shared. In the bargain, he hoped to learn more about the woman he'd married and would soon let go.

"Karly, this is Suede," he said, forcing himself to

smile as he led the mare over to where she sat. "She'll be your horse for as long as you're here at the ranch."

"She's awfully tall," Karly said, slowly rising to her feet. He noticed she was careful to keep him between herself and the gentle mare.

Trying not to laugh, he handed Karly the reins. "While you two get acquainted, I'm going to saddle Boomer."

"You're going to leave me alone with her?" she asked, sounding alarmed.

"Trust me, Karly," he said, trying to make his tone as reassuring as possible. "If I thought there was even the slightest chance you would get hurt, I wouldn't let you get anywhere near this horse." Before he could stop himself, he reached out to cup her cheek with his palm. "I promise you'll be just fine, sweetheart."

As she continued to stare up at him, he felt the ever so slight sway of her body toward his. That was all it took to send his good intentions right out the window and before he could stop himself, he leaned forward to cover Karly's mouth with his. Soft and every bit as perfect as he remembered, her lips molded to his and when her mouth parted on a soft sigh, Blake's heart took off like a racehorse out of the starting gate. He couldn't have stopped himself from deepening the kiss if his life depended on it.

Tracing her lips with his tongue, he slipped inside to reacquaint himself with her silky inner recesses. Every one of his senses sharpened and his lower body came to full arousal faster than he thought was humanly possible. Her taste and the tiny moan that she couldn't quite stifle caused him to groan with frustration. They were in a barn holding a horse by the reins. Not exactly the ideal situation to start something he knew damn well he wouldn't finish anyway.

When he felt himself fighting the urge to pull her into his arms and kiss her until they were both utterly senseless, he dropped his hand and took a step back. "You trust me, don't you?"

Apparently as stunned by the intimate moment as he had been and just as reluctant to comment on that kiss, she stared at him for several long moments before she finally nodded. "Y-yes. But if you're wrong about me and this horse, I swear I'll come back and haunt you."

He laughed out loud as much to relieve the tension gripping him as at the humor of her threat. Her quick wit was one of the things that he'd found so damn attractive about her. And he took her humor now as a good sign; she was becoming more relaxed with him again.

"If you want to score points with Suede, scratch her forehead and talk to her," he said as he turned to go get Boomer out of his stall. When he returned, he was glad to see Karly had graduated to patting the mare's neck.

"I think we've come to an understanding," Karly announced as Blake saddled the gelding. "I'm not going to upset her."

When she paused, he smiled. "It sounds to me like you've worked things out."

Nodding, she added, "We're both going to blame you if I do make the mistake of doing something she finds offensive."

"Now, why doesn't that surprise me?" he asked, grinning as he led Boomer over to where she and the mare stood.

"Probably because you're the one insisting that I have to ride a horse," Karly retorted as he handed the gelding's reins for her to hold as well as the mare's.

"Wh-what are…you doing?" she asked, her voice filled with panic once again.

"Don't worry, Boomer is just as well behaved as Suede," he called over his shoulder as he entered the tack room to get a rifle. They didn't have a lot of trouble with predators, but it was always wise to take protection along on a ride just in case.

"Just remember—"

"I know," he interrupted, returning to where she and the horses stood. "If something happens it's all my fault and you're going to haunt me for the rest of my days." He couldn't help but chuckle as he slid the rifle into the tooled leather scabbard attached to Boomer's saddle, then took the reins from her to lead the horses out of the barn to the round pen. "I guess it's fortunate for all concerned that I'm a damn good teacher."

"It's nice that you're humble about it, as well," she said, grinning.

Tying Boomer's reins to the top rail of the round pen, Blake turned to face Karly. "No brag, sweetheart. It's just a fact." He nodded toward the mare. "Now let's get you up in the saddle so you can start learning how to ride."

Her apprehension was apparent when she put her boot in the stirrup. But her expression changed to relief when she shook her head and lowered her foot to the ground. "This isn't going to work."

"Why not?" he asked, wondering what excuse she was going to come up with this time.

"I can't possibly climb up into the saddle with my knee under my chin," she said, shaking her head. "I guess you'll have to ride up to the pasture alone."

"That's an easy fix," he said, moving to stand behind her. "While you pull yourself up by the saddle horn, I'll give you a boost."

The offer had been an innocent one, but when he placed his hand on her delightful bottom to help lift her, he felt like the world came to a screeching halt. The feel of her body nestled in his palm sent his hormones racing through his veins like the steel bearings in a pinball machine.

He quickly helped her up into the saddle, stepped back and took a deep breath. Had he lost what little sense he had left? He wasn't looking for anything more to come from her visit to the ranch than finding out what had changed in the few days after they parted in Las Vegas. He was still recovering from his first heartbreak. No way did he want to start something new with Karly. So, considering the effect she still had on him, he'd do well to keep any kind of physical contact between them to a minimum.

If he hadn't known that before, he sure as hell did after that kiss and that touch.

"Dear Lord, I'm a lot farther off the ground than I thought I'd be," Karly said, her voice a little shaky.

"A little taller than that pony at the grocery store opening?" Blake asked, thankful for the distraction from his wayward thoughts.

"That would be like comparing a two-story house to the Seattle Space Needle," she retorted.

He chuckled and handed her the reins, then, taking hold of the mare's bridle, he led the gentle animal through the round pen's gate. "Just relax and move with her," he instructed as he stroked the horse's tawny neck. He showed Karly how to rest her boots in the stirrups with the heels down and the toes pointed slightly outward. "And when you feel comfortable enough, loosen the death grip you have on the saddle horn."

She shook her head doubtfully. "That's easy for you to say. You have both feet firmly on the ground. You're not the one sitting up here looking down at how far you're going to fall."

Blake grinned as he started leading Suede around the perimeter of the round pen. "Do you honestly think I'd let you fall and not catch you?"

Karly nibbled on her lower lip, causing him to bite back a groan. "I believe you would try. But what if you couldn't react fast enough? Or I was too heavy for you to hold on to?"

He frowned as he glanced up at her. "Did you see anything slow about my reflexes when you watched me ride bulls in Vegas?"

"Well, no…but—"

"Then why do you think I'd miss doing something as important as catching you if you fell?" he asked. "And for the record, I've been tossing around bales of hay that weigh more than you do every day since I was fourteen or fifteen years old. The day you're too heavy for me to catch is the day they bury me."

"But what if—"

"You can't let all of the what-ifs in life hold you back, Karly," he interrupted. He let go of the mare's bridle and continued to walk beside her as they made another trip around the inside of the round pen. "If you don't take a chance once in a while, you're just marking time. You're not living."

It was something his grandfather had always told him and Blake firmly believed it was true. It was one of the reasons he'd been so quick to ask Karly to marry him. He'd known what he wanted and he'd made her his. It was also the reason behind him asking her to stay at the ranch while he tried to find out why she'd been hell-bent on divorcing him. He might not like what was behind her abrupt decision, but at least he'd know for sure why she'd decided he wasn't the one for her.

Karly stared at him for several long moments. They both knew he was talking about more than her riding a horse. But she didn't seem willing to talk about it and he wasn't going to press her on the issue just yet.

Smiling, she finally shrugged. "If I didn't step out of my comfort zone once in a while, I wouldn't be on this horse now, would I?"

"And you're doing a great job of riding her on your own, too," he commented, holding up both hands to show her she was riding the mare independently.

"Oh, dear Lord!" From the look on Karly's pretty face, he knew she was a hair's breadth away from all-out panic.

"Don't freak out," he said calmly. "I haven't been leading Suede since the first trip around the pen and you've done just fine." When they reached the gate, he opened it and stepped out to untie Boomer while the mare continued to walk slowly around the inside of the pen.

"B-Blake?"

"I'm just going to get Boomer so I can ride beside you," he reassured her. Swinging up into the saddle, he guided the gelding into the pen and caught up with Karly and Suede as they made another trip around the inside. "There are a few more things I want to show you, then we'll be ready to leave the round pen and start the ride up to the pasture."

"Are you sure that's a good idea?" Karly asked. "I'd hate to have to spend eternity haunting you."

"I'll take my chances on that, sweetheart," he said, laughing.

As he showed her how to guide Suede by doing nothing more than touching the reins to either side of the mare's neck, he noticed that Karly began to relax. She sat looser in the saddle and actually started moving with the mare instead of remaining as stiff as a ramrod.

On the third trip around the inside of the circular fence, Blake nodded toward the open gate ahead. "It's time we take this show on the road."

Karly looked doubtful. "I really don't think—"

"Good idea," he said, grinning. "Don't think. Just do it."

When they rode the horses out of the round pen, he could tell by the tightening around her mouth that Karly was anything but confident. But he admired her willingness to give riding a try. He just wished she had shown that kind of consideration to giving their marriage a chance.

By the time she and Blake reached the pasture where the herd of steers had spent the summer, Karly was feeling a little more sure of herself. Suede had proved to be as docile as Blake had promised and once Karly relaxed in the saddle, riding the mare wasn't bad at all.

"Are these mountains part of the Rockies?" she asked, gazing at the splendor of the high mountain meadow.

"Yup. The Laramie Mountain range is part of the eastern edge of the Rockies," he answered, stopping his horse to look at the black cattle on the other side of the river that wound through the valley.

When she looked over at him inspecting the animals, she realized that he'd been right not to give up his way of life to move to Seattle with her. Blake Hartwell wasn't a man who was meant to be a city dweller. She could tell he loved living on this ranch, loved watching over the animals in his care. He was as deliciously rugged as this beautiful land and she couldn't imagine him living anywhere else.

As she continued to admire the man who had swept her off her feet eight months ago, she spotted the butt of a gun attached to his saddle that she hadn't noticed before. A sudden thought had her looking cautiously at the tree line surrounding the vast clearing. "Are there grizzly bears in the region?"

Grinning, he shook his head. "Black bear, mountain lion and bobcat, but no grizzlies."

All three species were prominent in the mountains surrounding Seattle and normally black bears and bobcats weren't overly aggressive unless startled or if they were being protective of their young. Although she was extremely cautious when she was in an area where they were known to be, she wasn't as concerned by them as she was by the mention of mountain lions. They were an entirely different matter. They were more aggressive and so silent, one could be within a few feet and a person might never realize the animal was there until it pounced.

Blake must have realized she was worried about the predators that might be close by. “Don’t worry, the big cats and bears in the area don’t normally wander down from the higher elevations unless there’s a drought or a shortage of the game they prey on.”

“What keeps them from making these cattle their next meal?” Karly asked as she gazed at the herd of steers grazing on the thick prairie grasses.

“Unlike grizzlies, black bears are too opportunistic to bother with hunting larger game,” he explained. “They’ll eat whatever is available—roots, berries, bugs, carrion. They’ll even eat garbage or whatever else they happen to find along the way.”

Karly laughed as she nodded. “They really aren’t very discerning when it comes to what they eat. Sometimes one will come down from the Cascade Mountains into one of the suburbs surrounding Seattle and everyone has to secure their trash cans. If they don’t, they risk having the trash strewn all over their yards show up on the evening news as a warning to others to take precautions.”

“Yeah, bears like an easy meal,” he agreed. “But mountain lions are natural-born hunters. We do have a problem occasionally with one of them straying down here. If we see one or find tracks too close to the herds or ranch buildings, we try to call the Fish and Wildlife Service and they send one of the game wardens to deal with a nuisance cat.”

"Do they kill the animal?" Even though the predators scared her outside the confines of a zoo, she hated that something might be killed because it had the misfortune to wander into the wrong place.

To her relief, he shook his head. "Not always. They first try to trap it for relocation to a more remote area. Exterminating the animal is a last resort unless it's known to be a threat to humans or livestock."

"Is that what the gun is for?" she asked, eyeing the hardwood stock sticking out of the leather holder. "For protection in case one of them becomes a threat to us?"

His expression changed to one of determination as he nodded. "It's always better to be safe than sorry. I told you I'd protect you no matter what and I meant it." He gave her a look that caused her insides to quiver. "I give you my word that as long as there's a breath left in my body, I won't let anything happen to you, Karly."

The intense promise in his dark brown eyes stole her breath and reminded her of the kiss they'd shared in the barn. Neither of them had seemed to want to acknowledge that the chemistry they'd discovered between them in Las Vegas was just as strong, if not stronger, than it had ever been. As she continued to gaze into the fathomless depths of his eyes, she'd never felt as safe and secure in her entire life as she felt at that moment.

They both remained silent for several more moments before they started across the pasture toward the trail that led back down to the ranch. There wasn't a doubt in her mind that he would do whatever it took to protect her from any and all dangers.

Her heart skipped a beat as she thought of how difficult it was becoming to keep him at arm's length. He'd acted just like the husband she'd always dreamed of, even though she'd presented him with divorce papers to end their union. And it was getting harder and harder to remember why it was the best for both of them to go through with the divorce.

She sighed when she glanced at him from the corner of her eye. He might be prepared to protect her from the four-legged predators that could hurt her. But who was going to protect her from the forcc of nature that was Blake Hartwell?

Four

"I told you riding isn't as hard as you thought it would be," Blake said, smiling as he helped Karly dismount the mare.

"I think I need to join a gym," she commented as she patted Suede's neck and moved away from the horse. Karly's wince and the way she walked told him that she'd spent too much time in the saddle for her first time riding.

His smile faded. He could have kicked himself for being an inconsiderate jerk. A new rider needed to condition their thigh and back muscles on shorter rides before they attempted long hours in the saddle. Otherwise they risked soreness much like what someone would expect after a strenuous workout. How could he have been so thoughtless?

He'd been so caught up in showing her the ranch and his way of life, he'd forgotten all about her being new to the experience of being on a horse. Now she was paying the price for his oversight.

"Why don't you go on up to the house and try to relax while I take care of the horses?" he suggested.

"I think I'll take you up on that offer," she said, nodding. She smiled. "I may be out of shape, but you're right about the riding. I can't believe I'm going to say this, but I actually enjoyed myself."

As he watched her turn and walk slowly toward the house, he knew what he would do if they were at the main house. He'd make sure she took a nice long soak in the hot tub, then give her a massage with a good soothing liniment. His body tightened at the thought of once again touching her satiny skin as he ran his hands over her thighs and back. Then he would turn her over and sink himself…

"You're one sorry son of a bitch, Hartwell," he muttered as he brushed down the horses. Karly was hurting from his insistence that she ride a horse and his carelessness about the hours she spent in the saddle. They'd both signed divorce papers that she was eager to file. But all he could do was think about what a pleasure it would be to make love to her again. If that didn't make him a prize jerk, he didn't know what did.

Blake took a deep breath to relieve some of his building tension. She obviously didn't want him touching her that way and if he wanted to preserve what little sanity he had left, he shouldn't want that, either. But as long as he kept his hands to himself, he could drive her over to the ranch house for some time in the hot tub to ease her discomfort.

Of course, that would require introducing her to Silas. Blake wasn't worried about the old guy telling her that Blake was the owner of the Wolf Creek Ranch. He knew that if he asked Silas to keep that information to himself, the old man would take it to his grave before he told a soul. But introducing his soon-to-be ex-wife and then keeping secrets from her was going to add a lot of fuel to the fire of the many lectures Blake would have to endure before Silas found something else he felt compelled to preach about.

With his mind made up, Blake took the saddles and bridles to the tack room, brushed down the horses, then led them back to their stalls. Giving them generous scoops of oats and flakes of hay, he reached for the cell phone clipped to his belt as he left the barn.

"I'm bringing Karly over for supper," Blake said when the old man answered.

"So you decided I'm decent enough to meet your bride after all?" Silas queried, his tone filled with sarcasm. "What changed your mind, boy? Did you finally fess up and tell her you own this spread?"

"You ask a lot of questions," Blake complained.

"Well, I would never find anything out if I didn't," Silas retorted. "So did you tell her?"

"No."

"Tarnation, boy! Why not?" The old man grunted his disgust. "The way I see it, that little gal's got a right to know just who she's hitched up to."

"I told you, I don't want my net worth influencing her decisions," Blake said, irritated that they were having the same argument they'd had every time he'd talked to Silas since Karly arrived on the Wolf Creek.

"Not every woman is as money-grubbin' as that heifer your daddy married or as connivin' as that little tart that tried to rope you into marryin' her by claimin' you were gonna be a daddy," Silas insisted. "All this gal did was take a trip down the aisle with you. And she did it so fast she must not have cared if you had millions or if you were flat broke."

Blake groaned at the mention of the fiasco with the buckle bunny that had taken place several years ago. He didn't like thinking about the hell he'd gone through proving that he wasn't Sara Jane Benson's baby daddy. Just the fact that he'd given the rodeo groupie a reason to accuse him had been bad enough. There were some women a man could have a good time with and then there were the ones that when they came toward him, a man would do well to turn around and run like hell. Sara Jane fell into the latter category.

But he'd been a little drunk that night and pissed off over his stepmother's latest refusal to sell him his family's ranch. He'd regretted his lapse in judgment the following morning, but he'd been fit to be tied when Sara Jane showed up a month later claiming that he'd made her pregnant. When he finally discovered that Sara Jane had lied—that there wasn't a baby and never had been—he didn't think he'd ever been more relieved in his entire life. After he confronted her, the woman had finally admitted it was all a ruse to try to get money from him after she discovered that he wasn't just a dust-covered rodeo rider. But aside from narrowly missing the trap she'd set, the incident had taught Blake a valuable lesson about letting anyone know that his family owned one of the largest private ranches in the state of Wyoming.

"She may have married me fast," Blake finally answered. "But she divorced me just as fast. I'll tell Karly when the time is right."

"When's that gonna be?" Silas persisted. "You know the longer you wait, the bigger the chance of somebody tellin' her for you."

"The chances of that happening are slim," Blake said confidently. "The men have been leaving before daylight to make sure the fences are ready for the herds when we bring them down from the summer pastures. And I know I can count on you not to say anything."

"It ain't my place to tell that little gal," Silas said, sounding affronted that Blake even mentioned the possibility. "But what are you gonna do when you take her over to the Rusty Spur for that barbecue day after tomorrow? What if one of the Laughlins says somethin' about it? What are you gonna do then?"

"I'm going to call Eli and fill him in before we go over there," Blake stated. "Neither Eli or Tori will say a word about it."

He'd given it some thought on his and Karly's ride back to the house and he knew he could trust his friends not to mention that Blake owned the ranch, or pass judgment on him for wanting to keep that fact from Karly. Eli Laughlin and his wife, Tori, had their own unorthodox tale of how they'd met and married, not to mention the obstacles due to secrets of Tori's past and Eli's trust issues that they'd had to work through.

Tired of arguing with the old cowboy, Blake decided it was time to bring the conversation to an end. "Go ahead and set the table. We'll be over in about fifteen minutes."

Ending the call before Silas could come up with more of his endless questions, Blake took a deep breath. He might be irritating as hell, but Silas was right. Karly had married him because she wanted to, not because she thought she could get something from him. And even though they were headed for a divorce, it was becoming more difficult to defend his stance on not telling her.

A sudden thought stopped him dead in his tracks. Could she have rejected him and their marriage because she thought just the opposite about him? When she got back to Seattle, had she decided that he didn't make enough money to support her and the kids he had hoped they would one day have?

Blake shook his head as he climbed the back steps and started into the house. Either way, he needed to find out what her reasoning had been for ending things with him. Once he knew that, he could put this marriage fiasco behind him. Until then, he'd simply wait and see what he could find out.

When Blake drove his truck up the asphalted driveway toward the huge log lodge, Karly caught her breath at the sheer size and beauty of it. "This is absolutely gorgeous," she said, falling in love with the way the home and the rugged landscape complemented each other so perfectly. No other style of house would have looked as natural with the vastness of the land surrounding it. "Can you imagine living in a place like this?"

"You like it?" he asked, staring straight ahead as he parked his truck in front of the porte cochere covering the entrance to the house. Made with the same huge logs as the main structure, it provided shelter from the weather as well as added to the grandeur of the home.

"Who wouldn't love this?" she asked, noticing a small waterfall cascading over boulders not far from the stacked stone steps. It emptied into a little pool by the bottom step and looked so natural that it took a moment for her to realize it was man-made.

"Everything about it is perfect." She frowned. "But shouldn't we be going through the back entrance?"

"Why would we do that?" he asked, sounding confused.

"It's not like we're invited guests," she said, shaking her head. "The owner—"

"He isn't staying here right now and even if he was, he wouldn't care." He grinned as if finding something humorous about her question. "He's a pretty easygoing guy."

She had a hard time believing anyone would want an employee and his guest taking advantage of their good nature. "And you're sure he won't mind us just walking in like we own the place?"

He laughed and shook his head as he got out of the truck and walked around to help her down from the cab. "Take my word for it, sweetheart. He doesn't have any problem at all with us making ourselves at home while we're visiting the main house."

When he lifted her from the truck seat and set her on her feet, he kept his hands resting at her waist as he gazed into her eyes. Her breath caught and her pulse sped up. He was going to kiss her again and heaven help her, she wanted him to do just that.

Mesmerized by the heated light in his incredible brown eyes, she could only watch as he slowly began to lower his head. But just when she thought his lips would cover hers, he took a step back and smiled down at her. "Silas is expecting us."

Not entirely certain whether she was disappointed

or relieved that he hadn't kissed her, she blinked. "Silas?"

He nodded. "I think I'd better warn you," he said as he put his arm around her and guided her toward the steps. "The housekeeper here is ornery, opinionated and downright disagreeable at times. But the old cuss has a heart of gold and if he thought you needed it, he'd give you the shirt off his back."

"Does he know…about us?" she asked hesitantly. She'd only told a couple of her friends at work about what had taken place on her Las Vegas vacation. But he hadn't mentioned telling anyone.

Blake nodded. "Keeping anything from Silas Burrows is damn near impossible. But don't worry. He's won't say a word to you about it, unless you bring it up."

She doubted that would happen, but she forgot all about her concerns or the housekeeper's opinion when they reached the entrance doors. Hand-carved images of black bears and pine trees overlaid the glass and added to the appeal of the lodge.

But when Blake opened the door and they stepped into the foyer, Karly couldn't believe the rustic beauty of the home. "This isn't just a log home, it's a mansion," she said as they walked into the great room.

With a vaulted ceiling and massive fireplace made of river rock, the room had a surprisingly cozy feel for such a large space. But when she noticed the panoramic view of the mountains through the wall of windows on the opposite side of the room, it felt as if the room opened up to the landscape beyond.

"Do you like it?" Blake asked.

She nodded in awe as she continued to look around the room. Even the interior walls were made of logs. "It's gorgeous."

"I'll give you the grand tour after supper," he said, smiling as if her approval pleased him.

"I'd like that." As an afterthought, she added, "As long as you don't think the owner would mind."

"Not at all." Blake's sexy grin sent a shiver up her spine. "Trust me, he'll be fine with it."

"Supper's ready and if you want it hot you two better get in here."

Turning, Karly spotted an older man who looked like every child's favorite jolly old elf. On the portly side, his thick hair and long, full beard were snow-white and although he wore jeans, his green suspenders and long-sleeved red shirt would have convinced young and old alike that he might very well be Santa Claus.

As they walked toward him, Blake made the introductions. "Karly, this is Silas Burrows."

"It's nice to meet you, Mr. Burrows," Karly said, extending her hand.

He stared at her for several moments before he gave her a wide grin as he shook her hand. "Just call me Silas or Si." He motioned for her and Blake to follow him. "I fixed beef stew and sourdough bread for supper. It ain't fancy, but it's hot and there's plenty of it."

"If it tastes half as good as it smells, I'm sure it's going to be delicious," she said when they entered the kitchen and the smell of baking bread and the rich aroma from the bubbling pot on the state-of-the-art range assailed her senses. "Is there anything I can do to help you finish getting it ready?"

Silas shook his head. "Not really much left to do. While I slice the bread, I'm gonna let Blake pour us all glasses of iced tea and we'll be ready to eat."

After Blake guided her over to the large oak table across the room and held her chair for her to sit down, he whispered close to her ear, "It looks like you've got a fan."

"What do you mean?" she asked, barely able to keep from shivering when his warm breath feathered over her sensitive skin.

"I haven't seen Silas grin this much since the former owner's second wife sold the ranch to his son," he said, nibbling a kiss along the column of her neck as if it was the most natural thing in the world for him to do.

Startled by his show of affection, her heart pounded against her ribs and she tried not to think about what it might mean as he crossed the kitchen to pour their drinks. To distract herself, she looked around. She loved to cook when she had the opportunity and someone to cook for. Unfortunately, that only happened a few times a year—usually when she and her coworkers had a potluck lunch at the office. But if she had a kitchen like this one, she might be tempted to cook more. All of the appliances were commercial grade and top-of-the-line. And she absolutely loved the spaciousness and convenience of the entire room's layout. Cooking, even if it was just for herself, would be a joy in a kitchen like this.

As the two men finished putting the food on the table, Karly suddenly realized just how hungry she was. She and Blake had had an early lunch before her riding lesson and trip to the upper pasture. Glancing at the digital display on the microwave, she was surprised to see that had been almost seven hours earlier.

When both men brought the food and iced tea to the table, Silas filled their plates with thick stew. Seating himself, he pointed to her plate with his fork. "You'd better eat up, gal. There's more where that come from." He grinned. "And I made a chocolate cake for dessert."

"I'll be sure to save room for a piece," Karly said, picking up her fork. "I love chocolate."

Smiling, Silas nodded. "Most women do."

"How would you know what women like?" Blake asked, frowning.

Silas grunted. "Just why do you think men give women chocolates on Valentine's Day, hotshot?"

"I don't ever remember you having a girlfriend," Blake said, sounding doubtful.

Silas shook his head. "Don't go thinkin' I didn't

have my pick of the women in my day, boy. I used to be quite the lady's man about forty years back."

Karly couldn't help but laugh as she listened to the good-natured banter. It was like a game of verbal one-upmanship and she could tell the two men thought the world of each other. Blake treated Silas like a favorite uncle or beloved grandfather and it was clear the old gentleman cared just as much for him.

By the time the meal was over and Silas served them all slices of the chocolate cake, Karly couldn't remember the last time she'd laughed as much. "You two are hilarious. How long have you known each other?"

"I've known him and his brother since the day they were born," Silas said, taking a bite of cake.

"You have a brother?" Karly asked, turning to Blake. He hadn't mentioned having a sibling. But then they hadn't really talked about family, or much of anything in their lives, when they were in Las Vegas.

He nodded. "Sean's a couple of years older than me."

"Does he live close by?" she asked, wondering what it would be like to have someone who shared the same memories of family and growing up. Being an only child, she'd never experienced that and she couldn't help but feel that she'd missed out on something meaningful.

"Sean has a ranch about twenty miles to the

north—on the other side of the mountain," he answered as he took their empty plates to the sink.

"That must have been nice, having someone to play with when you were little," she said, unable to keep from feeling wistful about it. "I always wanted a sister or brother, but I guess it wasn't meant to be."

While Silas loaded the dishwasher, Blake poured them each a cup of coffee and rejoined her at the table. "I take it you are an only child?"

"Back in December, we didn't get around to talking about family," she admitted, nodding.

He eyed her over the rim of his coffee cup for several long moments before he set it on the table and reached to cover her hand with his. "There were a lot of things we should have discussed, but didn't."

The feel of his warm calloused palm covering her hand made her feel heated all over and she found herself longing for the way things might have been between them. Before she could give in to that longing and do something she shouldn't, she pushed her chair back. "I…suppose I should help Silas with the dishes," she said, needing to put distance between her and Blake in order to regain her perspective.

She hadn't traveled all this way to rekindle what they'd shared in Vegas. She'd come to put an end to it once and for all. But unlike the certainty she'd felt in Seattle when she'd first made the decision, the thought of ending it after this lovely visit made her want to cry and she wasn't entirely certain why.

But when she started to rise from the chair, her

thigh muscles were so stiff and sore, her legs threatened to fail her. "I shouldn't have sat that long," she said, slowly getting to her feet.

"That's another reason I wanted to bring you over here," he said, starting to lead her into the great room. "You'll feel better after some time in the hot tub."

Karly stopped to stare at him. "Blake, are you out of your mind? I can't get in the hot tub."

He looked thoroughly confused. "Why not?"

"For one thing, I don't have anything to wear." She motioned toward the double glass doors leading from the great room to the stone patio beyond. "And for another, I know the owner of this place may be good-natured, but I'm sure he would draw the line at having someone he doesn't know taking a dip in his hot tub."

"Trust me, sweetheart, he won't care," Blake said, guiding her out of the house toward the in-ground pool and spa. "I have free rein here, which means you do, too. You can slip out of your clothes and soak for a while in the hot tub and no one will be the wiser."

"I'm not going to go skinny-dipping in a stranger's spa," she said, looking around as they walked outside. If the owner had a hot tub, she certainly couldn't find it.

The sun had already gone down and the lights around the stone patio and pool made it look as if they were standing on the edge of a tropical lagoon. At one end, a waterfall cascaded down a huge natural-looking rock formation into the pool. But when she looked closer, she realized that the hot tub was set behind the curtain of water, as if it was inside a hidden cave.

He pointed toward the waterfall. "It's completely private. And I promise it will help to soothe your aching muscles."

Relief from the stiffness in her thighs and lower back did sound like heaven. "The owner—"

"Won't mind at all," he interrupted. He grabbed a couple of bath sheets that were sitting on a lounge chair they passed on the way to the waterfall.

"Where did those come from?" she asked, beginning to realize he had this planned all along.

"I laid them out when we first got here," he answered, looking smug. "It was while you were surveying the kitchen."

"You had this planned when you invited me up here for dinner," she accused.

He nodded and grinned. "Now take your clothes off and hop in."

Five

When Karly continued to glare at him, Blake frowned. "What?"

"I'm not taking my clothes off in front of you," she said, stubbornly crossing her arms beneath her breasts.

He tried not to remember how perfectly those breasts fit in the palms of his hands or how responsive her nipples were when he teased them with the pads of his thumbs. Obviously, he hadn't considered the full effect of the temptation she'd present when he'd come up with this hot-tub idea.

"Why not?" he asked, grinning and putting aside thoughts of her lovely breasts. "We did a lot more than just take our clothes off in Vegas and I don't remember either one of us having a problem with that."

If looks could kill, she would have dropped him right there where he stood. "That was different," she insisted.

He raised one eyebrow. "How do you figure?"

"We were married."

He shook his head. "Not at first we weren't. If you'll remember I ran into you in the hotel lobby in Vegas on Monday morning just as you were arriving to check in." He smiled. "And I made love to you for the first time that night. We didn't get married until the following Saturday night."

"That was a long time ago," she said softly.

"Not really." Reaching out, he cupped her soft cheek with his palm. "Sweetheart, we're still married and I'm still your husband until a judge says I'm not. There's no reason for you to feel shy with me."

Her expression softened a little, but she was apparently going to stand her ground. "We haven't been together in over eight months, Blake." She shook her head. "And in three months we'll be divorced."

There was a sadness in her eyes that he hadn't expected. Was she regretting her decision?

The notion that she might be having second thoughts caused a hitch in his breathing and he didn't want to consider why. But he immediately abandoned the likelihood that she had changed her mind again. Just because she might be sorry for what had—or more accurately hadn't—taken place after they left Las Vegas, didn't mean anything. In light of the choices she'd made and the way things had turned out, he had his own doubts that it would have worked out between them, as well.

Fighting to keep from lowering his head to kiss her slightly parted lips, Blake dropped his hand to his side. "Follow me. There's an entrance at the side of the waterfall. Going in that way will keep you from getting your hair wet." Once they entered the secluded area, he flipped a switch, turning off the underwater lights in the custom-made, sunken tub. "You can put your clothes over there to keep them dry," he said, motioning toward a lounge chair a couple of feet away. Turning his back to her, he added, "Let me know when I can turn around."

"I still can't believe your boss won't have a problem with someone using his hot tub without permission," she said.

He started to tell her she was beginning to sound like a parrot, but the words lodged somewhere between his vocal cords and open mouth when he heard the rustle of clothing being removed a moment before her jeans and T-shirt landed on the end of the lounge chair. Blake swallowed hard. Then he took a deep breath when her lacy panties and bra landed on top of the pile. Just knowing she was as naked as the day she was born and standing right behind him was enough to send his blood pressure sky-high.

The sound of her stepping into the spa caused sweat to pop out on his forehead. He hadn't anticipated remembering how he'd sipped water droplets from her satiny skin when they'd showered together. He gritted his teeth and tried desperately to think of anything but how her lithe wet body had felt against his.

"Oh, dear heavens that feels good," Karly said, her tone appreciative. As if it was an afterthought, she added, "You can turn around now."

Thankful that he had switched off the submerged lights to keep her from seeing the obvious evidence of how she still affected him, Blake sat down on the side of the lounge chair and took his time pulling off his boots and socks. Maybe if he gave himself a few minutes before he got into the water with her, he could get a grip on his suddenly nonexistent control.

When he stood up to unbuckle his belt and release the button at the waistband of his jeans, he thought he heard her moan softly. "Are you all right?" he asked, unzipping his fly to shove his jeans and boxer briefs down his legs.

He couldn't help but chuckle when Karly sent a little wave of water over the rock edge of the tub as she quickly whirled around to look away from where he was undressing. "I-I'm just…amazed at how wonderful this warm water feels."

"I think you'll have to agree, the hot tub was a good idea," he said, knowing that wasn't the real reason behind her moan.

But he kept that knowledge to himself. Pointing out that she was no more immune to him now than she had been in Las Vegas would only put her on the defensive and prevent him from learning why she had changed her mind about them.

By the time he had removed his clothes, he felt a little more in control of his body. So he walked over to the side of the heated spa and stepped into the bubbling water. Lowering himself to the stone seat beside her, he closed his eyes and took a deep breath as the soothing, heated water swirled around them. Just knowing that her nude body was only inches away from his was playing hell with his good intentions.

"This is an unusual hot tub," she commented. "I don't think I've ever seen one made out of stones. It looks so natural."

Nodding, he opened his eyes. "The owner told some pool designer what he wanted and the guy made it happen."

"Well, whoever the designer was, he did a wonderful job." She looked toward the curtain of water separating the hidden room from the pool. "This feels like we're in a tropical paradise."

"I'm pretty sure that was the plan," Blake said, smiling.

Her appreciation for his home and for the attention to detail that he'd put into it pleased him more than he would have thought. The fact that he had wanted to share it with her for the rest of their lives made her approval bittersweet.

Deciding it was a good time to get a few answers

about why she'd changed her mind about them, he asked, "Have you always lived in Seattle?"

She turned her head to give him a puzzled look. "Where did that question come from?"

"Just wondering," he said, shrugging. He didn't want to give her the impression she was being interrogated. And asking her the questions he hadn't asked in Vegas would be a good way to keep his mind away from thoughts of her nude body.

"To satisfy your curiosity, I was born in New York City and with the exception of living in a small town in the Midwest for a few years, I was raised there," she said, answering his question. "From what you said about going to school in Eagle Fork, I assume you've always lived around here?"

He nodded. "Yup. And I take it the pony ride happened while you lived in the small town."

"Yes." She laughed. "I don't think I've ever heard of a market in Manhattan that has pony rides during their grand opening."

"Why did your family move from the city?" he asked, making sure to keep his tone from sounding too interested.

"My father was an industrial engineer and the company he worked for sent him to study and improve the productivity of one of their manufacturing plants." She stared at the waterfall. "He loved it in the Midwest, but my mother hated it."

"What about you?" he asked. "How did you feel about it?"

"To tell you the truth, I was really too young to have much of an opinion one way or the other," she commented. "And when my mother decided she'd had enough of small-town life, she took me back to New York and that was that."

"Your parents divorced?" he asked gently.

She nodded. "Unfortunately, I only saw my father a couple of times after we moved. He was killed in a car accident within a year after the divorce."

Without a second thought, Blake put his arm around her bare shoulders and pulled her to his side. "I'm sorry, Karly. I know how hard that is on a kid. I lost my mom when I was ten."

"I was only six when he died and all I really remember about him was that he worked a lot and he took me for ice cream more than my mother wanted him to," she said, her voice somber. He could tell it bothered her that she couldn't remember the man who helped to give her life.

"Dads have a tendency to do things moms would rather they didn't," he said, chuckling. "I remember one time my mom gave my dad a hard time for taking my brother and me to Cheyenne Frontier Days and letting us eat so many corn dogs and so much cotton candy that we were sick for two days."

"My mother wasn't as afraid that I'd get sick as she was that I would gain weight," she explained. "Martina Ewing was an editor for one of the premier fashion magazines before we moved to the Midwest and she was determined that I would be in the industry, as well." She shook her head. "It never occurred to her that I might want to do something else with my life."

"Did your mother resume her career when you returned to New York?" hc asked when she fell silent. He sensed there might be something about her parents splitting up that was relevant to their marriage situation. He just couldn't put his finger on what it was.

"She tried going back, but she'd been out of the loop long enough that she'd lost her place in the industry," Karly answered. "She blamed my dad for the loss of her career and never forgave him for it."

They both fell silent for a few minutes and Blake knew beyond a shadow of a doubt that her parents' marital problems had been a big influence on Karly. He wasn't sure exactly how it had factored into her decision to pursue a divorce, but he had every intention of finding out.

As he sat there pondering her reasoning, one thing became very apparent. He was sitting in a bubbling hot tub with her soft, nude body pressed closely to his. The lighted waterfall cast a dim glow into the tiny room, which only added to the intimacy of the moment. His reaction was not only predictable, but it was also inevitable.

With only a fleeting thought to the consequences, Blake pulled Karly closer and lowered his head. The feel of her water-slickened body rubbing against his was enough to send him into orbit, but the moment their mouths touched, a smoldering heat filled his lower belly and quickly sent liquid fire streaking through his veins. He briefly wondered how he could burn to a cinder while sitting in a tub of water.

When she sighed and brought her arms up to encircle his neck, it didn't even occur to him to resist deepening the kiss, and as he stroked her tongue with his, her sweet taste and eager response only heightened the need building inside of him. It was like nothing had changed since they were in Vegas. He was as hot for her now as he had been then. And he could tell she wanted him just as much.

Unfortunately, his timing was lousy. Making love to her right now could very well scare her into leaving the ranch without him getting to the bottom of what went wrong between them. Besides, he wasn't prepared to protect her. He hadn't come to the hot tub with seduction on his mind. And an unplanned pregnancy now would only add another wrinkle to an already complicated situation.

Easing away from the kiss, Blake held her close as he took several deep breaths. His hormones were racing through him like a herd of mustangs at a wild horse roundup and knowing there were no barriers between his body and hers wasn't making his decision to pull away any easier.

"It's probably time we got out of the hot tub and headed back to the foreman's cottage," he said half-heartedly.

"I—I think…you're right," she said, sounding just as reluctant as he felt.

Leaning back, he stared into her incredible blue eyes. "Karly, what…" He stopped and cleared his throat to keep from asking her what went wrong with them. Instead he declared, "I'll get out and get dressed first. Then I'll wait for you out by the pool."

"That's a good idea," she agreed. "Thank you."

Damning his nobility, Blake got out of the hot tub before he could change his mind, quickly toweled himself dry and got dressed. Picking up his boots and socks, he made it a point not to look back at Karly, who was still sitting in the spa as he left the man-made cave. If he had looked back, he wasn't sure he would have been able to walk away.

As he sat down on the foot of one of the lounge chairs by the pool to pull on his socks and boots, Blake told himself he was doing the right thing—that making love to Karly again would only make things worse when he watched her drive away in a few days. But that reasoning didn't do a thing to lessen the need for her that still burned in his gut.

Rising to his feet, he took a deep breath. He might as well face facts. He wanted her—had never stopped wanting her. If he hadn't known that before, he sure as hell did now.

He rubbed the tension at the back of his neck. He could see a lot of cold showers in his near future and the first one would be tonight—as soon as they returned to the foreman's cottage.

* * *

"Blake, I think I'll leave to make the drive to Lincoln County after we have breakfast tomorrow morning," Karly said as he drove the truck away from the log mansion.

"I thought we had that settled," he said, staring straight ahead. "You were going to wait until the strike was done and fly to Spokane."

"I just think it would be for the best," she said, unwilling to admit out loud that she was in real danger of falling under his spell once again.

Sitting in the hot tub next to him, having him put his arm around her and feeling his naked body against hers had almost been her undoing. Even though she hadn't been able to see much in the dim light of the little cave housing the hot tub, her memory had filled in the blanks. In her mind, she had seen every well-defined muscle, every plane and valley of his impressive physique. Remembering how his strong arms had held her so securely and how gently he made love to her was overwhelming, and she shivered as a wave of desire coursed through every part of her.

"I know I shouldn't have kissed you." He took a deep breath and added, "Either in the barn or tonight in the hot tub. But it felt right and I'll be damned if I'm going to apologize for it."

She couldn't in good conscience allow him to shoulder all of the blame. "You wouldn't have kissed me if I hadn't let you."

His deep chuckle sent heat pulsing through her veins. "Yeah, I noticed you weren't protesting."

"That's the problem." She sighed. "I should have."

He glanced over at her. "Why didn't you?"

"I...wanted you to kiss me," she admitted.

"But you didn't want to want me kissing you." It wasn't a question.

"No."

"Sweetheart, a wife wanting her husband to kiss her is allowed," he said, reaching over to take her hand in his. The moment their palms touched a delightful tingling sensation streaked up her arm.

She did her best to ignore it and tried to focus on what he'd said. "That's the problem, Blake. Three months from now we'll be divorced. I shouldn't want you kissing me, not anymore."

He gave her hand a gentle squeeze. "Have you asked yourself why you do?"

His question took her by surprise. But as she tried to think of an answer, she decided it probably wasn't wise to delve too deeply into the reason behind her wanting his affection. If she did, she was certain she wouldn't be all that comfortable with the answer.

"You're only going to be here a few more days, Karly," he said pragmatically. "And I give you my word that nothing is going to happen between us unless that's what you want. But I'm not going to lie to you and tell you it isn't what I want."

As he drove the truck up the lane to the foreman's

cottage, Karly thought about what Blake had said. What *did* she want?

Eight months ago, she'd been confident she was making the right decision when she'd said yes to his marriage proposal. She had been certain at the time she married him that she loved Blake and wanted them to spend the rest of their lives together. But when she'd returned to Seattle her practical side had taken over. That's when she'd known ending things was the right call—for both of them.

She'd questioned falling in love with him so quickly and feared that their feelings for each other might not last. Then she'd thought about her parents. Her mother had been in love with her father, but in the end it hadn't been enough for her. She'd become bitter and resentful, and Karly had borne the brunt of that bitterness.

Karly loved her own career as an import buyer—loved the travel to foreign countries—and feared that love might not be enough for her, either, if she had to give up all of that. Had she been wrong about her feelings for her job? Could she have been happy being the wife of a ranch foreman in a remote part of Wyoming when all she'd ever known was living in a city with conveniences just steps from her apartment door?

She'd been so sure of everything when she left Seattle to come to the ranch for him to sign the new set of divorce papers. But then she'd seen him—

stayed with him, had him treat her like his wife—and the doubts about her decision had set in.

She might have been able to keep things in perspective if she hadn't been stranded on the ranch by the airport workers' strike. She'd have gone back to Washington, filed the papers for the dissolution of their marriage and resumed her career with the confidence she was doing the right thing.

The trouble had come from seeing him again, being in his arms and experiencing the magic of his kiss. It all reminded her of what she'd wanted when she'd walked down that aisle in Vegas—what she was giving up—and had her questioning herself at every turn.

Had there been serious flaws in her reasoning? By insisting they continue with the divorce was she making the biggest mistake of her life? Would he even give her a second chance if she did want for them to try to make their marriage work?

Karly glanced over at Blake when he parked the truck beside the foreman's cottage. The way he held her—kissed her—he seemed open to rekindling what they'd found together in Las Vegas. But he hadn't once mentioned wanting her to change her mind. He'd even signed the divorce papers without a word of protest or even the slightest hesitation.

She sighed when he got out of the truck and she waited for him to walk around to open the passenger door. She wasn't nearly as sure of everything as she'd been when she arrived here. And the only way she was going to determine what was best would be to stay with Blake on the ranch and give herself the time to sort it all out.

Six

On Sunday morning when Blake walked back into the foreman's cottage after getting their breakfast from the bunkhouse cook, Karly was seated at the table waiting for him. "I thought you'd still be asleep," he said as he set the containers of food on the kitchen island.

"My phone woke me," she said, her tone pensive. He noticed her tightly clasped hands resting on the table in front of her. Her knuckles were white and she looked like she had something pretty heavy on her mind.

Without giving it a second thought, he walked over to where she sat, took her hands in his and pulled her to her feet. "What's wrong?" he asked, loosely holding her to him. He wasn't sure why, but it bothered him to think she might be worried about anything at all.

Instead of her backing away as he thought she might, she wrapped her arms around his waist and laid her head against his chest. "The strike at the Denver airport is over. The airline can get me on a flight out of Cheyenne tomorrow morning."

She didn't sound overly happy about it and he took that as a sign that despite what she'd said last night on the way home from the main house, she wanted to stay with him a little longer. And that was just fine with him. He told himself that he was okay with it because he hadn't yet discovered what had originally changed her mind about them. But if he was perfectly honest with himself, he would have to admit that he wanted to spend more time with her before he had to say goodbye and watch her drive out of his life for good. The way he saw it, having one more day with her was worth whatever hell he would have to face of a lifetime without her.

"You don't have to leave." He put his index finger beneath her chin to tilt her head up until their eyes met. "Why don't you stay a few more days?"

"I can't afford to miss work," she said, shaking her head. "I only have a couple of vacation days left and I'll need to use those for the stop in Lincoln County to file the…d-divorce."

She stumbled over the word and he would bet

nearly every dime he had that she was starting to second-guess her decision. "Can you work from here?"

She looked thoughtful. "You mean telecommute?"

He nodded. "The signal here is good, but it's a lot better over at the main house. You could work from there."

"As nice as your boss is, I'm sure he'll draw the line at some stranger using up all of his bandwidth," she stated.

Blake shrugged. "Like I said, he's not staying there right now. When he had the Wi-Fi installed, he made sure it was unlimited usage with no slowdowns." He purposely omitted that Blake himself was one of the internet company's principal shareholders.

She looked thoughtful a moment before she shook her head. "I didn't bring my laptop."

"Not a problem," he said, smiling. He knew she was giving it serious consideration and he was determined to convince her to stay on the Wolf Creek Ranch a little longer. "You can use mine."

"Are you sure?" she asked. "You might have something on it that's private."

He shook his head. "I only use it for breeding records and to keep track of the cattle we'll be sending to market. There's more than enough room on the hard drive for anything you'll be doing and if you need a special program we can always download it."

"I'll have to call the office on Tuesday morning and explain that I'm going to be working from here for a few days," she said, her expression thoughtful. "I've telecommuted in the past, so it shouldn't be a problem to set it up. And I'll need to email one of my coworkers to have her send me a couple of files I'll need."

"Then it's settled," he said, refusing to acknowledge just how important it had become to him that she extended her stay. "After breakfast we'll go over to the mansion and get everything arranged in the office."

She frowned. "Blake, I know you say your boss is easygoing and won't mind, but I'm sure he'd have a big problem with me using his office."

"There's a writing desk in one of the upstairs bedrooms," he said, thinking quickly. "We'll just move over to the mansion and you can work out of that bedroom."

"That's even worse, Blake," she said, shaking her head. "We can't just move into your boss's home." She stared at him. "Who is this man and why do you insist on taking advantage of his good nature so often?"

He took a deep breath. He should tell her the truth. He'd boxed himself into a corner and he had nobody to blame but himself. If he told her now that he was the owner of the Wolf Creek Ranch she thought he was taking advantage of, she'd think he had been playing her for a fool or, worse yet, that he had been trying to hide his assets from her because of the divorce. But the longer he waited, the worse it was going to be when she did find out.

Deciding he needed to dial things back a little while he tried to figure out the best time and way to tell Karly he was the man in question, Blake backtracked. "You're right. We don't want to take advantage while he's away from the mansion. But there's one place that I know he won't mind you using."

"Where's that?" she asked, seemingly distracted from finding out who the owner was—at least for the time being.

"There's a table in the library just off the family room that would be the perfect place for you to work," he said, bringing his hand up to twine his fingers in her silky blond hair. "It's quiet in there and you won't have to worry about anyone interrupting you or you using a room the boss would find objectionable." He lowered his head to brush her perfect lips with his. "And when you take a break for lunch all you'll have to do is walk down the hall to the kitchen and Silas will make you something to eat."

Unable to resist, he gave in to temptation and settled his mouth over hers. He knew he was playing with fire and would most likely get burned by his weakness for her. But he couldn't seem to control himself when he was around Karly. It had been that way in Vegas and it was that way now. Whenever he was with her, all he could think about was holding her close, kissing her until she sagged against him and making love to her until they both collapsed from the sheer pleasure of being together.

As he deepened the kiss, she put her arms around his neck and melted against him. Her soft curves pressed against his rapidly hardening body and the sweetness that was uniquely Karly caused his heart to thump against his chest like a jungle drum. No other woman had ever fit against him so perfectly or responded to his kiss as readily.

When she moaned softly and snuggled even closer, he realized that she felt his arousal straining against his fly. The fact that she was as hot for him as he was for her sent adrenaline pumping through his veins at the speed of light. Whatever caused her to want out of their brief marriage apparently had nothing to do with her desire for him. That was as strong, if not stronger, than it had been when they'd taken that trip down the aisle at that little chapel on the Vegas strip.

Barely able to resist the urge to take off both of their clothes and make love to her right there in the kitchen, he forced himself to ease away from the kiss. "Sweetheart, as much as I'd like to take this all the way to a satisfying conclusion for both of us, I think we'd better take a time-out."

Her smooth porcelain cheeks wore the blush of passion and he sensed that if he hadn't called a halt to things, she probably wouldn't have, either. That's when he knew beyond a shadow of doubt that there was every likelihood they would be making love before she left. And soon.

"I, uh, y-yes." She looked a little dazed. "I'll get flatware and coffee mugs."

While she walked over to get the items from the cabinets, Blake took a deep breath and set the two plates of bacon, scrambled eggs and hash browns on the table, along with a thermos of coffee. How the hell could a man feel like he'd done the right thing and, at the same time, regret doing it?

He wasn't sure. But he knew now that he needed to come clean with Karly and tell her that he owned the ranch before things progressed any further between them. Karly was intelligent and she'd already started questioning why he kept taking advantage of the mysteriously absent ranch owner. It was just a matter of time before she figured it out or someone unwittingly told her.

And the worst part of all, his reasons for keeping it from her were making less sense, even to him, with each passing day.

Karly sat at the library table in the log mansion and looked around at the volumes of books on the shelves lining the room. The owner's tastes were eclectic and included ranching manuals, nonfiction, autobiographies and novels by some of the most popular, bestselling authors of the past one hundred years.

As she continued to look around, she couldn't help

but smile. Unlike a lot of home libraries, which felt gloomy and heavy with the knowledge of the ages, the room felt cozy and extremely inviting. So much so that she could imagine herself spending endless hours on a rainy or snowy day curled up with a good book and a warm, comfy afghan on the big leather sofa in front of a crackling fire in the stone fireplace.

She rose to her feet and walked over to look out one of the windows at the surrounding mountains. Now that she'd visited the ranch, she could understand why Blake had told her he couldn't leave Wyoming for life in a bustling city. The land was beautiful and although she loved the green beauty of both the Cascade and Olympic Mountains, she couldn't look out any of the windows in her apartment and see them. If she wanted to enjoy the lush scenery, she had to take a ferry across Puget Sound or drive out of the city to the thick forests beyond.

But here on the Wolf Creek Ranch, every window had a spectacular view of the Laramie Mountains and experiencing nature took little more than walking out the door.

She sighed. When she had returned to Seattle after their whirlwind courtship and wedding, she had reasoned that living so far from a city would eventually end her and Blake's marriage the way it had with her parents'. She'd even convinced herself that she was doing what was best for both of them—that there would be less emotional pain by ending it so early in the union than there would be a few years down the line.

But she had to admit that although most of her conclusions made sense, they weren't her only motivation for insisting on a divorce. The main, most compelling reason that she'd refused to move to Wyoming with her new husband had been due to fear—not that he would fail her, but that she would fail him.

She had been afraid she would eventually feel about Blake the way her mother had felt about her father. And that was something she wasn't going to let happen. She cared too much for him to blame him for things he had no control over.

Martina Ewing had become a bitter, resentful woman once she returned to New York and learned she had lost her place in the world of high fashion. Until her death just a few years ago, Karly's mother had blamed Karly's father for the loss of her career, her unhappiness and just about everything else unpleasant that happened in her life. She still managed to find fault with him, even though he'd passed away not long after they divorced. Karly sometimes wondered if her mother had even blamed him for leaving her saddled with a child to raise.

But in Karly's attempt to protect Blake from the possibility that she would turn out to be as unreasonable as her mother, had she allowed her fear to deprive them of a real chance at happiness?

"It's beautiful, isn't it?" Blake asked, wrapping his

arms around her waist and pulling her back against his solid chest.

Startled, she jumped. "I didn't know you had returned to the house."

After they'd finished breakfast, he had given her his laptop and driven them over to the mansion to set up her workspace in the library. Once he'd made sure the internet connection was the speed she needed, he'd told her he was going out to see that the indoor arena's floor had been properly prepared for the training of a new stallion and left her to familiarize herself with his computer and to download a couple of programs she would need to do her job. But she suspected that had been an excuse to give her the time and space to think about the direction her visit had taken and what she wanted to do about it.

They were both aware that the chemistry between them was as strong as ever and that it wouldn't take much to send it spiraling out of control. It had almost happened last night in the hot tub and then again this morning when he kissed her.

"Did you get everything ready to start to work?" he asked, sending a wave of goose bumps shimmering over her arms.

She nodded. "And I went ahead and sent the email to my coworker so it's waiting for her when she arrives at the office Tuesday morning."

"I'm glad you'll be here at the mansion." He brushed her long hair out of the way to nibble kisses down the column of her neck. "I have to start working in the arena with the new stallion and I'd hate for you to spend the day alone over at the foreman's cottage."

"I was going to ask you about that," she said, attempting to get her mind off how good he was making her feel. "Why are the barns and corrals at the foreman's cottage instead of here at the main ranch house?"

His low chuckle caused her knees to wobble. "Sweetheart, in the warmer months, having the barns and livestock a quarter of a mile away makes entertaining guests out on the patio a lot more pleasant."

"Oh, I hadn't thought about the dust and the noise the animals make," she commented.

"Along with Essence of Barnyard floating on the breeze. It doesn't inspire people to attend a cookout or pool party," he said, laughing.

Smiling, she nodded. "It makes perfect sense now." She frowned suddenly and turned in his arms to face him. "But the barn is no more than fifty yards from the cottage and I haven't noticed a lot of dust or barnyard odors at the foreman's cottage."

"When the owner's family established the Wolf Creek Ranch back in the late 1800s, they made sure to build the barns and outbuildings downwind of the house." He shrugged. "I think that held true for most ranches back then. They figured out which way the wind usually blows and planned their layout accordingly."

"So the foreman's cottage was the original ranch

house?" she asked. She hadn't really thought about it before, but he had mentioned the owner building the mansion after he bought the ranch a couple of years ago.

He nodded. "I think every generation has remodeled and built onto it, but the original homestead is in the foreman's cottage somewhere."

"How do you know so much about the ranch?" she asked, puzzled by his knowledge of its history.

He looked a little taken aback by her question. "My family has lived here…as long as the owners have." Although not overly common anymore, she'd heard that in years past it wasn't all that unusual for generations of cowboys to work for the same ranch.

"By the way, I don't recall hearing you mention the name of the man who owns the ranch," she said, frowning.

She hadn't much more than gotten the words out than Blake lowered his head and pulled her to him. With his mouth moving so masterfully over hers, it suddenly didn't matter who owned the ranch. All she cared about was having him continue to hold her to his broad chest, kiss her until she was breathless and so much more.

That thought should have had her pushing away from his secure embrace. Wanting to make love and wanting their marriage to work out were two entirely different things. Or were they?

But when Blake deepened the kiss, Karly abandoned all thought in favor of losing herself in the way he was making her feel. A delicious warmth flowed throughout her body the moment his tongue touched hers and as he explored her with such tender care, her knees failed her completely. He caught her to him and the feel of his rock-hard body sent waves of longing all the way to her core.

Lost in the overwhelming need he was creating, her heart skipped a beat when he brought his hand up along her side to gently cup her breast. The feel of his thumb teasing her through the layers of her T-shirt and bra only intensified her desire, making her restless and impatient to feel his calloused hands touching her bare skin.

When he broke the kiss to nibble his way along her jaw, then down her neck to the hollow below her ear, Karly couldn't stop herself from vocalizing what she wanted. "Blake, please."

"What do you want, Karly?" he asked as he continued to tease her.

"You. I…want you."

"And I want you, sweetheart," he said, leaning back to look at her. His brown gaze held hers as a slow smile curved his lips. "Let's go back to the foreman's cottage."

Needing him more than she needed her next breath, Karly let him lead her through the mansion and out the front door to his truck. On the ride back to the foreman's cottage, reality began to intrude and by the time Blake parked the truck at the side of the house, she had begun to question her sanity. She longed for him to make love to her—and, to her own surprise, she longed for him to *love* her again—but she needed him to understand the depth of the fears and insecurities that had held her back for the past eight months. Before they could move forward into a future together, she had to explain about her past.

When he got out and walked around to help her down from the passenger side of the truck, she had to let him know about her apprehension. She had to try to make him understand so he could forgive her for not believing in them. "Blake, we need to talk before we do anything impulsive."

He stared at her for several long moments and the heated look in his dark brown eyes stole her breath. "Karly, do you want me?"

"Y-yes. B-but—"

"I give you my word that we'll talk later," he said, putting his arm around her waist and tucking her to his side as he walked them into the house. "But not now. I haven't made love to my wife in over eight months and I've needed you every second of every day since we left Vegas."

His words sent a fresh wave of longing from the top of her head to the soles of her feet. She hadn't realized it before she came to Wyoming, before she'd spent this time on the land he loved so much, but she felt the same way.

She needed him with every fiber of her being. She didn't know how she'd gone these long eight months without him. And after they made love they could discuss why she had refused to join him here, why she'd insisted a divorce was the right decision. They could figure out where they were headed in the future after they made love. Right now, she craved the magic of his touch and the overwhelming pleasure of being one with him.

She could hardly believe what she was about to say. But as she stared up at him, she knew that from the moment she'd decided to bring him the divorce papers in person, she'd never really had a choice.

"Blake, please take me upstairs and make me forget how long it's been."

Seven

When Blake opened the door to the room she'd been using since her arrival at the ranch, memories of the first time they'd made love caused Karly's stomach to flutter with anticipation. It had been so long since he'd touched her and for the past eight months she'd lain in bed every night missing the feel of his skin pressed to hers, their bodies entwined in an embrace as old as time. A shiver slid up her spine and her heart skipped a beat at the thought.

When he closed the door behind them, he reached for her. Neither of them said a word as they stood with their arms around each other and simply enjoyed the moment.

As he drew back to look at her, he placed her

hands on his shoulders for support before he removed her boots and socks, then pulled off his.

"Karly, I want you to know there hasn't been anyone since we left Vegas," he said, his brown eyes reflecting the truth in his words as he straightened to his full height and took her back into his arms. He brought his hand up to gently caress her cheek. "When we got married, I vowed that I would be faithful to you. And as far as I'm concerned, I'm still your husband until I receive papers telling me otherwise."

She nodded. "That's the way I felt about it, as well."

Leaning forward, he brushed her lips with his. "I promised you we would talk about all that later, and I meant it. But right now, I intend to get reacquainted with my wife's beautiful body." Her pulse sped up when he reached for the hem of her T-shirt and slowly pulled it up and over her head.

"I can't let you be the only one having all the fun," she said, tugging his chambray shirt from the waistband of his jeans. She unfastened the top snap and slowly, methodically released the closures. She placed her hands beneath each side of his open shirt to brush it from his shoulders and her breath caught. She'd always found the hard ridges and valleys of his well-developed chest and abdomen fascinating. "Your body is perfect."

"If you want to talk about perfection—" he paused and reached behind her, releasing the clasp of her bra "—you're the one who's stunning."

The appreciation in his dark eyes stole her breath. But when he cupped her breasts with both hands, then kissed each hardened tip, her knees wobbled and she had to place her palms on his chest to steady herself.

The moment her fingers came into contact with the thick pads of his pectoral muscles, he shuddered and she knew he loved having her touch him as much as she loved having him touch her. Inspired to give him as much pleasure as he was giving her, she continued her exploration of his body and let her hands drift down to his belt buckle.

When she paused to glance up at him, he grinned. "Don't stop now, sweetheart. This is just starting to get interesting."

"That's one of the things that I've always found amazing about you," she said, unbuckling the tooled leather strap of his belt.

"What's that?" he asked, his breathing sounding a bit labored.

"You openly encourage me to do the same things to you that you're doing to me," she said, releasing the button at the top of his jeans.

"That's a big part of making love, sweetheart" he said, teasing her nipples with the pads of his thumbs. "It's about trust and the freedom to learn what we like and how to bring the most pleasure to each other."

She wasn't all that experienced, but she had a feeling not all men were willing to be vulnerable with their partner. Her heart swelled with emotion at the thought that Blake was secure enough in his manhood to trust her that much when they made love.

When she smiled and took hold of the tab at the top of his fly, he drew in a deep breath. "Don't get me wrong. I love what you intend to do," he said, his smile so sexy it sent her pulse racing. "But an excited man and a metal zipper can be a real bad combination."

She gazed up at him as she eased one hand inside his jeans between his cotton underwear and the zipper. "Maybe this will keep you safe," she said, delighting in the heat she detected in his eyes as she eased the offending zipper down over his insistent erection.

But she hadn't anticipated the effect his arousal would have on her. The feel of the hard ridge against the backs of her fingers caused heat to flow through her veins and her insides to feel as if they had turned to warm pudding.

By the time she finished the task of unzipping him, she felt as if she might go up in a puff of smoke. But when she looked up at Blake's handsome face, his eyes were closed and a muscle worked along his lean jaw as if he might be in pain.

"Are you all right?" she asked, concerned.

He opened his eyes and his slow, sexy grin sent a shiver up her spine. "Sweetheart, do you have any idea what it does to a man when a woman touches him like that?"

"Even through your underwear?" she asked playfully.

Laughing, he nodded. "It's a thin barrier and a real sensitive area. I'd have to be a eunuch not to react."

Moving her hands to his sides, she carefully pushed his jeans and boxer briefs down his lean hips and muscular thighs. When she lowered them to his ankles, she caressed the backs of his knees and strong calves. Rewarded with his deep groan, she realized that something as simple as skimming her hands down the backs of his legs could bring him pleasure.

When he stepped out of the denim and cotton, then kicked his clothing to the side, she bit her lower lip to keep a tiny moan from escaping. "You're absolutely beautiful. I've always thought so."

Shaking his head, he pulled her to him. "Women are all gentle curves and soft, smooth skin. That's beautiful. But men are too angular, hard and hairy to be anything but passable at best."

"Don't sell yourself short," she said, gazing up at him.

He surprised her when he raised one dark eyebrow. "Really? I'm standing here without a stitch of clothes on and you had to mention the word *short*?"

In truth, he was a man who had nothing whatsoever to be insecure about and the humor in his eyes told her he knew it. She couldn't help but giggle as she placed her hands on his wide chest.

"I suppose that was a poor choice of words. But do

you really want to talk about my word choices now?" she asked, running her index finger down the shallow valley between his chest and navel.

"No." He kissed his way from her cheek down her neck to her collarbone. "I fully intend to take the rest of your clothes off, lay you on that bed over there and spend the rest of today and tonight loving every inch of you."

When he lifted his head, his gaze caught and held hers as he reached to release the button at her waist, then lowered the zipper. His smile held so much promise as he ran his index finger along the elastic waistband of her bikini panties, Karly thought she might melt right then and there.

As he began to ease her jeans and underwear over her hips and down her legs, the tantalizing abrasion of his calloused hands on her skin caused her heart to skip several beats and a delicious shiver to run through her. When she stepped out of the garments, the heated appreciation in his dark eyes took her breath away.

"Gorgeous," he said, stepping forward to wrap his arms around her.

The feel of her breasts pressed to his hard, hair-roughened chest caused her knees to give way. But when he caught her and pulled her more fully against him, his strong arousal nestled against her soft lower belly. The feel of it made Karly's head spin.

Without a word he led her over to the bed and pulled back the comforter. "I'll be right back," he said, walking over to where their discarded clothing lay on the floor.

As she watched, he picked up his jeans to get something from his wallet. When he returned, he placed a foil packet on the bedside table and stretched out on the mattress beside her.

Gathering her into his arms, he smiled. "I'm assuming you still aren't on any kind of birth control."

"There hasn't been a reason for it," she said honestly. She'd intended to talk with her doctor about it once she returned from Las Vegas, but when it seemed that their marriage had ended she hadn't bothered.

"It's not a problem," he said, kissing her forehead. "It's my job to take care of you and protect you, even if that protection is from me."

"Thank you," she said, touching his lean cheek. She'd been so caught up in the moment, she hadn't given protection a second thought.

He stared at her and the look in his eyes was breathtaking before a slow smile curved his lips. He lowered his head to kiss her with a tenderness that brought tears to her eyes. No other man had ever shown her so much reverence or been as devoted to bringing her pleasure as Blake. And in that moment, she knew that no other man ever would.

When he deepened the kiss, he brought his hand up to cup her breast and tease her nipple with gentle care. Her pulse sped up as ribbons of desire coursed through every part of her and an ache began to form deep inside. A mixture of impatience and anticipation filled her as he moved his hand to caress his way down her side to her hip then her knee.

As he continued to stroke her tongue with his, he slowly moved his calloused palm along the inside of her thigh. When he touched her, it felt as if an electric current skipped over every nerve in her body and she couldn't stop a tiny moan from escaping.

Needing to touch him as he was touching her, she moved her hands from his wide chest down his abdomen to his lean flanks. She felt him shudder against her and, encouraged by his reaction, she moved her hands lower. When she found him, she stroked his length and tested the heaviness below. He suddenly went perfectly still a moment before a deep groan rumbled up from his chest. He broke away from the kiss to take several deep breaths.

"Sweetheart, as much as I hate to say it, I think you'd better stop…and let me catch my breath," he said haltingly. He trapped her hands in his and placed them back on his chest. "If you don't, you're going to be disappointed and I'm going to be real embarrassed."

"It's been so long," she said, knowing that if they didn't make love soon she was going to go out of her mind with longing. "I need you, Blake."

"And I need you, Karly," he said, reaching for the foil packet he'd placed on the bedside table earlier. Arranging their protection, he nudged her knees apart and rose over her. "I promise next time it won't be as rushed."

If she could have found her voice she would have told him that she couldn't have waited any longer. But words were impossible when he guided himself to her and she felt him slowly begin to fill her.

As her body stretched to accommodate his, her chest tightened with emotion. She had never felt as complete as she did when Blake made them one. It had been that way in Las Vegas—it was that way now. And she knew in her heart that's the way it would always be. He was her man—her other half—and no amount of time or distance or fear or insecurity would ever change that.

Her heart stalled as she realized she'd fallen in love with him all over again. But as she stared up at his handsome face, she knew that wasn't true. If she was honest with herself, she'd have to admit she'd never fallen out of love with him.

"You feel so damned good," Blake said, oblivious to her realization.

Deciding to think about her sudden insight later, Karly noticed his clenched jaw and the strained expression on his handsome face. It reflected his struggle for control and his determination to bring her pleasure before he found his own.

"Please make love to me, Blake," she said, wrapping her arms around him as she arched her body into his.

Groaning, he lowered his lips to hers and to her

delight, he began to rock against her. Slow and gentle, she was certain his movements were calculated to bring her the most pleasure he possibly could. He made her feel as if she was the most cherished woman on earth and that it was his privilege to be with her.

But all too soon the tension he was building within her gathered into a coil of longing in her most feminine parts. Blake must have sensed her readiness because he increased the depth and strength of his strokes. Just when she thought her body would shatter from the exquisite tightening inside of her, she was suddenly set free. Pleasure flowed through every cell in her body and she felt as if she might faint from the beautiful sensations that seemed to go on forever.

As she slowly began to drift back to reality, Karly felt Blake's body surge into her one final time. He tightened his arms around her as if she was his lifeline and held her to him as he found his own shuddering release.

When he buried his head in the pillow beside her, she stroked the dark brown hair at the nape of his neck and reveled in their differences. His weight felt absolutely wonderful pressed against her and she felt surrounded by his much bigger body.

"I'm too heavy for you, sweetheart," he said, levering himself up on his forearms. He brushed a strand of hair from her cheek as he smiled down at her. "Are you all right?"

"I'm wonderful," she said, nodding.

"You can add *amazing* to that, as well as *exciting* and *beautiful*," he stated, brushing her lips with his. When he moved to her side, he pulled her to him and covered them both with the comforter. "It's been so long since I made love to you, I'm afraid my control wasn't what it should have been. I give you my word that the next time I'll make sure to give you more pleasure."

She shivered with anticipation at the thought of having him make love to her again. "As much as I love that idea, I think it would be best if we discussed a few things first," she said, knowing that even though this had been wonderful, everything had become a lot more complicated.

When he failed to respond, she moved her head from where it was pillowed on his shoulder to look up at him. His eyes were closed and she could tell by the movement of his broad chest that he had fallen asleep.

Karly kissed his chin and closed her eyes. He was probably exhausted from working with the stallion he had been training most of the day.

She yawned and snuggled closer to him. It might be for the best that he'd fallen asleep before they could talk. She needed to come to terms with the newfound knowledge that she was still in love with her husband, as well as decide what she wanted to do about that insight.

Did she have the courage to ask him to put the

divorce on hold for a while to see if they could make their marriage work? Was that what she really wanted? Could he forgive her for the mistake she'd made in thinking their marriage would lead to her resenting him as her mother had resented her father? What would she do if she asked him for another chance and he decided that wasn't what he wanted?

She yawned again and felt the shadows of sleep begin to tug at her. Maybe if she rested for a while, she'd be able to think more clearly and the answers would come to her. They had to. Happiness for the rest of her life might very well depend on it.

The following evening, Blake took a swig of his beer as he watched his wife chatting and laughing with Tori Laughlin across the patio at the Rusty Spur Ranch house. Karly seemed to be having a good time, and he couldn't help but wonder if she would be around for the next get-together with his friends and their guests.

They hadn't talked about the future beyond agreeing that she would stay a few more days and she hadn't seemed any more ready to discuss what would happen after that than he was. Before they made love, he had promised her they would talk afterward. But they'd both fallen asleep and when they woke up together in bed, nature had taken its course once again. They'd spent the rest of the night reacquainting themselves with each other's bodies and that morning they had awakened just in time to get ready to leave for the late-afternoon barbecue.

"You've really got it bad for her, don't you?" Eli Laughlin asked, walking up to stand next to Blake.

"Yeah, I guess I do," he admitted.

"She seems real nice," Eli commented. "When did the two of you meet?"

"During the Nationals Finals in Vegas before Christmas," he said, never taking his eyes off Karly. He took another swig of his beer. "That's when we got married."

When he'd called Eli a few days before to tell his friend he would be bringing a guest to the get-together, Blake had explained that she wasn't aware he owned the Wolf Creek Ranch and that he'd like to keep it that way. As he expected, Eli had immediately agreed. But Blake had known that at some point he'd need to explain his strange request and tell Eli that he and Karly were married.

In the middle of taking a drink of his beer, Eli choked and Blake reached over to pound him on the back. When his friend stopped coughing, he stared at Blake like he'd sprouted another head.

"You got married," Eli repeated as if he couldn't quite believe what Blake had just said.

Blake nodded and explained the events leading up to the current situation he and Karly found themselves in. "But filing for the divorce is on hold—at least until the end of the week."

Eli nodded. "That gives you a little time to figure

out how you're going to ask her to stay—and how to tell her you own the Wolf Creek. You're also going to have to tell her why you kept that from her in the first place."

Watching his wife play with the Laughlin's two-year-old son, Aaron, Blake tried to imagine having a family with Karly. If her interaction with the toddler was any indication, she loved kids and would be everything he could possibly want for the mother of his children.

"Any suggestions about how I should go about handling all of that?" he asked, grinning.

Blake had known his friend would be the last to pass judgment on the way Blake and Karly met and married. Eli and Tori hadn't gotten together in the usual way, either. And Blake had been confident that Eli wouldn't question his reasoning for keeping his wealth out of the equation. Before he met Tori, Eli had dealt with his own share of unscrupulous women going after his bank account.

Eli laughed. "You know better than to ask me for advice when it comes to women. I'm sure you remember what a stubborn jackass I was when Tori and I got married. I just thank the good Lord above that she loved me enough to give me a second chance."

"And look at you now," Blake agreed, laughing with his friend. "You're still a jackass, just a little less stubborn than you used to be."

"It takes one to know one," Eli retorted.

"What are you two laughing about this time?" Tori asked.

Looking up, Blake grinned as he watched the women and the toddler walking toward them. "I was just agreeing with your husband that he's a jackass."

"I was telling him that it takes a jackass to know one," Eli explained.

Tori laughed. "Well, it's nice to know some things never change. But right now, I need to steal Eli for a few minutes. The band has arrived and he needs to let them know where to set up while I take Aaron inside for a few minutes to change him into his pajamas."

"She said he'd be asleep before the band finished their first song," Karly commented as Tori carried the little boy inside the house.

Putting his arm around her shoulders, Blake pulled Karly to his side. "Are you having a good time?"

When she smiled up at him, it caused a hitch in his breathing. He suddenly wished they were back at the foreman's cottage, where he could spend the rest of the evening making love to her.

"I'm having a wonderful time," she said, sounding happy and relaxed. "I really like your friends. I'm just sorry I didn't get to meet your brother. Tori said he was supposed to be here, but was called away on business."

"Sean used to be a special agent with the FBI," Blake said, nodding. "They still get in touch with him sometimes to act as an independent consultant on certain types of cases."

"That sounds fascinating," she said, sounding genuinely interested. "Is your brother still involved in law enforcement?"

"Yes and no," he answered, setting his empty beer bottle on one of the patio tables to take her in his arms. "He's a private investigator now. But when he was with the Bureau he was a crisis negotiator. He gets calls from law enforcement agencies all over Wyoming and the surrounding states when they have a situation that requires his expertise." He leaned close to nibble kisses along the side of her neck. "But I don't want to talk about Sean right now. I want to discuss when you think it would be acceptable for us to leave for home."

She shivered against him and he knew she was anticipating the night ahead of them the same as he was. "I think we could leave after a couple of dances, since we have an hour-and-a-half drive to get back to the ranch."

"I'll be right back," he said suddenly as he released her and started across the patio to where the band was getting ready to start playing. When he reached the frontman, Blake pulled his wallet from the hip pocket of his jeans and took out a couple of hundred dollars. He handed the money to the man. "I'd really appreciate it if you could make the first couple of songs slow ones."

"Hey, for two hundred dollars we'll make the

whole first set slow ones," the man answered as he pocketed the money.

"After the first two, you can play whatever you want," Blake said, grinning. "Just make sure what you play is slow and good to dance to."

The man nodded. "You got it."

Blake walked back to where Karly stood and draped his arm across her shoulders. "Two slow dances and we're out of here."

"You didn't," she said, her voice filled with laughter.

"Yup, I sure did." He brushed his lips over hers. "I wasn't leaving anything to chance."

When she rose up on tiptoes, she whispered, "Don't tell anyone, but I'm not the least bit sorry."

Ten minutes later, when the band broke into a popular slow country love song, Blake led Karly out to the section of the patio that had been designated as the dance floor. Taking her into his arms, he swayed her back and forth in time with the music. The feel of her body aligned with his and the sensual brushing of her lower stomach against his steadily growing arousal had him wishing it had been one and done, instead of the two dances they'd decided were socially acceptable.

His heart stalled when she put her arms around his neck and pressed herself closer. "You're making me a little crazy, sweetheart," he warned.

"Only a little?" Her sexy smile sent his blood

pressure sky-high. "I guess I'll just have to try a bit harder to make you a lot crazy."

Blake swallowed around the cotton clogging his throat in order to get his vocal cords to work as he looked around to find the Laughlins. When he spotted them talking to some of their guests, he took her by the hand and started toward the couple.

"Where are we going?" Karly asked, sounding like she already knew.

"To thank Eli and Tori for having us over." Giving her a quick kiss, Blake grinned. "Social conventions be damned, sweetheart. We're heading back home where we can both be as crazy as we want to be."

Eight

The moment he closed the door to the master bedroom in the foreman's cottage, Blake took Karly into his arms and captured her mouth with his. The hour-and-a-half drive from the Rusty Spur Ranch had taken its toll and he was wound up tighter than a two-dollar watch. Every nerve in his body was on high alert and he ached with the need to once again claim her as his wife.

His wife. Even the words felt right and if he'd had any doubts about marrying her before, they had been erased this evening. Watching her with his friends—seeing her play with little Aaron—had been enough to convince him that Karly was the woman for him. She fit in perfectly and he could tell that she and Tori would end up becoming best friends.

If this was even a glimpse of what their lives would be like as husband and wife, he'd be the happiest man alive for the rest of his days. And he fully intended to make sure she was the happiest woman.

Deepening the kiss, he gently stroked her tongue and explored her soft, sweet recesses. Her taste and eager response to the caress were all he could have hoped for. Reaching down, he tugged the tail of her T-shirt from the waistband of her jeans.

Her warm, satiny skin was like a fine piece of silk beneath his calloused palms. Easing away from the kiss, he skimmed his lips along her jawline and down her neck to the fluttering pulse at the base of her throat. "Sweetheart, I'd like to go slow and love every inch of you. But I need you so much right now, I'm not sure that's going to be possible."

She caught his face with her delicate hands and lifted his head until their gazes met. "You can go slow the next time, Blake. I need you now."

"Thank God," he said, burying his face in her silky blond hair. "I don't think I could wait much longer, even if my life depended on it."

"I feel the same way. I thought I would burst into flames when we were on the dance floor and I felt how much you needed me." She shivered and he knew it had nothing to do with being chilled. "But I want you to do something for me."

Without a second thought, he nodded. "Anything for you, Karly."

"Let *me* make love to *you*," she said, giving him a look that sent his hormones racing through his veins at the speed of light. "Do you mind?"

What man in his right mind would turn down a beautiful woman doing incredibly sexy things to his body?

"I need you to promise me something, Karly," he said, pulling her close for a quick kiss.

"Wh-what's that?" she asked, sounding a little short of breath.

"If I tell you to stop whatever you're doing, can you give me your word that you will?"

She looked confused. "All right. But I don't understand—"

"I want us to finish this race together," he said, grinning.

He could tell she understood his meaning when she smiled. "I want that, too. I promise."

"Good." Stepping back, he held his arms wide. "I'm all yours, sweetheart."

Karly wasted no time in pointing to the side of the bed. "If you'll sit down, I'll take your boots off."

Looking forward to seeing what she had in mind, he did as she requested. He swallowed hard when she turned her back to him, straddled one of his legs and bent over. But when she started tugging on his boot and her delightful little bottom bobbed mere inches in front of his face, Blake was pretty sure he was going to have a coronary. By the time his boots and socks lay on the floor beside the bed, sweat had popped out on his forehead and his upper lip, and he felt like he just might need CPR.

"Sweetheart, why don't we take off our clothes and get into bed," he said, forcing himself to breathe as he stood up to unbuckle his belt. "Otherwise, I'm not going to last long enough to get to the main event."

"I think that would be a good idea," she said, sounding a little winded herself.

"I give you my word that I'll let you take my clothes off me another time when I'm not so revved up," he said, making quick work of his clothing.

He made it a point to keep his gaze averted while she removed hers. If he hadn't, he wasn't sure he wouldn't have gone up in a blaze of glory.

As Karly got into bed, he reached into his jeans for one of the condoms he'd remembered to get from his medicine cabinet when they were over at the mansion the day before. Placing it on the bedside table, he stretched out beside her.

When he started to pull her to him, she shook her head. "Remember, this is all about me giving you pleasure," she said, her smile causing another wave of heat to course from the top of his head to the soles of his feet.

"Just keep in mind that I'm only human and I do…have my limits," he said, feeling like he had been branded when she placed her hand on his chest.

When he cupped one of her perfect breasts, she closed her eyes and nodded. "I've almost reached mine, as well."

Just knowing that she was as turned on as he was had him clenching his teeth in an effort to slow down his overly active libido. But when she reached over to take the packet from the bedside table and carefully opened it, Blake closed his eyes and held his breath. He'd never had a woman do what Karly was planning to do and he could only hope that he had enough strength to hold on to what little control he had left.

At the first touch of her fingers to the most sensitive part of his body, Blake felt like he'd been treated to the business end of a cattle prod. He groaned and tried to think of something—anything—to take his mind off what the woman of his dreams was doing for him.

"Are you all right?" she asked when he let loose with a deep groan.

He nodded as he reached to take her hands in his. "I think you'd better give me…a minute."

"You need to catch your breath?" she asked.

"Yeah, we can…call it that," he said, breathing deeply in an effort to release some of the tension gripping him. When he felt like he had regained a degree of control, he warned, "I'm not going to be able to take much more, sweetheart."

"I can't, either," she said, rising to her knees.

His heart stopped completely when she straddled his hips and guided him into her. As he watched, she lowered herself onto him and just the sight of her body taking him in was mind-blowing. But the feel of her warmth surrounding him caused his body to respond with a tightening that left him feeling light-headed.

He watched her close her eyes as if she savored being one with him. Humbled that a woman as loving and beautiful as Karly would even want to be with him, he knew beyond a shadow of doubt that he still loved her.

It made him more determined than ever to find out what happened after she returned to Seattle. Whatever it was they'd find a way to work through it. And he could only hope she'd be able to forgive him for not telling her about himself sooner and give him a chance to make it up to her.

But he didn't have time to dwell on what he was going to do about his self-discovery and whatever obstacles they still faced. As he watched the woman who owned his heart, she opened her eyes, gave him a smile that caused his chest to tighten with emotion and slowly began to move against him.

He placed his hands on her hips and held on as the friction of their bodies increased the pressure building inside of him. He could tell Karly was experiencing the same sensations from the blush of passion on her porcelain cheeks and the rapt light in her big blue eyes.

As he felt himself reaching the point where his satisfaction was inevitable, Karly's tiny feminine muscles tightened around him a moment before her head fell back and she gasped from the intense sensations flowing through her. That's when Blake took control of the pace and did his best to give her as much pleasure as he possibly could before his own release set him free. Groaning, he shuddered as he gave up his essence to the woman he loved.

When Karly collapsed on his chest, he wrapped his arms around her and held her to him as their bodies cooled and their breathing returned to normal. "Are you doing okay?" he whispered close to her ear.

"That was incredible," she said, raising her head to kiss his chin.

"You're incredible." He enjoyed the feel of her lying on top of him and the connection they still shared. "Next time I promise you can take my clothes off and have your wicked way with me," he said, chuckling. "But I was so turned on, I wouldn't have lasted five minutes if you'd taken your time."

When she remained silent, he realized that she had fallen fast asleep. Kissing her cheek, he rolled them to their sides, pulled the comforter around them and held her close. He wasn't sure how he was going to explain why he hadn't been entirely honest with her about owning the ranch or the fact that neither of them would ever have to work another day in their lives if they didn't want to.

But it was past time he told her everything about himself and the reasons he'd felt compelled to keep the information from her. He hoped she'd understand his past experience with his gold-digging stepmother and the years she'd held his family's ranch hostage in her attempt to get the most money she could out of it. He also hoped Karly would be able to do the same when he told her about that buckle bunny, the one claiming he had made her pregnant in an effort to extort money from him, and how it had left him deeply suspicious of women's motives, as well.

When she murmured his name and snuggled into his embrace, he kissed her forehead. He wasn't sure how she would react to his revelations. But tomorrow he was going to tell her everything, pray that she understood and ask her to stay with him for the rest of his life.

The morning after the barbecue at the Laughlins', Karly sat at the table in the mansion's library, staring at the screen on Blake's laptop. She was supposed to be finishing up a purchase order for novelty items from one of the import companies in Hong Kong. But she couldn't have cared less about cases of rubber ducks, plush finger puppets and inflatable plastic beach balls. Her mind was on what would happen at the end of the week when it was time for her to leave the Wolf Creek Ranch. Blake hadn't mentioned anything about wanting them to stay married and have her remain in Wyoming with him. And she hadn't told him that she would like to stay and be his wife.

Nibbling on her lower lip, she thought about her reasons for refusing to join him at the ranch after they left Las Vegas and how she felt about that now. After she and Blake parted eight months ago, she had returned to pack up her apartment and quit her job. And that had been when her doubts set in. She had worried that she might move to the ranch and discover that she couldn't stand the quiet remoteness or that she would miss having a productive career. She had been so afraid of being unhappy that she'd convinced herself not to even take the chance.

But now that she'd spent time on the ranch, she found that she loved the peace and quiet. And it came as no small surprise that she found feeding a couple of orphaned calves much more rewarding than keeping a warehouse stocked with rubber ducks and plastic beach balls.

She sighed. She'd watched her mother sink into a deep depression after they returned to New York from the Midwest, especially after Martina hadn't been able to resume her career in the fashion industry. Her mother's misery had left a lasting impression on Karly and one of her biggest fears had always been that she would turn out to be as dissatisfied and resentful as her mother.

But looking at things objectively, Karly could never remember a time when her mother had been truly happy—not before they'd moved to the Midwest or after. Martina Ewing had been dissatisfied before her husband moved them away from New York. She'd been unhappy living in a small town in Middle America and when she and Karly returned to New York, she hadn't been content there, either. It was a hard truth to face, but her mother had been one of those people who always searched for something to make her happy and when she couldn't find it, blamed someone else. She had never discovered that true happiness comes from within and that just being with the people she loved was a real blessing.

But this time with Blake had convinced Karly of that truth. No matter where they lived or whatever job she needed to work to help with their finances, she knew she would be truly fulfilled as long as they were together. And she finally felt ready to create a life of happiness with him. She hoped he was ready for that, too.

"You wouldn't happen to know where Blake is, would you?" a man's voice asked from just inside the door.

Unaware there was anyone else around, Karly jumped and placed her hand on her chest as if that would slow down her racing heart. "Oh, dear heavens!"

"I'm sorry," the man said, stepping forward with his hands outstretched in front of him as if to stop her from panicking. "I didn't mean to frighten you." He looked contrite as he hooked his thumb over his shoulder toward the hall. "I would have asked Silas, but he's taking his afternoon nap and it's easier to wake the dead than to try to rouse him once he's asleep."

"Silas does seem to be able to sleep through anything." She'd noticed that fact while working to set up her workspace in the library a couple of days ago. Feeling calmer, Karly smiled. "Blake is out in the arena working with a new stallion."

The man nodded. "Thanks." He turned to leave, then turned back. "By the way, I'm Sean Hartwell, Blake's brother."

Once he'd introduced himself, she could immediately see the resemblance between the two men. About the same height, Sean had the same dark brown hair and brown eyes as Blake.

"I'm Karly Ewing," she said, not sure if Blake had mentioned he had a wife.

"Are you his new secretary or assistant?" Sean asked.

She wondered why Blake would need an assistant. It suddenly dawned on her that Sean must have meant to ask if she was the ranch owner's new secretary.

Smiling, she shook her head. "No, I'm staying with Blake for a few days over at the foreman's cottage."

Sean surprised her when he frowned. "Why are the two of you staying over there? He hasn't lived there since he built this place and moved in almost two years ago."

Karly stared at Sean for several long moments as reality began to sink in. "I-I'm not sure," she said slowly. "I suppose you'll have to ask him."

"You can count on it," he said, nodding.

"Do you and Blake own the ranch together?" she asked, feeling as if she had a knot the size of her fist in her stomach.

"No. My ranch is about forty-five minutes away on the other side of the ridge," he said, apparently unaware of his brother's ruse. He pointed toward the laptop on the library table. "I'll let you get back to whatever it is you're doing. It was nice to meet you, Karly. I hope you enjoy the rest of your visit to the Wolf Creek."

"It was nice to meet you, too, Sean," she murmured when he turned toward the door.

As she watched him leave, her chest tightened and it was extremely difficult to draw air into her lungs. Why would Blake lie to her? Why hadn't he told her he owned the Wolf Creek Ranch when they were in Las Vegas?

Of course they hadn't talked about much of anything personal. But that didn't explain why he had failed to tell her when she arrived to have him sign the new set of divorce papers.

A cold wave of sadness suddenly swept over her. He hadn't asked her to sign a prenuptial agreement. When she told him it would be best for them to end their marriage, Blake had obviously been afraid she would try to get part of his ranch.

She looked around the library and it became crystal clear that Blake had to be extremely wealthy. Log homes were some of the most expensive types of houses to build and one the size of this mansion would cost several millions of dollars just for the construction. The custom-built furnishings for a place this size would cost at least that much more. Then there was the pool area, with its waterfalls and tropical oasis hot tub. No telling how much that cost. Factor in a huge indoor arena and heated stable, the house and barns down the road and thousands of acres of land…

"Oh, my God," she said, sinking back down onto the chair at the table. "He thought I would try to take…" She covered her mouth with her hand to hold back a sob. His assets and hanging on to them was obviously more important to him than telling her the truth. He hadn't even given her the opportunity to assure him she had no interest in taking anything away from him.

Yes, she'd broken her promise to him when she'd asked for a divorce, but never once had she deliberately lied to him.

Standing up, she hurried into the foyer, threw open the massive front door, ran out to the ranch truck Blake had been using and got into the driver's seat. He made a habit of leaving the keys in the ignition whenever they were on ranch land and she was thankful he did.

When she started the truck and drove down the lane to the road, she didn't look back in the rearview mirror. Blake had made it crystal clear there was nothing back there for her.

She'd made her own mistakes by giving into her

fears and not telling him the real reason behind her asking for a divorce. But what he'd done had been far worse. He had deliberately misled her and had no intention of asking her to stay with him to see if they could work things out. He'd probably been relieved when she called to tell him she wouldn't be moving to Wyoming with him. That would certainly explain why he hadn't been more insistent that she give their marriage a chance.

Tears streamed down her cheeks as she drove the short distance to the foreman's cottage, she went inside to retrieve the things she'd brought with her from Seattle and loaded the rental car. It was just as well that she'd found out about his ruse. Even if he had finally come clean about what he'd been trying so hard to hide, she didn't think she would ever be able to trust him.

Sobbing, she drove down the mountain road toward Eagle Fork. She hadn't been after his ranch, his money or anything material. Whether Blake was as rich as sin or as poor as a pauper, all she'd ever wanted, all she'd ever cared about, was having him love her.

"Hey there, bro," Blake said, riding the stallion over to where Sean stood just inside the arena doors. "You missed a great party last night over at the Rusty Spur."

His brother nodded. "I was on my way back from a situation up in Sheridan."

"Anything you can talk about?" Blake asked.

"Some guy is robbing banks all over the state and I was asked to review the details of his latest robbery," Sean answered.

"If he's been at this a while, I'm surprised they haven't called you in before now," Blake commented.

"This was the first time somebody got killed," Sean answered.

When his brother fell silent, Blake knew that was all Sean would say on the matter. Blake wasn't surprised that Sean didn't go into more detail about the case. He never talked about the work he did for the FBI and Blake never pressed for more than his brother was willing to tell.

"So what are you up to this afternoon?" Blake asked, dismounting the horse.

"I came by to see if you want to go fishing with me tomorrow." His brother shrugged. "But after I met your houseguest, I decided you probably wouldn't be interested."

"You met Karly?" Blake asked, hoping the subject of who owned the ranch hadn't been a topic of conversation.

"Yeah, she seems real nice," Sean commented. "But why are you two staying over at the homestead?"

"It's...complicated." A knot began to form in his gut as he realized Karly must have mentioned where they were staying. He asked, "Did you mention that I own the ranch?"

Sean stared at him for what seemed like forever before he finally nodded. "She asked and I wasn't going to lie to her." When Blake cut loose with a string of cusswords that had his brother raising his eyebrows, Sean asked, "Care to explain what brought on that little display of profanity?"

"Have one of the men take care of Blaze," Blake said, handing Sean the stallion's reins.

"What's going on?" Sean demanded when Blake took off across the yard toward the house.

"I'll tell you later," he called over his shoulder. "I have to go talk to my wife."

Blake knew he would face an interrogation from Sean later on but he'd worry about that when the time came. Right now, he needed to talk to Karly and explain why he hadn't told her everything months ago.

Running across the patio, Blake started calling her name as soon as he entered the house. When his calls went unanswered an icy dread began to settle in the pit of his stomach.

His heart stalled when he went into the foyer and found the front door ajar. Looking out, he really couldn't say he was surprised to see the ranch truck gone and along with it, his wife.

By the time he went back inside to get the keys for one of the vehicles in the garage, his brother met him in the kitchen. "What the hell's going on?" Sean demanded.

"I don't have time to get into it," Blake said, heading over to the key rack. "I have to get over to the foreman's cottage to stop Karly."

"My truck's out front," Sean said, starting for the door. "Come on, I'll drive you over there. And on the way you can explain when you got a wife and why she didn't have a clue that you own this spread."

As they drove away, Blake explained about their marriage in Vegas, Karly showing up with the new set of divorce papers and his reasoning behind not telling her up front that he was more than a ranch foreman and part-time rodeo rider. "I had planned on telling her when she moved here, right after Vegas. Then there seemed to be no real reason to share the truth, when we were headed for divorce. After the past few days…I had planned to tell her everything this evening after supper and ask her to stay with me."

His brother nodded. "Sorry I spoiled your reveal."

Blake shook his head. "Not your fault. I knew I was running out of time." He groaned as Sean parked beside the ranch truck. The little red sports car was gone. "She's headed back to Washington." He paused as he tried to think. "I'm just not sure if she's headed for Seattle or Lincoln County."

"What's in Lincoln County?" Sean asked.

"The divorce court," Blake answered, explaining the reason Karly intended to file there instead of in Seattle.

"Let me make a couple of phone calls," Sean said, reaching for his cell phone.

Blake knew if there was any chance of finding Karly, Sean had the connections to do it. But finding her was only half the battle. Getting her to listen to him was an entirely different matter.

While his brother tried to track down where Karly was headed, Blake went into the foreman's cottage to see if Karly had taken her luggage. He wasn't surprised to see that she'd taken the things she'd brought with her, but left the clothing, hat and boots he'd bought for her on their shopping trip to the Blue Sage Western Emporium.

Blake walked back downstairs and met Sean on the back porch. "She just called Cheyenne and made reservations for a flight to Denver. From there she's headed to Seattle."

Blake took a deep breath. He'd caught a break. "What time does her flight leave Denver?"

"Not until around six this evening," Sean said, grinning. "She's going to miss the earlier afternoon flight by about an hour."

Blake checked his watch. "Can you get me down there to catch that early flight?"

His brother snorted. "If I can't, I'll turn in my license to fly helicopters." Sean had earned his pilot's license during his stint in the marines and because of his work with the FBI, regularly flew himself into Denver to catch flights to wherever there was a situation in need of his expertise.

Without another word, they both headed for Sean's truck. As his brother drove toward his ranch on the other side of the western ridge surrounding the Wolf Creek Ranch, Blake called to reserve a seat on the earlier flight to Seattle.

He didn't have a clear-cut plan, but he wasn't overly concerned. He had several hours before Karly's flight arrived and by then, he had no doubt he'd have something in mind.

When Karly called eight months ago, he'd told himself he was doing the right thing when he let her go without putting up a fight. It was what she wanted and he'd reasoned that pushing her would have done nothing to change her mind. But he wasn't going to make that mistake again. This time he was going to pull out all the stops.

He had no idea how long it would take to convince her, but one thing was certain. Blake wasn't returning to the Wolf Creek Ranch without her.

Nine

As Karly walked through the terminal toward the baggage claim area, she watched people as they met up with their loved ones and friends. It seemed that everyone else had someone there waiting to greet them. As usual, she had no one.

Tears threatened and she blinked several times to chase them away. It had never bothered her that she didn't have anyone to welcome her home after a trip. She had always collected her luggage, caught a cab and hadn't thought twice about being alone.

But that had changed with her trip to Wyoming. She'd never felt more alone in her entire life than she did at the moment.

Picking up her bag, she had to admit that wasn't

quite true. The only other time she had felt such a keen sense of loneliness had been eight months ago when she'd returned from her vacation in Las Vegas and she was facing the night alone without Blake to hold her.

Her breath caught on a sob and she hurried out of the exit to the line of yellow cabs, waiting to take travelers to their destinations. While the driver stored her bag in the trunk, she settled into the backseat and prayed that the man wasn't overly chatty. She really didn't think she could talk to anyone without making a fool of herself. All she wanted to do was go home to her apartment away from the prying eyes of strangers and cry herself into oblivion. Thankfully it was dark enough that even if she did lose control, chances were the man wouldn't notice.

When they reached her apartment complex, she paid the cabdriver and pulled her travel bag along behind her as she slowly walked the short distance to her ground-floor apartment. But once she approached the door, she spotted a man sitting in the shadows on her porch step. Unsure whether to proceed and demand that he leave or turn around and run for help, she stopped dead in her tracks. That's when he looked up.

Her heart pounded and drawing a breath was all but impossible. "Blake?"

"This isn't safe," he said, shaking his head. "There should be lights along these sidewalks and dusk-to-dawn security lights on every building."

"I left the front-door light on," she said defensively. "It must have burned out."

"I don't like you living in a place where the security is this lax," he said, rising to his feet as he looked around.

"Oh, really?" She shook her head as she reached inside her handbag for her key. "How safe it is where I live isn't any of your concern anymore."

"Like hell!" When she pulled the key from her bag, he took it from her trembling fingers and unlocked and opened the door for her. "You're my wife. Your safety is of the utmost importance to me."

His attitude and his reference to her as his wife infuriated and broke her heart at the same time. How could he claim to want the best for her when he hadn't trusted her with the truth?

"Get real, Blake." She brushed past him to enter her apartment and turn on one of the lamps at the end of the couch. "The most important things in your life are your precious ranch and your bank account. I doubt that I even make the top ten on your list of things you value."

"That's not true," he said, following her into her small living room. "You're more important to me than my next breath."

"Whatever," she said, dropping her purse on the coffee table. She turned to face him. "I don't know why you're here or what you think you're going to accomplish by following me to Seattle, but—"

"I came to talk to my wife," he said, closing the door behind him.

"I don't see that there's anything left to say." She shook her head. "You had ample opportunity to talk to me while I was at the Wolf Creek Ranch and you chose not to. And stop calling me your wife."

"I'm here now to set things straight," he said stubbornly crossing his arms. He stood like a stone statue and she realized he had every intention of making her listen to what he had to say. "And why shouldn't I call you my wife?" he asked. "We're still married."

She rubbed at the tension, causing her temples to pound unmercifully. "Please leave, Blake. I'm exhausted and you're not helping my developing headache."

He took a step toward her. "Sweetheart, I'm—"

"Don't call me that," she said, shaking her head as she backed away from him. "That's an endearment and one that you obviously don't mean and never have." She took a deep breath. "Now, will you please leave and go back to Wyoming, where you belong."

"I belong where you are." He walked over and sat down on the couch. "And I'm not leaving until we work this out."

Frustrated with his persistence to the point of tears she absolutely refused to let him see, she pulled her travel bag to the bedroom door. "I'm not going to argue with you any longer. I'm going to bed and I would prefer that you're gone when I get up in the morning. Please lock the door on your way out."

Without looking back, she walked into the bedroom, closed and locked the door, then leaned back against it. She couldn't imagine what Blake thought he could say to explain his actions or why he even cared to try. On the flight back to Seattle, she'd faced the brutal reality of the situation. No matter what he'd told her, Blake had never intended for their marriage to work. He'd never even told her what his life in Wyoming was really like! For that matter, she couldn't imagine why he'd married her to begin with He'd probably been immensely relieved when she'd refused to join him on the ranch eight months ago.

It suddenly occurred to her that he might be here now to make sure she wasn't going to go after his money or try to take part of his ranch. The divorce wasn't final yet, after all.

"He doesn't need to worry," she murmured as she walked into the adjoining bathroom to brush her teeth. Even if he offered her a settlement, she would tell him what he could do with it. She had never wanted anything from him but his love, his respect and his honesty.

But even though he hadn't given her any of that, her heart had stalled and she'd barely resisted the urge to run into his arms when she first saw him sitting on her step. Nothing would have made her happier than to have him hold her close and tell her that it would all be all right and they could work things out.

As she looked in the mirror at the miserable woman staring back at her, Karly couldn't help but wonder if she'd lost her mind. How could Blake possibly look so darned good to her when he was the last person in the world she should want to see? Or trust?

Sitting at the small table in Karly's breakfast nook, Blake shifted in his chair in an effort to relieve the kinks in his back from sleeping on her couch. Sometime around midnight, he'd decided the damn thing should be certified as an instrument of torture. Not only had both of his feet gone to sleep from hanging over the end of it, but there was also a definite sag in the middle that had his back feeling like it had been broken in several places.

But as uncomfortable as it had been, there was no way he was going to leave this apartment until she heard what he had to say—even if he had to sleep on that damn couch all week. After he'd laid it all on the line, then if she still wanted to kick him to the curb, he'd somehow find the strength to bow out of the picture—even if it killed him—and let her go. The bottom line was and always had been that he loved her and wanted nothing but her happiness. He could only hope that happiness included him.

"I thought you'd be gone by now," she said when she walked into the tiny kitchen carrying a box of tissues. Her eyes were red and puffy and he knew she'd spent most of the night crying. Just knowing he was the cause of her distress nearly killed him.

But as he continued to look at her, his heart stalled. With her long blond hair slightly mussed from sleep and wearing a nightshirt that was at least two sizes too large and about as shapeless as a tow sack, he didn't think he'd ever seen her look sexier.

He took a sip of his coffee and shook his head as he tried to focus on what he needed to say to get her to listen. "I'm not going anywhere until we talk."

"I have to go to work," she said, placing the box on the table and walking over to pour herself a cup of the coffee he'd made earlier.

"I'll be here when you get home." He shrugged. "Whether it's now or later, we are going to discuss this, Karly."

She stared at him for several long seconds before she closed her eyes as if trying to find patience. When she opened them, the emotional pain he detected in the blue depths just about tore him apart. The thought that he was the cause of that sadness was more than he could bear.

"Blake, I don't know what you could possibly say that's going to make a difference," she said, sinking into the chair across the table from him. "You obviously didn't want me to know that you own the Wolf Creek Ranch or that you're quite wealthy."

Guilt settled across his shoulders. "Karly, there were a couple of reasons I didn't tell you about my assets when we first met."

"I remember you telling me about the owner's stepmother being a gold digger and how hard it was to get the ranch back," she said, sounding defeated. "I just wasn't aware you were talking about yourself and the difficulties you had with her. But I had nothing to do with that."

"I know." He slowly set his coffee cup on the table. "Sean and I had hints of the way she was after Dad married her, but when he passed away she took the gloves off and made it clear she was going to do everything she could to cut us out and keep us from inheriting anything she thought she could turn into cash."

"It's unfortunate that she turned out to be so ruthless and I can understand you becoming suspicious of other women's motives." Karly shook her head. "But I didn't know anything about you having money and you had no right to blame me for crimes I didn't commit. And for that matter, never would commit."

"I know, sweetheart, and I can't tell you how sorry I am for that."

He stared down at his loosely clasped hands resting on the table a moment before he took a deep breath and met her accusing gaze head-on. She needed to know all of the reasons behind his caution, even if those reasons were something he was less than proud of.

"I also had my own run-in with a woman several years back who tried to extort money from me," he said, cursing himself for being such a fool.

"Once again, I had nothing to do with that," she reminded him. He hadn't expected her to make his confession easy on him and he deserved nothing less than her condemnation.

"I realize that, but I owe you an explanation and an apology." He took a deep breath. "About six years ago, I was at a rodeo in San Antonio and won the bull-riding event. Instead of celebrating with a can of beer and a good night's sleep like I should have, I went out on the town."

"You got drunk," she said, cutting right to the heart of the matter.

Blake nodded. "Yeah. And I should have stopped with that and gone back to the hotel."

"But you didn't," she mused.

"No. I went back to a cheap motel close to the bar." He hesitated. "I was with one of the buckle bunnies."

"What are those?" Karly asked, taking a sip from her coffee cup. Her doubtful expression hadn't changed, but she was at least showing an interest in his explanation.

"Rodeo groupies," he answered, wishing he'd never heard of them, either. "Some of them are harmless, but others want to sleep with rough stock riders who win."

"Why?" she asked, frowning.

"For the bragging rights," he said, disgusted with himself for falling into that trap. "It's like a feather in their cap to say they've slept with this or that rider." He shook his head at his foolishness. "Anyway, I spent the night with one of them and a month later she showed up claiming I had made her pregnant."

Karly's eyes widened. "You have a child?"

"Good God, no," he said hurriedly. "It turned out that she wasn't pregnant at all. She had asked around and found out that I had money and was in line to inherit at least part of the Wolf Creek Ranch. She decided I was an easy mark for a big payoff."

"She thought you would pay her to end the pregnancy?" Karly asked, looking affronted.

He nodded. "Just about the time I offered to raise the baby on my own, I learned she wasn't pregnant and never had been."

Karly looked thoughtful for a moment as if she was processing what he had told her. "I suppose something like that would leave you with an overabundance of caution."

"It had been my experience not to let people know that I was more than just another dust-covered cowboy trying to make a living off riding bulls and herding cattle," he said, nodding. "Then I met you and before I found a way to tell you about myself, we got married and started making plans for you to move to the ranch."

"Why didn't you tell me then?" she asked, her tone accusing. "Was it because you failed to get me to sign a prenuptial agreement before the wedding ceremony?"

"Not at all." He had to make her understand. "I had plans to tell you when you joined me at the ranch. I thought it would be a nice surprise learning that we'd never have to worry about finances the way other couples do when they first start out. You'd have the option of continuing with your career, work part-time or quit and be a full-time ranch wife. Whatever you wanted to do."

"Only I called and told you that if we stayed married, you'd have to move to Seattle," she said slowly.

"Yeah." He stared down at his empty cup. When he looked up, he added, "But I wasn't the only one with a secret, was I?"

"What do you mean?" she asked, frowning. "I've always been honest with you."

"Sweetheart, from what you've told me about your parents and their divorce, I think that carried a lot of weight in your decision not to come to Wyoming eight months ago." He reached across the table to cover her delicate hand with his. "The only thing I don't know is how it influenced you and why."

She had opened up about her parents during their conversation in the hot tub and he was positive their divorce had somehow played into her choices about them. But he needed to know how their problems had become her problems. How were they holding her back?

When Karly remained silent, he got up to round the table. He picked her up and sat down with her on his lap. "I know I screwed up by not telling you everything about myself and the reasons I felt I had to be cautious. But you've left out some important information about yourself, too. What we've got is good and worth fighting for, Karly. Talk to me. Tell me what held you back and why you were so frightened—why you're still frightened."

"You won't understand," she said quietly. She shook her head. "I'm not even sure it makes sense."

"Why don't you tell me and maybe we can make sense of it together?" he suggested, loving that she was in his arms again and wasn't pushing away from him.

She remained silent for a minute before she finally spoke. "From the moment we moved to the Midwest my mother hated it and before it was over with, she despised my father as well." She turned her head to give him a pointed look. "After she and I moved back to New York she blamed him for everything that went wrong in her life—the loss of her career, her unhappiness. Sometimes I even think she didn't like me because I was part of him."

When she fell silent, Blake kissed her cheek and hugged her close. "I'm sure she loved you, sweetheart."

She shrugged one slender shoulder. "Whether she did or not, I was afraid that if I discovered I didn't like living outside of a city the same thing would happen to us." Tears filled her blue eyes when she looked at him. "I care too much for you to let that happen, Blake. You deserved better than to be resented and blamed for something you had no control over."

Giving her a kiss that left them both breathless, he raised his head to smile at her. "I love you, too, sweetheart. I always have and I always will."

That was all it took for the floodgates to open and when she lay her head on his shoulder, Blake held her while her tears ran their course. He hated seeing a woman cry, but Karly's tears were especially gut-wrenching. She was crying for the child who had doubted her mother's love, as well as what her parents' mistakes had almost cost the two of them.

When she raised her head he handed her a tissue from the box on the table. "Feel better now?" he asked, smiling at the only woman he had ever loved.

Her cheeks turned a rosy pink. "I'm sorry. I hate being so emotional."

"You don't have to apologize to me, Karly," he said, kissing her forehead. "It's my job to be here for you during the bad times, as well as the good."

"I love you so much, Blake," she said, throwing her arms around his neck.

"And I love you, Karly," he said, hugging her tightly against him.

They sat that way for some time, content just to be in each other's arms.

"So where are we going to live?" he finally asked.

She sat back to give him a strange look. "I...assume we'll live in Wyoming at your ranch."

"Only if that's where you want to live," he assured her. "As long as I have you, I'll live anywhere and make a trip back to the ranch periodically."

"Blake, I was wrong," she said, placing her soft palms on his cheeks to gaze into his eyes. "I love your ranch."

"Our ranch," he amended. "It's yours now, as much as it is mine."

She shook her head. "All I want is you."

"Do you really want to argue about this now?" he asked, laughing.

Smiling, she shook her head. "I want to live with you on the Wolf Creek Ranch. That's where I want to ride Suede and help you feed bucket babies and raise our own babies." Her smile faded. "I know we haven't talked about it, but you do want a family, don't you?"

"There are a lot of things we haven't talked about," he said, nodding. "But now that you're coming home with me, we have plenty of time to share our hopes and dreams." When she continued to look at him, he grinned. "Yes, Karly. I want a family and I'll be more than happy to give you all the babies you want."

"I love you so much," she said, snuggling against him. "I can't wait to go back home."

His chest tightened with emotion at her reference to the ranch as home. "There's something else I intended to do for you after we got married in Vegas."

"What's that?" she asked, kissing his neck.

Her lips sent a flash fire blazing through his veins and he had to take a deep breath in order to answer her. "The ceremony we had in Vegas wasn't very fancy and I want to see that you have the wedding of your dreams."

"Oh, Blake, I would love that," she said, tears filling her eyes once again. "But we'll have to wait until spring."

He frowned. "Why would we have to do that?"

"I'd really like to renew our vows out on the patio by the waterfall," she said, looking hopeful. "I think it would be beautiful if we could have a sunset wedding."

"We can make that happen," he said, nodding. "It's warm enough right now. How about this coming weekend?"

"We don't have time to arrange everything," she said, looking doubtful.

"Sweetheart, you'd be surprised how quickly things can be arranged when you have the money to do it," he said, laughing.

"How about the following weekend?" she asked. "I really need time to think about what I want."

"That sounds good to me," he said, standing up with her in his arms.

"Where are we going?" she asked as he carried her across the living room.

"I'm going to take my wife into her bedroom and make love to her," he said, kissing her soundly. "Then while you go to work, I'm going to try to get some sleep. Do you know how uncomfortable that damned couch is?"

Her laughter was one of the sweetest sounds he'd ever heard. "After we make love, I'm going to call and tell my boss that I won't be coming back. Then I'm going to stay in bed and take a nap because I didn't get much sleep last night, either."

As he placed her on the bed and stretched out beside her, Blake kissed her soft, perfect lips. "Are you sure you want to quit your job, Karly? I don't want you doing anything you might regret."

"I'm positive." She reached for the snaps on his chambray shirt. "Now, will my husband please make love to me?"

They could plan their wedding and discuss her decision to quit her job later. Right now, he had his beautiful wife asking him to make love to her and she wasn't going to have to ask him twice.

"I love you, Karly Ewing Hartwell. You own me, heart and soul."

"And I love you, Blake. More than you'll ever know."

Epilogue

Two weeks later, as Karly stood in front of the mirror in the bedroom she'd used at the foreman's cottage, she waited for Tori Laughlin to work the tiny buttons through the decorative loops at the back of her long, white satin and lace strapless wedding gown. "Is Eli here with the carriage?" she asked.

"He just arrived," Tori answered, finishing with the buttons on Karly's dress. She walked over and picked up the veil they'd laid out on the bed earlier. "Thank heavens Blake got the road asphalted these past two weeks. I'd hate to see your beautiful dress covered in Wyoming dust."

Karly nodded. "I couldn't believe how quickly the

crew from the construction company finished surfacing the road from here to the main house."

"It doesn't take long," Tori said as she pinned the tulle and lace to the back of Karly's loosely upswept hair. When Karly's new best friend stepped back, she smiled. "You're going to knock the socks off Blake when he sees you in this."

"That's the plan," Karly said, smiling as she looked at herself in the full length mirror.

After she and Blake returned to the ranch from Seattle, Karly had gone into full wedding mode and, with Tori's recommendation, hired a wedding planner from Cheyenne. The woman had been nothing short of a miracle worker and once Karly had told her what she wanted and the date, all that had been left for Karly to do was decide on the perfect dress. Fortunately, she found what she wanted at the first bridal shop she and Tori visited and once the alterations were completed there really hadn't been all that much for her to do.

A knock on the door signaled that it was time for Eli to drive them over to the main house for the ceremony that would renew Karly and Blake's wedding vows. When Tori opened the door he grinned. "You ladies look beautiful." Eli kissed his wife. "Blake and I are the two luckiest guys this side of the Great Divide."

"And don't you forget it," Tori said, kissing her husband's cheek. Turning to Karly, she asked, "Are you ready?"

"I'm more than ready," Karly said, picking up the bouquet the wedding planner had delivered earlier.

As they made their way downstairs and out to the white horse-drawn carriage that would take them over to the main house for the ceremony, Karly couldn't stop smiling. She felt a little like Cinderella and knowing that her very own Prince Charming would be waiting to help her down from the carriage once they arrived at the ranch house made her impatient to get there. She hadn't seen Blake since earlier in the day when Tori arrived to take them to get their hair and nails done down in Eagle Fork and she'd missed him terribly.

When Eli drove the carriage up the drive to the log mansion, Karly's breath caught at the sight of Blake waiting for them at the end of the sidewalk leading to the patio. Dressed in a Western cut tuxedo, black snake-skin boots and a wide brimmed black hat, he truly was the man of her dreams.

"You're gorgeous," he whispered close to her ear as he lifted her down from the carriage.

"You clean up real nice yourself, cowboy," Karly said, rising on tiptoes to kiss his lean cheek.

"Are you ready to become Mrs. Hartwell?" he asked as he tucked her hand in the crook of his arm and started walking toward the waterfall where the minister and his brother Sean were waiting on them.

"I'm already Mrs. Hartwell," she said, loving her new last name.

He nodded. "But this time it's permanent, sweetheart."

As she glanced toward the Western sky, the sun was just beginning to sink behind the mountain peaks and it was time for her sunset wedding to begin. "I've never been more ready for anything in my entire life," she said as they walked past over a hundred guests assembled on the patio.

As the last of their wedding guests drove away from the ranch house, Blake took Karly in his arms and kissed her until she sagged against him. "I've got a surprise for you," he said, taking her by the hand to lead her around to the other side of the pool.

When he stopped by the fire pit where he'd lain a small amount of kindling, the woman he loved more than life itself looked up at him like he'd lost every ounce of sense he possessed. "Seriously? Do you really want to build a fire now?"

Happier than he'd ever been, he grinned. "Trust me. I think you'll like this."

"I was looking forward to going upstairs to give you a wedding surprise of my own," she said as she continued to stare at him.

"I promise this won't take long," he said, lighting the dry wood. When the fire began to crackle, Blake reached into the inside pocket of his tuxedo and pulled out an envelope. "I thought we could get rid of these together."

A look of understanding sparkled in her pretty

blue eyes and a smile curved her lips. "The divorce papers. I had forgotten all about them."

"I hadn't," he said, removing the documents from the envelope. He gave them to her, then just as they'd done when they cut their wedding cake, he covered her hand with his and they tossed them onto the fire together.

As they watched the papers curl and turn black as they burned, Blake held Karly close. "Now that we have that taken care of, what's this about you having a gift for me?"

Her lovely smile sent his blood pressure sky-high. "You'll have to wait until early summer for the actual gift. But I can tell you about it."

He leaned forward to press his lips to hers. "I'm listening."

"It's going to be small and loud at times," she said, grinning. "And you're probably going to lose a lot of sleep because of it."

Blake had no idea where she was going with this, but she definitely had his full attention. "Okay," he said cautiously. "Would you like to tell me what *it* is?"

"I don't know yet." Something about the look in her eyes caused the air to lodge in his lungs a moment before she grinned. "But as soon as we find out, we'll be redecorating the room across the hall from the master suite in either pink or blue."

"You're pregnant."

"No, we're pregnant," she said, laughing. "*We* got

me into this together and *we're* going to get me out of it. Together."

He suddenly couldn't stop grinning and he was pretty sure he looked like a damned fool. He couldn't have cared less. They were going to have a baby.

Pulling her in his arms, he kissed her until they both gasped for breath. "It happened the morning we worked things out."

She nodded. "We were so caught up in the moment, that's the only time we forgot about protection."

"I love you, Karly Hartwell," he said around the lump clogging his throat.

When he swung her up into his arms and started toward the house, she cupped his face with her soft palm. "And I love you, Blake. Now, please take me upstairs so I can show you just how much."

* * * * *

TERMS OF A TEXAS MARRIAGE

LAUREN CANAN

I owe my love of telling stories to my dad.
Without his inspiration and encouragement, my journey to become an author would never have begun.
This story was possible because of the love and support of my critique siblings, Angi, Jan, Jen and Kathleen, who were always there with a shoulder to cry on when I needed one. To the best literary agent in the world, Jill Marsal, who has the patience of a saint.
To my dearest friend, Laurel, whose belief in me never wavered. And to Terry, my own real-life hero. He taught me the true meaning of love and happily ever after.

One

Shea Hardin had to admit the man didn't look like the devil. No horns sprouted up through Alec Morreston's thick, expertly styled, mahogany-brown hair, although a few defiant tendrils fell lazily over his forehead. The wide mouth and well-defined lips, while appearing unrelenting, didn't make it to a complete snarl. The near-perfect white teeth, seen briefly in the forced smile as introductions were made, didn't include fangs. In fact, the sculpted features of his face had the potential to be exceedingly handsome, but the lack of any emotion other than cold indifference reduced that potential to tolerable. Just.

She'd sensed his glance several times since entering the conference room adjacent to her attorney's office. She didn't need to look in his direction to know he watched her, silently, recording his first impressions, probably sizing up her abilities, weighing her strengths, discreetly alert to any hint of weakness.

Feminine instinct told her his assessment wasn't limited to her ability to handle this situation. He was also taking in every curve of her body, noting every breath she took, watching every move she made. It was a frank and candid assessment of her female attributes without any effort to conceal his interest. Intuition told her here was a man who knew what a woman needed and exactly how to provide it. His subtle arrogance was at once insulting and alluring.

She tried to swallow but her mouth had gone dry. Endeavoring not to appear affected by this man, she crossed her legs, shook the hair back from her face and fixed her eyes on the old pendulum wall clock. But in spite of her determination to ignore him, there was no denying the heat radiating throughout her body, inflaming her senses, fueling the unwanted need pooling in her lower belly.

Picking up a pencil, she scribbled furiously on the open notepad. She was reacting like a besotted teenager. How could she possibly feel any attraction whatsoever to this man? His chosen path in life was destroying the past; tearing down the treasured remains of bygone eras, replacing them with cold glass and steel fabrications. And this man wanted her ranch. The awareness of her body's traitorous response both stunned and angered her.

She was not going to be intimidated—or enticed—by him or his attorney. The very reason they sat across from her should be enough to dispel any thoughts that Alec Morreston would ever be someone she'd want to know better.

"If everyone is ready, I suggest we begin," said Ben Rucker, her attorney and longtime family friend. He switched on a small tape recorder sitting on the polished conference table amid the varying papers, notepads and legal documents.

"Today is April twenty-sixth. The purpose of this meeting is to address the issue of tenancy concerning the home and land currently occupied by Shea Hardin. In attendance are Alec Morreston, owner of the property, his attorney, Thomas Long, Shea Hardin and myself, Ben Rucker, legal counsel for Ms. Hardin."

Shea smiled at Ben. His tired but astute gray eyes reflected his concern over the situation. He'd practiced law for almost forty years, and she had complete confidence in his abilities, as her father had before her.

"At the turn of the nineteenth century, five thousand one hundred and twenty acres of land running along the western boundary and into what is now the National Forest and Grassland Reserve in Calico County, Texas, were acquired by William Alec Morreston. Later that year, he transferred the entire parcel to a widow, Mary Josephine Hardin. Since that time, descendants of Mary Hardin have continued to live on the land, today licensed as the Bar H Ranch."

Ben reached for his glasses, placed them on his nose and picked up his copy of the original paperwork.

"Rather than a purchase, this transfer of land was handled in a manner similar to what we today call a lease." He glanced over the top of his glasses. "I believe you each have a copy of the original paperwork?" When everyone nodded, he continued. "You'll note the duration was ninety-nine years with a renewal option.

"The first lease term was renewed by Cyrus Hardin, Shea's great-grandfather. The second term, currently in effect, is due to expire at the end of this month—in five days, to be precise. Ms. Hardin would like to retain possession of the property. Mr. Morreston has indicated a desire to reclaim it for his own use. This can be achieved only if Ms. Hardin has not, or does not meet all of the renewal requirements by the end of the month."

Shea glanced at Alec Morreston and once again encountered the full intensity of his gaze. A powerful energy emanated from him, the full force of it focused directly on her. She swallowed hard and looked away, ignoring the increasing tempo of her pulse.

"We didn't inspect the house and outbuildings," Mr. Long advised without preamble. "But we are satisfied that everything appears in satisfactory condition. We concede all stipulations relating to the condition of the property have been met."

Shea closed her eyes as relief washed over her. Reaching out to Ben, she squeezed his arm and then looked at Mr. Long and Alec Morreston. So grateful they'd been honest in their findings, she even managed to send a stiff smile of thanks in his direction. He hesitantly tipped his head as if to say *you're welcome*, but she couldn't help but notice the raised eyebrow and the hint of a smirk in the hard lines of his face, almost as if he knew something she didn't.

Shea returned her attention to Ben. He wasn't smiling, and didn't appear to share in her feeling of relief. No one switched off the tape recorder. No one stood up. It was as though a silent warning had begun to flash in a quickly ascending elevator, indicating the bottom was about to drop out.

"In addition to the condition of the property," Ben said, still not meeting her glance. "Apparently the ancestors of Ms. Hardin and Mr. Morreston believed it necessary to add what I would describe as a personal clause."

"Personal clause?" Frowning, Shea began to page through her copy of the old, handwritten document.

"On page four, about two-thirds down the page." Ben removed his glasses and put down the paper as if he could recall the words from memory. His voice was quiet, his manner unusually gentle. "It states in addition to the actual upkeep, if the renewal of the lease is awarded to a woman, she must be legally wed by or before the expiration of the lease."

Her head snapped up, staring at Ben's face.

"What?" Her jaw dropped in astonishment. She frowned, not understanding or wanting to believe the implications of what she'd just heard.

"It further states—" Ben again donned the thick glasses and raised his chin, a motion that enabled him to use the lower, bi-focal portion of the lenses. "'If the female lessee has no husband or betrothed, the oldest adult male, unmarried, in the Morreston family will be joined to her in matrimony, legally and spiritually, and they shall live as husband and wife for a period of not less than one year to ensure her protection against any and all perils, assist her with all ranching endeavors and ensure she is given fair and equal consideration.

"'The failure of either party to meet these terms will result in the forfeiture of the property to the other. If a marriage does occur between the principal parties, such marriage can be terminated at the end of one year, and at such time the land will go to the Hardin family for another ninety-nine-year duration.'"

He sat back in his chair and tossed the documents onto the tabletop. "You gotta love the Morreston family chivalry."

Silence momentarily filled the small room.

"For what it's worth, Shea," Ben said, "I'd guess the families were very close, and this was their way of ensuring the safety of any woman who might be single and head of household when the lease expired. As you know, it used to be a man's world and a woman by herself didn't have much of a chance. The one year marriage provision was probably intended to ensure she had full support with the ranch. If either didn't want to stay married after that, they wouldn't be required to do so. Ironically—" his eyes narrowed as he looked at Alec Morreston "—the clause was probably intended to protect any female of the Hardin family from the *crooks* who might try and take advantage of her."

The only reaction from Alec Morreston was a deepening of the tiny lines around his eyes, a silent indication he found amusement in Ben's assessment.

"But…" Leaning forward, she placed her elbows on the table for support and rubbed her fingers against her temple, willing her brain to click back into gear. "You're saying… You're telling me the lease can't be renewed because I'm a single woman?"

"If I may," Thomas Long interjected. "What it means, Ms. Hardin, in the simplest terms, is that in order for you to renew the lease you must currently be married or you must agree to marry Alec within the next five days and remain married for at least one year. If you don't agree, the lease cancels. If Alec does not agree to such a marriage, should you choose that option, the lease will be renewed."

For a few moments, speech was impossible. Her eyes remained fixed on Mr. Long as her mind tried to make some sense out of his words. She was stupefied.

"You've *got* to be kidding. This is a sick joke. It's archaic." Although attempting to remain calm, her resolve was quickly slipping away. "This kind of thing isn't legal." She looked at Ben, who sat quietly, tapping his pencil on the tabletop. "Is it?"

Ben hesitated for a few seconds as if trying to formulate his answer. "As far as I've been able to determine, the owner of the property could place any clause, requirement or restriction in the lease that he wished within the existing laws of the time. If the lessee agreed, it became a binding agreement. As to the question of whether it's binding by today's laws, it may very well not be."

Hope flared within her.

"But the problem is, if we sue to have that clause stricken, the courts could declare the entire contract null and void, in which case Mr. Morreston is under absolutely no obligation to renew the lease. And, if the courts didn't find the clause unlawful, by the time they handed down their decision, the deadline would be past. Either way..." Ben made a small gesture with his hands, his palms turned upward, indicating the hopelessness of the situation.

Shea sat back in her chair and stared out the large picture window. How could such a beautiful spring day suddenly turn so bleak and ugly? She trained her eyes squarely on Alec Morreston.

"You knew about this, didn't you?"

"Yes," he replied, his voice deep and throaty. "Thomas caught it and advised me a couple of months ago. You might want to ask your attorney why he didn't see fit to inform you. Since he was obviously aware of your single marital status, it might have saved all of us a lot of time."

Her glance swung to Ben, who shrugged and shook his head. "I'm sorry, darlin'. I thought Mr. Morreston would view the outlandish clause for what it is. It never occurred to me he'd use it to his advantage to try and reclaim possession of the land."

"I don't believe it," she muttered. "I don't believe any of this. Are you all trying to tell me I've got to take this… *insanity* seriously? That I'm going to lose my home, my ranch, everything my father and his father before that worked for, because I'm not married and won't marry *him*?"

The tone in her voice clearly painted the "him" as something disgusting and vile—which, at that moment, was spot-on. In spite of his sexual charisma, her conscious mind told her Alec Morreston was nothing more than a cold-blooded opportunist. And as far as this…lease…how could anyone in his right mind possibly make up such a stipulation?

"Your loss was taken into consideration, Ms. Hardin." Alec pointedly ignored her outburst. His composed voice resonated through the thick silence that had temporarily blanketed the small room. "I'm willing to provide reimbursement for the structures on the property, including the house, as well as compensate for one year's ranch income. And, of course, the proceeds from the sale of your livestock and equipment will be yours, provided you choose to sell rather than relocate."

Shea glared at him, afraid to speak for fear it would release the torrent of fury welling up inside her. Comparing this man to the devil had been much too kind.

"In addition," Morreston continued, "I'm willing to provide adequate time for you to find another residence. We understand the relocation process will take longer than the standard sixty days."

"Alec is making a most generous offer, Ms. Hardin," added Thomas Long, as though he felt compelled to point that out.

Ignoring the attorney, she focused directly on the source of this insanity, on the devil incarnate. Sitting casually back in his chair, he appeared relaxed and completely indifferent to what amounted to the end of life as she knew it. Her basic principles, her education, her future dreams, pride in her family—all of it rested within the boundaries of the ranch. She couldn't imagine what her life would be without it.

"Why are you doing this?" Her voice was firm and unwavering, but her heart pounded and her stomach tied itself into knots.

"It's nothing personal, Ms. Hardin." He tipped his head to one side as his eyes roamed over her face. "It's just business."

"Oh, really?" she challenged. "That's what you call it? Destroying a person's life is 'just business?'" She shook her head in amazement. "You must think you'll make a small fortune on this deal."

"That's always a possibility," he admitted, shrugging his broad shoulders.

"I'm curious. What's it going to be? A dude ranch for your city friends or cheap housing that will fall apart in ten years?"

"I don't think Alec's future plans for the land need discussion at this—"

"It's good land in a prime location," Alec answered her, interrupting his attorney. "And the time for its development has come." His eyes never left her face, his tone hard and unemotional.

She couldn't help but speculate if they would have been

having this meeting if her dad were still alive. But common sense told her Morreston wanted the land and would have found other reasons to decline the renewal. This little "personal clause" was convenient and tailor-made to suit his purposes.

"You could omit the clause and renew the lease."

"I could," he admitted openly. "But I won't."

Silently she studied the hard, chiseled features of his face.

"Then there is no more to say, is there?" Standing, she gathered her papers and slipped them into the manila folder. She wouldn't grovel before any man, especially some arrogant stranger from New York, particularly when she knew it would do no good. Her hands were trembling due to shock, but she refused to let these contemptuous strangers see any weakness.

"Ben." She pressed her lips together to cover the trembling. "I assume you'll be in touch about what needs to be done?"

On seeing his nod, she gave a tight smile and walked out of the room. Somehow, she cleared the outside door without slamming it. Only when she reached the sidewalk did her vision blur with unshed tears of anger and frustration. Seven months ago, she'd buried her father. And now, in the space of less than an hour, she'd learned she was losing her home.

She swallowed back the overwhelming sense of panic. The ranch was her haven, her security. It was her past as well as her future. Her father had entrusted it to her care and she'd promised him in his final moments that his efforts—and the efforts of all the Hardins before them—would not be in vain.

She was the last, the only one remaining, who could carry the Hardin legacy into tomorrow. Two hundred years of struggle and sacrifice, of unwavering strength, bravery and determination by her forefathers to fashion a better life from this small piece of earth, and now, the future rested squarely on her shoulders. The weight of it was staggering.

Slipping behind the wheel of her old Chevy pickup, Shea tried recalling elements of the discussion. Even though Ben had conducted the meeting, she knew Alec Morreston had carefully orchestrated and controlled the entire presentation. Right down to her walking out of the room. The deliberate downplay of some factors of the contract, the strong focus on others. He was good. She had to give him that.

But there was one thing she'd bet Morreston hadn't taken into account. Her father had always said she was an obstinate, hardheaded female who never knew when to admit defeat. She had no intention of admitting failure so easily and giving in to that arrogant, money-grubbing son-of-a-bitch.

Maybe she would lose her home. But maybe she wouldn't.

Ben had said she must be married before the contract expired. He hadn't said she must be married to Alec Morreston, as his attorney had implied. Somewhere out there was a man who would agree to marry her for one year as a strictly business arrangement. She was going to find him.

She squared her shoulders with renewed conviction and started the truck. There was a lot to do and a very short time in which to do it.

Alec and Thomas gathered their respective documents and prepared to leave Ben Rucker's office. Ms. Hardin's abrupt exit from the meeting, while anticipated, had ended any further need for discussion.

Alec had to admit, he was impressed with Shea Hardin. She was not at all what he'd expected. In her midtwenties, she presented herself as having the maturity of someone much older. Even though this must have been devastating to her, she hadn't shouted or cried or otherwise made a scene as so many others in her position might have done.

She'd been upset, but that was understandable. Her parting words, quietly spoken to her attorney just before she'd left the room, indicated acceptance of the situation and what was to come.

But had she really given up? His success in business was due in large part to following his gut instincts. Rarely in his thirty-six years had those instincts let him down. Right now they were screaming that Shea Hardin had done anything *but* admit defeat.

From the top of the silky blond hair that fell in tousled disarray around her head to the tight jeans hugging her slim waist, then molding her sexy, feminine curves and long, slender legs, she was trouble with a capital T. If you added the delicate, almost angelic features of her face and the wide-eyed innocence of those amazing blue eyes, you had the makings of one hell of a problem. Shea Hardin would have no difficulty finding and persuading some spineless, misguided male to marry her for a year. She had five days to do it. And if she succeeded, he could kiss this project goodbye.

Alec regretted it had to be this way: that this young woman had to be forced out of her home. He'd experienced an uncomfortable twinge of regret even before her attorney had informed her of the hopelessness of her situation.

With a grimace, he tossed the last manila folder into his briefcase and closed it. Regret hadn't been the only thing he'd felt. He couldn't remember his libido ever reacting with the speed and intensity it had to Shea Hardin. A flash of insight told him sex with her would be hot and intense, mind-blowing in its fervor. Illogical anger flared at the idea of her marrying another man, lying in his bed. He shook his head to dispel the irrational notion. Under the circumstances, he'd be the last person on earth she'd ever let come near her.

As he snapped the locks on his briefcase closed, the idea

ran through his mind that he should find her, apologize for this seizure of the land and…what?

He wasn't backing away from this venture. He couldn't. Too much time and money already had been invested. So, what good would it do to apologize? She would soon be out of a home, and no apology would change that fact.

As they walked out of the building and toward the parking lot, Alec couldn't shake the idea that he shouldn't be leaving just yet. And if he was honest, he didn't know if it was concern about the land issue or a ridiculously illogical reluctance to walk away from Shea Hardin.

"Thomas," he said as they reached the car, "drop me off at the local car-rental agency, then drive back into Dallas, to Dallas-Fort Worth International, and go on to Boston. Meet with Rolston in the morning and finalize the plans for construction of his new hotel. You know what we need. Get the contracts signed, and I'll see you back in New York in a couple of days."

"You're staying here?" Thomas's brows rose in surprise. "You really think that's necessary?"

"Yeah. I have a feeling Ms. Hardin is not going to give in this easily."

"Well, keep me posted." Thomas opened the car door and tossed his suit coat inside. "Alec, don't start feeling bad about this woman's situation. You've offered her a lot of money that you didn't have to and you've given her virtually all the time she needs to relocate. Hell, it's *your* land."

"Yeah, I hear you." Alec nodded his head. "We're on the same page. I should be here only a couple of days. I'll call tonight and check on Scotty. Mom had the zoo scheduled for today. I have a feeling by now she should be about ready to go home."

"Your mother is keeping your son?"

Alec nodded. "Ms. Bishop quit. And after just two weeks, her replacement was already looking a bit frazzled." Alec shrugged. “Mother offered to come and stay with him. I flew her in from St. Petersburg just before we left to come here.”

Thomas chuckled. “That boy is four going on twenty-four.”

Alec smiled. “Don’t I know it.”

After arranging for a car, Alec eased the large sedan into the lane of traffic heading north. He should be on his way to Boston or back to New York. Instead, he was stuck in a rural north Texas town full of coyotes and cowboys, boots and brawls, dirt roads and bumper stickers proclaiming the South would rise again. He didn’t belong here. He didn’t want to be here. But he had to protect his right to this land. If it hadn’t been mentioned in the reading of his grandfather’s will, he wouldn’t have known of its existence. Now that he knew, he wasn’t about to let it slip through his hands.

The logical thing to do was to bring in a couple of his staff to keep an eye on things. But before the idea could begin to formulate, Shea Hardin’s face drifted into his mind, and he squelched the plan before it had a chance to develop.

“Thanks for coming over, Leona.” Shea pushed the screen door farther open, welcoming her neighbor onto the wide enclosed porch at the rear of the house. “I really do need your help.”

Three days had passed since the meeting in Ben’s office and Shea still hadn’t come up with a solid plan to save the ranch.

“Are you all right?” Leona squinted and gave Shea a cursory inspection. “You sounded terrible on the phone. Kinda scared me. I was afraid you’d gotten kicked by that damn stallion again.”

“I’m fine.” She smiled at the older woman. “At least physically. Come on in and I’ll fix us both a glass of tea.”

Leona Finch was the closest thing to a mother figure Shea had since her own mom died when she was five. Shea loved Leona dearly. In her midsixties, the sun-browned features of her face bore the wrinkles of a lifetime spent on a working ranch. Her speech was as rough as her skin. But she was sensitive, perceptive and in spite of her limited education, profoundly wise.

"So, if you're not hurt, what's the deal?" Leona walked into the kitchen, pulled out a chair and sat down at the table as Shea filled two glasses with ice.

She poured the freshly brewed tea and added a sprig of mint. Setting the glasses on the table, she took a seat across from Leona.

"I've…I've got a problem," she began. "A big one."

"Well, hell." Leona took a sip of the tea and sat back in the chair. "There ain't a problem that can't be fixed. You tell me what's got you so upset, and then we'll figure out how to put it right."

Shea gave her friend a strained smile. She was glad to have Leona on her side. She needed to hear a few of her unceasingly positive assurances that things would work out.

"I'm not sure exactly where to begin. Three days ago I was called to a meeting in Ben's office. It's so bizarre…" Her voice trailed off as she shook her head. Shea looked into her friend's face.

"It seems I've got to find a husband," she told Leona straight out. "And I have less than two days left to do it."

Two

"You've got to do *what*?" Leona leaned forward and Shea saw her eyes narrow as she searched for any sign of a joke.

Shea took a steadying sip of tea. "If I don't get married by the last day of this month, I'll lose the ranch."

"Says who?" Leona's tone was guarded.

Shea recounted the highlights of the meeting in Ben Rucker's office three days earlier. She still had a hard time believing it herself.

"I have no intention of just walking away from everything I love and everything Dad worked so hard to accomplish." Her finger made circles in the condensation forming on the frosted glass. "I've spent the last three days on the phone trying to track down some of my friends from college. The ones I did manage to locate are married or involved with someone. Between the years I was away at school and then Dad's illness, I've lost touch with most of the people I knew in high school."

There had been two loves in her life. The first had been a high school crush who was now married with two kids. She'd met the other, David Rollins, her second year in college. For a while, they had been inseparable and even had talked about marriage. But eventually they both had realized they wanted different things in life. David's plans hadn't included living on a ranch in north Texas. Shea hadn't been able to see herself living anywhere else. She'd tried desperately to reach David, but without any luck. A few of her friends had heard he was living back East, but no one knew exactly where. Some had offered to make calls to try to reach him, but so far he hadn't called.

She pulled a legal pad from under some *Western Horsemen* magazines that lay on the table. "I've made a list of a few possibilities, but—" she shook her head in frustration as she passed the pad to Leona "—it's been a long time."

Leona took the list and set it aside, her eyes locked on Shea's face. "You're not seriously thinking about asking some man to marry you." It was more a statement than a question.

She shrugged. "What else can I do?"

"Do you have even the slightest idea what you'd be letting yourself in for?"

"It will be a business agreement, strictly platonic."

"Yeah, sure it will," Leona muttered, rubbing her hand over her face. "God Almighty. This is the damnedest situation I've ever heard of."

Leona picked up the list, gave her a weary look and began to scan the names. "Tommy Hall. Are his parents John and Grace?"

"Yeah." Shea nodded.

"He got married two weeks ago. One of our hands was his best man." Leona picked up a pen and crossed off his name.

"Duncan Adams. Drinks," she recalled. "A lot. You don't need that grief. Cecil Taylor? I hear he loses more than he makes on the horses over in Bossier City. Unless you're willing to bankroll his gambling, you can scratch him off the list."

One by one, Leona crossed off each man until, of the fourteen names, only one remained.

"What about Tim Schultz?" Shea asked, trying not to sound desperate.

Leona looked at the last name on the list. "Maybe. Isn't

his father the preacher over at that little church east of town?" She frowned in contemplation. "I've never heard nothing bad about him. Kinda quiet. 'Bout your age, right?"

"Yeah," Shea confirmed. "His family only moved to this area a few years ago, but I had some classes with him in college. He's nice enough, I guess."

"So, how do you plan to approach him with this little plan of yours?" Leona laid the pen and pad on the table. "You gonna just walk up to him and say, 'Howdy. Will you marry me for a year? Oh, and by the way, it's strictly business.' I'd sure like to be a fly on the wall when you throw that little tidbit in his direction."

"I'll explain the circumstances, of course." She hadn't rationalized this part of the plan, but obviously it would be necessary. "I'll have to."

"Girl, use your head. Maybe if you talked to that Morreston fellow again—"

"No." Sitting back in her chair, Shea crossed her arms in front of her. Alec Morreston. The mere mention of his name caused a hot blush to spread over her neck and face. The look of male want in his eyes was still vivid in her mind. She'd never experienced anything like it, but even after three days, she knew she hadn't imagined it. And neither had she imagined his cold insensitivity to the havoc he'd caused in her life. She resolutely shook her head. "I can promise you, it would do no good. He's a developer. He lives in New York, probably in some posh penthouse. He doesn't care about the land. He doesn't care about anything but making more money. Probably never got his hands dirty in his life."

"What if you turned the tables on him?" Leona asked, taking another long drink of her tea.

Shea frowned. "I don't understand."

"Well, Ben told you, according to that contract, if you

weren't married by the end of the month, Morreston had to marry you or agree to renew the lease. Right?"

Shea nodded, suddenly afraid of where this was going.

"So tell him you want to marry him."

Shea could only gape in horror.

"Put the problem back on his plate," Leona reasoned. "Think about it. He's a city fellow. He's not going to agree to marry you and live on this ranch. He thinks he's got you bluffed into doing just exactly what you're doing—refusing to use him as a way out."

Shea stubbornly shook her head. "No way, Leona." The idea was beyond bizarre. "Absolutely no way." She still had forty-eight hours.

"I sure wish your father was still alive," Leona muttered.

"So do I, Leona," Shea whispered as she stood and walked to the phone to call Tim Schultz. "So do I."

Shea sipped from the glass of ice water and tried to remain calm. Tonight, before midnight, she had to be married. Tim had finally returned her call this morning. No doubt sensing the urgency in her tone, he'd agreed to meet her at Barstall's City Diner at one o'clock. He was late.

What was she going to say? All the rehearsing in the world couldn't prepare her for what she had to discuss with him. How would he respond? Would he laugh? Would he just walk out? Or, most important, would he agree to do it?

Before leaving yesterday, Leona once more had encouraged her to call Morreston's bluff. But Shea had held firm in her conviction that nothing on earth would make her so desperate to even contemplate such a thing. Heaven help the poor female coerced into marriage with that man.

Instinctively she knew Alec Morreston would be demanding, in bed as well as out. Even if the situation were different, a brief affair with a man like Morreston would take more from her than she could give. She suspected such a liaison would turn into an emotional roller coaster, and that was the last thing she needed in her life.

But it was a moot point. Morreston was long gone. It had taken him fewer than two hours to invade her world and turn it completely upside down. Then he had left, not even bothering to look back as she desperately tried to pick up the pieces from the devastation he'd caused. No doubt, he assumed she would just relinquish her home and quietly disappear. Well, he was in for a surprise—

"Hello, Ms. Hardin." Shea jumped at the sound of the deep voice directly to her left. Her head snapped around and her eyes immediately grew wide in astonishment. She could feel the blood drain from her face as she stared into the amber eyes of Alec Morreston.

"May I join you?"

Before she could respond, he pulled out the chair opposite her and sat down. As his eyes scanned her face, his lips twitched with unrepressed humor at her stunned look. For a long moment, she couldn't speak.

"What...what are you doing here?" she stammered, finally finding her voice.

"I'm about to have lunch," he said innocently, as though misunderstanding the true meaning of her question.

Shea glared at him.

Alec shrugged. "I decided to take a few days and see some of the area. Thought it might be...beneficial...to the future development of the project." He responded as if choosing his words carefully. "Have you ordered yet?"

"Have I...? No." She shook her head. "No. I'm meeting someone." She looked toward the front entrance, no longer sure she'd be glad to see Tim walk through it.

Alec regarded her silently for a moment. "I see. Well, then I'll certainly move to another table as soon as she—or he?—arrives."

If Shea had been nervous before Morreston's unexpected

arrival, that feeling was mild compared to what she was experiencing now. Suddenly, she could relate to every mouse ever caught in a trap that had looked up to find the cat walking in its direction. How on earth was she ever going to present her problem to Tim with Morreston hanging over her shoulder?

"The roasted chicken sounds good," he commented, scanning the lunch specials. "What do you recommend?"

"You really don't want me to answer that."

He glanced at her face over the top of the menu and feigned surprise. But the deepening of the tiny lines around his eyes told her he found her remark amusing.

Before she could deliberate on this newest chapter of the nightmare, another voice beckoned her.

"Um...excuse me. Shea?" Tim Schultz smiled his apology. "Sorry I'm late."

"Tim!" She smiled nervously. "That's okay."

She looked back to Morreston, hoping against hope he would just silently disappear. Apparently, that was not going to be the case. Politeness demanded she make introductions.

"Tim, this is Alec Morreston...Tim Schultz."

Alec stood as the two men shook hands. Over six feet in height, he easily towered over the younger man by several inches while his broad shoulders and lean waist hinted at a muscular, athletic build that made Tim appear almost adolescent in comparison. His reddish-blond hair and fair complexion seemed pale, almost sickly, as opposed to Morreston's dark features.

"Well, if you'll excuse me," Alec said, a grin tugging at the corners of his well-defined mouth, "I'm sure you two have a great deal to discuss. I certainly don't want to interrupt."

"Would you care to join us?" Tim asked, unaware of the situation.

"No!" Shea almost shrieked. Both men looked at her—one with curiosity, the other with increasing amusement.

"Thanks, Tim," Alec said, and Shea's heart all but stopped. "But I think Shea wants to speak privately with you. Maybe another time?"

He knows. He knows exactly why I'm having lunch with Tim Schultz. And apparently, he found the situation extremely amusing. That infamous smirk was firmly in place.

"You knew I was here, didn't you?" It was no coincidence Alec Morreston just happened to show up at the exact time she was meeting with Tim, even if it was the lunch hour and this was the only decent restaurant in town. When he didn't immediately respond, she added, "How?"

"I believe his name is Hank. Your ranch foreman? He said you might be having lunch here today."

Alec moved away from their table, giving her a quick wink as if to seal the private joke between them. She immediately turned away, biting back the angry retort that sprang to her lips. *Ignore him*, she told herself. *Just be thankful to be rid of him.*

But before she could enjoy a second of relief, to her utter dismay, Morreston pulled out a chair at a table next to them. In that location he'd be able to hear every word they said. Something akin to panic formed in her stomach.

"So," Tim began as he took the seat Alec had occupied. "How are you, Shea? Haven't seen you in what—three years? I was surprised to get your call. What's going on?"

She forced a smile and reached for the glass of ice water, needing something to steady her nerves. Her hand shook slightly, and a small amount of water spilled onto the table. As she fought to find the right words, her gaze wavered, and she found herself looking directly into the mocking face of Alec Morreston.

"Shea?"

She heard Tim's voice, but her gaze was captured by amber eyes.

"Shea? Is something wrong?"

She couldn't suppress the overwhelming desire to slam something as she stomped out of the restaurant. She was furious. No, she mentally corrected herself. She was beyond furious. She wanted to kill something. She wanted to kill Alec Morreston.

Each time she'd broached the subject of her meeting with Tim, Morreston had cleared his throat or apologetically interrupted to ask Tim a question or made some asinine comment. Between his little interruptions, he'd sat back in his chair and stared, never taking his eyes off her, exactly as he'd done that first day in Ben's office. That knowing smirk had remained etched on his lips, his tawny eyes alert to every movement she'd made, every breath she'd taken. For almost an hour, he'd made her feel like a bug under a microscope.

About the time she'd started to ask Tim if he would walk her to the truck, Morreston had folded his napkin, placed it on the table and leaned toward her lunch date to strike up a conversation. If they'd tried to leave, she'd known Morreston would have followed. Pleading a headache, she'd excused herself and asked Tim if she could call him later.

Now apprehension increased with each step as she made her way to her vehicle. Her time was almost up. It was down to a few short hours before she would lose the home she loved forever. She'd almost been tempted to stand in the center of the restaurant, loudly declare her problem and ask if there were any takers. If she didn't come up with a plan very soon, it just might come to that.

As she drove toward the parking lot exit, the front doors of the restaurant swung open and out walked Morreston—with Tim at his side. Seemingly engaged in light banter, only Morreston noticed her as she passed. He tipped his head to her in silent acknowledgment. She clutched the steering wheel in a death grip. Her hands itched to slap that arrogant smirk from his face once and for all. In the rearview mirror, she saw him turn to Tim, nod and laugh.

In that moment, she knew she never would have a second chance to speak with Tim. Morreston would see to it. That was why he was here. He knew what she was attempting to do, and he was determined to see her fail. The devil had just sprouted horns.

In the same instant, she also knew she'd reached the limit of her patience with the man and this bizarre situation. She slammed on the brakes and, without pausing to give her actions a second consideration, threw the truck into Reverse. It quickly roared backward before grinding to a halt directly in front of the two men. Their conversation immediately stopped and they both peered at her with curiosity.

She rolled down the window, a phony smile pasted to her lips. Alec watched her with guarded interest.

"Sorry to interrupt you gentlemen. But, *Alec*—?" She used his given name, implying a familiarity that was not there and never would be if she had anything to say about it. She gave him a look of pure innocence.

"You know, I've had a chance to think about our meeting earlier in the week. About the little problem we discussed?"

She had his attention.

"And, well, I think your attorney was right when he pointed out your family's unwavering concern that a single, unmarried woman can't possibly run a ranch…all by herself." The sarcasm dripped from her voice. Her tone was venomous.

Tim looked from one of them to the other, as if struggling to understand any part of their conversation.

"Since Mr. Long was so kind as to explain my alternatives and well…since you've gone to all the trouble to stay here in case I needed you, and in light of all the care and understanding you've shown, I think you're absolutely right." She looked directly into the golden depths of his eyes, an effort that challenged her sanity. "I will marry you, Alec. Under the circumstances, how can I possibly refuse?"

Only Alec comprehended the true meaning of her words. His head drew back, his eyes narrowed and her phony smile almost became genuine as she saw the flare of annoyance in those chiseled features.

"If you'll meet me at Ben Rucker's office in, oh, about an hour? I'm sure he can help us sort out any little details we need to address prior to the ceremony."

Before she switched her attention to Tim, she noted with satisfaction that the smirk was finally, effectively wiped from Morreston's face.

"Tim, I'm sorry I didn't have a chance to discuss this with you inside," she apologized. "But my reason for asking you here was to solicit your help in convincing your father to perform the ceremony on such short notice. Would you mind speaking to him for me?" She surprised herself at how quickly and convincingly the lie rolled off her tongue.

"No," Tim shrugged. If he believed this conversation to be as bizarre as it sounded, he managed to hide it well. "I'll see him this afternoon. When is the wedding? And where?"

"This evening. At my house." Her eyes returned to Alec's face and she noted, with immense gratification, he clearly showed signs of irritation. His jaw worked convulsively as he made a futile attempt to remain calm.

"Will eight o'clock be all right?" she asked.

For a long moment, Alec didn't answer. His eyes searched her face as if attempting to discern what she was up to, as though he couldn't believe what she had just said.

"Eight will be fine," he said finally.

If he'd refused, she'd have been surprised. She knew

instinctively that Morreston was not the type of person to back down after the first stone was cast.

She put the truck in Drive and smiled at Alec. His amber eyes narrowed in a silent declaration of war. While she suspected her triumph would be short lived, it would certainly feel good while it lasted.

"I can't let you do this," Ben Rucker stated for the third time. "Suppose the man doesn't refuse to marry you? What then?"

"Then we'll get married," she said firmly. "At eight this evening. Don't worry, Ben, you're invited."

"This is not a joke!" Ben pulled the glasses off his face and stood up from the desk. "For God's sake, don't do this, Shea. Take the money he's offered and buy land elsewhere. I'll help you. You can—"

"No, Ben. This is my home, my family home, for six generations. I can't just pack up two hundred years of memories and close that door behind me saying, 'Oh well.' If Morreston wants this land, *my* land, he'll have to fight for it."

Ben's eyes, full of concern, silently beseeched her to reconsider. "Is there no way I can talk you out of this?"

"Not unless Alec Morreston will renew my lease."

"Which he is not willing to do." The deep voice responded from the open doorway just behind her. Both Shea and Ben looked around in time to see the subject of their conversation walk casually into the room.

He had shed the sports jacket and tie, leaving his shirt open at the neck but still tucked into the navy slacks. They hugged his slim waist, hinting at muscular thighs beneath the fabric. Somehow, his shoulders seemed broader than they had only an hour ago. The strong line of his jaw was set in determination.

"Don't do this, Morreston," Ben pleaded.

"It's not completely my doing," he answered. His eyes focused on Shea. "Ms. Hardin had a choice, and apparently she decided on this option."

"You gave her no choice at all and you know it," Ben argued. "What kind of man are you to take advantage of her like this?"

Alec pointedly ignored the question. "I'd like to speak with Ms. Hardin in private." His eyes never left her face.

"You can discuss anything that needs saying in front of—"

"No, Ben. It's all right," Shea interrupted. This was her battle now. If she had any hope of making Morreston back down, she couldn't do it hiding behind her attorney. "Shall we step into the next room, Mr. Morreston?"

Alec followed her into the small, adjacent conference room and closed the door behind them with a resounding click. For a few moments they faced each other in silence.

"Are you really serious about this?"

"Yes," Shea replied without hesitation. "I am."

"You would marry a complete stranger in order to keep the land?"

"Yes."

"There is other land."

"Then perhaps you should go and find it."

Alec stared at her. "How much more do you want?" he asked quietly.

Had this man never loved anything in his life that didn't have a price tag attached to it? Could he not understand the legacy she was fighting to save?

"Two million," she said flippantly, and immediately saw a knowing look cross his face. The slight nod of his head indicated his initial acceptance of her outlandish but bogus demand. She was tempted to see how far he would go to buy her off but common sense came rushing forward.

"I don't want your money, Mr. Morreston. This is not

about money. It's about my home. My life. Family values and tradition. Things you, apparently, don't know anything about."

He shoved his hands into the pockets of his slacks and walked past her to stand gazing out the large window on the opposite wall. For long moments, he stood there, saying nothing. From the corner of her eye, she watched as he rubbed the back of his neck. His shirt did little to hide the muscular tone of his arms and back. The silky texture of his dark hair caught the subtle light coming through the window, accentuating deep auburn highlights. As he turned toward her, she quickly looked away.

"It won't work, you know." His voice had a slight raspy quality, which, under different circumstances, she might have found extremely sensual. "Even if I agree to this, no marriage can survive for a year under these circumstances. Eventually you'll concede defeat and the land will revert to me. It's inevitable. Why put yourself through it?"

"That's a very chauvinistic attitude, Mr. Morreston. What makes you so sure *I'll* be the one to call it quits?"

He didn't immediately answer as a look of indulgent amusement crossed his features. Then all traces of humor disappeared. Slowly, he closed in until barely a foot separated them. Without any warning, he reached out and stroked the side of her face.

She inhaled sharply and adjusted her stance at the unexpected contact but determinedly held her ground. His hand slid from her face to cup the back of her neck and, applying the slightest pressure, drew her even closer to him. She watched his gaze roam over each detail of her face before coming to rest on her mouth. She noted the faint shadow that darkened his face as he bent his head toward her. His lips, wide and defined, parted slightly as if intending to kiss her, but stopped a mere breath away, and only his thumb touched her mouth, tracing the curving fullness in an incredibly intimate gesture.

Time stood still. The close physical contact brought her challenge into clear focus. The pulse hammered in her throat. She swallowed back the overwhelming sensation of panic that rose within her and tried to look away.

Alec gently tilted her chin upward, forcing her to look into the golden depths of his eyes. The bittersweet fragrance of his cologne teased her senses. She could sense the disciplined power and virility of his body as he stood mere inches away from her. There was no doubt he was all male. Her stomach muscles involuntarily contracted as a shaft of sexual awareness shot through her. An intense heat seemed to envelop her as her breath became shallow, almost nonexistent. A little voice inside screamed to run while she could.

Three

"All right, Ms. Hardin." His throaty voice penetrated the silence of the room. "We'll play this one your way and see what happens. I'll honor the conditions as set forth by our ancestors and we will be married. And there will be no development on any of the land as long as the marriage continues or if this…union…should exceed one year."

He paused, tilting his head slightly as though studying her reaction. "But know this—" the tone of his voice reflected the seriousness of his words "—you *will* be my wife as stipulated in the original lease. Legally and spiritually, body and soul. You'll share my life, as well as my bed, for the duration. Do you understand what I'm saying?"

It was time to bail out. She knew it but couldn't seem to move. He was telling her exactly what she would have to agree to, up front. He was giving her every opportunity to walk away. She took a deep breath and hoped her strength was as unfailing as her stubbornness.

"I understand." Her voice was firm although barely above a whisper.

"Do you?" A sparkle glistened in Alec Morreston's amber eyes. "I guess we'll find out tonight, won't we?"

He released her and stepped toward the door but hesitated before pulling it open. "One more thing. I'll require a prenuptial agreement. Thomas should have time to fax one to your attorney's office before—"

"No."

His eyes narrowed, pinning her to the spot. "Excuse me?"

"You heard me. I said no."

"Ms. Hardin, do you really expect me to marry a woman I don't know and risk losing half of everything I have?"

"I'd say, after your earlier statement, you expect me to give up more than that. No prenup, Mr. Morreston. I want no part of anything you own, other than my ranch. You can trust me on that—" Shea eyed him coolly "—or you can book your flight home."

She could see the muscles in his jaw working overtime as he apparently strove to keep his temper from exploding.

"My personal holdings have nothing to do with this land issue. If, as you say, you want nothing but the land, then signing a prenup should not be asking too much."

"Neither is wanting to keep my home," she countered. "Nothing in the contract said anything about a prenuptial agreement. I refuse to sign one. If you refuse to marry me because of that, then I guess the land is mine. Your call."

Her heart beat so solidly against the wall of her chest she felt sure he could hear it from three feet away. She hoped she looked calmer on the outside than she felt on the inside.

Silence dominated the room. A barely perceivable change in his stance, from tense to an almost exaggerated casualness, conveyed the control he maintained on his emotions. His tawny eyes drifted over her as if trying to discover how much determination lay underneath. The burning strength of his gaze wandered insolently from her face to her breasts, down to her belly, to her hands—held tightly clenched at her sides—then down the legs of her jeans all the way to her feet. Shea could feel the blush spread across her face as he rudely inspected and silently weighed the feminine merchandise standing in front of him.

"All right, Ms. Hardin," he said finally, his tone suddenly menacing. "We'll play hardball if that's what you want. You just upped the stakes and I'd be a fool not to call your bluff. Be ready tonight, honey. Be ready for me."

He stepped back and opened the door. Shea shakily, but resolutely, walked through it. While temporarily disconcerted by his unexpected and candid proclamation, she knew the marriage would never be consummated. He was trying to intimidate her. That's all it was. He would do well to remember that two could play this game.

She had no intention of letting herself become physically ensnared and used by an egotistical maniac. She may have been forced into making a pact with the devil, but he would quickly find she was anything but a sacrificial lamb. Alec Morreston was city bred and raised. He had no concept of the sometimes harsh realities of ranch life, and she'd bet he wouldn't last a month.

In fact, she had just bet the ranch on it.

"Alec…" The heavy concern in Thomas's voice was clearly evident through the telephone line. Alec could picture him gripping the receiver so tightly his knuckles were turning white. He was almost sorry he couldn't be there in person to deliver the news of the pending wedding. "Are you certain you know what you're doing?"

Because their client-attorney relationship had grown into a solid friendship over the years, Alec wasn't insulted when Thomas questioned his sanity. Hell, in the past five hours, he'd begun to question it himself.

"I mean, what do we really know about this woman?"

"I think she's okay, Thomas."

"But what if she's not? What if this is all a setup? Do you have to *marry* her, for God's sake?" His tone was incredulous. "Maybe if you offered her more money?"

"She wouldn't take two million."

"She—" Alec heard Thomas Long swallow hard on that one. "My God! How much more does she want?"

"She says she doesn't want money. She wants the land. I believe, in her mind, she's telling the truth. She honestly thinks she can pull this off and make me back down. Unfortunately for her, I've committed to building this entertainment complex. The investors are already on board. I'm down several million and we haven't yet poured the first foundation. There is no turning back at this point."

"How about we try to find other land alternatives. I could put out some feelers..."

"A friend who specializes in real estate spent almost a year doing just that. I originally wanted to build in the East. He checked land possibilities within a hundred-mile radius of every major city near a natural waterway from New York to Florida. We encountered zoning restrictions, municipal politics, arbitrary city codes, small town gluttony. He found a two-thousand-acre tract just outside Cincinnati, but the deed was in probate. There was a five-thousand-acre tract in Virginia, but it was so far removed from civilization I didn't want to take the chance it might be *too* far.

"This location is perfect. A little farther west than I initially wanted, but it's actually working out even better than the original plan. It's centrally located in the US, only fifty miles from the Dallas-Ft. Worth International Airport and it borders the Red River."

Alec had already purchased land directly across the state line in Oklahoma and had most of the permits for that side of the river. "I've spent weeks restructuring blueprints to meet local building codes, obtaining land surveys for two states and finally have received a clearance from the EPA over some near-extinct bird they thought nested nearby. I refuse to spend any more time or money trying to find equivalent land just so Ms. Hardin can continue to raise her cows. Give me a few days, a couple of weeks at best, and I'll have her out of here."

"Okay." There was a moment of silence while Thomas,

no doubt, regrouped. "What about a prenup? You're potentially handing this woman a key to a very large door. Your bank accounts alone…" Thomas paused. "I'll have a basic agreement drawn up and sent to you in—"

"No thanks, Thomas."

"*No?* Alec—"

"We've already had this discussion. She refused."

Another stunned silence. "Then don't marry her. Let her have the damn land. Even considering how much you've sunk into the project, it isn't worth a fraction of your other holdings. Alec—"

"Thomas, look, I appreciate your concern. But I honestly feel if it should come down to a divorce petition for any of my current assets, the bizarre reason for the marriage—my being forced to take this route in order to regain the use of my own land—would supersede any claim."

"But we can't know that for sure."

How could he explain to Thomas his gut instinct said this would not be a problem? There was something about Shea Hardin, some glimmer of truth deep in those blue eyes. Nothing he'd seen gave him any reason to suspect she wanted any more than *her* ranch.

"I don't intend to remain married for one millisecond longer than absolutely necessary. In less time than it would take to battle this out, I intend to have her bags packed and be helping little Miss Tradition out the door. Then a simple annulment, give her something for her trouble, and it's done."

He'd been challenged by opponents a lot tougher than Shea Hardin and had come out on top. He grimaced at his own expression. Hell, in truth, on top of her was exactly where he wanted to be. He sensed the blood congregate in his loins at the mental picture and cursed his weakness. He had to keep his focus on the reason he was here and stop letting his imagination run wild.

Alec intentionally changed the subject. "I need you to call Valturego. See if he's ready to sign the contract for the construction of his casino. I'll contact him when I get back in the office."

"I'll call as soon as we're finished," Thomas promised. "But, Alec, back to the prenup thing—"

"Did Rolston sign the revised contract?"

Thomas grudgingly took the hint and began explaining the outcome of his meeting with the banker.

When their business concluded, Alec tossed his cell on the bed in the small motel room and glanced at the digital clock on the nightstand. After six. He probably should start getting ready.

The last time he'd taken vows, there had been more than fifteen hundred invited guests—some he'd known, most he hadn't. The planning had gone on for months. The fragrance from thousands of flowers had permeated the air, almost overwhelming the guests who'd gathered in the enormous church. He could remember the aura of hushed excitement that had filled the large sanctuary in anticipation of the spectacle to come.

Sondra had wanted it all and she had been relentless in making her desires come true. In hindsight, he should have seen what was coming. He should have picked up on the clues. She'd loved to party and her actions had made him suspect she'd crossed the line as far as using drugs. But he hadn't been able to prove it, had never found any evidence, and he'd never known about the other man until the day he came home and found the note. No excuses. No apologies. A strange woman waiting outside his door handed him a baby and said it was his. Suddenly he was alone with an infant son. A month later, Alec learned she'd died of an overdose. The man she'd left him to be with supposedly had provided the pills.

In the years since, the anger over her betrayal had diminished, but the lesson she'd taught him about trust had reshaped his character and would always be foremost in his mind. He'd sworn he would never again make the mistake of marrying. Anyone. For any reason. For almost five years, he'd kept that resolution. But in less than an hour, he would once again stand in front of a minister and make a pledge to love, honor and obey, and this time to a woman he knew nothing about.

Shea Hardin was a total perplexity. She didn't fit into any mold he'd ever come across. At first, he'd believed she was one of the members of Gold Diggers Anonymous he frequently encountered. But if those initial suspicions were correct, she was better than average at setting a trap, because he'd certainly taken the bait. She came across as completely sincere, candid and unwavering in her determination to keep the land.

She was a walking contradiction—intelligent yet naive, beautiful but unsophisticated, sexy as hell yet seemingly innocent. She looked fragile, sensitive, as though her poise and conviction could easily be shattered. But after today, he had the solid impression she was about as fragile as an oak tree, her temper as controlled as a glass vile of nitroglycerin.

She challenged him. She fascinated him.

And she had the most amazing blue eyes he'd ever seen.

Then there was her mouth—full lips that could give a man all kinds of grief, all kinds of pleasure. He'd almost kissed her in the attorney's office, drawing back at the last minute as he realized he wouldn't have wanted to stop with a single kiss.

No, his problem would not be intimidating Shea Hardin. It would be keeping himself from taking her while he did so.

Shea stood in front of her closet later that afternoon, staring at the few dresses hanging inside. Rarely was there any need for her to wear anything other than casual ranch attire and therefore her options were severely limited. She removed a simple paisley dress from the closet and held it in front of her as she viewed her reflection in the full-length mirror. Somehow, it didn't seem right.

She replaced it and reached for another. Wrong style. She bit her lip as she removed a dark green suit from the closet. Not right either. Red? Nope. Black? An impish grin crossed her face at the picture that would create. Quelling the urge, she hung the dress back in the closet and shook her head in frustration. There was no time to go shopping. Under the circumstances she should probably just pull on a clean pair of jeans and be done with it.

Thinking back on her day, she couldn't believe how fast everything had fallen into place for this wedding. Old Doc Hardy had done the blood work on the spot and Jane Simmons at the courthouse had gotten Judge Lamb to push the license through without the three-day wait. It was as unbelievable as her reason for being there.

Suddenly the mirror's reflection caught the motion of a large ball of orange fur as Pumpkin, the old tomcat, jumped onto the cedar chest that sat at the foot of her bed. She spun around and looked at the chest in speculation. Instantly memories of her childhood came rushing back. Memories of her as a little girl standing on top of the chest, trying to be tall enough so she could wear the long silky white dress her mother kept inside. It had been years since she'd reflected on the chest and its contents. On a whim, she set a disgruntled Pumpkin on the floor and then moved the miscellaneous items on top of the chest. A mild scent of cedar permeated the air around her as she raised the lid.

On top were pillowcases, handkerchiefs and small hand towels, their borders bearing floral designs embroidered by her mother. With a regretful smile, Shea set the linens aside. Underneath were two handmade quilts, their colors still amazingly crisp. She noted a date sewn into the corner of one: "A.H.—1812". Her great-grandmother must have made them. Maybe even her grandmother before that. She placed them on the floor next to the linens.

Kneeling over the now half-empty chest, she removed several more layers of tissue paper. Suddenly, there it was, and just as she remembered. Her mother's wedding gown. She rose to her feet as she lifted it out of the chest.

The material was an off-white satin. The years had slightly darkened the creamy color, but time couldn't diminish its simple elegance. The high, Victorian-style neckline, enhanced by delicate lace, covered the bodice and shoulders. Tiny pearl buttons ran down the full length of the gown with a matching row of buttons on each sleeve from the wrist to the elbow.

Tears stung her eyes as she was suddenly overcome with longing for the mother she'd never really known. She gently touched the delicate lace. Should she dare risk tarnishing the memory of her mother's wedding day by wearing it to the marital atrocity about to take place? But the thought of putting it back in the trunk and closing the lid didn't feel right. Something urged her to try it on.

Some ten minutes later, she stepped in front of the mirror and almost didn't recognize her reflection. The gown fit perfectly. Its simple style subtly created an aura of poise and sophistication as it gracefully cascaded to the floor.

She caught her lower lip between her teeth. Sadly, she wished hers would be a genuine marriage, one based on love and respect with hopes for a future. Not a contractual stipulation with an arrogant stranger.

Alec Morreston would no doubt have a good laugh if she appeared in a wedding gown. He'd be convinced she was every kind of crazy. She chewed her bottom lip. When she walked into the room for the ceremony would she feel like a total and complete fool? Circumstances being what they were, it probably was an idiotic idea. Still, a woman got married for the first time only once in her life. Right or wrong, this was it.

There was also the chance Morreston might think she was trying to play him and raise his guard, which could make getting rid of him more difficult. She let out a frustrated sigh. Wearing her mother's gown was fulfilling a dream she'd carried since childhood. If he laughed, why should she care? Let him scoff all he wanted, the hateful man.

"You know what, Pumpkin? Bizarre or not, this *is* my wedding day. I'm going to do it." As soon as she uttered the words, she knew she was making the right decision. There would be just enough time to freshen the dress before Morreston and the Reverend Shultz arrived.

But first, she needed to have a talk with Hank Minton, the ranch foreman. Quickly, she undressed, placed the gown on the bed and then pulled on a pair of jeans before heading for the main barn.

Four

"Do you, William Alec Morreston, take this woman as your lawfully wedded wife, to have and to hold from this day forward, for better or worse, for richer or poorer, in sickness and in health?"

Shea's head swam. This couldn't be happening. Perhaps if she blinked her eyes fast enough she would awaken from the nightmare.

Standing next to her in the old-fashioned parlor, Alec responded to the Reverend Schultz's questions with the reverence and sincerity of a man who was marrying the woman of his dreams. Raising her hand to his lips, he briefly kissed her fingers after slipping the diamond-encrusted wedding ring he'd purchased that afternoon onto the third finger of her left hand.

After the license had been issued at City Hall, Alec had insisted she accompany him to the town jewelry store to pick out rings. He'd ignored her suggestion that they use Band-Aids. In the shop she'd refused to voice any opinion whatsoever, seeing the sparkling gold-and-diamond jewelry as miniature handcuffs intended only as a psychological reminder that she would be shackled to the obstinate man for a year. Less, if she had her way about it, but even one day would be too much.

To the few well-wishers Leona had invited, his gesture probably appeared to be genuine. What would her friends say if they knew the truth? That this man planned not only to destroy her ranch land, but possibly bring about such catastrophic change it would send a tidal wave well beyond her borders and affect the lives of everyone standing in this room. She felt like a traitor hiding it from them. But Leona had agreed that to tell anyone the truth would only create unnecessary worry and add pressure on Shea she didn't need. Her sole focus had to be on the war against this man. And *when* she won, no one would ever be the wiser.

Consequently, Alec Morreston had been introduced as the long lost love she'd met while at college. Family concerns had taken him away but now he was back in her life and neither wanted to wait a second longer to marry. Shea could tell Alec had fought not to laugh when she'd told him the plan, but he'd agreed to it. And why not? He wouldn't be around to explain if this whole thing blew up in her face. She hoped she'd make it through this night without being sick.

"Do you, Shea Elizabeth Hardin, take this man to be your lawfully wedded husband…?"

As she reluctantly, obligingly recited her promise to love, honor and obey the irritating man, she glanced once in his direction and couldn't mistake the pursing of his lips as he fought to suppress a wicked smile from spreading across his face. She gritted her teeth as she shoved the gold wedding band onto his finger, not daring to look at him again. She wasn't near the actress she needed to be to pull off a convincing smile.

"By the authority vested in me, I now pronounce you husband and wife." The Reverend Schultz smiled at her before turning to Alec. "You may kiss your bride."

Reality became surreal as she looked at Alec, this stranger, who was now legally her husband. She had only seconds to comprehend the full impact of what she'd done before he pulled her into his arms and raised her face to meet his.

"Too late for any regrets, Mrs. Morreston," he whispered, as if reading her mind. He lowered his head and his mouth covered hers.

Like a bolt of electric current, something exploded within, causing her senses to whirl and the room to spin. She grabbed the lapels of his suit in an effort to steady herself.

With practiced skill, he parted her lips and his tongue entered the deeper recesses of her mouth. His hand cupped the back of her head, holding her to him, as he filled her mouth with his raw, male flavor. Despite her resolve to remain impervious to this man and unaffected by his touch, she found herself responding to the sensuous temptations he offered.

Her hand left his shoulder to touch the texture of his face, letting her fingertips glide along the strong line of his jaw until finally coming to rest at the point where his mouth joined with hers.

Then he withdrew from her and she couldn't deny a slight feeling of disappointment. With his thumb, he gently wiped the moisture from her lips as he studied her expression. A frown drew his dark brows together and he searched her face as if seeking an answer to a silent question. Had he been as affected by the kiss as she had?

Then a slow, sexy grin spread across his features and a knowing gleam flashed in the golden depths of his eyes before he stepped to her side to receive the offers of congratulations from the small group of people who stood smiling around them. She inhaled deeply, frustrated at her own momentary weakness.

Somehow, she managed to be pleasant as she introduced her new husband to her closest friends and neighbors, all the while praying they would never find out what was at stake beneath the façade of this marriage. The last thing she needed was concerned neighbors who feared for their own livelihood distracting her from her primary objective of getting rid of the man.

The photographer Leona had arranged through the local newspaper began to position them for their wedding photos. Someone made an off-color comment about the wedding night. Everyone joined in the banter and laughter abounded, but it only served to drive home the depravity of her situation.

A chill settled over her. What kind of man was Alec Morreston? Would he be understanding of her feelings or completely insensitive? She couldn't stop her eyes from straying to this man who potentially held the future of the ranch, as well as her own well-being, in his hands.

Alec glanced at his new bride. Immediately he noted the anxiety that was obvious in every delicate feature of her face, and he didn't have to be hit over the head to know the cause. His laughter faded as he recognized the depth of her apprehension. She was frightened.

Of him.

The fact should have made him happy. It was the first step toward making her leave. Such quick success should be sweet. So why did he feel sickened by her fear?

Their eyes met. The glistening blue of hers held him transfixed. Somewhere a light flashed, the brilliance challenging the intensity of the moment, capturing it forever.

Then, she seemed to gather her reserves and in a barely perceived movement, she straightened her shoulders and raised her chin. The near panic and vulnerability he'd caught a glimpse of moments before were now replaced with a look of pride and stubborn determination. With sudden insight, Alec knew that while he'd often admired beauty in other women, never had he appreciated their character or inner strength.

"Good one," he heard someone say. "Now if you'll both turn this way…and let's see some smiles!"

With the speed and brilliance of the camera's flash, Alec knew he was in trouble. He swallowed hard. While admittedly attracted to her, he'd previously ignored the sparks that ignited between them whenever their eyes found each other. He'd told himself he looked at all women the way he looked at Shea Harden. He'd just never noticed before.

He'd lied to himself.

He'd never been smitten by any woman. Whatever he'd felt for Sondra in the beginning was not even close to this. And the soft blush on Shea's face when she'd caught him staring told him the attraction was not one-sided.

There was definitely something between them. Like a force field of pure energy, it surrounded them. The air crackled every time they got close to each other. Where this put him in the overall scheme of things, he wasn't sure. He knew an affair would only complicate matters, but the temptation to throw caution to the wind was overwhelming.

As Shea closed the front door behind the last of the departing guests, she realized that for a few crazy minutes she'd actually forgotten about Alec. Reaching over to pick up a wineglass left on a nearby table, she took several steps toward the kitchen before she noticed him.

Leaning against the newel post at the foot of the stairs with his arms crossed casually in front of him, he had discarded his tie and unbuttoned his white dress shirt at the neck. The long sleeves were rolled up midarm and Shea noticed a gold watch nestled amid the sprinkling of dark hair on his tanned wrist. She also caught the dull gleam of the gold wedding band. The color drained from her face.

She clenched and unclenched her hands around the stemware as something close to panic settled into every inch of her body. She raised her chin in an effort to appear nonchalant as she crossed the room and entered the kitchen. Alec followed. Stepping up behind her, he reached around and removed the wineglass from the death grip she had on it, placing it on the counter next to the sink. The shrill ring of the telephone was a welcome intrusion. She hurried across the room and grabbed it on the second ring.

"I hear you've been looking for me," said a male voice. "It's about time!"

"David?" No. No. No. This could not be happening. Not now.

"Who else?" His voice was as jovial as she remembered. "How the hell are you, Shea?"

"I…I'm good. It's so good to hear your voice." *Understatement. Exclamation mark.*

"Right back at ya, Doc." The nickname he'd always used while she studied to be a veterinarian caused her heart to swell. She could sense him grinning. "So, I got a call from Marcy Allen. She said you've been trying to reach me. What can I do?"

Marry me, she wanted to scream. She closed her eyes as the irony washed over her. Why couldn't he have called yesterday? Or even this morning.

"Ah. Well…actually it's nothing. I mean, the problem has been resolved."

"Are you sure?"

Shea chanced a look in Alec's direction. Was that a smirk on his face?

"Yeah. I'm sure." At least as far as David was concerned. It was just after midnight and the bizarre marriage to Alec Morreston was in full swing. *Her* problem was just beginning.

They spoke for a few more minutes, then with a promise to keep in touch, they said goodbye. And just like that, the positive energy holding the tension at bay seemed to evaporate from the room.

"Old boyfriend?" Alec asked quietly.

She nodded.

"Gee. That's too bad. One day too late." He didn't sound a bit sorry as she crossed the room, returning to the sink, not certain what her next move should be. Alec followed and slowly slid his arms around her waist. His face rubbed against her hair, the heat from his body warm against her back.

"I like your friends that were here tonight," he murmured near her ear. His breath was hot against her neck. In such close proximity, his deep voice caused tingling sensations to dance over her skin. Shea clung to the edge of the counter for support.

She tried to remain calm. "They are good people."

"It was nice of them to come on such short notice."

"Yes. Leona…called most of them."

He stepped away and she heard the clink of ice. Glancing over her shoulder, she watched as Alec pulled a partially consumed bottle of champagne from its silver canister. Holding two crystal flutes easily in one hand, he poured the champagne with the other.

"To what shall we toast?" he asked as he handed her one of the glasses. "A long and satisfying marriage?"

She eyed him coolly. "How about to integrity?"

He pursed his lips as if to contain a devilish grin, then tipped his head and touched his fluted glass to hers. She downed the full contents, desperately needing the champagne's calming effect. She rarely drank alcohol, never champagne, and she wasn't prepared for the sensation. Her eyes clouded with tears and she couldn't stop the choking cough.

Still, the night that lay ahead made her hold the empty glass out to Alec. She ignored the knowing smile tugging at the corners of his mouth as he obligingly refilled it to the brim.

If it were within her power to disappear in a puff of smoke, she'd have done it. For one fleeting second the land didn't seem *that* important. Then the moment passed and she knew she'd see this thing through.

Somehow.

"It's been a long day," he said when she set her empty glass on the table.

"Yes." She readily agreed, some hope suddenly flaring in her chest.

"I suggest you show me our room."

Alec ignored any traces of panic that must have been apparent in her face and, without waiting for an answer, reached for her hand. His was large and warm, his grip firm and solid as he led her out of the kitchen and toward the stairs, turning off the lights as he went.

Lifting the long skirt of the gown with her free hand to ensure she didn't step on the hem, she followed him up the stairs. At the top of the staircase, he paused, silently indicating she should precede him into a bedroom. She walked down the hall, her head held high.

At the door to her room, she stopped. *I can't do this.* She felt light-headed. She could almost hear the chaotic beating of her heart as it pounded against her ribs.

Reaching around her, Alec turned the knob and effortlessly pushed open the door. She hesitated, swallowing back the vile taste of fear that rose in her throat. She could feel the warmth of his body against her back and the soft caress of his breath on her ear seconds before he kissed the sensitive area just below. Wild sensations tore through her. She spun around to face him, her hands braced against the muscled wall of his chest as she tried to keep him at arm's length.

"What's the matter?" he asked, tilting his head in mock innocence. "Wedding night jitters?"

"No." She shook her head. "No. It's just that…well, we…

we don't know each other. I mean..." She took a step back from him, placing her just inside the bedroom.

"I think I know a way we can remedy that problem." He began to unbutton his shirt. With his other hand, he reached out and flipped off the bedroom light leaving only the soft beams of moonlight that streamed through the window to challenge the darkness that now surrounded them. In the dim glow, he watched her, his gaze focused on her lips.

Shea slowly backed away but Alec advanced toward her, matching her step for step. With the last button released, his shirt fell open to reveal the muscular wall of his chest. She hadn't realized he was so powerfully built; so solid. Definitely not the body of a man who sat behind a desk every day.

"You surprise me, Mrs. Morreston. I had expected you to come down the stairs wearing boots and jeans. Instead, you walked into the room in that gown." The deep, velvety texture of his voice made her shiver. "If that was for my benefit, to ensure I knew what a beautiful and desirable woman I was about to marry, you can rest assured, it worked."

"It...it was my mother's."

"It's very nice. Very elegant." He continued to advance toward her. "But now it's time to take it off."

"No."

"No?" He mocked her. "Why, Mrs. Morreston, are you saying you intend to deny your husband on our wedding night?"

"I...I just think we need time to—"

"Don't worry, sweetheart," he cut in. "We have all night, and I certainly intend to take my time."

"No!"

"No? Might I remind you, Mrs. Morreston, you're now a very wealthy woman. You played a good hand and put me in a position of having to marry you in order to keep my own land. Almost diabolical when you think about it. But all the benefits don't swing in one direction. It's now my turn to see what I get in exchange for giving up my freedom."

"No."

"There's that word again." Alec didn't bother concealing his devious smile. "Are you saying you want to have our marriage annulled and give up so soon? I honestly believed your resolve to keep this place, no matter what, would last longer than the wedding night."

"And I hoped, as a gentleman, you would afford me an opportunity to get to know you before…before…"

"Who ever said I was a gentleman?" Shea could see the faint white of his teeth as he smiled in the darkness. "I've held up my end of this bargain, Mrs. Morreston. Now, I believe, it's your turn."

"Stop calling me that!" she snapped through gritted teeth as her inner turmoil exploded to the surface. This only succeeded in causing a bigger grin to spread across his face.

"But that's who you are, *Mrs. Morreston*." His fingers reached out and touched the tiny pearl buttons at the neckline of her dress. "It was your decision, remember?"

"Only to prevent you from taking my ranch."

"It was your decision."

Shea swallowed back the alarm that threatened to engulf her. He was right. He had warned her. And she had agreed freely.

Reaching for one of her hands, he began to unbutton the seam that ran from her wrist to her elbow, letting the satiny material fall away from her arm. Then, without a word, he moved to the other sleeve.

That completed, in a gentle but firm action, he turned her around and began to unfasten the back of the satin-and-lace gown. His hands moved slowly, methodically down the dress, releasing button after tiny button.

She caught their reflection in the mirror on the closet

door. The moonlight highlighted the silver-blond strands of her hair and softened the panicked features of her face. Alec's large, dark silhouette loomed behind her, his head bowed as he worked at his task. All traces of his earlier amusement were gone, replaced by a look of serious intent.

Standing practically nude before a strange man was not an experience she'd ever anticipated. The gown provided a frail armor, a subtle safeguard. In a few precious minutes, her lace panties and the white hosiery would be the only pieces of armor that remained.

Their eyes met in the mirror for countless seconds before he bent his head and placed his lips against the sensitive area beneath her ear. Her heart kicked into double time as Alec emitted a low growl, which sent electric sensations racing down her spine.

She spun around in an effort to break the contact. Rather than reach for her again, he removed his shirt, tossed it aside and began unbuckling his belt. The muscles of his shoulders and arms rippled in the moon's glow, the significant pectorals making him seem even bigger than he'd looked with his clothes on.

Taking another step back from him, her legs bumped against the bed. Her pulse tripled. Frantically her eyes searched the room, hoping to detect any means of escape from this reprehensible situation.

Before she could voice any more objections or seize on a reason to try to postpone the inevitable, Alec reached out to her. His hands cupped her face, compelling her to meet his gaze as he took the final step, closing the short distance between them.

Shea clenched her hands into tight fists at her sides, determined to resist this forceful male. In the pale light, she saw his eyes focus on her lips seconds before his mouth came down over hers hard, masterfully firm in its possession. His hands left her face as his heavy arms encircled her body like bands of steel. His sheer strength and size, coupled with the passion of the embrace, rocked her senses and snatched the very breath from her lungs. She was way out of her depth. A feeling of near hysteria enveloped her mind. With a small cry, she tore her mouth from his. He allowed her to pull back but kept her close, his large hands resting on her shoulders.

"I can't…I can't do this." Her fingers gripped his. "I know you said…I know I agreed that…but I…please…don't—"

"Shh." A frown drew his dark brows together. He had to see the frantic, almost terrified expression that must be on her face, mirroring the fear churning inside. "It's all right, Shea. I'm not going to hurt you," he murmured as his thumbs caressed the side of her face. "Just kiss me. That's all you have to do."

Shea scarcely had time to nod her agreement before his mouth once again claimed hers. This time he moved slowly, sensuously, with an easy gentleness that immediately began to tear down the walls of her resistance. His tongue licked and teased her lips, moistening them, as if readying her for a more intense joining.

With consummate skill, he encouraged her lips to open. His tongue slid deep into the cavern of her mouth, sending her heart plummeting all the way to her knees. The kiss was frankly intimate, shamefully enticing and custom designed to evoke a matching response from her. He tasted of champagne and his own uniquely delicious male flavor. It mingled with the bittersweet essence of his cologne, which silently affirmed the raw masculinity of the man who wore it.

His hands rubbed her back, working down her spine, slowly massaging away the last remnants of her inner turmoil. Sensual warmth began to spread though her, intensifying the heat pooling between her legs while a thread of confusion wove its way into her mind.

What am I doing? But the question was too fleeting to receive an answer.

Slowly but steadily, her fear began to change form, turning instead into a fundamental need that refused to be ignored. A fragment of her mind insisted this wasn't right. Her body screamed that it was.

Alec pushed the creamy fabric of the gown from her shoulders. It fell to the floor with a quiet rustle. She should have been shocked, but the realization weighed no heavier than the soft evening breeze entering the room through the open windows. For a few moments in time, she forgot the reality of her situation, of her pledged hatred of this man. Of their own accord, her arms slid up over his muscled chest to rest on his broad, powerful shoulders, letting her fingers play in the thick, silky texture of his hair. Alec's hands moved lower in their rotation until, reaching the fullness of her hips, he pulled her firmly up and against him. The hard, male ridge of his arousal pressed against the sensitive juncture between her legs and a jolt of pure sexual hunger shot through her. Her body jerked forward, uncontrollably, bringing a deep growl from Alec.

He began to alternately kiss and nibble the delicate contours of her neck and shoulder and, eyes closed, she tilted her head to allow him greater access. His hands moved to her breasts, kneading the firmness, making them swell under his touch. Then his mouth returned to hers in a deep, drugging kiss that brought a small whimper, an automatic response conveying the end of her struggle against the inevitable.

Five

Experience told Alec that sound signified her acceptance of what was to come. He knew, at this moment in time she was his, completely and totally. Raising his head, he looked at Shea's face, radiant in the moonlight. Her eyes were closed, her lips parted as if waiting for his mouth to return. As if beckoning his lips to return.

Heat coursed through his body, centering in his loins, making him throb against the restricting barrier of his slacks. A slight tremor reminded him he was about to cross the line. This was not the plan. Seducing her wouldn't accomplish anything except add to the problems he already faced and enormously complicate the entire situation.

He gritted his teeth, closed his eyes and fought for restraint. But even when he couldn't see, her fragrance assailed him, called to him and tempted him almost beyond his control. He knew her body craved fulfillment and her need only served to bring him closer to that moment of ultimate possession, a moment that should never happen. He ached with wanting. His libido screamed, *Take her*!

Suddenly, it was too much.

Damn the land. Damn that contract. Damn this situation. With a groan of defeat, he scooped her into his arms, laid her gently on the bed and followed her down, his mouth again finding hers.

Then, almost unnoticeable at first, a persistent sound of drumming broke into the moment. The sound, hesitant but determined, brought with it a cold reality that refused to leave.

Frowning, Alec raised his head, reluctantly separating his lips from hers. He inhaled deeply, fighting to regain cognizant thought. It sounded as if someone was knocking on a door. Silence. Then it started again. Another hard series of raps caused him to look questioningly at Shea while he fought to latch onto some thread of reality.

"Are you expecting anyone?" His voice sounded rough, even to his own ears.

She mutely looked into his face. Alec drew a deep breath and blew it out, pausing to regain what little mind he had left. Finally, he rolled off the bed and stood up. Taking another deep breath, he walked out into the hallway and down the stairs as the persistent knocking continued. He knew a sudden surge of fury as he reached the kitchen door.

Hank Minton, the ranch foreman, stood on the doorstep. He had his hat in his hands, and a worried look pinched the strained features of his face. He wouldn't look Alec in the eye. Instead he watched the bugs fluttering around the porch light, studied the doorbell and finally appeared to give significant attention to his old, worn boots.

"Hank." Suspicion set off a flashing red light in Alec's still-muddled brain.

"I'm sorry to bother you all with this," the old cowboy said. "Real sorry. Specially knowing it's your weddin' night and all. But we got a horse down and I think Shea's gonna need to take a look at him."

"I see," Alec replied. And he did.

There was no question in his mind that Shea had solicited Hank's help for this perfectly timed interruption. Alec was torn between a desire to toss the old man off the step or hug his neck and thank him for doing what Alec apparently lacked the strength to do himself.

Hank had just provided a plausible excuse for Alec to

stop, which was exactly what *he* should have done in the first place. Annoyance surged through him for his weakness and for letting his desire overcome his common sense.

He definitely should be grateful to Hank. Why, then, did he have the urge to break the old man's neck?

"Come in. I'll get her."

The old cowboy nodded and stepped just inside the kitchen, glancing at the sink, the overhead light, the chairs and finally back to his boots.

Shea sat on the edge of the bed in the darkened room as reality came slamming back. Willing her pulse to steady, she took a deep breath in a desperate attempt to clear her head. Her hand trembled as she ran her fingers through her hair. It had been close. Too close. His touch left the lower parts of her body swollen, unfulfilled and badly in need of something more.

He hadn't made love to her. Technically. Hadn't penetrated her body with his. She should be monumentally happy. Why, then, did she feel ridiculously disappointed?

She stood and felt her way to the closet, not bothering to turn on a light. Her legs were strangely weak. She quickly shucked her hosiery, pulled on a pair of jeans and a shirt and then descended the stairs. She couldn't help but grimace as the full impact of the situation settled over her.

She'd almost had sex with Alec Morreston.

Even worse, he hadn't forced her. He hadn't held her down or tied her to the bedposts. He'd kissed her. That was all. Apparently, that had been enough. She knew it. And worse, so did he. Alec was here to take away her ranch, her home, everything she held dear. She would do well to remember that. He was, inarguably, a very potent package with obvious experience to back that up. She had to be strong.

Alec pivoted from the open doorway as she entered the

kitchen. He didn't appear surprised to see her there. "It seems your presence is needed in the barn." His tone clearly said he was suspicious of Hank's timing.

"It's Crusty, Shea." Hank's voice carried to her from the doorway. "He's down. Me and Jason, we've been working with him almost an hour, but we can't keep him on his feet. I think it's colic." The old cowboy threaded the brim of his hat through his hands in a nervous gesture as he stared at his boots. "I'm real sorry about this. Real sorry."

"That's okay, Hank." Shea glanced at Alec. "I'm sure Mr. Morreston understands." The look Alec gave her clearly said he understood far more than just the claimed need for Shea's presence in the barn. "Give me a second to put on some shoes. Is he in the main barn?"

"Yes, ma'am. I'll go on back out there." He put his hat firmly on his head and turned toward the door. "I'm real sorry 'bout this. Real sorry." Hank closed the door behind him.

Shea ran up the stairs and into the bedroom, wasting no time as she pulled on socks and boots. Just as she stood and reached for her jacket, Alec walked into the room.

"Need any help?"

"No. Thanks anyway."

As she walked past him, he gently touched her shoulder, stopping her in midstride.

"Consider this…a wedding gift. We wouldn't want all of Hank's efforts to be for nothing. But, take fair warning, next time there will be no interruptions. You can accept that or you can prepare to leave here." There was a gleam of promise in his eyes.

His insolence was like a splash of cold water. A scant few minutes ago, she'd been on the verge of giving herself to this man. Now her only inclination was to put her fist firmly against his nose with the highest velocity she could muster. The combined emotions of frustration and humiliation propelled her anger to the surface.

Pushing past him, she almost ran down the stairs.

When she pulled open the heavy barn door, she found Hank holding the lead shank attached to a halter placed on one of the older geldings.

"Figured he might come with you," Hank explained. "Ole Crusty here looks like he just might keel over any minute. A city feller wouldn't know the difference." Shea smiled and nodded. "Was I convincin'? Did I do okay?"

"Yeah." She nodded her approval as she walked toward the old horse. "You did good, Hank."

Her plan had worked. The timing could have been a little better, but even so, good enough. So why wasn't she bouncing-off-the-walls deliriously happy? Why did she feel so incomplete? In all honesty, she had to admit deep down a part of her regretted the interruption.

Alec knew a woman's body. He knew exactly where to touch, precisely how to kiss and just what to do to make a female respond to him. To make *her* respond to him. From the beginning, she'd sensed he would be highly skilled in bed, but she'd never envisioned finding out firsthand. She could still taste him, could feel his hard body against hers. His masculine scent was heavy on her skin. The fire he'd lit still burned, refusing to die out. Taking a deep, shaky breath, she sat down on a bale of hay and rubbed her forehead in an attempt to clear her mind. But the remembrance of what had happened—of what had almost happened—stubbornly wouldn't go away.

"Missy, are you sure you know what you're doing?" Hank removed his hat and scratched his head, which left his thinning gray hair in a tousled mess on top of his head, then replaced his timeworn hat.

"Absolutely." She smiled bravely, confidently at the old cowboy. But she knew she was lying through her teeth.

* * *

Alec watched as Shea almost ran down the stairs. He raked his hand through his hair and took a deep breath. It had been too close. Three minutes, maybe less, and their bodies would have been locked in the most intimate act that could happen between two people and nothing on this earth would have made him let her go. He wasn't exactly sure how he'd allowed the situation to escalate as far as it had and he wasn't certain how to prevent it in the future.

The plan had been to frighten her with an overload of sexual intimidation, come on so hard and heavy that she'd run like a scared rabbit. But instead of running, instead of saying, *Okay, you win, I'll leave*, she had looked up at him with those damned amazing blue eyes and silently begged him not to hurt her, pleaded with him to give her time. And in that instant, with her enticing lips a mere breath away, and those eyes imploring him to understand, he'd made a choice. And that choice had almost irrevocably changed everything.

He couldn't remember ever losing control or being blindsided by the aura of a sexy woman. But this time his strength of will had flown out the window and he'd almost sacrificed everything for a young woman from the back woods of Texas with big blue eyes and one hell of a game plan. So much for his ironclad resolve.

He had to get out of here, at least for a while. Let things cool down and give himself time to regain his perspective, to reformulate his plan. With a grimace, he turned and walked toward the bathroom and a cold shower.

The sun was just peeking over the distant hills when Shea quietly made her way back to the house. The romantics of the world could say all they wanted about sleeping on a soft bed of hay. In truth, it was prickly and itchy and its stiff, needlelike projections could poke through even the thickest blanket right into your skin. She hadn't had a good night. But the few hours of restless sleep had been enough to restore her sanity. In the light of day, she knew the outcome of the previous night could have been much worse.

She could have made love to Alec.

She could be lying in that bed right now with his big, muscled arms securely around her, drowsy in the aftermath of their lovemaking. Feeling— *Stop*! With a muttered oath, Shea pulled open the back door.

When she entered the kitchen, to her surprise, Alec was already there dressed in dark slacks, a clean white dress shirt and tie. He looked disgustingly well-rested.

"Looks like you had a good night," he said, reaching out to pull some straw from her tangled hair. "You give an entirely new meaning to a roll in the hay. Sleep well, did you?" His mouth twitched in amusement as he gestured to the pot of fresh coffee.

Shea ignored his jibes, opened the cabinet and selected a mug. If he expected her to make any comment about what happened last night—or what *hadn't* happened—he could hold his breath until he turned blue.

She couldn't help noticing the way his shirt did little to hide the muscles of his arm as he lifted his cup to his mouth, or the way his full lips opened against the rounded edge of the mug as he sipped the steaming coffee. She quickly turned away as unsettling sensations began to send surges of heat through her veins.

"I need to return home for a few days," Alec said as she reached for the coffee. "I understand this might be viewed as deserting my wife on our honeymoon, but I'm afraid it can't be helped. As far as the contract, I don't recall any stipulation that I never leave the boundaries of the land, only that I ensure your protection from *any and all perils*. If you think you'll be *safe* for a few days—" his sarcasm was apparent "—I need clothes. And I need to make some arrangements. Do our attorneys need to become involved with this?"

In spite of the temptation to try to deny Alec the time he needed, she knew it wouldn't be right. And there was nothing in the contract to prevent him from leaving the property.

"No. But I wouldn't bother packing a lot of clothes. You won't be here long enough to need them."

At least his trip would give her the time she needed to form a better plan to make him leave permanently. With any luck, he wouldn't come back at all.

He watched her guardedly. "Want to come with me?"

"No, thank you," she quickly responded. "I've got things I need to see to here."

"I'm sure you do," he replied, tongue in cheek. "How's the horse?"

"The horse?" she frowned. It took a few seconds before she remembered the "sick" horse in the barn. "Oh. Fine. Good." She looked down at her mug and away from the scrutiny of those amber eyes, knowing she was incapable of telling a convincing lie. "I expect he'll make a full recovery."

"Oh, I have no doubt."

Alec walked to the counter where she stood and reached around her to place his cup in the sink. "Call a local furniture store and have them send out a larger bed. Get an entire suite if you like."

The surprise must have shown on her face.

"Is money a problem?"

"No." She shook her head. "But a larger bed won't fit into that room."

"Then have it put in a larger room." He cocked his head. "There *is* a larger bedroom, isn't there?"

"Yes, but…"

Alec watched her reaction. "But what?"

There were in fact three bedrooms upstairs. But moving

into the master indicated a permanency she did not want. She just wished he would stay wherever it was he was going and let her life return to normal.

"Nothing." She shook her head. "How long will you be away?" She didn't want to ask. To do so might imply she cared. But she had to prepare for his return.

"A few days. Possibly a week. I can't be sure. Why? Will you miss me?"

She snorted and took a sip of her coffee.

"I'll take that as a yes."

He tucked a loose strand of hair behind her ear before his head dipped toward her and his lips found hers. It was instinct rather than conscious thought that made her open to him. He deepened the embrace, kissing her thoroughly but briefly. Then, raising his head, he broke the contact but remained close.

"You're going to lose," Alec whispered. "But this challenge is becoming more interesting by the minute. I look forward to the next round."

Her expression strengthened into a cold glare. But before she could respond in kind, he turned and walked out the door.

The large private jet sliced through the white clouds en route back to Dallas from New York LaGuardia. After a week of reflection, Alec was no closer to finding a concrete plan that would ensure he maintained control of the bizarre situation.

So far, the only thing guaranteed to work was avoiding her altogether. But not only would that not serve his objective, it was not something he was willing to do.

He glanced at the child, asleep on the small bed across the aisle. This morning, when he'd picked up his bag and prepared to leave for the airport, he'd seen Scotty peeking around the corner of the kitchen doorway. He'd walked over to his son, lifted the four-year-old into his arms and given in to the overwhelming need to hold him close.

"Are you gonna be gone a long time?"

Alec had given him a regretful smile. "Maybe not too long this time."

"Good. Where are you going?"

"Actually, I'll be staying on a ranch."

"A ranch?"

"Yep."

"Do they have horsees?"

"I believe they do."

"And cowboys?" Scotty's eyes had been wide with excitement.

"And cowboys," he'd confirmed as an idea had formed in his mind.

It had been a spur-of-the-moment decision to bring him along, but even now, some three hours later, Alec still felt it was the right one. Scott's preschool was over for the summer. Alec spent far too much time away from his son because of the requirements of his work. This wacky situation actually might provide some time to spend with his son, an experience both he and Scotty would remember.

The only negative he could see was the possibility Shea and Scott might bond, which could be tough on the boy when it was time to leave. It was because of this concern Alec elected to not mention the marriage. To tell Scotty he had a mother only to take him away from her a couple of weeks later was just wrong. He wouldn't do that to Scott.

Alec's mouth quirked as he thought of Shea and the days ahead. As far as he knew, Shea had no children and possibly no experience with a four-year-old. This unexpected twist could prove very interesting.

He rose from his seat and entered the area of the plane set up as his office. They were still an hour out from DFW. He might as well get some work done while he could. He had a feeling his time away from the ranch had provided Shea with ample opportunity to put some plans in motion to try to make him give up and leave.

Good luck with that.

"Okay, that should do her," Shea said, removing the rubber surgical gloves and giving the mare's shoulder a pat. "Take her back to the stall and keep an eye on her."

"Sure thing, boss." Hank picked up his hat and slapped it against his leg to dislodge some of the dirt before fitting it firmly onto his head.

The mare carried one of the best bloodlines in a five-state region. It was the boost this ranch needed. That was the only reason Shea tolerated Bonnie Blue's ridiculous temperament every time the mare needed medical care. Thankfully, it didn't happen often.

With three cowboys holding the high-strung horse, Shea had still been thrown hard against the side of the barn when she'd attempted to inject a tranquilizer. Her shoulder had absorbed most of the impact, providing a painful souvenir she would no doubt carry for a few days. Once the tranquilizer had begun to take effect, it took no time to stitch the mare's cut, apply a topical dressing and give Bonnie Blue the added safety of a tetanus booster.

Shea bent to pick up the discarded cotton, linens and syringes, not bothering to watch the three lanky cowboys lead the now docile mare out of the paddock. When she again looked up, the breath died in her throat as she found herself staring directly into Alec's scowling face.

He'd gone from being like a character from a foggy, half-forgotten dream to suddenly materializing right in front of her as a crystal clear vision. And he was as disturbingly handsome as ever. His tall stature, the broad width of his shoulders and the sheer male essence of him seemed even more pronounced than she remembered.

As she approached the paddock gate, Alec swung it open and then closed it behind her.

"You want to tell me just what in the hell you were doing?"

"What do you mean?" She frowned, clueless as to what he could be talking about.

"You. That horse. You were almost killed."

Rolling her eyes, she moved to walk past him but the distinctive voice of a child abruptly shattered the tension of the moment, halting her in midstride.

"Boy, oh boy! That was *cool*!"

Shea's head snapped around in surprise. She focused on a small boy clinging precariously to the centerboard of the paddock fence, allowing the crown of his head and two large round eyes to peek over the top.

The child jumped from his perch and ran toward the gate to stand directly in front of Shea.

"Are you all right?" His small face held a look of genuine concern. "Did the horse hurt your arm?"

"No, I'm…fine." She sent a questioning glance at Alec.

"This is Scotty." He watched her face as if ready to gauge her reaction. "My son."

Shea blinked. More than twice. Alec had a child? Good Lord! Devils didn't normally produce such angelic-looking offspring, did they?

"Scotty, this is Shea."

She knew a look of disbelief covered her features as she leaned over, bringing her closer to eye-level with the boy.

"Hi, Scotty." She forced a smile and held out her hand. The boy placed his small hand in hers and produced a wide grin. Then, mysteriously struck with a bout of shyness, he stepped back to stand closer to his father, his arm around Alec's leg.

"You never told me you had a son."

Alec flexed his shoulders. "So now you know. As I was

about to leave I mentioned I would be staying on a ranch." Alec looked down at his son before returning those tawny eyes to her. "He wanted to come and see the horses and cowboys."

Are you freaking kidding me? She could only gasp as her blood pressure shot up to dangerous heights. Momentarily at a total loss for words, she forced herself to breathe deep and stared at the man standing four feet in front of her. He was insane. This child had no business on a working ranch. Not only had this conceited lunatic returned, but he'd brought an innocent child along as his backup. And she'd thought the situation couldn't possibly get any worse.

"Are you ready for the next one, Shea?" Hank asked from the side door of the main barn.

"Take a break, Hank." Her voice was unnaturally high even to her own ears.

"We need to talk." She shot an if-looks-could-kill glance at Alec and headed to the house, muttering under her breath.

Her shoulder throbbed. She longed for a nice hot soak in the tub and something to eat, but until she finished checking and treating the remaining horses, she knew she couldn't stop. The preliminary work for the annual fall roundup and branding would begin in earnest in just a few weeks. There was a great deal of preparation between now and then, and most of it rested on her shoulders. Alec couldn't have picked a worse time to return. Let alone with a child in tow.

Entering the kitchen, she tossed the dirty gauze into the trash bin before washing her hands. To give herself time to calm down she took a pitcher of tea from the refrigerator and set three glasses on the counter. Adding ice to two before filling them with tea, she then poured fresh milk into the third.

"Have a seat," she told Alec, indicating the kitchen chairs when he and Scotty followed her inside. Her eyes were drawn to the child. She guessed his age to be four or five.

He was a miniature of his father except his hair was several shades lighter than Alec's dark mahogany brown.

"If you look in the big jar on the cabinet, I think you'll find some cookies."

Scotty wasted no time in pulling a chair over to the counter and climbing up to reach the cookie jar.

"Can I have two?" He flashed a smile that would melt the coldest heart. She'd bet he'd learned that from his father.

"Sure." She tried to return his smile but wasn't fully convinced she'd pulled it off. "There are some paper towels next to the sink. Grab one and your cookies and follow me. You can watch cartoons while I talk with your dad."

"I like cartoons."

With Scotty contentedly watching TV and munching on the homemade cookies in the next room, Shea returned to the kitchen and joined Alec at the table.

He'd shed his usual business suit; snug-fitting jeans now hugged his muscled thighs and a tan sports shirt hung casually from his broad shoulders. Ostrich-skin boots completed the ensemble and to her surprise, they weren't new. His tawny eyes were as compelling and enigmatic as ever.

"You said you wanted to talk?" Alec sat back in the chair looking completely at ease.

"Yeah." She set the glasses of tea on the table and dropped into a chair opposite Alec. Where to begin? What to say to a complete schmuck? "This is a working ranch. What you saw out there today happens all the time. It's what we do. This is not a pony club or a dude ranch. We don't cater to novices who don't know the nose from the back end of a horse. A child could get hurt, especially a little one who has never been around livestock. I cannot halt the operations of this ranch to play nursemaid to either one of you."

He merely looked at her, his eyes sliding from her mouth

to her breasts and back to her eyes. It was unnerving. *He* was unnerving.

"Every year we usually find at least two poisonous snakes near the main barn or around the house," she continued, determined to ignore the pulsing sensation in the pit of her stomach. "Go into the forested sections and you're likely to find cougars or bear. There are wild boars that can take a man's leg off. This is no place for a child."

"Sorry. Maybe I misunderstood. Didn't you grow up here?"

She could only glare. What could she honestly say to that?

"I will not be held responsible if an innocent little boy gets hurt."

He shrugged. "I'll have a talk with Scott. Tell me his boundaries and I'll see he stays within them."

"Then tell him to stay inside this house."

"Don't be ridiculous."

"*Me* ridiculous?"

"I have a son I love very much. I do not intend to leave him back in New York or make him stay in the house for however long it takes you to pack your bags."

Her annoyance shot across the line to pure fury at his insolence. The wooden chair made a screeching sound as she bounded to her feet. Her hands rested on the table as she leaned toward Alec. "I can't believe you'd stoop so low as to bring an innocent child into this…insanity."

Alec met her angry glare and rose slowly from his chair like a mountain lion ready to pounce. His hands rested on his side of the table as he leaned toward her. "*I* didn't cause this. *I* was not the one who refused to relinquish possession of land that didn't belong to me!"

"Oh, yes," she hissed, her voice coated with vehemence. "Just try and convince me you're the innocent victim! Do you make a habit of throwing people out of their homes?

Do you get your kicks from watching them scurry around trying to find another place to live?"

"I offered you a sizeable sum of money to leave. Not exactly the same as throwing you out on the street."

"Money. All you seem to care about is money! I feel sorry for you, Alec. I pity your son that he must live the kind of life you deem appropriate when you don't even know what family or tradition is all about."

"Leave Scotty out of this."

"*I'm* not the one who brought him into it!"

"And you've made your feelings quite clear."

"Apparently not. You're still here."

A movement out of the corner of her eye told her they had an audience. Turning toward Scotty, she pasted a smile on her face.

"The cookies were good," he said, his gaze going back and forth from his father to Shea.

"Oh. Great." *Down shift.* "I'm glad you like them. Is the cartoon over?"

"Are you and Daddy always gonna fight at each other?" He tilted his head in a manner she'd seen his father do. Guilt quickly dissolved the anger as she realized this little boy had heard their heated exchange.

"I…I don't know, sweetie," she hedged and then decided to be honest. If she and Alec didn't kill each other before this was over, it would be nothing short of a miracle. "Your dad and I, well, we have a lot of things to work out between us. There's a lot *he* doesn't understand."

The child seemed to take the answer in stride.

"Freddy Correnski said his mommy and daddy used to fight all the time. Then Freddy and his mommy moved to another house. Are Daddy and me gonna live in your house with you?"

"Uh. Well. Yes. I guess you are," she answered, trying

to force happiness into her tone. Her eyes cut to Alec as she added, "For a while."

"Cool." He walked over to stand in front of Shea. "Sometimes Daddy gets sad and I ask him why and he says he's not sad, but I know he is 'cause he just sits there in his chair and looks real tired, but he says he's not tired but he won't get up." He took a deep breath and looked at Shea. "Will you make Daddy not be sad?"

For the life of her, Shea couldn't think of an appropriate reply. Alec, apparently, had no such difficulty.

"She is going to do her best, Scott," he said as a wide grin spread across his face. The mischievous twinkle was back in his eyes.

"Good. Can I have another cookie?"

Her voice seemed to have abandoned her, so Shea merely nodded her head.

As the youngster scrambled for the cookie jar, she whispered to Alec, "You can bring a hundred kids out here. A thousand. I'm still not going to let you have this ranch."

His eyes roamed over her face. "Why don't you show us where we'll be sleeping?" he suggested, choosing to ignore her blatant declaration. "It's been a long day. I have a feeling we're going to have an early night."

Six

Shea turned and marched toward the stairs. She didn't pause until she stood just inside the doorway to a second-floor bedroom overlooking the barn and paddock area. She crossed to the window and opened the blinds, letting the sunshine in.

"I think Scotty will be comfortable in here. If you had bothered to call and let me know he was coming, I could have had the room prepared. Yolanda, the wife of one of our ranch hands, comes in twice a week and helps with the laundry and general cleaning. She should be here soon to start dinner. I'll have her change the bedding and air the room."

"This is gonna be my room?" Scotty asked in delight, oblivious to the tension still hanging heavy between the adults. "Cool!" He ran to the bed and joyfully bounced on the springy mattress before bounding to the floor and running to the large double window. "Wow! Daddy! Look at this! Is that where you keep the horsees?" He pointed a finger at the barn.

"Some of them." Shea smiled down at Alec's son.

"Can I ride one?" He looked up at her, his bright, eager eyes hopeful.

She reached out and tousled his hair. "You'll have to ask your dad."

"He'll say okay. Won't you, Daddy?" Not waiting for an answer he added, "I like it here." He turned and surveyed the room, then nodded his head as if he'd made a great decision. "Yep. This is gonna be all right."

"I assume you brought extra clothes and personal items?" Alec nodded. "I'll get Jason to help you with your suitcases. Just tell him if you want to change anything around, move the bed, whatever."

"This will be fine."

"Hey, Daddy, where is your bed?"

Shea had started out of the room. This question, however, made her pause. Clearly, Alec hadn't shared the fact he'd gotten married with his son. She couldn't pass up the chance to see how he was going to handle this one. She turned toward him, eyebrows raised, her head tilted as she waited for the answer along with Scotty.

Alec stood staring down at the small child in front of him. He rubbed a hand over his mouth, sighed, then rested his hands on his hips. "Actually, I'm going to be sleeping… in another room."

"Where?"

"I'll be bedding down with Shea."

"How come?"

Get him, Scotty!

Alec put his large hands together, cracking his knuckles as he fought to answer that one. Then his head shot up, he glanced at Shea and back to his son. "She's afraid of the dark."

"Oh."

He did not just say that. She couldn't withhold a snort of laughter, which earned her a glare of warning from Alec.

"Okaaaaay." *Your son. Your bad.* "Well, I've still got a lot of work to do this afternoon. Yolanda will start supper about six." She again looked at Scotty. "What do you like to eat?"

"Hot dogs! With ketchup."

Her lips slid into a full, easy grin and Alec had to wonder if it had the same effect on his son as it did him. Damn, she was beautiful.

"I'll see what we can do."

As she disappeared around the corner, Scotty's voice rang out. "I *like* her, Daddy."

Alec nodded. His son had just answered his unspoken question and he wasn't surprised. He'd carried the far-fetched hope that returning to the ranch would dispel his initial attraction to Shea and he could chalk up the whole thing to stress.

No such luck.

He looked around the room. The wallpaper was faded, its edges peeling away from the walls in a couple of places. Slightly discolored stains on the ceiling indicated water had entered uninvited at some time in the past and left its murky calling card. The light fixture, a remnant from a bygone era, dangled precariously from the twelve-foot-high ceiling. The faint scents of mothballs and lemon touched his senses. But in spite of its worn appearance, this room, in fact the entire house, brought to mind childhood memories of home-baked bread and leftover meatloaf sandwiches. Of the big tree that had been outside his window, perfect for sneaking out of the house to go night fishing with Grandpa Jacob and old man Muldoon.

Alec moved to stand beside his son at the large window. Shea came into view directly below, walking toward the barn.

"Hey, Dad? Do you think she likes us?"

"Oh, I'm sure she does, son," he lied.

Shea was standing next to a big Appaloosa and a portable medic unit writing something on a form attached to a clipboard when Alec and Scotty walked into the paddock area near the main barn. The tension in her carriage was obvious. He was tempted to step over and give her shoulders a quick massage, but immediately decided against it. The last thing he needed was to get so close to temptation.

"What are you gonna do?" Scotty asked her, his eyes wide and curious.

"I gave him a shot that'll help keep him healthy," she explained simply. She patted the horse's shoulder. "Okay, Jason, take him away."

After making some additional notations she turned her attention back to Scotty. "Have you ever seen a horse get shoes?"

Scotty shook his head.

"No? Then, come with me."

Alec followed as they walked to the north end of the barn where a blacksmith had set up his rig for shoeing horses. The clang of his hammer rang out through the late afternoon calm. Alec stood slightly to the side, content to watch the interaction between Shea and his son. It appeared they already were bonding, a fact that both surprised and intrigued him.

"This is Charlie." She nodded toward the burly man dressed in a sleeveless shirt and jeans. A faded red bandana tied around his forehead kept the sweat from his eyes.

"What's he doing?"

"He's making a shoe for one of the horses." Smiling at Scotty, she selected a metal horseshoe from the trailer, handed it to him. Scotty held it as though it were made of gold.

"Each horse has different size feet, just like people do. Charlie selects a shoe close to the size of a horse's hoof, then heats the metal so when he beats it with the hammer it will change the shape a little bit until it fits. Then he cools it and nails it on."

"Doesn't it hurt?"

"Nope. He uses special nails. The horse can't feel a thing."

Scotty looked again at the metal shoe, then held it out to Shea.

"Keep it," she said. "Hang it on a wall in your room. Like this." She turned the metal shoe around so that it formed the shape of a cup. "It will catch good luck." Fascinated, Scotty smiled up at her. He took a few steps in Charlie's direction before stopping and looking back at Shea and his father.

"It's okay, son." Alec assured him. "You can go over and talk to Charlie. Just don't get too close to the horses."

He hesitated only a few seconds before walking over, proudly holding his horseshoe with both hands.

Alec was moved by the gentleness and attention she'd shown Scotty. It was something he hadn't anticipated. There was no hidden agenda he could see. Unlike some women, she certainly wasn't doing it to impress him. She seemed genuine, as though she not only enjoyed teaching Scott about the things in her world, but she honestly liked Scotty, as well. And his son seemed equally fond of her.

She glanced at Alec as she walked past to return to the medic unit.

"Thanks," he felt obliged to say.

She frowned. "For what?"

"For taking the time for Scotty."

She shrugged it off. "I like kids. He's a sweetie. There's no point in making him feel unwelcome. But you brought him. He's your son. Your responsibility. If he gets hurt, it's on you."

With that, she picked up the clipboard and began to check her data.

"How many cattle do you have?" Alec asked, glancing beyond the barn at the distant hills.

"On average the Bar H runs about three thousand head." She turned to him, her captivating eyes moving over his face. "The number, of course, drops after we ship in the fall, but is reestablished the first of the year when the calving begins."

"Shea?" Hank called from the doorway. "Where do you want Shonie?" He led a large painted gelding into the area.

"Bring him over here," Shea instructed, setting the clipboard aside.

"Is there something I can do to help?" Alec wanted something to keep his mind occupied, his hands busy. In the short time he'd been back, his body already had begun responding to her.

His question appeared to take Shea by surprise. "Have you ever been around horses?"

"Some."

"I've got eight more to check." She looked down the hallway. "The stalls are numbered. I'll need to see the ones in eight, twelve and fifteen next. Their halters, with leads attached, are hanging on the doors."

Finding the correct stall, Alec slipped the halter over the head of a docile mare and led her out of the barn.

Shea took the lead from his hands. "She's no problem. I can handle her by myself. While I check her out, go ahead and get Ransom. Number twelve."

She was just finishing with the mare when Alec arrived with the spirited bay gelding. The feisty animal nickered playfully and attempted to rub his head against Alec's shoulder.

"You seem to have made a friend."

"You sound surprised," he noted, turning to rub the neck of the striking animal. He appreciated quality and this big gelding reeked of good breeding, as did most of the horses he'd seen here.

"I am. Hold him here while I take Essie to Charlie. Her shoes need replacing."

* * *

On the horizon, fiery remnants of red and gold accented the darkening sky as Shea checked the last of the horses. When she brought the final one around the corner of the barn, she was surprised to see Scotty perched on top of one of the trail horses tied securely to the fence. Frowning, she looked at Alec, who stood next to the child.

"He's fine." Alec assured her, as though reading her mind. "Having the time of his life." His booted foot was propped on the lower rail of the fence, his jeans hugging his muscular legs and hips. His arms rested easily on the top rail. He looked lean and strong. She swallowed hard, fighting back the insane desire to walk over and step into his arms.

"I'm beat." She could hear the tiredness in her own voice, no doubt the cause of her temporary insanity. "I'll see you back at the house."

Alec nodded before she turned and headed toward the house. She refused to let her mind dwell on the night ahead and the possibilities it could hold. Entering through the kitchen door, she walked to the stairs and made it as far as the second-floor landing when she saw the open door at the end of the hall.

The master bedroom.

She stopped in her tracks.

The new furniture had been delivered, the bed prepared with clean linens and the door closed. It had remained closed—until today. Until Alec returned and opened it. Now it taunted her, dared her to enter and face the moment of truth.

She clenched her hands at her sides, fighting her growing panic. She turned and almost flew down the stairs.

Alec and Scotty were just coming in the door when Shea reached the kitchen. She grabbed her car keys and a manila folder containing information Leona had asked for a month ago.

"I'll be back," she muttered.

"Mind if I ask where you're going?"

"Um…I've got to take some records over to Leona."

Without waiting for any further comment, she quickly walked out the door.

The house was quiet when Shea stepped into the kitchen much later. Closing the door behind her, she dropped the car keys onto the counter and walked toward the stairs.

"Have a good visit?"

"Oh!" She spun around in the direction of Alec's voice. "You startled me." She clutched the neckline of her shirt.

"Sorry." He stepped out of the shadows. "I came down to get some water and heard you drive up. What are you doing back here?"

"I live here?"

He shrugged. "I just didn't think you'd come back tonight."

He didn't know how close he was to the truth.

Or maybe he did.

He was clad only in jeans, the ripple of hard muscle in his arms and chest apparent even in the semidarkness. She could sense the pure male aura that always seemed to surround him.

"Did Scotty settle in all right?"

"It took a while, but he's asleep."

Shea gave him a strained smile, nodded and together they climbed the stairs. When she stopped in front of the door to the bathroom, he proceeded down the hall without another word.

Stripping off her dirty clothes, she turned on the shower, stepped under the fine spray and let the hot water massage away the stress running rampant through her body. But she knew it would take more than hot water to make her relax. Alec had to go. Finding a way to make him leave was imperative and she had to do it quickly. She turned off the water and stepped out of the shower.

Her arm was tender from the bashing she'd taken from Bonnie Blue earlier. A large, reddish-purple bruise had begun to appear over much of her shoulder and upper arm. She carefully donned a worn-but-comfortable cotton T-shirt. After drying her hair, she applied moisturizer and brushed her teeth. With nothing more to keep her in the bathroom, she swallowed her trepidation and opened the door.

Two steps down the hall in the direction of the master bedroom, her feet suddenly reversed direction. Vivid in her mind's eye was the picture of lying in the bed, Alec's hands and mouth caressing her body, preparing her, priming her for the sex to follow. While she couldn't argue he oozed sex appeal, he was still a stranger: a cold man whose sole reason for being here was to take away her home.

Quickly, she made her way to her old bedroom, and quietly closed the door. With any luck, Alec would be asleep and never notice her absence. She pulled back the covers and climbed into bed.

She lay still, hopeful, watching the shadows from the leaves on the tree outside her window dance on the ceiling. She was so tired. Slowly, the tension began to leave, her muscles relaxed, and she closed her eyes and let sleep overtake her.

She was floating. Yet she could feel an iron brace holding her firmly against tremendous warmth. Groggily, she blinked open her eyes. She was being carried. Instantly she was awake, and just as quickly, she knew who was carrying her and where they were going.

Seconds later, Alec placed her on the large new bed. Before she could scramble away, he leaned over and placed his hands on either side of her, effectively preventing her escape.

"I told you in the beginning, you *will* sleep in my bed." She could hear the annoyance in his voice. "Unless you want to start packing right now, you'd better learn to deal with it."

Slowly he stood over her and Shea scurried to the far edge of the mattress, eyeing him with apprehension. He frowned, resting his hands on his hips.

"Where's your ring?"

The question threw her. "What ring?"

His mouth quirked. "Your *wedding* ring. Remember the little ceremony when you promised to love, honor and *obey*?"

"It's over there—" she nodded toward the dresser, deciding to ignore his taunt "—in that little box. I…didn't want to wear it while I worked in the barn."

He walked to the dresser and took the ring out of the case and then came back to the bed.

"Give me your hand."

With a grimace, she extended her left hand and he slipped the sparkling wedding band onto her third finger.

"Leave it on."

Without another word, he unzipped his jeans. Shea turned away, hugging the far side of the bed as close to the edge as she could get. He turned off the light and she felt the mattress shifting to accommodate his large frame. Then his heavy arm slid around her waist as he settled next to her.

"I missed you, Mrs. Morreston." His breath was warm against her ear, his voice deep and sexy. "I missed kissing you."

"Leave me alone."

"Remind me of what I missed."

"No." She tried to push his arm away, but her efforts were futile.

Alec's hand settled gently on her shoulder to turn her onto her back. She couldn't hold back a cry of pain when he touched the bruised area. He immediately released her. There was a faint movement and then light shattered the darkness.

"Let me see your shoulder. Take off your T-shirt."

She sat up. "It's nothing. Just a bruise."

"Now."

"No."

"Either you take it off or I will."

The hard lines of his face contained no sympathy, only determination. But she faced him with equal strength of purpose. "You have no right to make that demand. Nothing in the contract gives you the right. If I want to cut off my nose it's none of your concern."

"Does everything have to be a battle with you?"

She clamped her mouth shut and glared. He was about the most demanding man she'd ever met. Nothing in those rich golden eyes and handsome features showed the tiniest indication he would relent.

"I want to look at your shoulder," he stated evenly. "If you don't want me to see, then get dressed and I'll take you to the emergency room and have a doctor check it out. But I'm not going to ignore the fact that you're injured."

She searched his face, looking for any way to pierce the armor of his resolve. Finding none, she turned away from him and eased the injured arm out of the sleeve. Raising the tail of the shirt over her shoulder, she refused to meet his eyes.

Alec inspected her arm with a muttered curse. "You damn near broke your arm. You could have a fracture. I think you need to have it x-rayed. Why the hell didn't you say something?"

"I… It's not that bad." She shrugged. "It's not any more painful than being forced to live with you."

She heard him sigh. "What are you afraid of, Shea?" His raspy voice was compelling, tuning her senses to his every word. "I can feel you respond to me. I know my touch doesn't repulse you. Surely you've had sex before?"

Her head shot up, and she spun around on the bed to face him, pushing her arm back through the sleeve while glaring at him for his audacity. "I've *made love* before. To someone I knew and cared for very much." He watched her intently, his golden eyes again reminding her of a predator amusing himself with his prey while deciding if he was hungry. She turned away from his scrutiny. "I don't know you. And I certainly don't care for you."

He reached out, his fingers grasping her chin, turning her to him. His eyes held her there. "I have no intention of remaining celibate during our marriage. It'll be easier if you try to accept that. Accept me. The sooner you come to terms with it, the better off you'll be. Or you always have the option of leaving and bringing this craziness to an end."

Wrenching her chin from his grasp, she tried to swallow the feeling of doom welling in her throat. "I'm not going anywhere. Why don't you go visit one of your lady friends? I'm sure there must be *one* out there somewhere who isn't completely repulsed. Hell, you supposedly have money. Go buy one."

"Why would I do that when I already have a beautiful, desirable woman in my bed?"

He reached out to switch off the small table lamp, and she noted again his wide shoulders and large biceps. His bronzed skin gleamed in startling contrast to the white linens that barely covered his hips. She swallowed hard.

The light went out and the mattress shifted as he lay back.

"How long has it been, Shea?"

She jerked her head around to stare at him, even though now all she saw was a silhouette in the darkened room.

"How long has it been since a man held you in his arms, touched you…took you to the edge…made you crazy with wanting…then gave you release?"

His deep, throaty voice sent shivers down her spine.

"That's none of your business!" she snapped, her voice sounding hoarse to her own ears. His words planted images in her mind she didn't want to see.

"On the contrary, as your husband I think it's expressly my business."

"Think what you want." She was not about to discuss her sex life—or the lack of one—with him; she refused to give him any more ammunition. She lay down, facing away from him and adjusted her pillow.

"Why are you afraid of me?"

"I'm not."

He was still for so long, she found herself holding her breath in expectation of what he might do. But he made no further attempt to touch her or harass her. Shea lay very still, staring out into the darkness.

A man with Alec's experience would recognize the battle that raged within her every time he came close. She was painfully aware of her limited ability to withstand his sexual magnetism. She'd only ever been with one man and that experience was nothing close to what Alec's words described. His voice, his devastating good looks topped with his apparent expertise in bed made her traitorous body crave his touch. But common sense told her he would use her to his own end. Moreover, his tactics would be as low and cutthroat as he deemed necessary to prevail in this war of wills. She had to hold on.

The sounds of the night closed in around her. A distant rumble of thunder echoed the turbulence in her mind. Sleep, when it finally came, was uneasy. Visions swirled around in her head. The ranch, encased in a fog, began to disappear while the thunder rumbled overhead. Powerless to stop it, she cried out. Then she sensed comforting warmth surrounding her, holding her close and protected. The dream faded, and she knew peace.

Alec held the innocent warmth of her body against the ache of his own. The last time he'd held a woman—just held her—had been too long ago to remember. With other women, there was no reason to stay after their needs had been satisfied, and certainly no desire to hold them as they slept.

After Sondra's infidelities, he made certain his relationships stayed free of emotional entanglements. The women he chose knew the score. It was sex, mutually enjoyable, nothing more. With Shea, her claims to hate him one minute then passionately respond to his kiss the next affected him in ways he neither liked nor knew how to deal with. She was pretending. Acting. She had to be. She couldn't possibly be as naive as she was letting on.

A glimmer of speculation made him question if she could be for real. He hated that glimmer. He hated not knowing. But most of all, he hated the idea that he cared either way.

Sondra had acted completely innocent when she'd just come from the bed of another man. She'd shown him what she'd wanted him to see until the end when she'd displayed her true colors. He knew what women were capable of when they wanted something badly enough. Shea wanted this land. And, like Sondra, there were no rules as far as she was concerned. Nothing was out of bounds. Nothing off-limits. No holds barred until she got her way.

And he'd be every kind of fool if he didn't keep that at the forefront of his mind.

Seven

When Shea awoke in the predawn hours, the birds sang outside the window and for the first time in her life she scoffed at the sound.

Raising her head, she was shocked to realize she'd used Alec for a pillow. Immediately rolling away from him, she eased over to her side of the bed. Holding her breath in the hope her actions wouldn't wake him, she lifted the covers and swung her legs to the floor. His light snoring continued as she made her way to the door. Unable to resist she spared a quick glance at Alec. Even relaxed in sleep, he was an intimidating presence. She had to be strong. There was too much to lose if she didn't find a way to send him packing.

Entering her old room, she grabbed a clean shirt and a pair of jeans and made her way to the bathroom. Her right shoulder screamed as she pushed her arm through the sleeve of the fresh T-shirt. Her head felt as muddled as it had the night she'd tried to sleep in the barn. This was going to be a very long day.

She trudged to the kitchen, needing a strong cup of coffee. When she opened the pantry door to grab the coffee tin, she saw the jar of Yolanda's homemade hot sauce sitting on the same shelf. A smile kicked up the corners of her mouth as she grabbed both the coffee and the jar of liquid fire.

An hour later she sat sipping her coffee while the biscuits finished baking. Scotty had joined her and was busy eating his stack of pancakes. Her mind had finally cleared and was focused on any strategy that would get rid of her unwanted houseguest. She'd just stood to refill her cup when the subject of her thoughts walked into the room.

"Hi, Daddy!"

"G'morning, son. Shea. How'd you sleep?" Alec looked directly at his son.

"Good!"

Alec had anticipated Scotty waking him at least once due to the new and unfamiliar surroundings, but apparently he'd slept through the night. The tantalizing aroma of bacon and freshly brewed coffee stirred his appetite. He poured a cup and let his gaze settle on Shea, who was busy pulling a tray of golden-brown biscuits from the antique oven in the corner. Did she believe the old saying about the way to a man's heart being through his stomach? He smiled. If that's what she believed, who was he to correct her?

"Smells good. I never pictured you as Little Miss Homemaker." He smiled. "I think I could get used to this."

"Have a seat."

Pulling out the chair next to Scotty, Alec sat down. Within minutes, Shea set a plate of eggs and bacon on the table in front of him, followed by a basket of the biscuits.

"Aren't you going to eat?"

"Already have." She nodded to his plate. "You go ahead. Enjoy your breakfast."

With a brief nod of thanks, he dug in with relish. Shea stood to the side.

The first mouthful tasted as good as it looked. She was a damned fine cook. He shoveled a second helping of the spicy eggs into his mouth, but just as he swallowed, an odd sensation brought his chewing to a halt.

It wasn't the taste that gave him the first hint he'd been had. It was the pure liquid lava that scorched his mouth and throat and continued to burn all the way down to his toes that gave him his first clue.

His vision clouded with tears as he reached for his glass. An instant of surprised horror raced through his mind at the realization the glass was empty.

"Oops," Shea said in a bored tone. "I forgot to give you any juice. So sorry."

Grabbing one of the biscuits, still warm from the oven, he quickly bit down and almost broke a tooth in the process. One slam of the biscuit on the table told him he'd have done better biting into a rock.

And his mouth continued to burn.

"Are the biscuits hard?" She leaned over and lifted one out of the basket. "Huh. Guess I had the oven temperature too low."

He glowered at Shea, who still stood, a picture of innocence beside the table, before he ran for the sink.

Turning on the faucet, Alec leaned over and gulped at the cool tap. But instead of relieving the scalding sensation, the water actually increased the burning.

"Are you finished with your plate?" she asked from behind him, her tone indicating she saw nothing odd about her husband gulping water from the kitchen faucet while smoke had to be billowing out of his ears. "You didn't eat much of your eggs. I guess you weren't very hungry."

He could only glare at her, his tongue singed to numbness. She picked up the plate and dumped the remains into the sink. "I've got some errands to run. Jason needs some help with a couple of chores. I told him you'd meet him behind the main barn right after breakfast."

"Chores?" he asked, looking at her suspiciously, before reaching for a napkin to wipe his watery eyes and running nose. "Like what?"

"Some fences need mending. Stalls have to be cleaned. A couple of old trees, downed during the last storm, are blocking the north gate. They'll need to be chopped, split for firewood, hauled to the house and stacked."

"Anything else?"

She smiled. "Jason has a list."

The sound of steady clicking challenged the silence in the old house as Shea stepped into the kitchen. She'd intended to start supper as soon as she got home, but curiosity made her set the sack of green beans and new potatoes—a gift from Leona—on the table. A frown crossed her face as she followed the sound out of the kitchen and down the hall. Pushing open the door to her office, she was dumbstruck at the sight of Alec sitting behind the old desk typing on a laptop, his files and papers strewn all over, her ledgers and ranch records pushed to one side. Immediately her temper flared.

"What do you think you're doing?"

He spared her a quick glance. "Working."

"You're in *my* office."

"There wasn't another one."

"You can't just barge in here and—"

"I have my own work to do. I'm not here solely to be your hired hand." He glanced at his palm and she couldn't miss seeing the multitude of blisters. He grimaced and then pulled open the drawer with his fingers. "I need a ruler."

She crossed her arms in a defensive gesture and refused to respond.

Alec shut the drawer. "Look. My own work can't come to a crashing halt simply because I've changed my address."

"Well, neither can mine! I can't work around you. You've buried my ledger underneath your junk!"

With a barely concealed sigh of frustration, he nodded his head. "All right, *dear*," he said sarcastically. "If you're going to work in your ledger, may I *please* set you up at the kitchen table long enough for me to send some emails?"

Emails? She relaxed her stance. His sarcasm was about

to change into something much more enthralling and she had a front row seat.

"Emails?" She saw him nod as he stood and began to gather her books. "How are you going to send emails?"

"What do you mean, how am I going to send…?" he began, his words dying in his mouth as realization settled in. "Tell me you have an internet connection."

Smiling, she shook her head. "Sorry."

"Well, this is just great." He sat back, rubbed his neck and then flinched from the blisters on his palms. "My cell is useless out here. I can't get through to my office on your landline until some talker named Ms. Hoover finishes the call to her sister."

"That would be Gladys."

"And now no internet."

He tossed the pencil onto the desk and stood up. "This is the twenty-first century and you people are still using stone knives and bear skins. It's amazing old Gladys doesn't break out the drums."

"Hey, if you don't like it…"

Muttering under his breath, Alec stomped past her and limped out of the room, the soreness in his body apparent. Score two points for her side.

The next few days were a repeat of the same routine. After Alec carefully tested the food before eating his breakfast, he and Jason would leave to complete the multitude of tasks needing to be done around the ranch. Because Shea had so much to do to prepare for the roundup—decisions only she could make—Hank had slowly transitioned to the role of part-time babysitter, a job both he and little Scotty seemed to enjoy.

Alec had taken time out to arrange for a wireless internet service. She'd seen the work trucks go up and down the main road indicating the installation of a new communications tower. She didn't even want to guess how he'd pulled that off. Or how much it had cost. He'd commandeered one of the unused bedrooms upstairs for his office. A new desk and chair had been delivered. After a long day of physical labor with Jason, he would often spend hours in his new office, sometimes working well into the night. Phone calls came in at all hours to his cell phone. If Alec wasn't there, the call would transfer to an answering service somewhere. Shea often went to sleep listening to him speak in various languages and wondered if he worked with people all over the world. She had to admit, having him at the Bar H was not turning out to be the total nightmare she'd feared. At least not yet.

A couple of weeks after Alec began working with Jason, Shea spotted the younger ranch hand as he walked toward his truck to go home at the end of the day. She'd been curious if Alec had been making an honest effort to lend a hand. She ran to catch up with Jason before he pulled out of the driveway.

"He's awesome," Jason replied to her question, grinning. "Alec works as hard as I do. No breaks. No hesitation to take on any job that needs doing. He's a great guy. You should have married him a long time ago."

"Thanks." She tried to keep the sarcasm out of her tone. "See you tomorrow."

As Jason backed his truck out of the gravel parking area, Shea wondered what Alec was up to. Why would he work so hard to make repairs on a ranch he wanted to level?

She rounded the corner and walked in through the back door of the old farmhouse. She found the subject of her thoughts standing in the kitchen, a bunch of wildflowers clutched in his fist. Her eyebrows shot up at the sight of the big, powerful man clutching a handful of wilting flowers.

"I picked these just before we headed back to the barn." He held the bouquet out to her. "I thought...well, maybe they might look nice on the table." She heard a touch of awkwardness in his voice, which was completely out of character for Alec. That surprised her as much as the offering of flowers. "The west pasture was full of them," he added. "Like a multicolored blanket almost as far as the eye could see. It was amazing. Anyway..."

Stunned, she accepted the offering. She looked from the blooms to Alec and couldn't stop the smile that widened her lips. It was a thoughtful gesture and one she never would have expected from him.

"Thank you," she said earnestly. "And you're right—the flowers are remarkable this time of year. You might want to stay clear of the blue ones. They're the state flower and I don't think we're supposed to pick them."

"Ah," Alec nodded his head, indicating message received. "Okay. Well, I need a shower."

As he left the room, Shea looked at the colorful bouquet. The mixed colors of yellow, orange, pink and blue would indeed make a pretty table setting. She selected a crystal glass from the cabinet, added water and arranged the blooms before placing the small arrangement in the center of the table.

Alec Morreston had brought her flowers.

He probably had a hidden agenda in there somewhere, but that thought couldn't diminish the delight she felt receiving the small gift. She'd be wise to keep up her guard and watch him like a starving hawk would a mouse. He had to be up to something. But for now, she would enjoy the flowers and consider this nothing more than a thoughtful gesture.

Later, when they all sat down for dinner, Alec spoke with enthusiasm about what they'd accomplished that day, asking her questions about the ranch setup or the livestock, but stopping just short of making any suggestions. Why try to improve something that, if he had his way, wouldn't be here in a year? But it let her see more of the man he was beneath the business suit. Locked away inside her where no one could see, a seed of respect for him had begun to take root and grow.

As she gathered the empty plates from the table and placed them in the soapy water, Shea was suddenly overcome with an intense wave of sadness. Between the gestures of kindness, the unspoken treaty between them for Scotty's sake and the camaraderie that had developed among Alec, Hank and the other ranch hands, it gave the illusion of one big happy family. The evening meals were a time of friendly banter, sharing humorous stories of the past and ideas for a future that possibly would never be. Even little Scotty played into the role of her loving son. And she was beginning to love him. She couldn't keep herself from forming a bond with such an adorable, bright child.

Each day seemed to intensify the illusion and it was becoming more difficult to remember that this was not a family. It was not a time for joking. There should be no camaraderie. This was not a game of pretend. It was war. And it was very real. A mandatory sentence forcing two opposing, equally determined individuals into a life-changing competition requiring constant stamina and strength of mind to win the grand prize, all within preposterous directives set up two hundred years ago by individuals unknown and for reasons she couldn't fathom. It was clearly a chapter out of a Stephen King novel.

At times she felt herself slipping into the illusion, letting it envelop her, as though something deep inside wanted it to become real with a desperation that was off the scale. The dangers of this were obvious. She had to remain focused. She had to remember that this illusion of a happy home with a handsome, caring husband and loving child was not reality. And never would be.

* * *

The ledger remained open awaiting a final calculation, but it was just a closing formality. She already knew the profit margin, while small, was clearly there. As long as the beef prices didn't take a sudden plunge before they shipped, the ranch would have a profitable year.

A soft knocking from the open doorway pulled her attention from the columns of figures. She glanced up to see Alec stroll into the room. His gaze rested first on her, then shifted to the collage of framed photographs hanging neatly on the wall to his left.

"Mind if I just look around?"

She shrugged. "Go ahead."

She tried to return her attention to the ledger but his presence presented a distraction she couldn't easily ignore.

"I noticed these right after I arrived." He scanned the wall of framed photographs. "Some of these pictures are really old."

"I think the oldest ones are from the mid-1800s."

Pictures of cowboys with their horses, branding operations, women dressed in styles portraying Western fashion almost two hundred years ago.

"Is this your father?" He pointed to a picture in the upper right corner of the grouping.

"Yes."

"Who are the two men with the longhorn?"

"My grandfather and his brother," she answered, never taking her eyes from the computer screen. She didn't need to. She knew the snapshots by heart. "They were one of seven families credited with bringing the longhorn back from near extinction."

Alec moved farther down the wall. "There's a kid on a horse getting some kind of award," he said, observing another picture. "Is it you?"

"Yeah." She saw no reason to elaborate.

"And what about this one?"

Shea glanced at the wall. He pointed to picture of a child astride a large dapple-gray thoroughbred. "That's me on Sir Raleigh at the hunter-jumper competition at Fair Park in Dallas. I was about twelve." She nodded to the next picture. "You might recognize the person in that one."

Alec leaned toward the picture. "Leona?"

She nodded, unable to restrain a smile. "It was taken several years ago during a Fourth of July party."

"She looks…different."

"She was smashed. Somebody spiked her watermelon punch."

Alec grinned. "These are fascinating pictures. I feel as though I'm looking at a wall in a cowboy history museum."

He glanced at Shea. In surprising contrast to the usual glare she sent in his direction, she was smiling. He walked over to the old leather wing-backed chair that faced the massive oak desk and sat down.

"When I was a teenager, there was a fairly large stable a few miles from our summer house in Saratoga County in upstate New York," he said, leaning back and resting one booted ankle on the other knee. "The Tall Pine Stables." He shook his head. "I haven't thought about it in years. My dad was determined his sons would learn the value of a dollar. I was given the choice of working in his office during the summer—" Alec nodded at the ledger "—which meant sitting behind a desk. Or I could find my own job. Most of my friends got summer work flipping burgers, sacking groceries or caddying at the country club. I was lucky enough to find work mucking out horse stalls."

"You?" Her eyebrows shot up and her eyes grew wide.

Alec chuckled. "Yeah, me. Not fun, as I'm sure you know. But I loved the horses, so I stuck it out. Went back the next two summers and the second year the owner began to supplement my pay with the bonus of exercising a few of the thoroughbreds. It was…amazing. I loved their spirit. I swore I would have one of my own someday."

"And did you?"

"Nah." He shrugged. "Just never worked out."

He envied Shea her life and the way she'd been raised. Close to the land and nature. It had always beckoned him, but he'd never stopped long enough to heed the call.

"That's really too bad." Her voice was soft, as though she was truly sorry he'd never seen that dream realized. "You've still got time. And I think Scott would love it. He seems to have inherited your love of horses."

Alec nodded. "Yeah. So it would appear." He was thoughtful for a moment. "I might never have known if we hadn't come here. Maybe I can work something out." He stood from the chair. "I'll get out of here and let you finish your work. Guess I'd better go and check on Scott." He walked to the door.

"Alec?"

"Yeah." He faced her.

"Thanks for sharing that with me."

She smiled and while it was cautious and hesitant, nonetheless something deep inside him felt very good.

It was almost midnight when Shea stretched and stood up, flexing her tired muscles. After Alec's visit, it had taken quite a while to regain her concentration on the work she'd needed to finish. To say she'd been surprised by his story of working summers at a stable was an understatement. She never would have pictured Alec Morreston mucking stalls. Or riding thoroughbreds. His professed love of horses seemed to contradict his intent to close the ranch. It was yet another layer of the complex man. It would be prudent to watch him even closer. Apparently there was much more to Alec than she'd originally thought and he could use any accrued knowledge against her, which brought back the earlier sadness and added to the growing stress she already was feeling.

At times, she felt as if she was a stranger in her own home. She wasn't used to not trusting people, to always being on guard, having to watch her every action and word, being alert to anything Alec did or saw as potentially giving him leverage to take the ranch. It was like walking a tightrope and even though she would never admit it aloud, it was taking its toll. Her nerves were shot to hell and frustration was building. She had to wonder how much longer this situation would last before it blew sky high.

With a sigh, she turned off the computer, returned the ledger to the bottom drawer of the desk, flipped off the light and left the office. A hot shower sounded wonderful. The few minutes of relaxation it would provide were definitely needed.

In the bathroom, she turned on the water and peeled off her clothes. Soon steam began to cloud the room as hot water jettisoned out of the nozzle.

Stepping into the shower, she reached for the bottle of shampoo. Empty. Muttering to herself, she stepped back out of the shower to grab a new bottle from the cabinet.

She'd not taken more than three steps when a slick spot on the tile floor sent both feet shooting out from under her. She landed in a sprawling, floundering heap, hitting the floor so hard she swore the earth shook from the force of it.

For a few moments, she lay in stunned silence, then slowly clambered to her feet and gingerly made her way to the cabinet. Grabbing the new bottle of shampoo, she limped back to the shower.

As she applied the soap, working up a good lather, she noticed the water didn't seem quite as hot as it had been just seconds before. With her eyes tightly closed, she fumbled with the taps, trying to adjust the temperature. It wasn't until she had turned off the cold completely that she realized there was no more hot water. At that very moment, the old pipes began to rumble and groan as if building in momentum, and half a heartbeat later, a spray of water from the icy depths of the well hit her squarely in the face.

A squeal of surprise tore from her throat. Sputtering and coughing, she managed to withstand the frigid temperature long enough to rinse out the shampoo, then immediately turned off the tap. Teeth chattering, goose bumps covering her skin, she stepped from the shower, careful to avoid the slick spot this time, and edged her way around the room to the linen cabinet.

She stared in disbelief. The shelves were empty. This morning, there had been at least a dozen bath towels in the linen closet. Now, all that remained were several washcloths and one hand towel.

Dripping wet and shivering, she grabbed the hand towel and began blotting the water from her skin and hair. This was no accident. It had the Morreston name written all over it. Oh, how she hated that damned contract. She wished she could go back in time and do something vile to the ancestor who'd added that insane clause. She combed the tangles from her hair, stepped into her panties, pulled on an oversize T-shirt and slowly counted to ten.

It wasn't long enough.

The bedroom was in darkness but in the soft glow from the yard light outside, Shea could see Alec's silhouette sprawled diagonally across the bed. Still shivering, she walked to the far side. His large frame lay on top of the covers and try as she might, she couldn't dislodge enough of the top sheet and blanket from under his sleeping form to give her even a small amount of warmth.

Suddenly, the urge to whack the horrible man with a blunt object overcame her common sense. A thirst for revenge compelled her to grab the edge of a pillow, yank it from under his head, raise it high and slam it down on top of the sleeping man with all the force she could muster.

"Hey!"

Again the pillow came down on his head.

"What the hell…?"

And again.

"Goddammit, Shea!" He caught her wrist and pulled her down onto the bed, fighting to control her flailing legs and arms. "Stop it! What the hell's the matter with you?"

"*You.* You're what's the matter with me!" she snarled. "Let me go!"

She pushed against him and tried to twist free. He easily controlled her efforts, throwing one leg over hers, catching and holding both her hands above her head and firmly pressing the parts in between against his muscled length.

"I want to know what brought this on."

"Nothing. Just…nothing. Let me go."

"Not happening."

She struggled against him, making one last all-out effort to free her hands before giving up and glaring at him through the darkness. She saw his focus move from her eyes to her mouth seconds before he lowered his head and covered her lips with his own. She tried to turn away, but he effortlessly held her in place. His lips were full and warm and totally enticing. Her mind let go of her earlier frustration and focused on Alec. His slow, lazy kiss made the need to get away from him seem not quite as important as it had seconds ago.

He raised his head and their gazes met through the dim glow from the lights at the barn. It was as though he was offering her a choice. When she didn't move away, he returned to her lips without saying a word, his mouth claiming hers in a deep and passionate kiss. His tongue entered her, filled her, and gone was any want for him to stop. With a sigh, she gave up the struggle. The passion escalated to raw, hungry need.

Her oversize T-shirt was twisted and stretched tightly over her breasts. She felt the warmth of his hand move up her side to gently squeeze the soft flesh. He lowered his head, placing his mouth over one taut nipple, licking and sucking through the thin material. Shea drew air deep into her lungs, her breasts swelling under his touch. His hot mouth moved to the other breast, bringing it to the same throbbing ache, an ache that shot straight to her core.

Taking one of her hands, Alec directed it down between their bodies, placing her fingers against his sex, holding it there when she would have drawn away. "No. Feel me, Shea. Feel what you do to me." His voice was low, gritty, as though the tight rein on his emotions was about to shatter.

She became lost in the sensation. Her hand couldn't fully encompass his girth, but he throbbed under her touch. His lips returned to hers, hungry, wanting. His hand slid down her belly, not pausing until he was cupping her most sensitive flesh. "Open your legs for me, Shea," he instructed, his voice raw. "Do it."

The final remnants of hesitation dissolved as she obeyed, raising one leg, allowing him access to the most private part of her. His skilled hands increased her need for penetration to a level of near desperation. All other motion ceased, her body paralyzed, completely enraptured by what he was doing.

Alec was on fire and close to losing it before he ever got inside of her. He wanted her with desperation he'd never before experienced. The sweet smell of her arousal flooded his senses. Her breath rushed in and out as her hands encircled his neck, holding him to her while her hips pushed against his throbbing erection, leaving no doubt in his mind she needed more.

Seconds, maybe less, before he permanently changed the entire situation, the cell phone he'd put on the nightstand began to ring. Its loud, shrill robotic tone infused the moment with cold reality.

All motion stopped. Breathing hard, he opened his eyes. *What in the hell was he doing?*

With a shuddering regret, Alec rolled to his side, his body protesting painfully, refusing to downshift. He had almost done it again. Making love to Shea was not going to accomplish anything except temporarily easing the pain of arousal. It would open a box full of complications neither one of them needed. He had little doubt that Shea didn't normally partake in one-night flings. This was something they would both regret, albeit for very different reasons, in the light of day.

The ringing stopped. As he lay next to her, willing his breathing to slow, she turned away from him, rolling onto her side. She didn't speak, and damn if he knew what to say. He'd honestly never been in this situation, wanting a woman beyond comprehension but knowing it was absolutely wrong, even as she lay in the bed next to him. He swallowed hard. He had to offer her something. He couldn't ignore her emotions.

"Shea?"

She was quiet for so long, he thought she wasn't going to answer. Then her voice reached him through the darkness.

"I understand, Alec."

Then maybe she could explain it to him.

"It's this whole horrible situation." Her voice sounded strained, as though she was struggling not to cry. He sensed a motion. Was she wiping the tears from her eyes? "I no longer know what's right and what isn't. I lost the map. I don't know how I should feel or what I should do. I want my life back. I want my dad not to have died." She drew a shaky breath. "I want to feel, even for a minute, that I'm not a stranger in my own house. That I'm not alone and fighting against the entire world."

"Hey." Alec gently pulled her into his arms, determined to relieve some of the heartache he had no doubt caused. Her head rested on his shoulder. She offered no resistance. "You're not taking on the world," he responded. "Just me. And from this side of the bed, you're doing a pretty damn good job."

He sensed rather than saw her smile and she sniffed back the tears. Beyond her beauty, she was an honest, caring woman who hadn't asked for any of this. He felt the urge to tell her she could have the ranch. But he couldn't. There was already too much invested, both time and money. There were too many people counting on this project for jobs and investors expecting something for their venture. For the first time since coming here, Alec wished he could just walk away. Let Shea's life return to normal. Hell, let both of them return to doing what made them happy.

That thought brought him up short. When *had* he last been happy? Before coming here, when was the last time he'd slept throughout the night without waking to pace the floor at 3:00 a.m.? How long had he been working such long hours that he didn't know if it was day or night? When had he taken the time to reflect on his childhood and his fishing excursions with Grandpa Jacob? When had he spent as much quality time with Scotty? Everything here seemed to move at a much slower pace. But he felt at home here, like a figurine that had found its way back into the mold. And it all revolved around Shea and this ranch. All the good and positive feelings.

"Shea?" Alec lowered his face to the top of her head. She had fallen asleep in his arms, her head on his shoulder, her arm resting across his stomach. He loved the softness of her hair, how it always smelled like the sweet blooms of the Ligustrum trees that grew in abundance here. He lay back on the pillow, his fingers playing idly in the silky strands of her hair, closed his eyes and drew her intoxicating aroma deep into his lungs. The softness of her breasts pressed against him, her breathing gentle on his skin. It felt so right. While this moment in time was nothing life changing, he knew it was a time he wouldn't soon forget.

For almost a month, he'd lain in this bed night after night, taunted by the temptation of her sleeping next to him. What had happened to his brilliant notion that he would have her gone in a few days? Things had changed. *He* had changed. He wanted her to like him. She stirred him as no woman ever had and they hadn't even been intimate. Although they'd damn sure come close. Too close.

What he wanted from Shea was more than sex—and that was a first for him. And he knew because of the land situation and that damned contract he had little-to-no hope of anything more between them ever coming to pass.

Eight

Shea had just finished drying the breakfast dishes when Scotty ran into the kitchen, eyes wide, excitement pouring out of every pore of his small frame.

"Shea!" He stood next to the table, looking as though he was going to explode. The fingers of his small hands knotted together and then unknotted over and over.

"What is it, sweetie?"

"Hank had to go into town and Daddy doesn't have to work with Jason on account of Jason taking his wife to a doctor and Daddy said he didn't have to work at his other job and we can go fishing and I've never been fishing but he doesn't know where the fishes are." He took a breath. "So...Daddy said to come and ask where you keep 'em."

She couldn't stop the grin from covering her face. Only one place came immediately to mind. Grady's Gulch. About a mile to the north, just past the lake, a ravine wound its way toward the Red River. In one spot near a huge granite bolder, the banks drastically curved, creating a deep cavity that contained some of the best fishing anybody could ever hope to find. Shea knew a moment of hesitation. Few people knew of the spot. Did she really want to share this special spot with Alec? But a second glimpse into Scotty's hopeful eyes made the decision.

"I know just the place," she said, smiling, as his eyes grew even larger. She bent over and grabbed a large empty coffee can from the cabinet under the sink. "Take this to your dad and tell him to dig for some worms in that shady area near the well house. I'll get the fishing poles and meet you guys at the truck."

Scott bolted out of the kitchen and tore down the path to the barn yelling "Daddy!" the whole way.

Within an hour, the three of them were bouncing their way across the meadow. As Shea pulled into a tranquil spot under one of the giant oak trees and killed the engine, Alec immediately heard the sound of rushing water. A small trail led in that direction. Grabbing the poles and can of worms, he nodded for Shea to lead the way.

While she spread the old blanket in a shady spot next to the river, Alec baited the hook. With a cork firmly attached to the line, he swung it out over the water and handed the pole to Scotty.

"Just watch the cork, son. If you see it dip under the water, raise the pole really fast with a quick yank." Scotty nodded his understanding, his eyes not straying from the bobbing red-and-white ball floating toward the opposite bank.

When Alec turned to the blanket, Shea was staring up at him as though he'd grown an extra set of ears. "What?" he asked and looked down at his shirt.

"Nothing."

"Not fair."

She shrugged. "I just find it amazing you know how to bait a hook and can give instructions on how to fish with a cork."

Joining her on the well-used coverlet, he leaned back against the large tree trunk. "You think because I live in a city I've never been fishing?"

"Something like that. At least not without some fancy rigging."

"Well let me set the record straight. When I was just

about Scotty's age, my grandparents lived in a rural area a lot like this. I spent my summers with them. Gramps was big on fishing. He would cut his own cane pole, tie a string to the end, dig some worms and off we would go." Alec couldn't help but chuckle at the thought.

"You talk like those memories are…like they're special to you."

"They are." Alec frowned, not immediately understanding why she would say that.

"Yet you've never taken Scott fishing?"

Alec dropped his head and nodded. "You're right. Kept telling myself I would take him someplace special next week or next month but something always came up and it just never happened." And it was a regret Alec had carried with him for a long time.

"Well, you're doing it now."

He nodded and gave her a smile. "Yeah, I am. Thanks to you."

Shea shrugged as though none of this was her doing. Alec knew different. "How did you know about this place?"

"Because right over there—" she pointed to a granite boulder on the other side of the river "—is where I caught my first fish. Not many know about this place. Dad and his father and uncle guarded it as though the bottom was paved in gold. People tried for years to find out where Dad always managed to catch all the fish he would bring to a fish fry. I don't think they ever did."

Alec tilted his head. "But you were willing to share it with us."

Shea held his gaze, neither speaking nor nodding, and for a few brief seconds in time, the rest of the world ceased to exist. She had placed her trust in him, shared one of the special places in her life and some happy memories she treasured. She'd given Scotty a day of fun and Alec a small measure of relief from the guilt of not spending enough time with his son. He felt a kinship with the rich earth, with the cool water as it splashed against the huge boulders on its way downstream, the towering trees providing shade, their tallest branches catching and swaying in the gentle breeze. In spite of the animosity between them and her fierce determination to keep this ranch, Shea had shared something special with a virtual stranger who would take it all away.

Alec swallowed hard and closed his eyes. He wasn't used to her world and accepting acts of kindness wasn't in the game plan. Her small benevolences knocked him completely off balance. Other than Scotty, his mother and brother, he wasn't used to trusting people. But in that moment, he knew he could trust Shea with anything, including his son. And a shadow of guilt for what he was attempting to do with regard to the ranch seemed to put a dark cloud over the day.

"Daddy! It's gone! The fishies got it!"

Quickly getting to his feet, Alec hurried over to assist his son with the pole. In a matter of seconds, Scotty had landed his first fish. When he held it up, the fish still thrashed about on the end of the line and the boy wasn't certain exactly what to do with it. They should have brought a camera…

"Alec, do you have your cell phone?"

"Yeah, why?"

"Does it take pictures?"

Alec grinned. Of course. Why hadn't he thought of it? "It most certainly does."

Reaching into his pocket, he pulled out the small black phone, changed the settings and handed it to Shea.

She snapped away as father and son posed for a "first fish" picture, then continued to take shots as Alec patiently removed the hook and held the prize catch for Scott to touch.

"How about we let it go today?" Alec suggested. "Then

you can come back and catch it again sometime when we want to have fish for supper."

Without a word, Scotty vigorously nodded his head, clearly still amazed at the entire process.

They lingered next to the small river until the sun dropped low in the sky. It was as though they'd formed a truce and had silently declared this a place of neutrality where legal contracts and land development had no admittance. While Scotty waited for his next fish to grab the hook, Shea and Alec exchanged stories of their youth. The more she told him about special places and times on the ranch, the tighter the knot in his belly grew.

His planned development wouldn't reach this far out from the Red River. Maybe there was something he could do to let her keep at least part of her home. For months, the investors had been maneuvering about where they wanted this or that and adding more and more to the overall size of the project. It was his project and he maintained control, but his professional integrity insisted he consult with them on any major changes. For the first time he seriously considered reducing the overall scope of the project. It was certainly worth looking into.

The telephone rang as Shea entered the kitchen the next morning. She grabbed it on the second ring.

"Morning!" Leona's familiar voice hailed her from the other end of the line.

"I guess," she replied.

"Everything all right?"

"I suppose. So far. I haven't seen Alec or Scotty this morning."

"Well, I called to tell you they're both over here. Rode over with Hank. Alec is getting a tour of the spread, and the boy is with my grandson, Cody. They're playing with the new puppies."

"Oh, that's right. Maggie had her pups, didn't she?"

"Yep," Leona confirmed. "Did you remember tonight is the party to celebrate Ms. Annie's birthday?"

Annie Philpot was considered the matriarch of the Calico Springs ranching community. She'd married and lost two fine husbands, and then, by herself, had raised her nine children and carried on the tradition of producing fine horses and prime beef cattle. Through it all, she'd still found time to care for the friends and neighbors she loved. In times of sickness or when a new baby was about to make its presence known, Miss Annie had been there. In recent years, she'd reached out more via telephone than personal visits, but nonetheless her heart remained with her extended family.

"Oh, Leona, I'd completely forgotten."

"Figured you might have, what with the way your life has been here lately. It's been a while since you've seen everyone. Most of 'em are about to bust open with curiosity about Alec. Try and make it over here, if you can."

"Absolutely." She would have plenty of time to make a pie. Everyone always brought a dish or dessert to these gatherings. But something else tugged at her mind.

"Leona, does anyone know?" If rumors were flying about Alec taking her ranch and his plans for the land, she needed to know before they walked into the party.

A numbing pause followed the question.

"You mean about Alec?"

"Yeah."

"No. At least nothing's been said to me. Whatever he's planning, he's kept to himself. There has been some talk of a big entertainment complex gonna be built across the river in Oklahoma. People are generally either excited about the idea or don't much believe it. Is that what he's doing?"

"I honestly don't know." Alec had never told her and she hadn't asked. Shea wasn't sure she wanted to know. Whatever he had in mind was not going to happen and that was as far as her mind had gone on the subject. Let him build his magical kingdom in the adjacent state if he wanted. Just keep it off her ranch land and out of the community. "Thanks, Leona. We'll see you about eight."

By six o'clock Alec had returned and by seven thirty they were on their way to Leona's house. At least fifty adults and maybe a dozen kids were already enjoying the festivities when they arrived. The aroma of hickory smoke from a huge grill invited all new arrivals to bring their appetites around to the back of the house. Several long tables were set up, complete with red-checkered tablecloths. Shea placed her pie on the table with the other desserts.

One hello led to another and another until most of the party guests had met Shea's new husband. Alec dutifully shook hands and repeatedly answered the questions of the evening: "Where are you from?" and "How did you meet?" He surprised her by responding to their inquiries in a manner both believable and flattering to her.

In essence, he lied.

They paid their respects to the guest of honor, wishing Miss Annie a most happy eighty-ninth birthday. Then they joined Hank and Leona in the chow line and came away with their plates heavily laden with home-cooked fare. Scotty wanted to eat with Leona's grandson and several other kids his age. A table had been set up just for them.

When darkness fell, candles and lanterns cast their soft glow over the crowd. Several strands of white twinkle lights strung in the lower tree branches gave a strange, almost mystical, ambience to the festivities. With an area under the lights cleared for dancing, couples filled the space as the soft melody of a country ballad drifted through the cooling night air.

At the edge of the sphere of soft light, some of the children, including Scott, held sparklers, running back and forth, waving their arms, making circles and glowing formations against the darkness. Their laughter blended with the music and the cheerful mood of the adults, most of them lifelong friends, who'd gathered to celebrate another year of life of one of their own.

Shea knew total relaxation for the first time in a very long time. She sat quietly, eyes closed, listening to the music. Unexpectedly, a warm hand touched her shoulder. She looked up to find Alec standing beside her.

"Dance with me."

Without waiting for an answer, he took her hand and led her to the edge of the dancing couples, drawing her into his arms.

The music flowed in a soft, slow tempo. His arms encircled her, holding her close while they moved together to the rhythm of the song. It seemed the most natural thing in the world to rest her head against his shoulder. She closed her eyes, intoxicated by the musky scent of his cologne, warmed by the sheer strength of the arms around her.

This is so wrong. She shouldn't be dancing with this man—shouldn't be taking pleasure in his arms. By getting to know Alec, by seeing him as something other than the enemy, it was becoming more and more difficult to ignore her growing attraction to him. She liked him. A lot, in fact. Amazingly, the realization wasn't so painful.

As they danced, his thigh intermittently rubbed against her lower belly. She found herself holding her breath when he moved away until another shift in their movements again caused the hard contours of his body to press against her.

His fingers threaded through her hair, cupping the back of her head as he gently encouraged her gaze to meet his. She saw the flames of controlled passion in his darkening eyes before he lowered his head and settled his mouth on hers.

The kiss was pure seduction. A ball of searing heat shot

straight to the juncture between her legs while the world around them ceased to exist.

Alec made a slight adjustment and his swollen shaft pressed solidly against her belly. For a moment, instinct took over and she succumbed to the blinding need to forget everything but the urge to satisfy the ache his touch created. She gave in to her body's natural reaction and pushed against him. She heard his sharp intake of breath followed by a low growl. He lowered his hands to her hips, pulling her solidly against him, and wanton desire scorched the skin beneath her jeans.

The loud snapping of firecrackers close by made her jump. She tore her lips from his as reality came crashing back with ferocity. It was as if someone had suddenly turned up the volume to the music and the voices around them. Her eyes lingered on his mouth. The temptation to return and seek the pleasures it offered was overwhelming.

Blinking, she stepped back and looked around her, feeling as if she'd just come back from another time and place. Desperately she willed her mind to reengage.

They were in the midst of some twenty dancing couples. Glancing around, she was thankful to see that no one appeared aware of the sensual drama unfolding in their midst. She chanced another look at Alec's face, and in the depths of his eyes she saw awareness of her internal battle. He knew how close she was to losing.

"I should go...and help Leona."

"Leona has all the help she needs." He gently smoothed a stray lock of hair back from her face. "Let's go home."

His deep, husky invitation was almost her undoing. "I..." Her eyes roamed over his face while he waited patiently for her decision. He wanted her. He wasn't using coercion or bribery. There were no threats. He was putting it out on the table and she could say yes or she could say no.

She couldn't make love to Alec. Could she? He was still

her enemy. Wasn't he? She didn't believe in casual sex. For Shea, intimacy had to be between two people who honestly cared for each other. And even if she felt that way toward Alec, could she justify one night of ecstasy with a man who was bent on destroying everything she had?

"I…I've got to go." She pushed out of his arms, walked in the direction of Leona's house and didn't look back.

Shea wasn't sure what was happening between them, but at the very least, she knew she already had broken her number one directive: hating Alec Morreston.

"It looks like you two are having a good time," Leona remarked as she entered the kitchen. She handed Shea a dishtowel.

Shea nodded and picked up a plate, unable to meet Leona's eyes. "I guess."

"Things going any better?"

She shrugged. Alec wasn't the adversary she'd initially expected. Either his tactics weren't as cutthroat as she'd first feared, or the man was tremendously subtle and highly skilled at manipulation. Probably both. But since his return from New York with his son, she'd glimpsed another side of the man. Even Scotty was a revelation, providing insight into the complexities of Alec's character. It was as if he were two different people. One was the enemy, a cold and ruthless man bent on destroying everything. The other was a caring and loving father who had gained her respect and was well on his way to becoming someone she cared about.

In spite of what he'd threatened that day in Ben's office, in spite of his determination to force her from the land, he'd given her time. Conversely, the more time he gave her, the more she contemplated what it would be like to love such a man. Lovers with no future, engaged in an affair that was sure to end badly. Who did that? Was she so foolish to fall in love with the very man who would take away everything she'd ever loved?

She picked up another plate and began to rub it with the towel. Leona snatched it from her hand.

"You're drying a dirty plate," she said, her eyes narrowing. "You haven't heard a word I've said for the last five minutes. Do I get to guess where your mind is?"

Blushing, Shea shook her head.

"Just be careful," Leona cautioned.

Shea nodded and reached for a clean plate.

With the few nondisposable dishes washed and dried, and the remaining food covered and put away, Shea stepped outside. She spotted Hank and Alec and walked in that direction. Detecting her presence next to him, Alec reached out to her, his arm settling around her shoulders. "Scott and Cody are going to sleep in their fort tonight. Steve Laughton said he'd stay out here with them and make sure they got inside the house if it starts to rain. Are you ready to go?"

"I guess. Good night, Hank."

The old cowboy nodded and touched his finger to his hat. Alec's hand remained at the back of her neck as they walked to his car. He seated her inside the luxury sedan, then took his place behind the wheel. She sat back in the plush leather seat, her head on the cushioned rest while the car easily ate up the miles to the Bar H. She glanced at the multitude of lights on the front console, then let her eyes move to the large man behind the wheel. He caught her glance and returned it.

"You have some nice neighbors," he said. "I enjoyed meeting them."

"They liked you, too." She turned her head to stare out into the seemingly endless shadows of the night. "It's too bad..."

"It's too bad...what?" he prompted.

"Well, I can't help but wonder what their reaction will be when they discover your plans for my ranch and ultimately this area. Most of these folks are third- and fourth-generation farmers and ranchers. They won't take kindly to some out-of-towner plopping a housing development in the center of their grazing land or paving their neighbor's pasture for a parking lot."

Shea chanced a quick glance in his direction. Alec continued to look straight ahead, seemingly without emotion, but in the dim light from the driver's panel, she noted a brief grimace cross his features.

"For your information, I have no intention of building a housing development here or anywhere else. That's not what I do."

"Maybe not, but you're a commercial developer," she stated, daring him to deny it. "That means destruction. If it's not a housing development, it'll be something else equally as bad."

"Not all change is a bad thing," Alec reminded her. "Sometimes it's for a good reason. It fulfills a need."

Shea swallowed uncomfortably. "And what about people who like things as they are?"

"Change is part of life. Most people are willing to accept it if they understand the reasoning behind it, especially if it benefits them in some way. You're painting me as the bad guy before you even know what my intentions are for this place."

"Oh, I see." She looked at Alec. "I should let you take over my ranch and trust you to develop it in a manner you think is—"

"Shea, it's not *your* ranch!"

"The hell it's not!" she muttered.

"Then show me your name on a deed."

"How can you be so…two-faced? How could you talk and laugh with the people there tonight, sit at their table, share their food, all the while knowing what you plan to do to their community if given the chance?"

"You make it sound like I intend to rob them!" Alec responded, his tone incredulous.

"Stab them in the back would be more accurate."

"For God's sake. You've got to be the most narrow-minded, bullheaded woman I've ever come across in my life!"

"Well, as my grandfather used to say, that's the pot calling the kettle black."

He turned off the main road onto the winding driveway leading to the old farmhouse. As Alec swung into the parking space, Shea grabbed for the door handle and was out of the car before he could turn off the ignition. She walked through the kitchen, up the stairs and into the bedroom, slamming the door behind her.

Angrily, she paced the floor until, finally realizing the futility of the situation she changed her clothes, brushed her teeth, switched off the lights and climbed into bed. A few minutes later, Alec joined her, arranging his pillows but making no attempt to acknowledge her presence. He lay on his side facing away from her. Instead of being relieved, she was irritated, and that was crazy. She should be glad. But she wasn't and she refused to dwell on why.

The distant rumble of thunder shattered the serene silence, waking Alec from his sleep. The sky was still dark even though the clock on the nightstand said it was almost five in the morning. Faint flashes of lightning intermittently lit the room for a few brief seconds as the increasing winds surged around the corner of the old house. He immediately thought of Scotty. Steve would have both boys inside Leona's house by now. It was a new and comforting realization that he could leave his only child in the care of near strangers and trust, without any hesitation, that his son would be well taken care of. Such trust was almost unheard of in his world.

Alec started to turn over, but immediately felt a soft, warm body snuggled against him. The aura of innocence and trust as Shea slept was alien to him. Hell, everything about her, about this place, was so different than what he was used to. Yet, at the same time, it often felt as though he'd come home.

With his sexual frustration at its peak, his body ached with desire every time she came close and now was no exception. He didn't know how much strength remained before his good intentions would go out the window. He'd never have believed he could become this damned infatuated with anyone, especially after Sondra. With a groan of frustration, he eased Shea onto a pillow and got out of bed.

The few days he'd originally anticipated being here had rolled into weeks. He'd surprised himself by actually finding a way to continue his own work and still enjoy the physical labor the ranch required. Ironically, it was in that labor he found an inner peace. A fresh breeze on his face, sweet scents in the air and the sun on his back. Beat the hell out of any gym.

He pulled on some jeans and grabbed a shirt and his boots. He needed to put some space between himself and Shea. A lot of space. One last glance at the bed where she slept was all it took to confirm in his mind what his body had been telling him. He wanted her. Desperately. And the frazzled strength of the single thread of determination that held him at bay was about to snap.

Nine

By six o'clock the rainstorm was over and the morning dawned clear. The eastern sky lit up in glorious color, heralding the sun's imminent appearance. Alec threw the last of the coffee down his throat and turned away from the kitchen window, stepped outside and meandered toward the barn. As he got close, the scents of alfalfa and pine shavings permeated the air. Soft nickers greeted his approach, bringing a smile of contentment to his face.

Entering the barn, he followed the bank of stalls until he came to number twelve. The big bay gelding was licking the last remnants of breakfast from his feed trough.

"You're up mighty early."

He turned to see Hank amble in his direction.

Alec nodded.

"You want me to throw a saddle on him for you?" Hank asked.

He hadn't thought about going for a ride, but the idea immediately took hold and it was too perfect to pass up.

"I'll do it," Alec replied. "Where's the tack?"

A few minutes later, Alec rode the big horse out the main gate and headed north. Ransom was excited about the outing, dancing against the firm hold Alec kept on the reins. Hank had mentioned the old homestead and provided general directions. It sounded like the perfect place to think.

The rutted path eventually grew less and less visible as the big bay continued to carry him through the trees and over the rolling hills. After an hour, Alec began to relax. The serenity of the countryside, the wind blowing softly through the leaves of the trees, helped clear his head. He honestly loved it here. He again experienced a twinge of regret over the changes that would soon come. For the first time in his life, the jubilance of building something great was overshadowed by the nagging uneasiness over the fact that he was about to destroy something very special.

Not surprising, his thoughts turned to Shea. Her determination to keep this spread should be an obstacle to overcome, not something to admire. But that was before their wedding night when she'd been so gut-wrenchingly beautiful and so damn sensual. It was before he'd seen her laugh, before she'd received hugs from his usually standoffish son. Before she'd shared her concerns about the ranch and had begun to trust him enough to open up and talk to him about things that troubled her. Before he'd seen her schoolgirl-like grin over a bunch of silly wildflowers.

It was before she'd become someone special in his life. Hell, they hadn't even had sex. But the longer he was around her, the more he had to remind himself their marriage was based on a very bizarre two-hundred-year-old contract. Becoming involved with Shea wasn't something that should happen. But his gut instinct told him it was too late. He'd already crossed that line.

Shea sat alone in the kitchen watching the morning unfold. She fixed a piece of dry toast, poured a cup of the not-too-old coffee and decided she could afford to take the time to enjoy part of the day. It was only five weeks until fall roundup but all of the preparations had been made, the equipment checked and ready to be taken to the site.

After clearing away the few dishes, she set off in the direction of the barn. Finding it empty, she walked down the main hall toward Hank's house. As soon as she rounded the corner, she saw him sitting on the wooden porch, leaning against a post with a wide-eyed little boy hanging on his every word. Apparently Hank had picked up the boy from his overnight stay at Leona's and from the lingering smell, they'd already enjoyed a breakfast of bacon and eggs.

"…So he lays real quiet-like and crawls on his belly—*real* slow—over to the fallen log. But just as he reaches fer his gun, this old owl comes screeching out of the trees and swoops down right at him."

"Wow…" Scotty's voice held the excitement of the moment. "What did he do?"

"Well, Roy reckons that old owl done give away his hiding place, don't ya see, so he pulls his gun from the holster, counts to three, then jumps out from behind the log with his gun a blazin'. Old Treach figured that owl was after a mouse so he never knew what hit him."

"Boom! Bang! He shot him! Didn't he, Hank?"

"He did fer a fact. Got the reward of all that gold and built him a little cabin right there on the bank of that river. Some people say his ghost still walks along the riverbank to this very day, protecting his gold."

"I wouldn't never go there 'cause he might think I was gonna steal it and I sure wouldn't want him to shoot at *me*!" Scotty shook his head, speaking in whispered excitement. Then he noticed Shea for the first time. "Did you ever see him? Old Roy?"

"Once. When I was about your age." She smiled and winked at Hank.

"Man…"

"How was your campout?"

"It was good!" Scotty answered, his eyes full of excitement. "We got hot dogs and cooked marshmallows on a stick. Mine got on fire."

"You had a campfire?"

"Uh-huh. And we heard the owl way deep in the woods.

Then we hadda go in the house cause of the rain. But it was *cool*."

Smiling, Shea turned her attention to Hank. "Where's Alec?"

"Said he was going to ride out to the north and see if he could find the old original homestead. Left here a couple of hours ago."

"Ride out…on what? You mean on a horse?"

"He saddled Ransom."

"Ransom!" He'd never make it back in one piece. Shea was incredulous. "And you let him? That horse could—"

"He's a big boy, Shea." Hank squinted up at her. "I watched him saddle the gelding and swing up like he'd been doing it all his life. Didn't seem to have any problem with him." He shrugged and bent his head, his attention focused on the small stick he'd been whittling.

Alec told her it had been a long time since he'd been on a horse. To handle Ransom as proficiently as Hank described, he would have to be a skillful horseman. A feeling of unease ran down her spine. She turned and quickly made her way back into the barn.

The stalls were empty. Hank must have moved the horses to the other barn in preparation for the drive. She marched straight down the main hall and back toward the house. Her truck was missing. She supposed Jason or one of the other hands had borrowed it, which wasn't unusual. She didn't see Alec's car either, which *was* unusual. Maybe Alec had let one of the hands use it to run into town. It wouldn't be the first time. She climbed into the only remaining vehicle in sight, the old white Jeep.

She wouldn't sit around and wait for Alec to come back. Something could happen. It was of equal concern that he was nosing around the old home site. It was a sacred place to her. She put the Jeep into gear and headed toward the big gate that opened to the northern pastures.

It was a bright, sunny day with not a cloud in the sky. All indications of the thunderstorms that had blanketed the area in the predawn hours were gone. Thanks to all the rain they'd had this spring, the grass was a deep, rich green. Shea should have enjoyed the outing. The old home site was her favorite place where the world couldn't come crashing in. It was a special place. A private place. Why had Alec headed there? With a grimace, she punched the pedal, and the Jeep bounced along the dwindling path into the deepening timber.

The trail cut through the forested area for several miles, skirting the vast grasslands to the west. It wound its way through the trees, over a rise and down into a small valley. The cooling waters of a small lake glistened in the sun as a gentle breeze sent small waves to lap against the shore. It was just past this tranquil setting that one would find traces of the original home site.

Shea shifted to a lower gear as the vehicle climbed the rise past the lake. As she topped the hill, she spotted Ransom, his front feet tethered, contentedly munching the tender, knee-high grass.

Pulling up a short distance away from the remains of the old foundation, she killed the motor and stood up in the seat. Immediately, she became aware of the silence. Somewhere in the distance, a meadowlark sang. The trees, touched by the gentle breeze, danced to its song.

Leaving the Jeep, she walked purposefully in the direction of the old home. There was very little left of the original structure. Not surprising since fire had raged through the timbers, followed by the ravages of the elements for two hundred years. The giant cinder blocks supporting the foot-thick oak timbers and roughly hewn floorboards were still intact. Three walls, log and mortar, and a corner of the original lower roof remained, their edges bearing traces of the fire that had claimed the house. The tall, sturdy chimney rose impressively as if daring anyone to challenge its right to be there.

"It's incredible." Alec's deep voice beckoned from behind her. Shea spun around, watching him casually walk toward her.

"Yes," she replied warily. "Is this where you're going to build your shopping mall?"

Alec ignored her taunt. He looked at the ancient dwelling. "Tell me about the house. Did they bring in the logs or were there trees this size on the land?" He looked up at the remaining roof.

"The logs for the house were all cut from here. The stones used in both the chimney and for some of the floor support were gathered from the creek bed." Shea pointed to the east. "Down there." Alec nodded, silently encouraging her to continue.

"The house had only two rooms and a loft. The kitchen was separate, over there." She nodded in the direction of the far side of the structure. "It used to have a covered breezeway linking it to the house. You can still see some of its foundation."

"What happened?"

She shrugged. "I'm not sure exactly what caused the fire. Dad tried to find out once, but there were no records. He believed lightning struck the roof. I think he said that someone died. There wasn't a lot anyone could do to save the structure. The remains you see here are probably thanks to a few buckets of water from the well."

"So, after the fire, your family rebuilt in the present location?"

"Yeah." Shea pushed away a strand of hair the wind had blown in her face as she looked at him with curiosity. "Why are you so interested? I mean, what does any of this matter to you?"

Alec turned away, looking out over the surrounding area.

"If you'll remember, it was my ancestors' land. They lived here, too."

She couldn't argue with that. He had as much a right to seek his heritage as she did.

"Behind the house—" she pointed west "—on top of the far rise is the old family cemetery. I think one of your relatives might be there, as well."

"I'd like to see."

Together they walked to the small burial ground. The names and dates on the long-standing headstones were partially obscured, some more than others. The men and women who had come to this land, driven by a desire to build a future and the courage to tame the raw wilderness, now rested in peace on this small patch of earth. At the edge of the area, two headstones stood slightly apart from the others.

Alec read one of them. "'William Alec Morreston. Born 1780. Died 1848.' My great-great-grandfather."

Shea reached out and gently touched William's stone. "Odd he was buried here. He was originally from the north, wasn't he?"

"Yeah." Alec nodded. "My grandmother used to tell me stories of how her grandfather loved the West. He came out here as a young man and fell in love with this part of the country. There was a young woman he met here. Alyssa, I think. He wrote that they were to be married, but she died before it could happen. Eventually, he returned to the family home in New York but I guess this is where he wanted to be laid to rest."

"At least someone in your family had some sense," Shea couldn't resist saying. She glanced at Alec in time to see a grin pull at the corners of his mouth.

"I have some old letters indicating he was a trapper. He used the river for his transportation and supposedly built a cabin, probably more of a shack, not far from here. Does the property reach as far as the river?"

She nodded. "Yeah. About a mile in that direction."

"You up for a hike?"

"We could take the Jeep."

"Let's go."

It took only a few minutes to reach the river's edge. Together, they walked along the high riverbank looking out over the wide expanse of the Red River. Appropriately named—the red clay, seen in the shallow parts of the riverbed and in the steep canyon walls flanking each side, cast a pinkish glow in the late afternoon sun.

"I don't think I'm going to find anything." He stood, hands resting on his hips, gazing out over the scenic terrain. "I'm sure the river has changed its banks dramatically in the last two hundred years. Erosion probably destroyed any remnants long ago." He sounded regretful.

"You're probably right, but it never hurts to look."

Alec's interest in his heritage surprised her. The questions he'd asked about the Hardin home site and now the interest in his own ancestral home didn't fit the image of the modern builder who wanted to level everything. She couldn't stop from watching him as he continued looking out over the scenic waterway. From his tawny eyes and full lips to the strong, deep set of his jaw, his face was temptation run amuck. Add intelligence sprinkled with a sense of humor, and it all added up to an irresistible combination.

In a moment of clarity, she realized she had come to respect Alec. He was a successful businessman and builder, a great father and a man of his word. But the reason he was here sent a twinge of sadness inching its way to her heart.

At that moment, he turned toward her and she made the mistake of looking into his eyes. The smile faded and his eyes darkened to the color of molten topaz. She knew he saw the awareness in her face. She swallowed hard.

The cry of a hawk circling overhead broke the spell.

"It's getting late. The sun has almost set. We'd better get back," she whispered, turning away.

In silent agreement they climbed into the Jeep and headed back to the home site and the trail leading home.

Ransom was still contentedly munching on the knee-high grass when the Jeep pulled up near the old homestead. Alec approached the big gelding and ran his hand down the glossy neck, then looked at the last rays of the setting sun in the open western sky.

"Is it true a horse can find his way back home on his own?"

Shea pursed her lips to hide a grin, nodding. "They usually know where the food is. Go ahead and unsaddle him and turn him loose. You can ride back in the Jeep. We wouldn't want Scotty to think his dad doesn't know which way is up in the dark."

"Ha. Ha."

With the saddle, bridle and tether removed, Ransom acknowledged his freedom by kicking his heels in the air and running for home, his tail held high above his back. Alec put the tack in the Jeep and climbed into the passenger seat. She slid in behind the wheel and turned the key. The engine caught, but immediately sputtered and died. She tried again, but it refused to start. Pumping the gas pedal did no good either.

"Mind if I have a try?" They switched places, but Alec had no more luck getting it started than she had. He walked to the front and opened the hood. "Everything looks okay," he muttered. "How much gas did you have?"

"I filled up last week and haven't really gone anywhere except over to Leona's. It should have plenty."

"Well, it doesn't." Alec closed the hood.

It was miles back to the ranch house. By the angle of the

sun, it would be dark in less than an hour. A quick glance revealed he was thinking the same thing.

He walked over to a small crevice, kicked at the grass, then looked out over the far hills as if deep in thought. He smiled, shook his head, then he began gathering rocks, placing them in a circle around the indention.

"Are you building a fire?"

"Yeah. It might get cold later tonight." He looked at her. "Unless you know of a better way we can keep warm?"

She ignored his teasing. "Hank will know something's wrong and come after us. You don't really need to do that."

Alec dropped more sticks into the circle. "It might be a while. Are there any matches in the Jeep?"

"Not that I've ever seen but I'll look." She walked to the front of the vehicle. Opening the glove box, she found not one, but two lighters and a small box of matches.

"I don't know how these got there, but here you go," she said, tossing him a lighter.

"How about water?"

"We don't keep water in the Jeep. If we're headed out to a branding or mending a long stretch of fence—something that will take a day or more—we load a couple of big ice chests and some ten-gallon coolers in the supply trailer and pull it to the site."

He nodded. "Would you humor me?"

With a shrug, Shea returned to the back of the vehicle. Moving aside Ransom's saddle and an old tarp, she immediately spotted two jugs of water. Frowning, she looked at Alec.

"And…?"

She pulled out the two gallons of water. "I don't understand—"

"It's just a guess, but I think Hank knew we would need matches and water before you ever left the ranch."

"What? What are you saying?"

"This." He gestured with his hands. "Our being out here alone…stranded. It was a setup. It was planned."

"No." Shea denied his words, but at the same time, her heart increased its rhythm. "Hank…wouldn't do something like that."

"Okay." He squatted next to the small pile of wood, tearing dried grass and shoving it underneath the smaller sticks.

"I've known him all my life. He just isn't the kind of person to…to…"

"Play matchmaker?"

"Exactly."

"Take a look in the back. I'm betting you'll find some blankets. While you're there, you might check and see what we're having for dinner."

Shea opened her mouth to argue but closed it again without a word. She set the containers of water on the ground and turned back to the Jeep. Partially hidden farther under the tarp were a sleeping bag, two pillows, a couple of blankets and a small ice chest. A thermos and a few foam cups completed the stash.

"I don't know of anyone else who would drain the gas tank and load the Jeep with supplies two people would need for a night," Alec said, walking over to where she stood. "Do you?"

She was dumbfounded that Hank Minton, of all people, would do this. But it could be no one else. "No." When she got back to the ranch, he was going to get a piece of her mind.

Shea watched the last of the sun's glow surrender to the multitude of stars in the night sky. The wood in Alec's campfire popped and hissed as the flames danced over the dried branches, releasing the tantalizing aroma of hickory and pecan into the still night air.

They ate in companionable silence. The sandwiches in

the small ice chest went quickly, along with the slices of apple pie and coffee.

Finally, unable to hold any more, she dropped the remains of her meal into the baggie. Leaning back against a big rock, she stretched out her legs and pulled the blanket around her shoulders. The temperature had begun to drop as the sun disappeared.

"Want another cup of coffee?" Alec sat next to her, his arms resting on his knees as he, too, looked up at the night sky.

"No, thanks." She leaned her head back against the boulder. "I still can't believe Hank set us up."

"He's from the old school," Alec replied. "Married people don't live separately. They don't argue all the time—"

"They don't leave their wife the morning after the wedding."

"And the wife damn sure doesn't spend her wedding night in the barn."

"You're right," she murmured. "Hank did it."

"I'll bet he had help."

She turned to look at him. "What do you mean? Who?"

"A couple of nights ago, when I tucked him in, Scotty voiced some concern about having to leave here. I hadn't said anything about him returning to New York, and I didn't understand what would cause him to worry about it. He must have figured if we didn't get along—"

"Then he'd have to leave." Shea finished the thought. "Set up by a four-year-old."

"He's smart, capable of a lot more than you'd expect for his age," Alec replied. "Which is another reason I wanted him here with me." He chuckled. "He's run off two nannies so far and his grandmother is on her last nerve, even though she would never admit it."

"Hank mentioned he's been asking about a horse."

"I know," Alec replied. "He's talked about little else since he got here."

"Alec, I'm hesitant to mention this because I still worry over Scotty's safety, but we have a gelding. Been around here forever," she ventured. "He's a small horse, older than I am, and as gentle as they come. He loves people. If you want Scotty to learn to ride, he couldn't be any safer than on Marty. I think Scotty would like him. He's a paint and kinda flashy."

Alec appeared to consider the suggestion. He glanced toward her, grinned and nodded his approval. "I appreciate your offer. I think that would be great."

For a while they sat back listening to the fire crackle. Somewhere out in the woods a pack of coyotes made its presence known.

"Alec, I…I never asked if there was someone special in your life. I mean, it's a little late now, but—"

"No." Alec shook his head. "No one special."

"But you were married…?" she prompted, hating herself for showing any interest at all, but unable to contain her curiosity.

"Yes. I was married. For just over a year." Alec hesitated, as if debating whether to say anything else. Finally, he said, "It wouldn't have lasted that long if she hadn't gotten pregnant. Scotty was the only good thing to come out of it."

He was quiet for a few minutes. "It didn't take her long after we married to realize the role of wife and mother was not for her. I never knew about the other man until after she'd walked out. For whatever reason, she decided to go through with the pregnancy. For nine months, I lived with the possibility that the baby wasn't mine. Then one day, I came home to find a stranger standing outside my door with a baby in her arms. She handed him to me and said he was my son. My ex didn't even bring Scotty to me herself.

After that I heard she started partying pretty good. A few months later, she was dead of an overdose."

"Oh, my gosh! Alec. How horrible. I'm so sorry."

He shrugged as though it was nothing, but Shea sensed it had affected him deeply. It must be a terrible thing to find out the person you love had betrayed you. Alec deserved respect for raising his son alone, giving the baby all the love he needed. Scotty was proof positive Alec was a great dad.

"What about you?" he asked. "Any broken hearts because of this situation?"

The image of David's face popped into her mind, and she couldn't help but wonder what course his life had taken. It couldn't possibly be as bizarre as the direction hers had gone.

"No."

"I find that hard to believe."

Shea shrugged. "There was a guy in college. He was the one who called the night we were married. Haven't seen him in a long time but he's still a good friend. We talked about getting married but we both knew it wouldn't work. We wanted different things out of life. Then Dad got sick. I left school to take care of him and run the ranch. There was just never any time for…anything else."

"What was your major?"

"Veterinary medicine."

"You're a vet?"

She shook her head. "No. I got as far as my master's. That's when Dad became ill, so I came home. I'd hoped to have a practice someday. But things don't always work out like you plan." She shook herself out of somber thoughts that would serve no purpose and smiled at Alec. "Do you have any other family? I mean, besides Scotty?"

"One brother, Mike. And my mother lives with her sister in St. Petersburg, Florida."

"Do they know you're married?"

"No. I wrestled with the idea, but didn't exactly know how to explain our situation."

Shea nodded her understanding. "What's your mom like?"

Alec appeared to think on that for a while. "My mother. How do I describe my mother?" He shook his head. "She's a character. As hardheaded as you are." He shot her a grin. "In fact, the two of you together could make a guy absolutely crazy. She's smart, good-natured, has a terrific sense of humor, but she also has a strength. After my father died, she kept me in school and had the patience of a saint. I have her to thank for where I am today."

She sounded like someone Shea would love to meet, but sadly that probably would never happen. She now understood where Alec got his dogged determination. It also was obvious he loved his mother very much. Apparently they had a close relationship. Alec was, indeed, like an onion, and with every layer Shea peeled away, the more exceptional he became.

He was not a cold, heartless adversary as she'd initially thought. He was a man who respected family values. And despite the situation over the land, he had a good heart. In fact, she couldn't imagine herself ever finding a man better suited to her and to this life.

And that realization was very unsettling.

"I'm hesitant to bring this up," Alec remarked, absently dragging a small stick over the ground. "I keep waiting for a good time to mention it, but...I doubt if such a time exists."

Shea's heart missed a beat. There was only one thing he would be so hesitant to mention. The future of the Bar H. "Well, you have my curiosity roused. Go ahead." She forced a smile but refused to look at Alec.

"There's a meeting scheduled at the end of the month at a hotel in Dallas. All the investors will be there. Probably some of the local jurisdictions represented, as well. We're building a resort, Shea. Hotels, casinos, a theme park, some restaurants on the Oklahoma side. A water park, golf course and a couple more restaurants in Texas." He was quiet for a moment. "I'd like you to go with me to the meeting."

Shea immediately shook her head and swallowed the huge lump that formed in her throat. "That is not where I want to be."

"Shea, it's going to happen. The change is inevitable. You need to come to terms with the possibility that—" Alec stopped midsentence. "Look, maybe there's a way both of us can get what we want. Compromise might be a possibility. I'm open to trying, but you have to see the plans—with an open mind—then tell me if you think something can be worked out."

She looked above her to the millions of stars in the black velvet sky and shook her head at the hopelessness of her plight.

"So you think my cattle can skip the fall roundup and spend a few days at your resort?" She took in a deep breath. "We both know there is only one way this will end, Alec. One of us has to leave."

"So…you refuse to even try to see if there is an alternative." It was as much a statement as a question.

"I don't see how there could be."

"And you won't unless you attend the meeting. See for yourself." Alec tossed the small stick into the fire. "If I were in your place, I would want to learn everything I could about the enemy and their intent."

She shot him a look of surprise.

"Maybe," she finally agreed. *And maybe not.*

She heard him sigh. "It's late. We have a long walk in the morning. I suggest we bed down in the corner of the old house." He stood and poured out the last drops of his coffee. "I don't care to wake up in the morning and find one of your country varmints in our bed."

While they'd been sharing a bed for some time there was something about sliding into a sleeping bag with Alec that screamed disaster. And she needed some time to come to grips with what he'd just told her. A large resort would be worse than a shopping mall. But she didn't have a clue what her friends and neighbors would think of such a thing.

"Do what you want. I'm sleeping in the Jeep," she said. "Take the bedroll. I'll be fine with the blanket."

His eyebrows rose in quiet speculation, but he said nothing as she retraced her steps to the Jeep. It took some maneuvering, but she finally managed to shift around enough junk to make a reasonably sized sleeping space. She tossed him the bedroll and a pillow and climbed in.

"I heard rumblings of thunder earlier," Alec said. "There's no top on the Jeep. Are you sure you want to—"

"Yes, I'm sure," she quickly assured him. The whole day had been bright and sunny without a cloud in the sky. How gullible did he think she was?

She settled under the warm folds of the blanket and tried to get comfortable in the tiny space. By the time the first rays of the sun broke over the distant hills, she would be halfway back to the house.

And the first thing on her to-do list when she got there was find Hank Minton.

And maybe start looking for another place to live.

Ten

The uncomfortable sensation of cold water running across her face and down her neck woke her from a sound sleep. Brushing the moisture away with her hand, she blinked her eyes and pushed into a sitting position. It was dark. So incredibly dark she couldn't see her hand in front of her face. And it was raining—gently, but steadily. As she came fully awake, she noted the blanket was drenched, as were her clothes.

Muttering to herself, she climbed out of the Jeep. The wind had picked up, dropping the temperature, and she shivered as she stumbled in the direction of the homestead and what shelter it offered. The dying embers of the campfire provided just enough light to see the last few steps.

As she approached the old log structure, the skies opened up in a downburst. Climbing onto the floorboards, she followed the wall of the building to the back of the structure where a section of the roof remained.

"Over here." Alec spoke from the darkness.

Cautiously she followed the direction of his voice until her toes found the edge of the sleeping bag. Squatting down, she felt for the edge of the bedroll.

"Here," Alec said, and suddenly his hand held hers. "Shea, you're soaked. Get out of those clothes. Don't argue."

Teeth chattering, she unbuckled her belt, unzipped the wet denim and struggled to push her jeans down her legs. Finally, Alec grabbed the end of the legs, and with one hard tug, she was free of the soggy pants. She scooted inside the soft fleece lining, still warm from the heat of his body.

"And the shirt," he said, not bothering to wait for an argument. He efficiently pulled it over her head, tossed it away and lay down next to her. His heavy arms wrapped around her and their legs entwined, as he began rubbing her arm and shoulder, the friction bringing much-needed warmth.

"No 'I-told-you-so's?'"

"Not this time."

The rain surged, pelting the wooden roof above them. The moist air carried the heavy scent of pine, and in the distance a lone coyote called out to its kinsmen. Alec's hands eventually stilled and merely held her next to the warmth of his body.

Her mind whirled, preventing the return of sleep. Alec was as complex as a jigsaw puzzle whose pieces were upside down. One minute he came off as hard and unrelenting, but the next minute he lay in the shelter of a centuries-old, burned-out building, holding her in his arms, ready to protect her from whatever might be out there. And he seemed completely comfortable in either role.

In fairness, she had to question her own sanity. Here she lay in the home of her ancestors, the last surviving heir, held warm and protected in the arms of the enemy, the very man who would destroy it all.

The low, rumbling thunder gradually became louder, the flashes of lightning brighter. Alec lay in the black shadows, holding Shea as she slept. Lowering his head, he breathed in the sweet scent of her hair.

A long, increasingly loud rumble of thunder was followed by more flashes of light. Shea turned her face into his neck and covered her ears with her hands.

"Shea?"

"The storm."

"It's all right, hon." He tried to soothe her.

"I hate storms. Please try to start the Jeep again." Her voice was high, frightened, her words partially muffled by his shoulder.

"It doesn't have any gas, remember?" His arms resumed their circular motion on her back. "We'll be all right. This old house has weathered more bad weather than you and I will ever see."

Another loud crack of thunder shook the floor. She raised her head and, through the flashes of light from the storm, he saw the fear in the blue iridescence of her eyes. Her sensuous lips parted slightly and desire charged through his body like a bolt of the lightning from above.

Slowly, she reached out and placed her hand against the side of his face as if making certain he was there. He didn't move, didn't breathe, afraid that doing so would break the spell that held them. She leaned forward, moistening his lips with her tongue before kissing him fully. The blood pounded in his head, surged straight to his groin.

He responded without thinking as passion flared. He didn't know if she actually wanted him or if she was half-asleep and didn't realize what she was doing. But whatever the reason, she didn't pull away. And despite his earlier resolve, neither could he.

With a last surge of willpower, he set her away from him.

"Alec?"

"Shea, listen to me." His voice was rough, even to his own ears. "I can't do this anymore. It's no longer a game. All bets are off. If you don't want me to make love to you, then move away. Now."

In the ensuing silence, he assumed she realized how close she'd come to losing her resolve, that there would be no turning back. The bedroll moved as she shifted her body. But instead of turning away, she kissed his chest, her teeth nipping his skin, her tongue tasting his heated flesh.

Like a man driven by forces beyond his control, he pushed her fully onto her back, pressed her down into the thick bedroll. Warm and pliant, her flesh conformed to his like the rain that filled each tiny crevice of the parched earth.

In that moment, he knew it was no longer a bluff to get her to leave. She was his wife, regardless of the circumstances. And he wanted her. Oh, how he wanted her. He needed to feel his hard flesh sheathed inside. She was his. And he'd make damn sure she knew it. His mouth found hers, plunging his tongue inside, loving the taste of her, the feel of her. And this time Shea kissed him back.

With a moan of defeat, Alec kissed her deeply, urgently, with a hunger that threatened to consume him. He heard her whimper, and the blood pounded in his ears. His hand followed the exquisite contours of her body, cupping her perfect breast, his thumb teasing the taut nipple. He left her lips, kissing down her throat to the supple flesh he held in his hand, teasing the small nub. She arched her back, pushing her chest toward him with a soft moan and he gave equal attention to her other perfect breast. With his hand, he traced over her belly, then lower to the silken curls that framed the center of her desire.

"Alec," she whispered, need heavy in her voice as she pushed against his hand.

The pain in his loins became unbearable as raw, primitive instinct took over.

He moved fully on top of her and she opened to him. His hand fisted her hair, drawing her head back, allowing him greater access to her mouth, and like a starving man, he fed.

Alec raised his head and through the flashes of radiant light, he looked into the blue iridescent depths of her eyes and with a hoarse, almost feral growl, he pushed inside.

The thunder rolled, escalating in power, mirroring the intensity of their joining. Shea struggled to accept him, her body stretching as his power filled her. She knew no fear of the storm. Her mind and body were consumed with Alec, all senses tuned to him. She could no longer think. Only feel. And the feeling was incredible. Every movement of his big, powerful body propelled her higher. Her arms slid up and over his broad shoulders to circle his neck, her fingers gripped his thick hair.

Alec's lips returned to hers, his tongue pushing deep. His hands cupped her head, holding her where he wanted her to be and a pressure inside began to build, causing a need that was almost painful in its intensity.

"Alec!" she cried out against his lips.

"I know, babe. Let it happen."

Rotating his hips, he pushed hard and suddenly her desire crested and her mind shattered into a million brilliant pieces. She cried out his name as wave after wave of complete and total fulfillment coursed through her body.

He kissed her again with animal hunger. He began to move with a driving force, bringing her to the edge of mindless release for a second time. She clutched at his broad shoulders as his hands moved to cup her hips, lifting her, filling her, until, with a wild growl, he reached the summit of his own release. He shuddered against her as the spasms of his completion vibrated through him, and pushed her over the top yet again.

Spent, he collapsed on top of her. His heavy weight made it difficult to breathe, but she never would have asked him to move away. Surrounded by his musky scent she could feel the rapid beating of his heart. Wrapped in the warmth and protection of his arms, she floated slowly back to earth. Outside their shelter the rain continued to fall.

It was as though neither of them was inclined to move for fear they would somehow lose this sweet accord, this exquisite joining of their bodies and souls. She wanted this moment to go on, for him to hold her like this forever.

Rising up on his arms, his eyes captured hers, his thumb gently tracing the contours of her lips. In those moments, time stood still.

Finally, he eased from her but held her close.

"Did I hurt you?" he asked, bringing her hand to his lips.

"No." She smiled and gently touched his face.

She knew the pain would come later.

When this situation was over and Alec said goodbye.

"Shea—" Alec's voice called to her, bringing her back from the blissful realm of sleep. "Shea, hon, wake up."

She moaned her disgruntlement and attempted to snuggle back into the heavenly cocoon of their soft makeshift bed.

"Come on, sweetheart." Alec kissed her before pulling the warmth of the bedroll away from her. "I think we're about to have company."

Before she could respond, a piercing light shattered the darkness, followed by the sound of an engine and tires bouncing through the small pools of water in the rain-drenched earth.

Struggling to sit up, she pulled the top of the sleeping bag around her. "What is it?"

"I think we're being rescued."

"Rescued? What time is it?" The rain had slowed to a drizzle, but the sky was still black.

"Just after midnight."

"You both all right in there?" Hank's voice called from the truck as he pulled up in front of the foundation. "Got kinda worried when the storm broke. Figured I'd better come out and check."

Her eyes locked to Alec's, she didn't immediately move.

Then, with a grimace, he rolled onto his side and reached for his jeans.

Shea found the blanket he'd been using, pulled it around her, gathered her wet clothes and stood up. Hank's arrival had effectively melted away the sweet fantasy and slammed her back to reality.

What had she done?

She didn't look in Alec's direction as she walked toward Hank and the truck.

The trip back was made in silence, her earlier intentions to wring Hank's neck now overshadowed by confusion. She must be crazy. How could she have made love with the man who threatened to take away her ranch and everything she cherished?

A slight tremble ran down her spine and she pulled the blanket more tightly around her. Alec reached out and turned up the heater. But it wasn't the temperature in the truck's cab making her feel chilled to the bone.

Entering the house, she went straight upstairs. Maybe, with any luck she could be in bed and feign sleep when he got there. She quickly grabbed a clean T-shirt and panties, entered the bathroom and turned on the shower. Stepping under the spray, she leaned forward, placing her forehead against the shower wall, and let the hot water stream down her back.

Had she been wrong in making love to Alec? She didn't love him. She couldn't. She *wouldn't* fall in love with him. It had been hormones. Or the rain. Or momentary insanity. She gritted her teeth. This would only make everything worse.

Shower finished, she dressed for bed and pulled open the bathroom door. Alec stood in front of her, very tall, very imposing and very male. He was clad only in a towel slung low around his hips. He must have showered in the bathroom downstairs. He watched her with those cat eyes, alert to the emotions she tried to hide.

She forced a smile and moved to step around him. He caught her arm as she passed, gently halting her forward motion.

"Do we need to talk?"

She kept her vision focused on the floor. She didn't want to see the mockery in his eyes or the smirk that would be back on his face. "No."

He placed a finger under her chin, forced her to look into his eyes. Her gaze dropped lower, to his mouth, full, defined and capable of so much passion. There was no mockery. No contempt. No smirk.

"I disagree. I just made love to my wife, and now she doesn't want anything to do with me." He watched her intently, his head tilted in question. "I'd like to know why."

She shrugged. "I… It's awkward, Alec. For me. I mean, I'm not sure—"

"Where we go from here?"

She nodded. "Yeah."

He moved forward, resting his hands against the wall, his well-muscled biceps on either side of her head, and leaned down to her. "I say we take it one day at a time." His raspy voice was deep and wonderfully disturbing. He moved to her neck, nipped at the sensitive skin just below her ear. "I can't tell you I'll call off the project," he murmured, his breath hot against her skin. "There is already too much time and money invested and too many people involved," he murmured before moving to the other side of her neck and repeating the wildly arousing little bites. "But there has to be a way to work this out."

Every nip sent tingles of hot current jolting through her. He was doing it again. He was seducing her with his touch and his voice. Oh, how she wished they'd come together under different circumstances. But right then, she couldn't quite remember why it mattered.

"But for now I see no other immediate changes that are required." The look on his face told her he was serious.

As they stood in the shadows with his face so close she could touch her lips to his with minimal movement, the concern over the ranch faded somewhat. Yet she knew the only thing they'd truly accomplished was admitting their mutual desire for each other.

Mutely, she nodded, and his mouth came down over hers. The stubble of his beard scratched her skin, but she didn't care. God help her, at this moment she didn't care.

With a barely concealed moan, Alec scooped her into his arms and carried her to their bedroom, kicking the door closed behind them.

Eleven

The distant rumbling of thunder announced the approach of yet another summer storm. The humidity was high, the air thick. Alec found Shea in Scotty's bedroom, opening a window to allow the gentle breeze to penetrate the room's stuffiness.

"Does it always rain this much in Texas?" he asked from the doorway.

"Summer showers," she replied, turning to smile at him. "By mid-August we'll be wishing for some of this rain."

"Hey, Dad! Look what I won at the fair!" Scotty ran into the room fresh from his bath. Just after breakfast, Hank had taken him and Cody for a day at the county fair, giving Alec and Shea the entire day together without distractions. They hadn't wasted a second.

Scotty proudly grabbed a huge stuffed owl from atop his dresser. The oval face, covered in gray feathers, framed two huge round eyes. "Isn't it cool? Cody just won a stuffed bear. Boy, I was lucky, wasn't I, Daddy?"

"You sure were, son," Alec replied, smiling at Scotty.

"And I got to ride with Hank on his horse in the parade, and we ate hot dogs with ketchup, and we got some of the candy they threw from the...uh...uh..." He looked at Shea.

"Floats," Shea supplied.

"Yeah, from the floats. Then we saw the biggest pig get a ribbon, and Leonard Mabry let me brush his goat." He actually stopped and took a breath. "It was cool, Dad."

Grinning, Alec leaned over and placed a kiss on his son's head, then rustled the soft hair. Shea turned down the covers of the small bed. "Okay, in you go, cowboy."

Scotty ran to the window and carefully placed the owl on the windowsill. "Hank said this old owl will bring me luck. I'm gonna set it here so it will see me when I ride Marty."

The day after they'd been stranded at the old ruins, Hank had introduced Scotty to his first horse. Marty had indeed been a perfect choice, moving slow and gentle as though he knew his young rider was just learning. After only an hour of simple instruction, Scotty had been off and riding, making endless circles around one of the larger corrals.

The boy turned and jumped into the center of the mattress with a squeal and a giggle. Alec smiled and leaned over to tuck in his young son for the night.

Shea slipped out of the room, giving father and son some bonding time. The wind had picked up, and the sheer draperies fluttered gently inside the master bedroom. Suddenly, the rain began to fall, pelting against the top of the house, falling in heavy sheets from the edges of the roof. She walked to the dresser and took out a soft cotton T-shirt in preparation for her shower.

Large hands came to rest on her shoulders, their grip a welcome deterrent against the rain's sudden chill. Alec's arms came around her, pulling her back against his chest. His chin rested on her head.

"Thank you," he said quietly.

"For what?" A quizzical frown covered her face as she turned to her husband.

"For all you do for Scotty. And for me." He grinned. "Or, maybe I should I say *to* me."

"Both are my pleasure." She beamed.

"Come here," Alec whispered, pulling her down onto the bed and settling himself next to her. He began unbuttoning her blouse.

"I would like to know the name of the idiot who invented buttons," he muttered. "And why my wife insists on wearing clothing with them on it."

"What would you have me do? Wear nothing but T-shirts?"

"You've got it partially right. Just leave off the T-shirt."

She laughed, and he leaned over and placed his lips on hers.

She was so focused on Alec at first she ignored the cool, wet sensation on her forehead. As the feeling persisted, it became an irritant, breaking her focus and causing her to push Alec away. She sat up and wiped at her temple, noting the moisture on her hand.

Before she could assimilate her thoughts, another drop of something cold and wet hit her head then trickled down her scalp underneath her hair.

"Shea, what's wrong?"

She swung her legs to the side of the bed as another droplet of water splattered onto her shoulder and ran down her arm. She sprang from the bed. "Oh…Alec, it's—"

At that moment, with a sickening groan, a section of the ceiling above the bed collapsed, sending a downpour of accumulated rainwater squarely onto Alec's head.

With a shriek, she scampered back from the bed as a flash of lightning illuminated the room. Startled, she took in Alec, sitting on the bed, his hands held ineffectively above his head as a river of water cascaded down.

"Cool!" Scotty called out as he opened their bedroom door, no doubt hearing the loud crash as well as her shriek. His eyes were wide at the spectacle in front of him. "Hey, Dad, can I—"

"No!" Alec didn't give him a chance to finish the question. "Go into the bathroom and get a towel," he barked as he rolled off the bed, sending Scotty running down the hall.

Shea stood to the side, staring incredulously at her husband, who appeared to be in shock. He placed his hands on his hips and stared up at the heavily dripping ceiling, a look of amazement on his features.

Shea clenched her fists in a weak effort to contain her amusement but lost the battle as a fit of giggles overpowered her and she gave in to a moment of full-fledged laughter. Scotty returned with the towel, his giggles joining hers at the sight of his father standing drenched beside the bed.

"It's not that damn funny," he growled, which brought an encore of laughter from both of them. Alec snatched the towel from his son's hands and began to blot his head and neck.

"Hey, Daddy, you want some soap?"

Shea clamped her hand over her mouth and turned away from Alec as she fought to restrain the laughter. Suddenly, she was hoisted up into his arms.

"You think it's so funny?"

Before she could answer, she was tossed through the air, landing with a splash on top of the completely soaked mattress. There were matching screams and giggles from Scotty as he came to rest on the bed next to her.

"Why? Why go to the trouble of checking the foundation of a house you only want to tear down?"

Shea watched as Alec checked the flashlights while he waited for Jason to arrive.

"Because I want to know that it's safe. Obviously we won't be moving out as quickly as I'd originally anticipated." He shot her a knowing glance, his lips pursed to subdue the grin. "As old as this place is, it could be a death trap. I'm not about to endanger Scott's life—or yours—by taking that chance."

"Well, I think you're making this bigger than it is. You're going to extremes."

"I don't care. There may not be anything holding this

house together but the paint and even that's beginning to crack. I'm going over every square inch. It obviously needs a new roof."

"Oh yeah? How can you tell?" They'd spent the night in her old room and while it was not as comfortable as their new bed, especially for a man of Alec's size, Shea had slept peacefully. The cold rainwater shower hadn't dampened his sexual appetite, and after they'd managed to get Scotty back to sleep, Alec had wasted no time proving it.

"Yeah, Daddy," Scotty chimed in. "How can you tell?" A quelling look from his father did little to silence his giggles, but he scooted out of his chair. "I'm gonna go see what Hank's doing."

"Breakfast will be ready in an hour," Shea called. "Tell Hank to have you back here by nine."

"Okay," he replied, as the door slammed behind him.

"This is serious, Shea," Alec said as he poured another cup of coffee. "How long has it been since this house was checked?"

"Checked for what?" She put the strips of bacon into the large iron skillet. The sizzle and aroma immediately filled the air.

"Wood rot. Termites. Faulty wiring. Leaking pipes. Any number of things."

She shrugged. "I really don't know."

"How long since the roof was replaced?"

She again shrugged her shoulders. "Dad always said he was going to have it repaired, but I don't think he ever got around to it. We've had some leaks from time to time, and the roof was patched in those areas." She'd hoped that would suffice until there was money for a new roof.

Alec grimaced. "Then you don't know how much water damage there's been?" Shea shook her head. "What about the foundation?"

"What about it?"

"How long since it's been examined?" He looked at Shea's blank expression. "Never mind. I think I can guess. There's been virtually no protective maintenance. In two hundred years. Amazing. I intend to find out exactly what's going on. I'm afraid the incident last night was only a hint of other problems."

Shea turned the bacon over in the pan and mentally crossed her fingers. If Alec found serious damage, she didn't know where she would get the money for the repairs.

When breakfast was over, Alec went to find Jason, impatient to get started. The two men took the soaked mattress downstairs, Alec still muttering about the roof as they went. Then he located a ladder, loaded two flashlights with fresh batteries and they were off. She knew Alec was more than qualified. Inspecting the house would be like child's play to him.

She called a local roofing company to come out and give an estimate on repairs. For the rest of the day, she stayed close to the house, finishing laundry, preparing a brisket and waiting for the arrival of the roofers.

A few minutes before Shea was about to call Alec and Scotty in for supper, Alec came into the kitchen. He was covered in dirt and grime from his head to his feet. A scowl was firmly in place.

"Give me a few minutes to get cleaned up," he said and walked toward the stairs.

A short time later, Alec reentered the kitchen.

"So, how bad is the roof?"

"It's not good."

"It can be repaired where it fell in and—"

"It's not just the roof, Shea," he cut in. "There's major wood rot and termite damage everywhere. I found extensive destruction to most of the load-bearing walls on the first floor, and the foundation is crumbling. The house has already begun to shift. Its ability to remain standing for much longer is highly questionable." He rubbed the back of his neck. "That aside, the wiring is sixty years old. The plumbing needs replacing, the gas line is highly suspect and I'd guess most of your heat during the winter flies out the old single-pane windows. Did you know several are cracked?"

"So, what are you saying?" She wanted him to spell it out. "If…if it's the cost, I could replace one thing at a time over the next few—"

"Shea, the house isn't safe." His words caused a sick feeling in the pit of her stomach. "We shouldn't even be inside right now. It's not safe for you—or any of us—to stay here. I don't know how much clearer I can make it."

She'd known the old house was long past need of repairs, but because the money wasn't there, she'd ignored the problems. Apparently, her father had done the same thing.

"So…what are my options?"

He shook his head. "The *only* option is tear it down and build a new one. But under the circumstances, that would be ridiculous."

Under the circumstances?

Her mind whirled, not wanting to believe what that meant. Was this his way of telling her it was over? She'd thought they had found something special between them. They made love every night. She'd even begun to believe the marriage was real—or had a chance to become so. Had he been plotting all along? Looking for a bona fide reason to make her leave?

Had he only been pretending he cared for her? If she'd been wrong to start trusting him…if he had only been using her while he waited for an opportunity that would allow him to reclaim the land, she didn't know how she would ever deal with that. She felt her heart drop to her knees as that possibility threatened to knock her off her feet.

She'd let herself believe he cared about her as well as the land. She'd let down her guard. Reality and disappointment hit with the force of a sledgehammer. With her pulse slamming through her veins, she removed the rolls from the oven, set the tray on top of the stove and stared at him. Suddenly it was overwhelming. The news about the house was bad enough. Her life was here, her past as well as her envisioned future rested on this small piece of earth. Everything she knew revolved around this ranch. She had nowhere else to go. Tears burned the backs of her eyes; her breath died in her throat.

But to think she would lose Alec as well, that she'd merely been used to relieve his boredom, that she meant nothing to him. How was she ever going to come to terms with that?

"Shea?"

Covering her mouth with her hand to try to muffle a cry of despair, she ran from the room as the tears spilled over.

Curling up on the end of the old bedraggled sofa in the den, she faced the worn recliner that sat in the corner of the room. Her father's chair. She could visualize him kicked back, his feet resting on the stool as he read his afternoon paper. He was gone now. This house was the only connection she had to him and to her mother. Every room, every space under its roof carried precious memories. She could feel the love from the generations of family who had lived here before. Her dad's boots still sat in a corner of the mudroom. Her grandmother's handmade quilts were spread over the beds upstairs. It was as if the house gave her the strength to carry on alone. It was unthinkable that she had failed to protect it.

"Shea?" Alec entered the room. He stood just inside the open doorway, his hands resting on his hips.

She didn't want to talk with him. She couldn't. He might confirm that she was right in suspecting him.

"In the morning, you need to pack some clothes. I'll

make arrangements for us to stay in a hotel in Dallas for a while."

"And then what?" She gazed at her hands clenched tightly in her lap. "What happens next, Alec?"

"That's something we need to talk about. But regardless of what you decide to do going forward, staying here is not an option." He moved farther inside the room. "I'll still keep the promise I made that day in Ben's office. My original offer still stands. I'll buy you out. You can go back to school, get your doctorate and become a veterinarian. Fulfill that dream. You don't have to live here to do it. You need to be reasonable."

"Reasonable? Define reasonable. Is it unreasonable to want to stay in a place you love? A place you've based all your plans for a future around?"

"Maybe it's time for a change. Perhaps you should consider—"

"No." She shook her head defiantly. "No! Alec, you don't understand. I'm telling you I will not let this house be destroyed. Where would I go?"

"Anywhere you wanted."

"*Here* is where I want to be." *With you.*

Alec nodded, then shrugged. "Then you and your world will fall apart together. But I'll have no part of it."

Obviously, she'd been wrong when she'd assumed he cared about his ancestors, those who had so loved this land. The day they'd roamed around the old homestead and he'd asked all the questions. He'd wanted to see where his great-great-grandfather had been laid to rest. He'd commented that the area, the old cabin, were incredible. He'd shown what had appeared to be genuine interest. Had it all been a ploy to make her think he cared?

Had there ever been anything between them other than sex? She'd fallen in love with Alec, but he'd never said he felt the same. She swallowed hard as that realization hit.

Total humiliation washed over her, followed by a heightened sense of anger at herself for being so stupid. So gullible. Alec didn't love her. He never would. How could she have become so delusional as to believe a man like Alec Morreston would want any kind of permanent relationship with her?

She stood to face him. "I will not leave this house. You think you've won, but you haven't."

He reeled back as if she had slapped him. For a moment she thought she saw pain in his eyes, but it was gone so fast she knew she must have imagined it. The devil didn't have feelings.

"Won? Is that what you think this is about? Winning?"

She refused to answer. She knew what it was about and it wasn't their relationship. There was no relationship. There never had been. She'd played into his hands. He knew it and now so did she.

"If that's what you think, there's nothing more to say."

She walked to a nearby table, pulled a couple of tissues from the box. Wiping her eyes, she took a deep breath, struggling to control the pain running rampant through her body. She'd fallen in love with Alec, so much so she would have given him anything. But his only concern was getting her to vacate the property.

Suddenly, he was in front of her, his hands clutching her upper arms. His face was set in stone, his eyes narrowed. She could clearly detect the underlying thread of exasperation bordering on fury. "You're going to listen to me," he told her. "Tomorrow, you are going to start packing your bags because we are leaving this place—all of us."

"I'm not going anywhere—"

"And you're going to face the reality that life as you've known it is over. It's finished."

"No." She struggled, but he easily held her.

"Shea, stop! Listen to yourself. Take off the damn blinders and look at the truth that's right in front of you."

All she saw standing in front of her was the man she'd fallen in love with. A man who didn't love her, didn't care about anything but making more money. A man who'd done whatever was required to regain the land. Her first impressions had been correct. He was ruthless. She'd just never imagined how truly merciless he could be.

He turned and walked toward the door. "I had hoped that..." He shoved his hands into his jeans pockets and clenched his teeth. "I'm going to contact a building inspector. If you won't believe me, you can hear it from him. And I'm going to call the county. This house needs to be condemned."

She winced.

He paused at the door, his tawny eyes narrow and forbidding. "I'll have my jet readied for takeoff by tomorrow. I'm taking Scott back to New York. I'd like you to come with us, but that's your choice."

What would I do in New York?

The man who stood before her was ruthless and determined, powerful and unyielding, with the money and the resources to back him up. How could she ever have been so foolish as to think she could challenge him and win? What had she been thinking to let down her guard and start caring for him? It was no longer an either-or situation; the goal of winning Alec and the land had become one in the same. With the old house condemned, Alec would be gone, as well.

"I hate you for this." Her voice was low and broken. She gripped the back of the sofa to remain standing. It was a poor attempt to place armor around her heart. The words, like a boomerang, came right back at her, cutting deeply.

The hands of time stopped as they silently faced each other. Then Alec turned and walked out the door. She heard his footsteps going up the stairs and toward Scotty's bedroom, leaving Shea in the center of a room spinning wildly out of control. The searing pain in her chest made her gasp for breath. But it hurt to breathe. This impossible situation had escalated into a nightmare of epic proportions and she was drowning, being pulled down into the center of a black hole from which she might never emerge. Alec was free to return to his own world. Old house condemned. Mission accomplished.

Early the next morning Alec left as he'd said he would, taking Scotty with him. Hearing the child's cries of "but why, Daddy?" and his tearful pleading to please let him stay had almost been Shea's undoing. She'd finally run out to the barn, unable to bear hearing his cries, unwilling to watch them walk out the door forever.

When she eventually returned, the house was silent, as though it knew its time had come, awaiting annihilation like a condemned man awaiting his execution.

The merriment and laughter of Scotty's voice no longer echoed through the halls. But Alec's absence was the hardest to bear. She didn't cry because she couldn't. The numbness wouldn't let her.

Finally, on the third day, she saddled one of the horses. All her life, she'd found solace in the land. It had been a refuge where she could work through problems that seemed far greater than she could possibly contend with alone. Other than her dad dying, losing her home was the greatest hardship she'd ever faced. And the loss of the man she loved, however convoluted that might have been, was earth shattering.

She swung her leg over the saddle, gathered the reins and urged the mare toward the piney woods and the old homestead beyond. She knew going there would renew the memories of the last time she'd been there—with Alec.

The gentle, even stride of the mare was soothing as she carried Shea through the trees and over the meadows. The call of a red-tailed hawk as it circled overhead seemed to mock the fact she was alone. After dismounting, Shea walked to the sacred ground where five generations of her ancestors lay in eternal sleep. Stopping in front of the grave of William Morreston, she wished she could ask him so many questions.

Eventually, she made her way to the old homestead. As she looked at the burned-out hull, she could visualize Alec's face, hear his laugh and feel his arms around her. As the sun set on the horizon, Shea curled up on the edge of the old floorboards a mere foot from the spot where they had made love, and succumbed to the pain shredding her heart into tiny pieces. Unable to hold back her misery any longer, the heartache broke through any lingering restraints and sobs of loss ran rampant through her body.

Twelve

It had been almost a week since Alec had left the Bar H to take Scotty back to New York. Now, en route back to Dallas, he still didn't know what he could say to make Shea understand her safety was his primary concern.

He'd known he needed to get Scotty to a neutral setting. The child didn't need to witness the argument that was sure to take place when Alec went back to the ranch and her hardheaded resistance collided with his single-minded determination that she leave there before she was injured. Or worse.

The onboard office was furnished with the latest computers and advanced communication technology, enabling him to conduct business from anywhere in the world. Anything and everything needed to handle virtually any crisis was at his fingertips.

Except the one named Shea Hardin-Morreston.

His fingers drummed impatiently on the desktop as he gazed out the small window at the darkening sky. He was used to long flights, usually working his way from destination to destination, continent to continent. It helped to pass the time. But on this flight, he was incapable of concentrating on anything except Shea and that damned old house.

Shea's refusal to accept the reality of the situation and see the futility of what she wanted made no sense. It was not just the issue of the house. This was about the safety of a woman he'd come to care about very much. She'd opened a door to a place he'd long forgotten, reminding him of the things he'd loved as a boy. A feeling of peace had surrounded him at the ranch, encouraging him to set aside the abstract world to which he'd become accustomed. It had been a free fall out of the rat race into a new reality of home and heart; he had taken a step back to the things and the people that mattered. And he wanted Shea to be part of his new reality. He'd not imagined it without her. But if she didn't care enough to trust him…if she wasn't willing to let go of the past and take a chance on a future with him, then both of them would lose.

Suddenly, visions of his first wife clouded Alec's mind. Sondra had also wanted it all. The big house, the expensive cars had never been enough. She'd continued the affairs, the parties, the drugs, even after she'd learned she was pregnant, because that had been what had suited her. She'd pushed aside her own safety and the safety of their innocent child for her own selfish wants. And Shea was doing the same thing.

Shea's drug was the ranch. It was as addictive to her as drugs had been to Sondra. Shea was attempting to make him conform, get him to spend millions to put the house back in working order, and then… He didn't want to speculate on what she would do then.

God, he wanted to be wrong about Shea. His feelings for her ran deep. He'd actually let himself envision a future together and he'd never thought he would feel that way about any woman again.

Surely, by now Shea must have accepted the truth that the house wasn't safe. But still, he had to acknowledge it was her home. It was the only one she'd ever known. As she'd said when he issued the ultimatum to get out of that building, the ranch was her life. It defined who she was. At least in her mind. To Alec, she was so much more.

Hopefully the time he'd been away had given Shea a chance to calm down, to realize that things had to change.

Even so, convincing her to leave her home would take every amount of skill he possessed. She had to understand he wasn't forcing her out because of that damned contract. It was for her safety. It was because he cared. He didn't have a clue how it had happened, but he could no longer deny that truth. He was in love with Shea Hardin.

The issue of the land remained a black cloud over both their heads. It continued to drive a wedge between them and that had to end. If he had to choose between giving up the entire project and losing Shea, the project was history. He'd never thought a woman like Shea existed, let alone that he would find her. She had taken away all the suspicions and internal rage that had burned a hole in his soul for five long years, and opened his heart to the possibility of a future of happiness. She'd made him whole again. He was not about to lose her. Not over this land. Not over anything.

He glanced again at his watch. Ten minutes later than the last time he'd looked. Still half an hour out from Dallas-Fort Worth. He wanted to pace, needed some way to let off the tension churning in his gut. He'd never felt this uneasy, never sensed the need to hurry as he did now.

I never should have left without her. That thought kept churning in his mind. *I never should have left her alone in that house.*

Once the jet landed at the airport, a helicopter was waiting, ready to take him back to Calico Springs. This time he would make her listen to him. At the meeting he'd scheduled to take place in four days, he was calling a halt to the project. It was worth any financial loss if it meant having Shea in his life. He needed her. Scotty needed her. And he believed Shea needed them.

The sound seemed to come from far away. Shea ignored it, not wanting to leave the dark recesses of sleep that had finally given her temporary peace.

Almost every day since Alec and Scotty had left, she'd saddled a horse and had come out to the ruins of the old homestead. She'd reflected on her limited options but unlike the previous times in her life, she'd found no solution. There was no peace. In the end, everything came back to Alec and what she would do without him in her life.

The sound grew louder, now joined by a voice calling her name. Blinking open her eyes, she sat up.

Thunder rolled across the sky as lightning flashed, challenging the darkness. The wind roared around the old structure, bringing the smell of the pending rain.

"Shea!"

It was Hank. As she stood up, she saw the truck about a hundred yards away heading toward her at a high rate of speed. He came to a screeching halt in front of the foundation.

"There's trouble," he told her without preamble. "Get in."

Recognizing the serious tone in his voice, she jumped into the vehicle without a word. He spun around on two wheels and they headed back over the rise.

"What?" She was almost afraid to ask.

"It's the house," Hank said. "It's on fire."

"What!" Shea couldn't immediately grasp the meaning of what he said. "The house…*my* house?"

She saw him nod, his mouth set in a grim line.

"How?" Her mind was reeling.

"Don't know," he yelled over the sound of the racing engine. "My guess is lightning. But as old as the place is, it won't take it long to burn down. That wood's like dry kindling."

Shea sat in stunned silence. Hank bypassed the trail and shot a straight line for the house, tearing through the wooded area a half mile away from it. They bounced over stumps and plunged through shallow ravines, sideswiping trees and boulders.

As soon as they topped the last rise, she could see the flames against the darkened sky. Fire equipment surrounded the house along with police and ambulance. Men were running in all directions, shouting to each other and scrambling to battle the flames shooting out the windows. A black wall of smoke engulfed the old composite roof; the large streams of water the firefighters were spraying onto its burning surface had little effect. Bright red, blue and white lights flashed and cast an eerie ambiance over the horrific scene unfolding around her.

She jumped from the truck before Hank came to a complete stop and ran toward the house. One of the firefighters caught her, bringing her to a stop.

"I'm sorry, ma'am, but you'll need to stay back."

"It's my house," she screamed over the commotion.

"Ma'am, you can't go inside." His tone had changed to one of understanding, but he remained adamant in his refusal to let her near the house.

"But—"

"Please, ma'am, you must stay back. The walls could collapse at any time. Please."

She turned away, unable to stop the flow of tears as they streamed down her face. She'd never felt so powerless in her life. The nightmare was coming true, playing out in full color right in front of her eyes. She stumbled to the far side of the three-story structure and watched helplessly as the flames continued to eat at the roof.

At least Alec and Scotty were gone and in no danger.

Then something caught her attention. It looked like a face in the upstairs window. Scotty's room. She brushed the tears from her eyes and looked again. Was Alec here? Had they come back? Was Scotty trapped inside? Between the darkness and the smoke billowing out of the window, she couldn't be sure. Sheer terror gripped her heart. She anxiously searched around her for any sign of Alec.

"Scotty!" Firefighters were pulling more hoses from the trucks, yelling instructions to each other while the anxious ranch hands and their families looked on. Then in the distance, on the very edge of the illumination from the flashing lights on the emergency vehicles, she spotted a white car. It looked like the sedan Alec had been driving while he was here. He'd come back! Frantically, she took one more look around her but couldn't spot Alec in all the chaos. Time was running out. She ran to the closest firefighter, tugged on his jacket to get his attention and pointed to the upstairs window. "There is a child up there."

She had to yell to be heard over the roar of the fire and the commotion on the ground. The man looked in the direction she indicated. A dark cloud of smoke still plumed out the open window.

"I don't see anyone, ma'am," he said, still looking. "We checked the house before the fire got to this stage. There was no one inside."

"But he's there!" She pointed to the window.

The man turned and hurried back to one of the fire trucks, yelling instructions to the others. She didn't have time to wait. Scotty didn't have time to wait. Without another thought Shea took off at a dead run toward the kitchen door. If she hurried, there was a chance she could reach Scotty in time.

Taking a deep breath, she bounded up the outside steps and pushed her way inside. The wall of heat was overwhelming. A thick blanket of smoke filled the room, whirling around her as the fresh air followed her into the kitchen. She quickly wet some towels, held them against her face, and ran for the stairs, taking them two at a time. The closer she got to the second floor, the more intense the heat became, surrounding her like a giant furnace.

As she reached the top of the stairwell, she heard a loud crackling sound and a cloud of dark gray smoke billowed down from the roof. She coughed violently as she urged herself forward. Just a few steps more.

"Scotty!" No reply. Crouching low to the floor, she crawled down the hall. The towels seemed of little help as the smoke burned her throat and lungs. The loud roaring from the inferno brought renewed terror. *Am I already too late?* The smoke burned her eyes, further restricting her sight. Feeling her way along the wall, she finally reached his room.

She hesitated in the doorway only a fraction of a second before plunging into the smoke and ash, not stopping until she reached the window where she'd seen the small face. Suddenly, the smoke swirled away from the open window. She gasped for a breath of air. It was then she saw it. *The owl.* It hadn't been Scotty she'd seen in the window. It was his stuffed owl. At that instant, a loud crash from another part of the house rocked the floor under her feet.

Turning, she began the arduous journey back down the hall. Approaching the doorway to her old room, she knew a moment of anguish for all the cherished things that would soon be lost forever. The linens, hand-embroidered by her mother, the wedding gown, pictures of her father and the family Bible. The only things left of the Hardin family were in that cedar chest. It sat not more than four feet from where she stood. She couldn't see it because of the smoke, but she knew it was there.

Acting purely on impulse, she lunged for the big chest. Grabbing the handle, she began pulling it from the room.

The smoke was thicker than it had been only a few moments ago and every breath was a horrific struggle. At the top of the stairs, she gave a hard push and the chest began to slide down, bumping over each step. It was almost to the bottom landing when the corner caught in the stair railing, halting its progress.

Climbing over the chest, she tried tugging from the

lower side. Suddenly, the railing gave way and the chest lurched forward. The motion threw her off balance and she fell, tumbling the rest of the way down the stairs, the heavy trunk crashing down on top of her.

As she teetered on the edge of consciousness, she pushed at the trunk, but it had become lodged between the newel post and the wall, effectively pinning her underneath.

Her ears were ringing. With each cough, her lungs filled with more minuscule particles of ash. She pushed frantically at the chest, trying to dislodge it enough so she could scoot out from underneath.

The roar of the fire, which now surrounded her, was almost deafening. It was so hot. For a moment, she gave up her attempts to push the chest away and covered her face with her one free arm, desperately trying to breathe. Unable to move, all she could do was look toward the ceiling as the nightmare continued to unfold.

She knew she was suffocating, dying a horrendously slow death. Her thoughts were of Alec, her mind encapsulating their time together. He was a good person. A good father. And she loved him with all her heart. Even if that love wasn't returned. The times he'd held her in his arms she'd been given a little taste of heaven on earth. She could see his handsome face in her mind's eye. His smile. The glitter of amusement in his golden eyes. She could hear his voice, so strong and deep. She was glad she'd had the opportunity to know him. To know what it was like to totally lose herself in his arms. What she wouldn't give for another chance to be with him without the issue of the land hanging over their heads.

There was so much more to life than history and tradition. Alec had shown her that. The really important things were the people you loved, not man-made structures. Even the land couldn't give you a glimpse of the stars and hold you close and protect when you floated slowly back down to earth. Material things couldn't make you feel safe while a storm of trouble threatened to tear your life apart. They couldn't give you hope for the future. They couldn't love you back. Why hadn't she realized it before it was too late? The way she missed her dad should have told her it was the people you love that mattered.

Tears slipped from the corners of her eyes. She could barely feel the moisture running down her face. It was so hot. If only she had a second chance she would make sure Alec knew he was the only thing that really mattered. Oh, how she wished she could somehow let him know.

"I love you Alec," she whispered as more tears joined the first. "I love you." Another crash pulled her attention to the area behind her. Craning her neck, she watched helplessly as pieces of flaming debris fell all around.

The thick cloud of smoke prevented her from seeing the flames on the burning ceiling above her, but she heard the loud cracking of the fire and the deafening shriek of the timbers as they lost their centuries-old struggle to hold up the roof. She heard her own scream, but it was lost in the loud crashing of falling timber. Then blackness swirled inside her head, dragging her down into the blissful realm of oblivion.

Almost as soon as the helicopter cleared the city lights of Dallas, Alec detected a yellowish glow on the darkening north horizon. It was a fire of some kind. While he prayed the cause was a farmer clearing out a brush pile, a churning in his gut told him it could be the house at the Bar H.

"Chuck, can this thing go any faster?" Alec asked the pilot through the headset.

The pilot nodded as if he sensed the urgency, sending them plunging ahead into the darkness. The closer they got to the yellowish glow, the more the fear churned in Alec's gut. Finally he knew. It was the old house.

I never should have left her in that house.

Before the chopper fully set down in an area near the barn, Alec jumped out. The sight of the old, three-story house ablaze against the blackened sky was surreal. His worst fears were confirmed. The firefighters swarmed around the structure, sending streams of water to the top and sides in a last-ditch effort to save even a portion of the building.

Alec looked everywhere for Shea but she was not to be found. As the sky opened and the rain began to fall in torrents, he spotted Hank. The ranch foreman was standing beside the Jeep, helplessly watching the firefighters' valiant efforts to contain the fire.

He raced to the older man. "Where's Shea?" Placing his hand on Hank's shoulder, he spun him around. "Hank! Where is Shea?"

Frowning, the old cowboy looked around. "She was just here. One of the firemen pushed her back from the house."

A quick glance told Alec she was nowhere in sight. An ungodly fear began to fester in his gut.

"I don't know where she went..."

The scream that pierced the night air was a sound that would haunt Alec for the rest of his life. Above the shouts of the men, the roar of the fire and the rumbling thunder overhead, one shrill scream from inside the burning inferno gave him his answer.

"My God, she's inside!" he whispered almost to himself. "Hank, Shea's inside. Get help!" He ran toward the house.

Before he could reach the porch, one of the firefighters grabbed his arm. "Sir, you can't go inside."

"She's in there. She's inside."

"Sir, no one is in the structure and we can't let you go—"

With one well-placed blow of his fist, Alec halted both the man's words and any further attempt to hold him back.

He sprang for the kitchen door, sensing others close behind who might try to stop him.

At first he didn't see her. The combination of searing heat, black swirling smoke and the demands from the firemen to get out almost made him turn away. Then Alec spied the chest at the bottom of the stairs and the still form lying underneath it. For an instant terror flooded his body and the vile churning of his stomach rendered him incapable of movement.

"There!" he shouted and lunged in that direction.

The men pulled the chest from over Shea's limp form. Alec scooped her body into his arms and ran for the door. A loud crash followed their retreat as the roof tumbled to the ground behind them.

Once he was clear of the building, Alec fell to his knees and laid her gently on the water-soaked earth.

Immediately, paramedics and firefighters surrounded her. One of them pushed him up against a fire truck and shoved an oxygen mask over his face, while the others focused their attention on Shea's still body.

The downpour continued as the lightning pierced the clouds overhead. For what seemed an eternity, Alec could only watch in stunned disbelief while the paramedics worked to bring life back to her fragile body. He ignored the rain, the fire, the shouts of the firefighters, every cell in his body attuned to the woman who was fighting for her life.

Finally, a small cough gave him some hope. She was alive. But she'd been in the smoke a long time. Maybe too long.

Within twenty minutes, EMTs had Shea strapped in and the Care Flight chopper lifted off, heading for the special burn unit at Regency Hospital in Dallas. Alec wasn't allowed to ride with her, but he followed in his own helicopter.

Shea was already being treated when he entered the ER. She was alive, but no one could tell him anything more than that. He called Leona. And he waited.

Two hours later, one of the doctors walked into the hallway.

"Mr. Morreston? I'm Dr. Clements. Your wife is stable, but we're going to keep her a few days just as a precautionary measure. She may have a few bruises, but considering the circumstances that brought her here, I'd have to say she was very lucky. The concern is her lungs. She has some indication of thermal injury to her upper airway and depending on the toxicity of the wood, it may take another forty-eight hours for any chemical injuries to become evident. We want to be sure she's okay before she's released."

With a comforting tap on his arm, the doctor left and Alec was once again alone with nothing but a handful of hope and a gut full of regrets to keep him company. He didn't want to think about what might have happened had he not returned when he had. He revisited that narrow escape in his mind a thousand times before the sun peeked over the far horizon.

Three days later, Shea and Alec made the ride in the limo from the hospital to the large hotel on the Dallas outskirts in silence. He sat beside her as he had in the hospital room. Not pushing her to talk, just silently offering his strength.

Shea was grateful to be alive. The fact that Alec was here with her tugged at her heart. They would have to talk eventually. She had to make sure he knew she would not make any further attempt to keep the land. It was his land, after all, and had been from the beginning. After everything she'd put him through, eating crow seemed the least she could do.

She'd been given the second chance she'd prayed for.

She had to use it carefully. She would not screw up again. Every cell in her body wanted nothing more than to fall into his arms and confess how very much she loved him. But while in the hospital, she hadn't been able to stop thinking about their situation, and it had occurred to her that a full confession of her feelings might not be the best way to go.

Apparently Alec had returned to the Bar H, no doubt intending to make sure she'd packed her bags. He hadn't counted on the house burning down. Rather than simply escorting her to the door, he'd been forced to save her from her own foolishness. It was bad enough that he'd risked his life for her; now her immediate homeless status effectively made her a liability. Again.

She wasn't sure how to approach him. Declaring her love could be awkward for him and cause him to feel responsible for her welfare. This was her last chance, her *only* chance, to get it right. She had to be strong, this time for Alec.

When the bellhop opened the door to the luxury suite, Shea glanced around at the opulent surroundings. Never could she have imagined such luxury. It suddenly washed over her: this was Alec's world. After his time at the ranch, she'd come to think of him not as a billionaire but just a nice, if somewhat stubborn, guy. Being here, seeing a sample of how he must usually live was…surreal.

She walked across the wide living area to the wall of glass that overlooked the vast expanse of Dallas.

"Are you hungry?" Alec inquired from behind her.

She shook her head. "No. But I would dearly love a bath."

"To your left through that door, Mrs. Morreston." A man in a hotel uniform stood just inside the doorway to the suite. "Please, allow me to draw it for you. How do you like the water?"

While Shea groped for an answer, Alec interjected, "Very warm. Thanks." When the man disappeared into the next room, Alec looked at her, his eyes glittering with amusement. "Hopefully you'll have plenty of hot water."

She couldn't help but return his smile. He was referring to the night Scotty had used all the hot water and she'd had to finish her shower in the icy tap from the well. In frustration she'd then gone after a sleeping Alec with a pillow.

"You'll find some clothes in the closet and bureau. I left it up to the salesclerk to send over what you'd need until you can replenish your wardrobe. If she missed something, let me know."

"Thanks."

The master bedroom was as spacious as the vast living area. It had the same wall of glass offering the million-dollar view, only it was dominated by a huge bed draped with silken linens so thick and luxurious it looked as if a person could completely disappear into the softness when she lay down.

The dressing room and bath were just beyond it. Shea was quite certain the oval tub could hold ten people. At least.

She emerged an hour later feeling clean and pampered and smelling of lilacs. Dressed in one of the comfortable new white T-shirts from the bureau, she walked directly to the bed and climbed in.

Exhaustion pulled her into sleep. She had a vague awareness that Alec joined her sometime in the night. His strong arms pulled her close, offering his warmth and security.

The rays of the morning sun filtered softly through the sheer draperies. Shea opened her eyes, remembering immediately where she was and all that had happened. On the far corner of the bed she spotted a deep red rose with a note underneath it. After picking up the beautiful flower, she inhaled the rich perfumed aroma, then grabbed the small piece of paper.

Knew you needed to rest so I didn't wake you. I'm in a meeting downstairs.

Coffee and juice on the side table. Back as soon as I can.

-Alec

He had no need to hurry. As far as his plans for the ranch, he would have to wait while she cleared the land of several employees—some of whom lived on the ranch—the horses and roughly three thousand head of cattle. It wouldn't happen overnight. In fact, she didn't quite know where to begin. But now that this stumbling block over ownership had been resolved, Alec could get back to his life and somehow she would have to find a way to get on with hers. Wherever that would be. Whatever it entailed.

Fanning through the new clothes that hung in the huge closet, she selected a simple yet elegant dress in robin's egg blue. There were some pumps with the name Trump in gold lettering on the insole.

As she sipped a cup of delicious coffee delivered by a hotel employee, she sat back and looked out over the city of Dallas, her mind on Alec and what to say to him before she left. It would be painful to say goodbye. She loved him so much. But she would not be one of those women who clung to men who didn't want them. Leaving was the right thing to do. The only thing to do. Maybe he'd stop by and say hello if his business ever brought him back to the area. The tears welled in her eyes but she forced them back. This time, for Alec, she had to be strong.

By late afternoon she needed a new space. She was not used to sitting idle. Around two, Alec called to explain he would be tied up for a while longer. She assured him there was no hurry and went out to explore the hotel on her own.

With a soft ding, the elevator door opened to the marbled lobby. Stepping out, she immediately noticed a large flat-screen television mounted on the wall behind the concierge's stand. It listed the various shops and meeting rooms and the locations of each. Beneath the Presidential Suite, one name stood out: Morreston.

A chill ran down her spine. Could this be the meeting Alec had mentioned about the development of the ranch? Without any conscious thought, she began making her way in that direction. After rounding the far corner, she took a small escalator up to the next level.

The royal-blue carpeted reception area was deserted. Her hands clenched into fists as she walked silently to the meeting room entrance and pulled open one of the mahogany doors. Immediately she was assailed with the buzz of conversation. About forty men and women filled the room. Some held flutes of champagne while others sipped coffee. Most stood in smaller groups, nodding or arguing some point they were trying to make. But the mood throughout the entire room was excitement.

Stepping inside, she searched for Alec, finally spotting him in the far corner. Like the other men in the room, he wore a dark suit and tie. From the way it fit, no doubt it was custom tailored and probably cost more than the ranch. Surrounded by eight or nine people, his hands moved as he emphasized the point he was making.

The churning in her stomach made her feel queasy. This was it. The meeting. And these were the people, the investors, who'd put up millions to develop the Bar H, putting their faith in Alec to give them America's grandest entertainment complex for their vested interest.

He was at home in this setting. So confident. So self-assured. These people were accomplished in their own right, yet they held Alec and his capabilities high on a pedestal, clinging to his every word. The more that realization sank in, the smaller she felt.

A white-jacketed waiter appeared next to her, offering

glasses of champagne on a silver tray. She shook her head in polite refusal. What was she doing here? Had she honestly thought something good would come of the affair with Alec? And clearly, that's all it had been. At least to him.

Her eyes fell on a large display table in the center of the room. She knew it was a scale model rendering of the future of the ranch. Strangely, she didn't care to look any closer. It no longer mattered. Alec would probably direct the project from his office in New York. When this meeting ended, Alec would be gone.

Tears stung her eyes as her entire body began to tremble. Her heart pounded in her chest as she tried to swallow back the nausea churning in her stomach. She thought she'd been prepared to accept the eventuality of his leaving and say goodbye with an understanding smile, keeping the agony of regret hidden deep inside. She hadn't foreseen that the pain of losing him would be so horrific. Now she had to wonder how she would ever get through this.

Feeling lost in the din of voices, she took one last glance toward Alec. A man separated himself from the others, placed his hand on Alec's arm and nodded in her direction. For an instant, their eyes met before the world tilted and the room began to spin.

Shea turned, making her way back to the lobby, away from the meeting room before her tears fell and she embarrassed Alec in front of his colleagues.

The elevator doors immediately opened when she pressed the button. As she stumbled inside, she heard Alec's voice calling her name.

"Shea!"

His deep voice exploded into the hotel suite. Despite the emotions running rampant, her heart still responded to the sound of his voice. Hastily she swiped the tears from her face.

"They have it wrong." He spoke to her from the bedroom doorway. "That scale model is not even close to what I intended. A few of the investors have a tendency to push things to the limit. What you saw is not going to happen."

"It's okay." Shea nodded and began folding the few items of clothing Alec had bought for her. There had been too many harsh words between them, too much pain, too many regrets in the few months they'd been together. She hadn't even seen the model. She hadn't wanted to look. Alec had already told her the way of life as she'd known it was over. The old house burning down had underscored his point. Changing the scale model wouldn't change anything. It wouldn't change how she felt about him. It wouldn't make him stay. She just needed it all to stop, needed this insane emotional roller coaster to come to a permanent end.

"It doesn't matter," she replied quietly, calmly. "It's your land. You can do with it whatever you want."

"Shea—"

She shook her head and forced a smile as she placed the remaining personal items in the small designer sack that would serve as a suitcase, holding all she had left in the world. Lifting it from the bed and pasting on a brave smile, she turned to face Alec. "Congratulations on your project. I mean that. I'm sure your venture will be a huge success. Your investors have confidence in you. They know you're the best."

She had to accept Alec would be leaving and never coming back. She knew once this was a done deal, the restraints of the old lease over and forgotten, she would never see him again. Fresh tears threatened to fall but she determinedly held them in check.

"Someday, if you're back in this area for any reason, be sure and stop—" She couldn't finish. She couldn't tell him to stop by and say hello. She had no idea where she would be. "Stop by Leona's. She'll know where to find me."

For a long moment, Alec watched her. He opened his mouth as though he wanted to say something, then apparently thought better of it. For that she was grateful. The only thing left was admitting her love for the man who stood so tall, so handsome in front of her. But she wouldn't do that. She would not push him from one awkward situation into another. She respected him too much to do that.

Then suddenly Alec moved, grabbing her arms and spinning her around so her back was against the wall. His lips were hard, almost cruel when they came down on hers. Hungrily, he took her mouth, consuming hers with a passion that threatened to devour her very soul. There was no gentleness this time, just raw need. And she gloried in the strength of him, the taste of him. She kissed him back with all the pent-up longing that had been tearing her apart for days, silently conveying her need for him. *One last time. One final glimpse of heaven in his arms.*

The thin straps of the dress prevented him from touching her. With little effort he dispensed with them and roughly pushed the dress to the floor. His hands cupped her bare breasts, molding them, kneading them, feeling them expand under his touch while his mouth continued to ravish hers. His mouth left her lips, kissing and nipping a path to her neck, then lower to suck the swollen buds of her breasts. She trembled, her hand fisted in his hair, holding him to her.

His hand slid down across her stomach, then lower, to the sensitive area between her legs. The surge of passion at his touch pushed her hips against his hand, confirming her need. Alec quickly removed the thin scrap of lace and stroked her. She moaned at his touch.

She heard Alec let out a low growl.

"I can't go slow," he rasped against her ear, his voice rough.

"I don't…want you…to."

He unfastened his pants just enough, then lifted her, positioning her to receive him. Without a second's pause, he pushed deep inside.

His hungry mouth swallowed her soft moans as her body strove to accommodate him, to accept and embrace him and the heated force that drove him. It was as though he needed to brand her as his. If only that were true. She wrapped her legs around his hips, holding him to her as he began to move, driving any coherent thought from her mind. His muscles hardened as he pounded into her, taking her hard, filling her.

"Oh, Alec. I'm…" She didn't finish the sentence, but he knew.

Grasping her hips, he pushed even deeper, again and again, until she cried out as her passion exploded. The final waves of her climax caught Alec in the storm of emotion and he followed her, pulsating deep inside her as he growled her name.

As the waves of passion subsided, she cupped the back of his head, smoothed the damp tendrils of his hair, kissed his neck and under his chin while he fought for breath.

"I love you, Alec," she said softly. "Forgive me, but I love you."

He raised his head and his eyes found hers. "Shea," he murmured her name, then kissed her again, passionately, silently sealing the bond between them.

He swung her into his arms. Without a word, he carried her into the bedroom, placing her on the soft mattress. Quickly shedding his clothes, he lay down next to her, pulling her close.

Her head resting on his broad chest, she listened to the strong beat of his heart. She was still reeling from his lovemaking and the fact he was here with her instead of at his meeting.

"What do you remember?"

She closed her eyes. She didn't want to do this. Not now.

She hadn't figured out exactly what to say to him. But she answered truthfully. "Everything."

"Why did you go into the house?" His hand played in the fine strands of her hair.

"I…thought I saw Scotty. Upstairs. In his bedroom window. I thought you'd brought him back." She pulled away and looked at him through the pale city light filtering into the room. "I couldn't find you in all the chaos, but maybe if I hurried, I could save him. When I got to his room, I realized it was his stuffed owl that I'd seen from outside. As I was running back to the stairs, I remembered the chest. I thought I could save it."

She lay back on her pillow, covering her face as the somber weight of total loss returned. "It was all I had…from my mother, the only pictures of my dad. After our wedding, when I folded Mom's gown and put it back in the chest, I thought it would be a safe place." Swallowing hard, she turned her gaze to Alec. "Why did you come back? How did you…? I don't understand."

"I intended to make sure you got out of the house before something happened. My timing could have been better. I was on my way back and saw the flames." A rueful smile touched his lips. "I'd anticipated evicting you would be a major hurdle, but I never anticipated having to carry you out unconscious."

She drew in a sharp but shaky breath. There was her answer. He had just eliminated any lingering hope. When Alec had asked her how much she remembered, it included his demand that she leave. And he'd just confirmed he'd meant it.

It had all, finally, come to an end.

In the slender moments before the light of a new day began to appear in the eastern sky, Shea made her way quietly through the suite and toward the door, glancing one last time at the sleeping man on the bed. He had come into her life so unexpectedly. But in the end, he'd given her so much more than he would take away. Now it was her turn to give him the freedom he needed to go forward with his life. And somehow, maybe, someday she could get on with hers.

Thirteen

The week she spent with Leona provided some time and space for Shea to try to work through all the emotions and grief eating away at her soul. Leona gave her plenty of room and didn't try to encourage her to talk but made sure Shea knew she was there for her if or when she needed her.

Alec had called every day, checking to be sure she was all right. She'd heard Leona assuring him that Shea would be fine. It was good to know somebody thought so.

This morning, Shea felt the time had come. The day dawned bright and beautiful, and she knew she'd avoided returning to the ranch long enough. She had to take the next step in saying goodbye. Had to deal with the memories of when she'd been happy, her heart full of hope.

She thanked Leona for her offer to accompany her, but this was something Shea had to do on her own. With quiet understanding, Leona held out the keys to her truck.

The site where the house had stood for so many years had been cleared, all remains of the old structure removed and the ground leveled. Parts of the small path that at one time had led from the kitchen door through the small back yard and out to the main barn were still visible. All of the various ranch buildings were intact. Only the house was missing.

She slowly followed the path across the yard and into the hallway of the main barn. The familiar scents of freshly cut alfalfa, leather and pine shavings filled the air. She stopped to stroke the silky necks of the horses housed inside. When she got to Ransom's stall, memories flooded her mind and pain gripped her heart anew. The day Alec had ridden the spirited animal to the old homestead. The small campfire where they'd talked and laughed and shared the meal Hank had prepared for them.

The rain.

The night that had followed.

Forcing herself away from the stall, she ambled on toward the tack room. Before she reached it, her eyes fell on an object that looked incredibly familiar. Sitting against the wall on the floor was what appeared to be the old trunk. But that was impossible. It had been destroyed in the fire. Frowning, she reached down and touched the top, almost afraid it would disappear. But it was real. The marks of fire damage were apparent on the top and sides, but overall, it was in remarkably good condition.

Immediately falling to her knees, she pushed open the lid. A faint pine scent touched her senses. Removing the layer of tissue paper she saw the family pictures. *How did they get here?*

Beneath the photographs were her mother's hand-embroidered linens followed by the two quilts bearing the initials A.H., and, finally, the wedding gown. She swallowed hard as she gently reached in, picked up the dress and held it to her heart. Alec was behind this. Somehow, he'd managed to save it all.

Memories of her holding the dress in front of her, trying to decide if she should wear it to their wedding, flashed through her mind. Tears burned the backs of her eyes. She was glad she'd worn it. With a sad smile, she gently folded the dress, intending to return it to the trunk. Then she noticed a loose board on the bottom. Frowning, she set the gown on the quilts and removed the thin piece of wood.

Beneath it...letters. Dozens of letters. Really old, yellowed with age. *What are these?* Picking up the one on top, she began to read.

April 12, 1814
My Dearest Alyssa, My Beloved...

They all were signed William Morreston. Alec's great-great-grandfather.

Glancing over the words, she quickly saw they were love letters. Another look inside the trunk and Shea saw an old photo among the letters. The tin-plated picture had two images: a young woman standing beside a tall, handsome man.

Suddenly, she knew what these were, the pieces falling together like parts of a puzzle. William Morreston had courted Alyssa Hardin, daughter of the widow, Mary Hardin. He'd courted her, fallen in love with her and they had planned to marry. Photographs were rare and costly back in those days. It had to have been taken for a very special occasion. Such as a wedding. The quilts, the linens...this trunk had been Alyssa's hope chest. And it was Alyssa who had perished in the fire at the old homestead. Before she could become William's wife.

One thought exploded inside her head: it had never been about the land. The contract written two hundred years ago, the clause that forced her and Alec to marry, all of it had been intended to bring two ancestors of William and Alyssa together.

It had been about Alec. All along, it had been about him.

An invisible hand gripped her heart. She couldn't breathe. Her body began to tremble as she tried to blink back the tears. But they fell down her face, dropping onto the letters clutched in her hand. Even though she'd left Alec with the best intentions, she'd walked out nonetheless. And even though he'd called to check on her, he wouldn't be back. That truth slammed into her like an airbag deploying in an unforeseen crash. He was gone. Forever. The pain in her heart was unbearable, the sadness so deep, so piercing she knew she would never recover.

Through eyes blurred with tears, she looked at the sparkling wedding ring on her left hand. It seemed like a lifetime ago, the night Alec had slipped it back on her finger and told her to never take it off. At the time, she'd counted the days until her twelve-month sentence would be over, when she would be free of him and could happily throw the ring in his face. But it had become a part of her, as had the man who'd given it to her. Subconsciously she'd never let go of the hope she and Alec could work things out. Now, she faced the grim truth.

She'd failed to keep the greatest gift that fate could bestow from slipping through her fingers. She'd lost the greatest man—the *only* man she had ever loved and would ever love as long as she lived. A man who but for a ridiculous clause in a two-hundred-year-old contract, never would have entered her life.

The tears streamed unchecked down her face and she had no will to hold them back as another wave of misery overwhelmed her. The tears blurred the image of the beautiful ring as she began to slide it from her hand. If only…

"I told you to leave that ring where it is," said a deep familiar voice from behind her.

With a gasp, Shea whirled around. Alec stood just inside the barn, looking big and rugged and entirely too handsome. Dressed in jeans and a white cotton T-shirt, he stood with one hand resting on a stall door, the other on his hip.

It took her a few seconds to find her voice. "Alec? What… what are you doing here? What do you…?"

"What do I want?" he asked, stepping away from the stall, his arms falling to his side. "I want to go back in time where the past few weeks never happened. I want to hold my wife in my arms every night and see her face when I wake up the next morning. Emphasis on seeing her the next morning."

She knew he was referring to the hotel in Dallas when she'd snuck out to come home.

"And I want to see her belly grow with my son or daughter." She noted a flare in his golden eyes at those words. His mouth then pulled into a serious line. "I've shelved the entire project, Shea. My stipulation to continue is it will be built completely across the river in Oklahoma. I don't intend for one rock, one blade of grass, one single drop of water to be disturbed on this ranch. I've spent the last week making damn sure that doesn't happen. If the investors go for it, good enough. If not—" he shrugged his broad shoulders "—I really don't give a damn. Nothing is worth losing you."

A frown crossed his face, his eyes conveying the seriousness of his words, and for countless moments, neither moved. "Why did you leave the hotel? Have I lost you, Shea?"

Shaking her head, she rose to her feet. "You could never lose me, Alec. I love you too much."

Then she was in his arms—strong, powerful arms that were gentle as he held her tightly against him. She gazed into eyes the color of topaz as he cupped her face and wiped away the tears with his thumbs. His lips, hot and oh so incredible, covered hers and she surrendered to the overwhelming love that had grown for this man in spite of all the reasons it shouldn't. The warmth and the feel and the taste of him filled her. The wonderful musky male scent of his skin surrounded her as his hard body pressed against hers. She kissed him back with all the love she had, the tears of misery changing to those of pure joy.

Finally, Alec raised his head, but stayed a mere breath away. She touched his face, amazed that she had a chance to love and be loved by such a man.

"Just so we're clear this time, I've been in love with you since the day you walked into Ben's office," Alec admitted as she looked into his eyes. "I admit I fought it, even after we were married. I told myself I was slitting my own throat, setting myself up for a hell of a fall because someone like you just didn't happen to someone like me. I can handle cutthroat tactics, lying, backstabbing from my adversaries, sometimes even my supporters. My world hasn't left much room for honesty and innocence. Trust is something new to me." His gaze traveled over her face. "But you've shown me I can trust again. I can love. And I love you, *Mrs. Morreston*, with everything I have inside me."

A glint of amusement flickered in his eyes, making Shea smile.

"You know, I think I might get used to that name."

"You'd better," Alec said, in a teasingly threatening tone. "Because you're stuck with it for the rest of your life."

She knew he was telling the truth. This man, this incredible man, truly loved her. He was her husband. Scotty was her son. And it didn't matter whether they lived in New York or Texas or someplace in between as long as they were together. That realization was sealed when Alec's lips again came down over hers in a deep, passionate embrace that left no doubts whatsoever.

His lips left hers, kissing his way to her ear. "Mmm." He growled and nuzzled her neck. "We need to be on our way back to Dallas."

"Back to Dallas?"

"Mmm. To the hotel. To the bedroom…"

Shea grinned, caught her bottom lip, and shook her head as she backed him through the open door of the tack room and toward the stack of blankets in the corner.

"That hotel is much too far away."

Alec's eyebrows rose, then a smile turned up the corners of his lips as he realized her intent and kicked the door closed behind them.

And there was no further talking for a very long time.

* * * * *

LET'S TALK Romance

For exclusive extracts, competitions and special offers, find us online:

facebook.com/millsandboon

@millsandboonuk

@millsandboon

Or get in touch on 0844 844 1351*

For all the latest titles coming soon, visit millsandboon.co.uk/nextmonth

*Calls cost 7p per minute plus your phone company's price per minute access charge